THE
PHOTOGRAPHER

PETRA DURST-BENNING

TRANSLATED BY EDWIN MILES

AMAZON CROSSING

Previously published as *Die Fotografin—Am Anfang des Weges* by Blanvalet Verlag in Germany in 2018. Translated from German by Edwin Miles. First published in English by Amazon Crossing in 2020.

Published by Amazon Crossing, Seattle

www.apub.com

Amazon, the Amazon logo, and Amazon Crossing are trademarks of Amazon.com, Inc., or its affiliates.

ISBN-13: 9781542008495
ISBN-10: 1542008492

Cover design by Shasti O'Leary Soudant

Cover photography by Richard Jenkins Photography

Unless otherwise noted, all interior images courtesy of a private collection.

Printed in the United States of America

To photograph: it is to put on the same line of sight the head, the eye, and the heart.

Taking photographs . . . is a way of life.

Henri Cartier-Bresson (1908–2004)

CHAPTER 1

Esslingen, February 11, 1905

"I would like to ask you, dearest Minna, if you would do me the honor of being my wife." Heinrich Grohe took Mimi's hands in his and gazed eagerly into her eyes.

Minna? Mimi thought. The only person who called her Minna was her mother, and then only when she was about to criticize her for something. Mimi fought back a nervous laugh. Heinrich was proposing marriage, and the only thing that occurred to her was to reproach him for not calling her by her nickname!

Taking care not to overturn the small bouquet of freesias between them on the table, Mimi pulled her right hand from Heinrich's and reached for her glass of sparkling wine. The tiny bubbles burst on her tongue exactly like the thoughts in her head, vanishing before she could grasp a single one.

He beamed at her. "That's caught you off guard, hasn't it? Now I know it's all a bit sudden, and I haven't spoken to your parents yet. But today's your birthday, and I thought to myself, well, this would be the perfect gift." He swept one hand in a grand gesture that took in the café in which they were sitting, the wine, the bouquet, and the two of them.

A marriage proposal as a birthday present? Mimi blinked a few times as if to reassure herself that she was awake. In the winter sunlight that fell through the milky glass of the café window, Heinrich's shock of blond hair glowed as if the good Lord had fitted him with a halo.

Heinrich had met her at work at the Semmer Photographic Studio at noon, just as he did almost every Saturday. Usually, they sauntered through town for a while, looking into the windows of the elegant shops, and then they would stroll through the park. At the start of the month, salaries in their pockets, they would stop at one of the inexpensive inns dotted around Esslingen's market square to feast on the traditional tripe dish of *Kutteln* or on roast potatoes and bacon. They generally split the bill because neither Heinrich, as the vicar in her father's parish, nor she, as an employee in a photo studio, earned very much. But what did it matter when you were young and in love? They made a handsome couple: Heinrich had blue eyes, a high forehead, and blond hair. And she, Mimi Reventlow, daughter of the parish priest, a year younger than Heinrich at twenty-six, had glossy chestnut-brown hair that she pinned up in an elegant style, and she always dressed as fashionably as she could afford. When they walked hand in hand through the streets of the old imperial town, people turned and stared. *Ah, to be so young again, with the future ahead of you!* Mimi read in their expressions.

When Heinrich had picked her up from the studio, Mimi had thought of nothing but their usual Saturday jaunt, with perhaps the one difference being that Heinrich, since it was her birthday, would pay for lunch. He had presented her with the bouquet, wished her a happy birthday, and kissed her on the cheek. Instead of going to one of the inns that smelled of oily food, he had steered her to a stylish café and ordered a bottle of sparkling wine. Mimi had raised her eyebrows at that. *Such an extravagance!* How would she feel after drinking all that alcohol? And also how—dazed by the alcohol—would she manage to get up the steep road to the Esslinger Oberstadt, the upper part of town? A number of thoughts had gone through her mind, but never in her dreams would it have occurred to her that Heinrich would ask her to marry him.

She still had not responded to Heinrich's proposal, however, and his broad smile was beginning to lose its courage. "Minna?" he said impatiently.

She giggled nervously. "This is quite a surprise."

"Yes. Aren't you happy?" He furrowed his wide brow. Just then, as if a set designer had taken his cue, a cloud passed in front of the sun in the wintry sky. The café instantly grew darker.

"Of course I am. What woman wouldn't be happy?" she defended herself feebly.

Heinrich's smile returned. "I thought so. At twenty-six, some might say it's about time you tied the knot, before you turn into an old maid." He gave her a wink. "But let them talk! I think it's a good thing that women fulfill their dreams before they marry. Who do you know who has a wife who's both graduated high school *and* finished an apprenticeship?" He nodded good-naturedly, then leaned across the table and took her hands in his again. "Your parents, I'm sure, will be overjoyed. We should go to them as soon as we're done here, and I can ask your father for your hand. It's just a formality—especially because there's even more news . . ." His eyes twinkled, and Mimi could see that he could hardly contain himself.

"Yes?" she said weakly.

"I'm to take over the parish in Schorndorf! We can visit your parents whenever we want, and vice versa."

Schorndorf? Now it was Mimi who furrowed her brow. Although the little town was not far from Esslingen, she had never been there. "Aren't the people there all Pietists who forbid dancing, music, and alcohol?" She glanced pointedly at the bottle of sparkling wine.

"You're right. We should drink while we still can." Laughing at his own joke, he refilled her glass. "But I can put your mind at ease. The influence of the Pietists in Schorndorf isn't nearly as bad as everybody says. The Protestant congregation there is much bigger than the Pietists'. Of course, as a Protestant priest, I'll also need to be open to the Pietists' concerns, which will naturally mean keeping to a more God-pleasing lifestyle. Cheers!" He raised his glass.

To have something to do, Mimi also took a mouthful, but the bubbles had lost their tingle. *As if cursed by a rigid Pietist,* thought Mimi. *What an ungrateful creature you are,* she chided herself silently. *Be happy!* A marriage proposal, after all, was meant to be one of the most wonderful moments in a woman's life. But instead of excitement or pleasure, she felt as if a large pill had lodged halfway down her throat and was dissolving slowly, spreading an acrid, damp chill in every direction. Didn't they say that everyone had to swallow a bitter pill occasionally? *Mimi, you're absurd,* she berated herself.

Heinrich seemed oblivious to her dejected mood. He set his glass down with a flourish. "I can take over the Schorndorf parish as soon as I finish in the vicariate this summer. The priest there now is almost eighty and can hardly wait to retire. It seems he's not in the best of health, so he won't be sticking his nose into the work too much. We'll have to look after him, at least a little. The parish expects it of us, but it goes without saying anyway."

"I see," said Mimi. She hadn't yet said yes to his proposal.

"I was in Schorndorf earlier this week. The parish is manageable—it's not as big as your father's—but I'll be looking at it as practice for bigger things to come. And the house we'll live in . . . well, it's no palace, I admit. A little dilapidated, actually, and the fittings and furnishings have certainly seen better days. No wonder, really. Father Weidenstock, my predecessor, never married, and doesn't seem to have had a housekeeper, either, so there was no one to tend to house and home. Once you've set your mind to it, though, I'm sure you'll have it back in shape in no time."

"But I'm no housewife!" Mimi protested. "I'm a photographer. I've never learned how to run a household, and I'm supposed to look after the old priest, too?"

Heinrich waved off her objections. "Don't worry! Women have that kind of thing in their blood. And if you're ever unsure about something, I'm certain there'll be someone in the congregation who's more than happy to help." His smile became rapturous as he continued: "Ah, Mimi, I can picture exactly how it will be—you in the front row in church and me in the pulpit. The Schorndorfers will be thrilled to hear my new, progressive sermons. The Lord gave people a brain with which to think, and I want my congregation to understand that he doesn't want meek little lambs. I will preach that progress and faith in God are not mutually exclusive, but go hand in hand. Your father was the best teacher I could have had—I feel both inspired and well prepared. He's going to be proud of me, I know, and when I visit the poor people, you must definitely come along. A priest's wife can do so much good. But who knows that better than you? You have probably the best possible example of that in your own mother at home. And speaking of home, did I mention that the house also has a small garden? At the end of the garden, there's a little creek, which will be useful for doing the washing, and something I'm sure you'll appreciate once we have children."

"I see," Mimi said again and imagined herself as a parrot. Children? What children? She instinctively pushed her chair back as if she wanted to put some distance between Heinrich's plans and herself.

Heinrich nodded. "You'll be able to hang the washing outside just like your housekeeper does in your garden at home. Isn't that wonderful? Washing dried by the sun and wind smells so much better, don't you think?"

"I couldn't really care less about the garden and the washing," said Mimi, unable to keep the prickly tone out of her voice. "What I'd really like to know is whether there's a photo studio in Schorndorf."

"A photo studio?" Heinrich looked at her as if she'd asked whether the emperor of China was living in the house next door. "I don't think so. I'd have noticed that, and—"

"Then how do you see this working?" she said, cutting him off. "Am I to take the train or the mail coach to work in Esslingen every day?"

"But, Mimi!" Heinrich snorted with laughter. "As a married woman, you don't have to work anymore. Old Felix Semmer can keep his dusty studio for himself. You'll be able to dedicate yourself heart and soul to the duties of a housewife."

The church bells rang out. Mimi's heart pounded in the same quick rhythm. She looked at Heinrich with her eyes wide. "Oh, three o'clock already! I have to go. I've just remembered a pressing appointment. Please excuse me." She grabbed her handbag so abruptly that it hit her in the hip. She smiled apologetically and hurried off.

"But, Mimi! You haven't even said yes yet!" Heinrich called after her.

No, she thought. *I haven't.*

CHAPTER 2

And now? A little dazed from the sparkling wine, Mimi looked around Esslingen's market square. She would not go home; that much was certain. The instant she set foot in the door of the parish office, her mother would rope her in for one charitable cause or another, birthday or not. Heinrich would probably materialize there as well and insist that she explain herself. He certainly would not approve of the way she had simply run off and left him sitting in the café.

It was too cold to sit on a bench in the park. The sun that had shone until midday, feigning a breath of spring for the citizens of Esslingen, had disappeared again behind mountainous clouds. Icy gusts tugged at Mimi's hair.

Feeling angry and helpless, she pulled her shawl closer around her shoulders. Darn it! All she wanted was to have a little time to herself—time to think things through, let her thoughts wander, listen inside herself, and hope for clarity.

She decided to go to a church. In the past, when she'd been upset or did not know how to make up her mind about something, God had given her an occasional piece of good advice. And if he couldn't do that now, then at least she would have a little peace and quiet. The Church of Our Lady was close by. Beneath its blue-and-gold ceiling she would be able to think.

Mimi was about to go in that direction when someone tapped her on the shoulder from behind. Heinrich? She turned anxiously but was confronted instead by a young woman. "Excuse me. I'm something of a stranger to Esslingen. I'm looking for the Hirsch Hotel on Ulmer Strasse. Could you tell me how to get there?" A pair of blue eyes so brilliant that even Heinrich's eyes would pale by comparison looked expectantly at Mimi.

Mimi pointed behind her. "Ulmer Strasse follows the Neckar. If you go down that way, you'll find it," she said to the stranger and smiled. The woman's blue eyes, perfectly arched brows, shapely lips—*how lovely she is*, Mimi thought even as she spoke. She wore her hair in an unusual fashion, too: her straw-blond locks were wrapped around her head in a wreath that looked like a crown. To photograph the woman here and now, that would be something! Mimi's hands positively itched.

The beautiful stranger beamed at Mimi. "No problem at all. Once I'm going in the right direction, I'll find my way." Lovingly, as if she were holding a baby in her arms, she stroked one hand over a parcel wrapped in thin linen. "My wedding dress," she said proudly. "I've just picked it up at Brunner's by the market."

Mimi let out a little cry and one hand rose to her breast. Was this the sign from God that she had been hoping to find in church?

"You don't think Brunner's is the best choice?" the stranger asked with a frown.

"Oh, I do, I do! Mathilde Brunner is an artist with needle and thread. Even the Stuttgart royal family comes to her," Mimi hurried to reassure her. "It's just . . ." She stroked her windblown hair nervously and said shyly, "I've just been proposed to myself."

The stranger's blue eyes widened. "No, really? How romantic! Congratulations!" Before Mimi knew it, the stranger had thrown her arms around her warmly.

"Watch out for the wedding dress!" Mimi cried, laughing.

The stranger let go of her instantly. "We must absolutely drink to this, don't you think? On my last visit, I found a pretty café in Maille Park. Shall we go there? My treat, of course. My God, I haven't even introduced myself. Where are my manners? I'm Bernadette Furtwängler from Münsingen in the Swabian Jura." The words poured from the young woman without so much as a pause for breath.

Mimi laughed. A little diversion might do her good. "Why not? One glass more or less today won't make any difference now," she said, which drew another look of surprise from the stranger. "I'm Mimi Reventlow, by the way. My father is the parish priest in the Esslinger Oberstadt. I'm a photographer." *I really am,* she added in silently.

"Then you must do my wedding pictures," Bernadette said with enthusiasm.

Mimi frowned. "That would be wonderful, but my boss thinks all I'm good for is making coffee."

"Men!" said Bernadette, and she rolled her eyes. Companionably, as if they had known each other forever, the two women linked arms.

"Our wedding is set for the tenth of May," said Bernadette after they had placed their order. They had decided against sparkling wine and chosen coffee instead. "I'd have preferred summer, but from the middle of May, everyone's busy with the shearing. After that, they're out wandering the mountains with the sheep." Bernadette screwed up her face. "It's always been that way. The damned sheep rule every moment of our lives. I'm going to be so happy to have that behind me. My fiancé is a teacher, you should know. Let them keep their stupid sheep."

Mimi laughed. She liked Bernadette's candidness. "So you're shepherds?" Mimi asked. She never would have believed that a shepherd's daughter would be able to afford to travel to town and have a wedding dress made.

"Heavens above, no!" There was a touch of conceit in Bernadette's laugh. "We own the biggest sheep operation far and wide. We've got thousands of sheep. Half the village works for us—shepherds, shearers, men who fix the fences, men who train the sheepdogs. When it's lambing season, we take on even more men. My father isn't just rich. He's a powerful man," she said proudly. "He's looked after me all these years like I'm some fragile crystal vase. It was almost the end of me, I'll tell you."

"What do you mean?" asked Mimi. She sensed that Bernadette wanted to tell her story to the end, and she was happy to sit and listen. She found this glimpse of a completely different world not only a diversion but also immensely enjoyable. Besides, while she was with Bernadette, she didn't have to think about her own dilemma.

Bernadette shrugged. "Most of the men have a lot of respect for my father, which means hardly any of them are willing to exchange so much as a 'hello' with me, let alone ask me to dance at one of the shepherds' dances. They don't want to incur Father's wrath. I've shed a lot of tears over it, and I was starting to think I'd end up as an old maid," she said, and then a note of triumph entered her voice. "But then Michael came along."

Heinrich had used the expression "old maid" earlier, Mimi recalled. In that moment, she had been almost paralyzed with fright, but looking back now, she was angry at herself for not having spoken up against him. *Typical*, she thought, *that such derogatory terms exist for women but not for men.* Then she forced herself to focus again on the young woman across the table.

"So your fiancé's name is Michael," she said.

Bernadette's bright smile was back. "Yes. He's the teacher in our village school. We met at the weekly market, and it was love at first sight." She sighed. "In any case, last fall, Michael asked me for my hand. As a teacher, he's respected, and he's not afraid of Father at all. Isn't it wonderful? I've been the happiest woman in the world ever since. But you know yourself how it feels." Bernadette gave Mimi's hand a familiar squeeze.

Mimi bit her lip. Happy? She was happy when her employer, Mr. Semmer, let her anywhere near the camera in his studio. She was happy in the darkroom when, developing pictures, the sharp smell of the chemicals told her that the magic that conjured photographs from silvered plates had begun its work. And she was also happy when, on Sundays after the service, she and Heinrich went walking in the forests of the Schurwald. But earlier, when Heinrich had proposed, every word had made her feel more and more anxious. Almost as anxious as she had been years ago, in the poacher's trap . . .

"There are many in the village who were surprised that I accepted when Michael asked for my hand in marriage. They were all convinced that I'd choose my future husband after the motto money marries money. In that respect, my father had already been active."

"You'd been promised to another man?" Mimi had only ever read about such dramas in novels.

"Not exactly 'promised,' but certain hopes had definitely been raised. In the previous year, a rich wool dealer had often been our guest at home. Suspiciously often. We would eat dinner together, and when we finished, Mother and Father always found some reason to exit the room and leave me alone with him. But nobody bothered to include me in their calculations! I'm not about to marry a man twenty years older than me just because he's stinking rich," said Bernadette.

Mimi nodded fiercely. Unthinkable! "How did you convince your parents that Michael was the right man for you?"

Bernadette's eyes were full of warmth and intimacy as she said, "The only thing that matters is love. It wasn't easy for Father to accept that, but for my sake he did." She laughed. "Since then, he's been a changed man. He's invited the entire village to the wedding! 'When my princess marries, it will be the party of the year,' he keeps saying. There'll be rivers of wine and beer, and roast lamb for everyone. And I've wished for a huge table covered with every possible cake and dessert." She sighed rapturously. "After that, finally, I'll be Michael's wife. I can hardly wait."

The depth of feeling in Bernadette's words! The happiness! Before Mimi knew what was happening, tears were rolling down her cheeks.

"Goodness, what is it? Did I say something wrong?" Bernadette handed Mimi an embroidered handkerchief.

Mimi accepted it gratefully. She sniffed loudly, then said, "It's not you. It's just . . . even if I wanted to . . . I can't marry now!"

CHAPTER 3

Between sobs, Mimi told Bernadette about the dilemma she found herself in, and Bernadette understood Mimi's despair. Both women still felt that fate had had a hand in them meeting when they had. A little later, when they parted, they did so reluctantly. One day, somewhere, they promised they would see each other again.

Mimi, with a heavy heart, made her way to the Esslinger Oberstadt. At home, she found her parents waiting expectantly. Her mother in particular looked as if she were ready to burst with anticipation. Did they already know something? Mimi certainly had her suspicions, and it would be just like Heinrich to talk to her parents first and then only afterward with her, although he'd said earlier that that was not the case.

Neither her mother nor her father gave anything away, however, and Mimi was suddenly no longer so sure of herself. Claiming she had a headache—which was no lie—she retreated to her room.

Heinrich and Mimi as husband and wife. Adieu, Esslingen! No more photo studio, no more darkroom. All her photographic dreams up in smoke. Mimi's stomach grumbled as if to remind her of its existence. She had not eaten since breakfast. For a moment, she was tempted to go downstairs and join her parents for dinner, but she knew that the conversation would turn to Heinrich's proposal, and that she would very likely find Heinrich dining with them, which he often did on weekends.

Her father would tell her, as he had many times, that in the conscientious, ambitious vicar he saw a younger version of himself. For him, Heinrich was the perfect son-in-law, and he would not understand that she had not yet said yes to Heinrich's proposal.

Her mother would go on at length about the duties to which a priest's wife had to wholeheartedly devote herself. With her extensive network of charitable causes, Amelie Reventlow could likely name every needy person in Schorndorf, Mimi thought with fleeting resentment. That was the last thing she needed to deal with now.

She didn't care if she starved—she was determined not to leave her room before she had found a solution to her mess. She rummaged in her handbag for the block of chocolate Mr. Semmer had given her that morning for her birthday. That morning . . . it seemed to Mimi to have been part of another life. Carefully, she unwrapped the foil from around the chocolate and snapped off a row.

For Heinrich, their future together was crystal clear, she realized as she let the chocolate melt slowly in her mouth. She was astonished that he had not spelled out the number of children he was expecting her to produce. What *she* thought of all his plans seemed not to interest him in the slightest. Rather, he assumed that she would be overjoyed and that she must think of his proposal as an act of divine providence.

So why couldn't she see it the same way? Why couldn't she be at least a little like Bernadette, proudly on her way home to the Swabian Jura with her wedding dress, hardly able to wait for the day she'd stand at the altar?

It was well after midnight, and Mimi still had not been able to sleep. *Uncle Josef,* she thought angrily. *He is to blame for everything.* And her stomach growled its assent. Without him, she would probably be an utterly "normal" young woman like Bernadette and most of the others. If she were normal, she would have dreamed for years of being proposed to and would now be appropriately delighted. But the truth was that, until today, she had pushed all thoughts of marriage aside. She had so much she still wanted to learn as a photographer.

Happy to have found a scapegoat in Uncle Josef, she sank her teeth into another piece of chocolate.

Josef Stöckle was her mother's older brother and one of the first traveling photographers. A good-looking man, courageous, and filled with the urge to travel. A daredevil with a gift for working with people. A magician behind a camera and master of his trade. It was he who'd awakened in Mimi a love of photography. Thanks to him, she had been one of the first women ever to learn the photographer's profession. Her parents had been horrified when she told them what she wanted to pursue professionally. Her mother's greatest wish had been that Mimi would follow in her own footsteps and dedicate herself to the needs of others. A teacher, that was the job for Mimi! Or even better, a doctor, if that profession were ever to open its doors to women. As a last resort, her mother would have been satisfied to see her become a missionary's wife. An old vow, however—and one that involved Uncle Josef—meant that her mother had felt obliged to accept Mimi's extraordinary choice of career.

If I look at it like that, no other human being has had such an impact on my life as Josef, Mimi thought. It was not as if he lived close by, either. With his mobile photo studio housed in a large horse-drawn wagon, he only passed through Esslingen a few times a year.

Mimi began to smile as she thought of Josef's Sun Coach—finished in glossy black with a golden sun painted in the middle. She could have spotted Josef's wagon among thousands.

When her uncle was in town, there was always some business to be taken care of. Sometimes it was a visit to the doctor or a trip to the Esslingen blacksmith to shoe his horse. Yet he always found all the time in the world for her. His visits had always been like a party, except for one occasion—she had just turned seven—when Uncle Josef was supposed to be looking after her. Back then, so much had gone wrong, although the turn of events later proved to be serendipitous indeed. But at the time, all hell had broken loose! Mimi's thoughts drifted back nearly twenty years.

CHAPTER 4

Why couldn't everyone just take a little more care when they walked over the red-gold carpet of leaves? Seven-year-old Mimi watched as the maid Rosa dragged a heavy green garland toward the vicarage garden. Rosa paid as little attention as anyone else to the colorful maple and beech leaves that covered the ground. Everyone stomped across the vibrant mantle, trampling the fine leaves until all that was left was brown sludge. Yet the tones and colors were all so gorgeous!

Mimi crouched and picked up one of the maple leaves. She stroked it reverently with her finger, tracing the fine veins that covered the ochre-colored leaf. It was so beautiful, she thought with a smile, to see the leaves drifting down like snow from the trees every autumn.

The next moment, she let the leaf fall to the ground. There was her mother! Finally! Mimi had been looking for her, but as was so often the case, her mother had been busy elsewhere. Today was the day they fed the poor at the parish fair, which took place in the vicarage garden every year on the third Sunday in October. The event had taken place for as long as Mimi could remember. "In many houses in the old part of town, and in the weaving quarter especially, the people suffer from poverty and hunger. Someone has to help the poor souls," her mother had explained, adding that there was much that Mimi could learn from her mother and that one day she, too, could do her own good deeds.

Of course, Mimi also wanted the hungry people to get bread and soup, but life was sometimes so exciting that she was simply distracted from all the charitable work. Like today. Mimi felt delicately inside the pocket of her skirt. Relieved to find that her treasure was still there, she looked up, but—oh no!—Mother had disappeared again.

A moment later, she heard her mother's loud voice through the open kitchen window: "Isn't the soup finished yet?"

Mimi's face brightened and she ran into the house. "Mother! Mother!"

"Mimi, child," her mother said absently as she peered over the shoulder of Elke Bieringer, the vicarage cook.

"Look what I found!" Bursting with pride, Mimi held out the fat caterpillar she'd discovered that morning among the colorful autumn leaves. "This is going to be an especially pretty butterfly one day," she said with awe. She could already see it in her mind's eye. It would have blue-and-pale-yellow wings with maybe a few red spots sprinkled across them. "Is there an old box I can have? I want to build a lovely cage for my butterfly."

"There are no lovely cages," her mother said gruffly. "Put that creature back where you found it. Caterpillars can only turn into beautiful butterflies if they've got room to move. Which, by the way, is no different for humans." With the door handle already in her hand, her mother looked sternly at Mimi. "What are you even doing in here? Didn't I tell you to stay with Uncle Josef? At least with him you'll stay out of trouble while all the busy bees here get on with their work."

Mimi looked downcast and felt miserable. She wasn't getting in anyone's way. And why couldn't she keep the little caterpillar?

The cook, who was just then chopping parsley, looked at the child and sighed. "Doesn't anyone have any time for you again? Come with me," she said and nodded in the direction of the pantry.

"Do you have a box for me?" Mimi trotted happily behind the cook.

"Not a box, but you can have a cookie." Elke stood on tiptoes to lift down the cookie tin from the highest shelf. "Here, take one with nuts. One for your uncle, too."

Would the caterpillar like a few crumbs, perhaps? "Thank you," Mimi murmured as she took the cookies in her left hand. She still held the caterpillar in her right.

Elke plucked at Mimi's sleeve where the fabric was so thin that her skin showed through underneath. "This has to be patched. And your skirt is filthy! Have you been crawling around on your knees again? Oh, girl, you wander around like a ragpicker's daughter. No wonder your teacher wrote a letter home."

"This is how I always look," said Mimi innocently.

"That's exactly the problem." The cook stroked Mimi's head and said quietly, "All the poor children in Africa, looking after the needy in the town, the new fund for hardship cases . . . The lady of this house takes care of so many things. It's about time her own daughter had some benefit from all her Christian charitableness."

With the caterpillar safely in her pocket again, Mimi walked down through the back section of the garden. Unlike the front part, where the poor would soon be fed, it was quiet back here. She heard the croaking of a few ravens and the monotonous beat of a blacksmith's hammer on iron. Had the blacksmith come to shoe Uncle Josef's mare, Grete? Mimi's face brightened. The smith's stories were almost as exciting as her uncle's.

Mimi ran toward the wagon at the end of the garden. "Josef Stöckle, Traveling Photographer," it read on the side. To Mimi, the wagon looked like something from a fairy tale. She thought the name her uncle had given it was perfect: Sun Coach.

"Well, Grete, looks like we can get on the road again." Josef gave his horse a contented pat on the neck. Then he dug a few coins out of his pocket and handed them to the blacksmith, who was packing his tools into his own wagon. "Thank you for coming at such short notice. Without new shoes for Grete, I wouldn't be able to go anywhere."

The men said a friendly farewell.

"You're going away again? I thought you'd spend the winter here with us." In her disappointment, Mimi struggled not to burst into tears.

"Winter is still a long way off. Between now and then, I'm going to visit Schwäbisch Hall. There are plenty of little villages around the saltworks there that don't have a local photographer. The people are thrilled to see me come through because I make a change from their usual routine. My pictures decorate the blank spaces on the walls in their houses. A traveling photographer is always a welcome sight, my child."

Mimi nodded, but she was troubled. "But you just came two weeks ago, and you were gone the whole summer," she said.

"Child, I'm a traveling photographer, and money doesn't rain from the sky. I have to keep moving if I want to work," her uncle said. He laughed. "Besides, I have to give the people something beautiful. Do you understand?"

Mimi nodded. But understanding and accepting were two different things. "Mother said you were supposed to look after me," she said with a pout.

"My favorite job of all," her uncle replied, stroking her hair. "I'm doing some retouching, and I know you love to watch. Come inside."

Mimi's eyes lit up. She followed her uncle eagerly into his wagon. It smelled so exciting inside—of the painted backdrops her uncle used for his pictures, of the chemicals he used to develop the photographs, and of the much-worn top hats that he attached to the inside wall of the wagon with rubber bands to stop them from banging against each other as he drove along. Lace parasols and fans were also fastened to the walls in the same fashion, but they didn't have any smell.

Her uncle used the top hats for his "worthy gentlemen" pictures, Mimi knew; the fans and parasols, similarly, were for his "fine lady" photographs. Her uncle had explained that the women were sometimes not very fine at all, but he could turn any farm wife into a noblewoman.

Mimi thought about striking a pose herself with a fan and umbrella; instead, she followed her uncle into the small darkroom he had set up in the front part of the wagon and which was separated from the rest of the vehicle by a black door.

"What are you working on?" Mimi whispered as she always did when she stepped into the mysterious darkness.

"It's a photograph of your neighbor Käthchen and her husband, Karl. Last week was their silver wedding anniversary." Josef Stöckle leaned back so that his niece could see the glass plate set in a frame. The anniversary couple stood upright and stern looking in front of a balustrade. Mimi noticed immediately that the balustrade was not real but had been painted by her uncle on canvas.

Josef tapped the glass plate. "Well, do you recognize your neighbors?"

"Yes!" Mimi laughed. "Mr. Wiedemann's fat tummy!" His stomach really did stick out like a camel's hump.

Mimi watched in fascination as Mrs. Wiedemann's face became more and more refined.

"People want to look beautiful, so I make them beautiful," her uncle explained. "Right, now I have to concentrate on my work. Why don't you sit out on the wagon steps until I'm done."

CHAPTER 5

Could this be any more boring? Mimi thought grumpily after sitting half an eternity on the steps of the Sun Coach. The autumn sun was now shining directly onto this patch of the garden. Mimi was hot, and her caterpillar was hot, too, and she decided to set up a nice home for it, regardless of what her mother had said. She listened one last time to the sounds from inside the wagon. Her uncle was whistling softly to himself, as he always did when he worked. He could go on like that for hours, Mimi knew from experience. He wouldn't miss her for a little while.

She slipped out through the back gate in the direction of the forest. She would find a box or crate soon enough, but now she wanted to collect what she would need to furnish it. The caterpillar should have things at least as lovely as her uncle's customers.

Her mother had made a point of forbidding her from going into the forest—she said there were poachers and other dangerous types in there. Mimi pinched her eyes almost closed. What nonsense! There was no one around at all. At the edge of the path, she discovered an empty snail shell. All she had to do now was find some moss and a few pretty leaves. Then the caterpillar would feel right at home and was certain to turn into a beautiful butterfly much faster.

Mimi continued walking.

Dark-brown acorns, chestnuts, a curiously formed root. Mimi looked down at the treasures gathered in her apron—that ought to be enough for the caterpillar's house. She had not quite completed the thought when her right foot sank deeper than it should. She cried out, but then the ground underfoot opened up and she plunged into the depths.

Her arm hurt, her head hurt, and she felt sick. She'd bumped her arm and head when she fell.

She blinked and tried to get her bearings. All around her was earth. It was cold and dark, and it smelled strange.

Leaves had covered the ground, so she had not seen the hole as she walked along. Why was there a hole in the middle of the path anyway? Perhaps it was a poacher's traps her mother had warned her about. Then she realized that she had strayed from the path on her search for a nice root. She felt automatically for the caterpillar in her skirt pocket. It was still there, still moving.

Mimi took a deep breath. She had to see to it that both of them got out of that hole as soon as they could, but how was she supposed to do that? Mimi swallowed a sob. She wanted to go home.

"Help! Help me . . ."

"I'm starting to run out of ideas," said the sergeant of the Esslingen police to the dozen or so volunteers gathered in the parish garden. "We've combed every cellar, every barn—not just here but in half the village." In the cold October morning, his words formed small clouds that rapidly dissipated.

The volunteers listened dispiritedly. None of them knew what to say. It was early Monday morning, and the priest's daughter had been missing since the day before, vanished like the proverbial needle in a haystack.

"Why don't we just check everything a second time?" said a young officer who'd been with the search from the first hour. Like most of the others, he hadn't slept at all during the night, and his eyes were red and half-closed. But his will to find the child was inscribed more deeply than his exhaustion.

"No. Searching the same places doesn't make sense." The sergeant gazed off into the distance, shaking his head.

Dozens had taken part in the hunt for the missing girl. Her parents, her uncle, the servants, and almost the entire parish had been searching for her. No one in the family had been able to say exactly when she had gone missing. Amelie Reventlow had thought her daughter safe in her brother's keeping, while Josef believed that Mimi had returned to the house.

"None of us knows God's plan, but our trust in him remains," said Father Franziskus Reventlow, but the concern on his face belied his words.

"God's plan?" Amelie Reventlow repeated. "God certainly can't want a child to simply disappear!" She buried her face in her hands, sobbing loudly. "I promise you one thing," she said through her tears. "When Mimi is found, I will do everything in my power to make sure she never lacks for anything again—whatever plans God might have!"

A dismayed silence settled over those gathered. What if Mimi's mother never had the chance to make good on her vow?

The young officer cleared his throat tentatively. "I know a man. His dog has the best nose for miles around. Maybe it could track down the child."

"A man?" said his sergeant with a sneer. "Why don't you just say what you mean? You're talking about one of those miserable poachers. As if those rats would work with us. All they're interested in is the price they can get for their plunder." The sergeant snorted.

"Then let us enter the church and ask God for his help," said Father Franziskus, doing his best to be encouraging.

While the sergeant and his men set off on their search once again, the congregation followed the priest into the church. The young officer, pensive, remained behind.

Mimi didn't know how long she'd been sitting in the hole. She had lost all sense of time. A day? A month? A year? Fear and despair, along with the confidence that everything would be all right, shook at her like an autumn storm rattling at the shutters of a house. A miracle. Anything less would not help her.

It was dark down here, almost as dark as in Josef's tiny darkroom in the Sun Coach. She was hungry and thirsty. And cold. She had no jacket, for the sun had still been shining when she set off. The chill was uncomfortable, but her thirst was worse. A glass of lemonade. Or a hot peppermint tea—Mimi would have given anything for hot tea. But the best she could manage was to run her right index finger across the earth to gather a tiny bit of moisture. She had felt the need to pee but held it in so long that her kidneys hurt. Only then did she squat in one corner of the hole and relieve herself. What would she do if she had to . . . ?

And what if the miracle never came? Her mother always had so much to do that she probably wouldn't even notice she was missing. Would she?

Then something else occurred to Mimi. God—he would notice. He'd always been there for her, awake or asleep, which meant he was also with her in the forest. She wasn't alone.

This revelation gladdened and soothed her. With her newfound calm, something else came over her: the sudden sensation of being gently cradled by something—something extremely light and delicate. Was it an angel's wing lifting her from the cold floor of the hole and warming her? Was it God's hand enclosing her like her warmest winter coat?

With her arms around her middle to fend off the cold, Mimi smiled. A little detour like the one she'd taken in the forest made no difference at all to either God or his angels. The miracle would happen. With that in her mind, Mimi fell asleep.

It was no angel's song that woke her, but the high-pitched yapping of a dog. Something was scratching up above, at the edge of her prison. Soil rained down on her, and she heard excited barking and, farther off, a whistle. The next moment, Mimi found herself looking into the amber eyes of a skinny dog. Spittle dripped onto her.

"The dog's found her!" she heard a man call out. The next moment, the man jumped down into the hole beside her and lifted her up to the top, where Uncle Josef embraced her.

"Child, I nearly died. I was so afraid we'd lost you." Mimi, confused and tired, looked over Josef's shoulder and saw the man with the dog disappearing quickly into the woods.

Laughing and crying at the same time, Josef carried her home, where Elke immediately heated some soup. Her father and mother wrapped her in their arms. "Thank the Lord, I was so worried about you," her father whispered in her ear.

Mimi, as hungry and cold as she was, looked at him in surprise. "Why were you worried? God was with me. He is with us on all our paths. You say so all the time."

Her father's eyes glistened as he gazed at her. "My darling child, we can all learn a lesson from you. You are braver and more devoted to God than the rest of us put together."

Mimi frowned. "What did I do that was brave? Dying would have been dumb. I want to give people the gift of beauty, just like Uncle Josef does, and if I want to do that, then I have to become a photographer one day."

Her mother looked at her father and shook her head. "You hear that? Mimi feels called upon by God to give people the gift of beauty." Tears flowed down her cheeks as she threw her arms around Mimi again and sobbed, "If that's still what you dream of being when you're older, then I will make sure your dream comes true. Even if I have to bang on the door of every studio in the region to find someone to train you."

CHAPTER 6

In the quiet of her bedroom, Mimi smiled. After all these years, she could still hardly believe her mother's overnight transformation. No more of Amelie's noble words about Mimi as the privileged daughter of a parish priest, duty bound to lead a charitable life in the service of the poor. From that day on, Mimi had been free to pick flowers, paint, and dream without a single word from her mother about being an "idle child." It was then that Mimi realized her mother loved her—and what a wonderful feeling that had been. Yes, sometimes something bad had to happen to spark something good.

At three in the morning, it occurred to Mimi that she had never stayed awake an entire night. Yet, somehow, this night was special. She snuggled under her bedspread. She had not pulled the curtains closed earlier and now she looked out into the inky winter's night. The darkness settled her agitated mind. For the first time since Heinrich had asked for her hand, she felt a sense of inner calm.

As a small child, she had been afraid of the dark. Uncle Josef, however, had taught her that it had to be pitch black whenever a photographer changed a glass plate in the camera, which was why he always threw a heavy black cloth over the camera when he did so. "If even the slightest bit of light touches the glass plate, you might as well throw it away," he'd told her. Mimi had once crawled underneath one of those cloths herself, just to see what it was like. "If you can't see anything at all, you have to make even better use of your sense of touch," he had said. Armed with that knowledge, Mimi had learned to like the darkness.

Once, when Uncle Josef had given her an old, worn-out length of canvas, she had constructed her own photo studio in her bedroom. Her dolls became her customers, and her children's table and the small chairs around it served as props. She had fashioned a "camera" by tying broken broom handles together and adding a large carton in which, front and back, she'd cut peepholes. When her mother first laid eyes on Mimi's camera, she turned and scurried away. Mimi remembered clearly how afraid she had been that her mother was again going to forbid her from playing her favorite game. But Amelie returned a few moments later, proudly holding a length of black cloth. "You'll need this if you want to change your dry plates," she said with a wink as she clipped the cloth to the back of Mimi's camera. Mimi had been in seventh heaven. She would never have believed that so much good could result from her mishap in the woods.

Despite Amelie's newfound support of Mimi's pursuits, however, Mimi hadn't always gotten exactly what she wanted. Half dozing, Mimi surrendered again to her memories.

"Whatever profession you decide to follow, finishing thirteen years of school will make things easier for you," her mother had announced when her daughter completed the tenth grade. "There are so many possibilities for women these days. It would be a shame for you not to at least stay open to them." Amelie Reventlow had held a train ticket to Berlin. "Unfortunately, our beautiful Württemberg is still extremely backward in these matters and won't offer girls the final three years. But Luise High School in Berlin is not just for boys—young women can also finish their schooling there. I would have given anything for a chance like this as a young woman."

"But, Mother, we'd decided that I'd be able to start an apprenticeship as a photographer when I finished school," Mimi had protested. "You were going to help me find a master to teach me."

"And that has not changed. A promise is a promise, but first you finish school," her mother had replied, her tone as rigid as iron. "Your aunt Elsa in Berlin has a room ready for you. In three years, we'll see where we stand."

Mimi had been stunned. Her mother had said it so casually: three years! She made it sound like a weekend visit to her aunt.

"Father, say something!" she had pleaded. "Are you really going to banish me like this?"

"My sister is looking forward to seeing you very much. It pleases the Lord when children use their minds to learn. Your dream will survive a short postponement, I have no doubt." He had looked at her as benevolently as if she were one of the straying sheep of his congregation.

In her distress, Mimi had turned to her uncle Josef, who was visiting at the time. "But finishing high school isn't necessary at all if you want to be a photographer, is it?"

Instead of supporting her, however, her uncle had merely winked and whispered to her: "There are plenty of photo studios in Berlin. When you've got some free time and don't have to study, you can go and see what the competition's up to. You'll also learn what it takes to be a woman of quality. I bet that your Berlin years will do you nothing but good."

She had no interest in bets back then. Besides, Josef's first prophecy had been off the mark, because she did not find many opportunities at all to explore the city. Both the school's rules and those set by her aunt Elsa had been very strict. In the end, Mimi had accepted her fate. Anyway, Berlin was too big and too loud, so she focused on her studies and hoped the years would pass quickly.

Josef, however, had been right in predicting that she would become a "woman of quality." Her father's sister had been horrified to see Mimi's neglected wardrobe. A moth hole here, a split seam there, and her underwear—items that should have been spotless white were instead stained or graying! When her aunt discovered that Mimi was used to washing her hair only once a week, her dismay only deepened, and she had actually called the parish household back home "depraved." Mimi had felt deeply ashamed. It was not that she was indifferent to looking well groomed, but she did not know things any other way. Her mother spent so much time tending to the needs of the poor in other parts of the world that she could not give Mimi's appearance the attention it needed. Her aunt threw herself with great zeal into the task of turning Mimi into a stylish young woman. Mimi showed her gratitude by soaking up everything Elsa taught her like a sponge.

When she returned to Esslingen in 1899 in a spotless outfit, her hair perfectly coiffed, and with a good report card in her pocket, her heart rejoiced. Home again! Finally! She had missed the half-timbered houses of her Swabian homeland, the gently melodic Swabian accent, and the view of the mountains of the Swabian Jura one had from the Esslinger Oberstadt in good weather.

Now her life would begin, she believed. At last, her dream of being a photographer's apprentice would come true.

Back then, when she was seventeen and on her way to Berlin, she had had to bend to her parents' wishes. *But what about today?* Mimi wondered as the night gave way to a pale dawn beyond her window. She was twenty-six years old. A grown woman. Wasn't it finally time to do what she truly longed to do?

How had Bernadette put it barely twelve hours earlier? *"The only thing that matters is love."*

It was high time for her to turn her mind to her great love once again.

"Heinrich asked me to marry him yesterday," said Mimi the following day, when she and her parents sat together for the Sunday roast and spaetzle smothered with gravy. *Thank God Heinrich isn't here,* she thought fervently. She would still have to talk with him, of course, but one thing at a time.

Under the pretext of needing more rest for her headache to fade, she had skipped the Sunday visit to church—something she had never done before—and slept late. Now, sitting down to lunch, she felt good, a circumstance that had less to do with her freshly washed hair or the fact that she had, after all, gotten a reasonable amount of sleep than it did with the clarity she had reached. She was facing a fork in the road, she knew. One way was clearly signposted, but the other she could see only vaguely. Still, she knew exactly which path she would follow.

Her parents exchanged a knowing look.

"We thought so," her mother said. "Oh, child, I'm so happy for you! You could not find a better husband." She squeezed Mimi's hand, then frowned. "But where is Heinrich? He usually eats with us on Sundays."

"I asked our vicar to leave us alone, just this once," her father said.

Mimi almost dropped her fork in surprise. "You did what? But why?"

Her mother was also looking at him in incomprehension.

Her father laughed. "Oh, child, I'd be a poor pastor if I did not see the state you were in when you came home yesterday. I wanted to give you the chance to talk in peace and quiet, just us. Heinrich let something slip a few days ago that made me suspect what he had in mind."

"Franziskus! What are you trying to say? One might almost think that you're not happy that Mimi will be Heinrich's wife. Who's been going on and on for years about his wonderful vicar?"

"I have the greatest respect for Heinrich, that's true. But this is not about whether *I* am happy, but whether our daughter is." With raised eyebrows, he looked at Mimi.

"But . . . I don't understand . . ." Amelie looked frantically from one to the other.

Mimi was deeply moved by her father's sensitivity. She stopped eating and put her fork on the table. Quietly, she said, "I also have the greatest respect for Heinrich. But I can't marry him."

"Excuse me?" Her mother released Mimi's hand as if she had grabbed hold of hot coals. "What exactly is that supposed to mean?"

Mimi sighed. How could she say in a few words all the things that had been on her mind the past few years?

"What I'm going to say to you might come as something of a surprise. But in truth, it isn't a surprise at all. On the contrary, I've had enough time to think it all through. You know it was always my dream to become a photographer," she said.

"And that's what you are, isn't it? What more do you want?" her mother shot back. "Nothing's harder than ingratitude, that's all I can say," she hissed accusingly at her husband. "Heinrich is such a good man. How can she hesitate even a minute?"

"Let the girl speak, and perhaps we'll all be a little wiser."

Mimi smiled sadly but thankfully at her father. "I *work* in a photo studio, but I am far from being a photographer. Mr. Semmer, of course, has taught me all I need to know to practice the profession, but I cannot *actually* practice it. From the first day of my apprenticeship, Mr. Semmer has seen me as no more than a docile assistant, someone to dust, polish the floor, clean the windows, make tea, and run errands. But to make up for that, when customers come to have their portraits taken, I get to straighten the women's hats and make sure every hair is in place." Her voice dripped with irony. "Oh, and I'm allowed to show our customers our sample album so they can choose how they want to be photographed from the array of poses and props we offer: Lady with bouquet in right hand, left hand on table— choose number one. Gentleman with top hat sitting at table, upper body leaning slightly forward—choose number two. Child standing with doll—that would be number three. Child, sitting with doll—number four." She shook her head. "It's all so trite. And so formal!" Mimi swallowed. She hadn't planned to get so upset, but now that she'd gotten started, it was hard to stop. "In any case," she continued, somewhat calmer, "in all these years, I can count on two hands the times Mr. Semmer actually let me touch the camera."

Both her parents frowned.

"He *is* the boss," said her father and helped himself to a slice of roast meat.

Amelie reached out for her daughter's hands again and squeezed them tightly. "But, child, don't you see that when you're Heinrich's wife, you'll finally have your say? Just look at me—have you ever seen your father try to meddle with my work?"

"Mother," Mimi said, and there was pain in her voice, "I admire you so very much for what you do, but I'm not you. Photography is what I love." *And love is all that matters,* she added silently.

"Do you really think you'll be better off in another studio?" her mother asked with disdain. "Is it off to Stuttgart now? Isn't Esslingen enough for you anymore?"

"I don't want to go to another studio. Nor to Stuttgart, at least not forever," Mimi said. Summoning all her courage, she said, "I would like to be a traveling photographer. I want to give people the gift of beauty. I want to photograph them outdoors, even with props, if that's what they want. But for heaven's sake, not always crammed into the same poses! I want to work with light and shadow and captivate people with the pictures I take—and I want to see some of the world, too."

For a long moment, there was an uncomfortable silence.

Then her mother let out a shrill laugh. "Have you completely lost your mind? Or has Josef been putting ideas into your head? Well, my dear brother had better watch himself!"

"You want to go traveling with Josef? When did you discuss that?" her father asked with a furrowed brow.

"We haven't discussed anything," said Mimi calmly. "Like you, I haven't seen Josef for ages."

"So it's just some harebrained scheme." Her mother nodded as if that was what she'd been thinking all along. "Well, you can shake that right out of your head again, my girl. I know my brother well enough to tell you he has no interest whatsoever in having you tag along on his travels. He treasures his independence far too much for that." As if that were the end of the matter, Amelie picked up her fork and knife and began to slice a piece of meat. "Eat!" she ordered her husband and daughter.

"I don't want to travel with Josef at all," Mimi said. "In fact, I will do my best to stay out of his way. I don't want to compete with him by turning up in the same places, after all." As casually as she had managed to say that, she had not previously thought the point through at all. Still, she believed that she'd sounded quite sure of herself. But was that any wonder, considering all the years she'd been pondering these ideas secretly? The notions came to her like ghosts when she was dusting shelves in the studio or developing Mr. Semmer's photographs in the darkroom. Her ghost thoughts even appeared when Heinrich told her about the inspiring sermons he wanted to deliver one day.

Her father stared at her in wide-eyed disbelief. "You want to buy a horse and wagon? Child! You don't have the first clue about horses, and you can't drive a wagon either. Even if you were an expert in both . . . a woman, alone, wandering the countryside? Sleeping alone out in the wilderness? You'd overtax even the most hardworking guardian angel. I'm sorry, but I think your mother is right—you really are out of your mind."

"I most certainly am not," Mimi said, her voice steady. "But I can reassure you that I have no intention of buying either a horse or my own wagon."

"Then what *do* you want?" asked both parents at once.

Mimi took a deep breath and began to put her dream into words.

CHAPTER 7

Mid-March 1905, Hanover

"Greetings and welcome to my emporium for photographic and optical devices. I trust your journey was pleasant? It is an honor to welcome customers who've traveled so far." Gustav Rüdenberg, proprietor of the eponymous company, ushered Mimi inside with a broad smile, reaching out to her with both hands.

"Thank you. I'm very happy to be here," said Mimi, her voice a little husky. *What a lovely place,* she thought. Glass cabinets stood in orderly rows around the walls. They contained dozens of pairs of binoculars, cameras, and other equipment. Overhead hung an enormous chandelier, in the light of which the cabinets gleamed alluringly.

"Mr. Stöckle, welcome! I've heard a great deal about you," the trader greeted Mimi's uncle.

"All good, I hope," Josef replied with a laugh.

Mimi glanced warmly at her uncle. When Josef had heard about her plans, he would not be deterred from traveling up from Bavaria solely to help her purchase a camera.

"Come and sit, please." With an inviting sweep of his hand, Gustav Rüdenberg indicated a large circular walnut table in the middle of the room. "I've prepared everything for your visit. A cup of tea or coffee, perhaps?"

Mimi thanked him but declined. Her hands were practically tingling, and she could hardly wait to get a closer look at the cameras, all of them a gleaming, inky black, that Gustav Rüdenberg had set out in the center of the table. *First-class equipment at genuine factory prices,* she read to herself from a large advertisement on the opposite wall. She could believe it—Mr. Rüdenberg and his elegant mail-order establishment radiated an aura of true expertise. *The long journey from Esslingen to Hanover was worth it,* she thought with satisfaction.

When they were seated and Josef had been served a cup of coffee, Gustav Rüdenberg turned to Mimi. "Madam, would you be so kind as to explain the purpose for which you require a camera? If I have understood correctly, you are a trained photographer, is that accurate?"

Madam . . . no one had ever called her that before. Mimi looked to her uncle, hoping for assistance. But Josef stirred his coffee as if none of this had anything to do with him.

Mimi pulled herself together. "Well, my goal is to be a traveling photographer, of a sort. I don't plan to have a mobile studio, though, but to rent space with local photographers for a certain period. A guest photographer, you could say." There, it was out. If the man decided she was crazy, so be it.

Gustav Rüdenberg merely nodded. "You're the second this year to try that. The first was a young man from Stralsund, and I had a customer last year with the same idea. An interesting development, I must say, taking place in our industry."

Mimi thought she must have misheard the man. "You mean I'm not the first to have this idea?"

Rüdenberg laughed heartily. "I'm sorry to disappoint you. Now, if the idea actually works, I can't tell you."

"That's exactly my argument," said Josef. "When *I* show up somewhere, the local photographers are far from enthusiastic about the competition. You'll probably be sent packing more than once. But what do I know? Times are changing, that much is clear." He gulped down a mouthful of coffee. "In ten years, we traveling photographers with our horses and wagons will probably be a thing of the past, replaced by other approaches to the business. I must say, I've also been thinking about opening a studio of my own."

"Really?" Mimi said, surprised.

"I'll tell you about it another time," Josef said. "Today, we're here for you."

Rüdenberg nodded and got down to business. Like a conjurer pulling a rabbit out of a hat, he reached beneath the table and produced a double-shutter camera. "My recommendation for you would be this."

"It's not much bigger than an iron," Mimi said. "Can you really take good pictures with it?"

Both men laughed.

"Next to that monstrous wooden bellows contraption your boss has in his studio, this camera certainly looks small," Josef said. "But once you've been carrying it around the whole day, you'll wish it were even smaller."

"I'm sure that's true," said Mimi, and a smile spread across her face. Even if she were to collapse like an old horse under the weight of her equipment, she was counting the days until her travels began.

"This camera is made of wood, although the construction is light," said Rüdenberg now. His eyes shone with pride and he ran his hand over the camera as if it were a living thing. "Finest mahogany. As far as the technology is concerned, it is surprisingly easy to operate and offers a photographer an excellent range of possibilities. The lens board itself is . . ."

Mimi focused on following the dealer's description. After all, if she decided on this model, she would have to be able to handle it by herself, starting the very next day. At the same time, she had to withstand the urge to pinch herself on the arm. Could it be that she was actually at one of the best-known companies for photographic equipment and buying her very own camera? If someone had told her this just a few weeks before, she would probably have declared them insane.

Once she had told her parents about her plans on the day after her birthday, everything had started moving very quickly. Her mother had shed a few tears for the "wasted opportunity," then she had sighed, stood up, and taken a cream-colored envelope out of a drawer in the sideboard. The ink was already a little faded, but Mimi could still read the words written on it: *Minna's Trousseau.* "Maybe you wondered why I never bought you anything for your trousseau," her mother said. "For one thing, I never really had the time to do that kind of shopping, and for another, I find the whole tradition old fashioned. I wanted you to be able to choose the things you wanted for yourself. So for the last few years, I've been putting away a bit of the housekeeping money every week," she went on, while Mimi's father listened in astonishment. "I always pictured you in the Tietz department store in Stuttgart, choosing a tea service and towels. Well, nothing's going to come of that now." She smiled. "But what of it! Now that you don't need cooking pots or bedding, you can at least use the money to get yourself a decent camera and whatever else you need. If there's anything left, then you'll have something to tide you over in the early times." Without making a fuss, as if she were dealing with a few coins for pocket money, she had handed Mimi the envelope. "Use it wisely, child."

Mimi had laughed and cried at the same time.

Getting through the conversation with Heinrich had been less pleasant. He had made comments that, for Mimi, were not at all what one would expect of a soon-to-be parish priest. She had tried not to take his insults personally but to attribute them to Heinrich feeling that his honor had been tarnished. Afterward, she was more sure than ever that she had made the right decision. Preaching freedom of spirit was one thing, but living that freedom of spirit in the real world was another.

Her talk with Mr. Semmer had also been anything but agreeable. When she handed in her notice and told him about her plans, he had laughed and laughed. With her lack of experience, she would never be able to make a living as a photographer, he'd predicted. Mimi had nearly told him that he alone was to blame for her lack of experience, but she did not get the chance. Instead of insisting that she remain to the end of the month, as her contract stipulated, Semmer told her to pack her things and get out. He had no use for "someone like her," he'd said in his most condescending tone.

Her heart wounded and her self-confidence shaken, Mimi had returned home. *Every dawn is dark,* she consoled herself, and held on tightly to what Bernadette had said. *"The only thing that matters is love."*

"I also have a five-part tube tripod, all metal, foldable and thus easily transportable." Rüdenberg smiled at Mimi.

She smiled back. "I can't do without a tripod, of course. But do you also have a bag to carry it all in?"

Gustav Rüdenberg gave her a cheerful wink. "Young lady, do you think I would let you walk out of here without a suitable bag? I have one that's custom made for this camera and tripod. You can comfortably stow everything inside, and it has a broad strap designed not to dig into your shoulder." He had already set a gleaming leather bag on the table in front of her. "It has a lock to keep things inside safe from light-fingered types, just in case you ever find yourself in a crowd. And it's lined top to bottom with red velvet. Your camera will lie as if on a bed of roses. In the compartment next to the camera, there's space for a dozen glass plates, which should keep you going for a while. A very well-thought-out unit, if I may say so."

The leather smelled spicy . . . *Like the freedom of the road,* Mimi thought. The velvet was as brilliantly scarlet as a Catholic priest's cassock, and as soft as silk to the touch. Mimi already knew that every time she opened the bag and saw that color, her heart would do a little somersault of joy.

She looked inquiringly at her uncle Josef. *Should I really?* He nodded encouragingly.

"I'll take it all!" said Mimi, and felt quite dizzy with delight.

An hour later, Mimi was 166 marks poorer but a complete camera kit richer. She could hardly believe her luck.

"There's a good inn near here. Let's get a bite to eat," said Josef. "My treat, to celebrate the day."

Mimi, her heart still pounding all the way to her neck, was certain that she wouldn't be able to swallow a morsel, but she agreed. She wanted to sit and talk with her uncle before they went their separate ways.

"You can put your camera on the floor, you know. It's not going to run away," said her uncle with a smile as they ate sauerbraten and potatoes—Mimi held her camera bag on her lap, protecting it like a treasure.

She looked around suspiciously, but the other guests were only interested in their food. No one seemed to be paying any particular attention to her or her camera, and she finally shifted the bag to the floor between her feet.

"Well, now you have a camera, but no husband," said her uncle between bites.

"Josef!" Mimi, shocked, looked at him over the rim of her water glass. "Are you going to start with that kind of talk now, too? I thought I'd left all that behind in Esslingen."

"All I want to say is that I hope you don't regret it one day," said her uncle with real concern in his voice. "As someone's wife, you'd be taken care of. When you're traveling, the fear of not being able to make a living is your constant companion. Oh, there are good times when you can hardly keep up with all the orders, but there are other times, too, when no one recognizes you exist. I've always been able to handle those kinds of things, but can you? There's a lot you'll have to put up with, and many things you can't take personally."

"If I'm cut even a little from the same cloth as you, I'll manage," Mimi said confidently. "Besides, I don't have a choice. I *have* to do this now. Do you know what I mean?"

Josef smiled mischievously. "I do know! Right now, I feel the same as you."

Mimi looked at him excitedly. "That photo studio you mentioned earlier—were you serious? You living a sedentary life. Somehow I can't imagine it."

"Neither can I," Josef admitted. "But I've met someone. A few years ago, actually. She's a widow, a wonderful woman. Her name is Traudel, and she lives in the Swabian Jura. It was providence that we met at all. I was on my way to Ulm when my mare, Grete, threw a shoe. Like it or not, I had to spend the night in the mountains—I could only get to a blacksmith the next morning. Traudel and I met that night. It was love at first sight."

How Josef's eyes shone! Just like Bernadette's when she talked about her future husband. Mimi sighed. *True love must be something very wonderful.*

"Traudel isn't interested in traveling with you?"

Josef shook his head. "To be honest, child, I've never asked her. And I admit I'm a little worn out, too. Not having to hitch up the horse and wagon every day and move on is looking more and more attractive. Traudel has a nice house with a huge garden, and I'd build myself a studio there, completely out of glass." His eyes sparkled, as if he were picturing it in front of him. "Grete can live out her last years in the garden. She's eighteen, you know. Not young for a mare."

Mimi nodded thoughtfully. "It sounds like a good plan. But it's strange, in a way—you settling down and me going on the road." Josef's words about feeling worn out made her uneasy, as did the slight shuffle she had noticed earlier in his gait. His shoulders seemed to curve farther forward than they had before, and he moved more slowly. How old was he? Sixty in August, she realized, calculating quickly. Yet he'd always been so full of energy, so adventurous. Did he really want to settle down and retire to the backlands of the Swabian Jura?

"Maybe it's exactly how it should be. Like a relay race, you taking the baton from me," Josef said with forced cheer. "Tell me—how does it feel to be a fledgling traveling photographer?"

"Can you ask me that again in a few weeks?" Mimi's stomach was so nervous just then that she was afraid she might have to make a run for the toilet. As much as she had wished a thousand times in recent years to be on the road like Josef—as free as the wind, her only duty to herself and her creative endeavors—now that she was at the threshold, she was afraid.

Josef had always been able to read her like an open book, and he grasped her hand in his. "You'll do fine! When it comes to competition, local photographers are probably more likely to open their doors to an attractive young woman than to a man. Your job is to convince them that if they give you space in their studios, they're getting an added attraction to offer, a boon and bonus for their esteemed clientele."

Mimi beamed. That was exactly how she'd imagined it.

"So you're going to have to think hard about the arguments you will use to convince those gentlemen to take you on."

"It's easy: because I'm a bit more daring than most photographers," she said. She felt sure of herself now—she'd certainly spent enough time thinking about this. "I don't want to use any head supports or body braces, but to see people in natural poses. I want to get away from that whole 'studio' flavor with the same old props, the same old postures and expressions. When I think of the deadly serious pictures that Mr. Semmer always took of children . . . Why can't children just be children in front of the camera?" Her creased brow reflected her irritation. "And why does the wife always have to docilely sit on a chair while her husband stands behind her with his hand on her shoulder, like she's a schoolchild. It's all so . . . stereotypical. There were so many

things I would have done differently, but Semmer wouldn't let me."
She stabbed a potato as if it were to blame for everything.

"Wanting to do everything differently—the prerogative of youth!"
Josef wiped his mouth with a napkin and laughed. "But I know what
you mean. You want to let the personality of every person you photograph shine through."

Mimi nodded vehemently. She knew that Josef would understand.

"Still, you must have noticed that many customers insist on a pretty
veneer. The farmer wants to look like an imposing officer. The nanny
wants to see herself as a lady of means. Just for a moment to be someone
else, to dream of living a different life . . . is that so terrible?" With his
head tilted to one side, Josef looked at his niece.

"Oh, I certainly don't want to take away anyone's dream," Mimi
said. "To be a different person, if only for a brief moment, well, that's
the magic of photography. If that means dressing up, or even posing
with some interesting props, then I'm not going to disapprove." Her
gaze wandered away into the distance as she said, "But people can also
be beautiful just as God made them. My dream, with the help of photography, is to show them that. Sometimes a smile on someone's lips or
a sunbeam on a face are worth far more than all the props in the world."

"You've set yourself quite a goal, my girl," Josef said affectionately.
"I've been trying all my life to get people to smile. Mostly in vain, I
might add. But quite apart from all your artistic ideas, do you feel you're
prepared technically for your new work?"

"More than you know!" said Mimi with a grin. "The fact that Mr.
Semmer never let me actually take pictures had *one* advantage. I was
able to study all his settings in detail and think them over for myself.
Later, when I was developing the pictures, I could see how shutter
speed, camera angle, and lighting affected the results. Theory and practice are two very different things, I know, but I can hardly wait to get
started!"

CHAPTER 8

"Remember, before you take a room at an inn, always go and check it first. If you get on a train, never sit in an empty compartment. Find one where people are already sitting, or you never know who's going to sit down next to you and start harassing you. And you should be settled in a guesthouse before dark. It's dangerous to go wandering the streets of a strange town by yourself, and—"

"Stop!" Mimi interrupted her uncle. She laughed. "I've survived twenty-six years, so you needn't worry. Besides, I've got a guardian angel watching over me wherever I go. You know that." She winked at him, but when she saw the concern still etched on his face, she added, "I'll still be extra careful, with everything. I promise."

It was the next morning, and they were standing together at the train station. Josef would take the train back to Ulm, where he had left his wagon and found a stable for his horse. He had several appointments there to take care of, and after that he was going back to see his sweetheart in the Swabian Jura.

Mimi, however, wanted to stay in Hanover and try her luck there.

"If any of the photographers give you any trouble, you tell me, agreed?"

"I will," Mimi said, with an affectionate glance at her uncle.

"You're sure you don't want to head south again and start there? Maybe around Würzburg, or the beautiful landscapes along the Rhine valley. Karlsruhe, Baden-Baden. I had good times there. Wherever they grow wine, the people are a cheerful and friendly lot."

"You and your wine-growing regions. That's probably why you're moving to the bleak old Swabian Jura," Mimi teased. "Don't worry, I'll be back down in Baden one day, but I'm here, and this is where I'm going to start. Going somewhere else now would be a waste of good time. Besides, Hanover is big, and the people here seem to be well off." She waved her hand, including in one gesture the train station and all the well-dressed citizens hurrying by.

Josef nodded. "That may be true, but my gut tells me the people here like to keep to themselves. You're cut from different cloth. When it comes to the modern world, the good citizens of Hanover don't strike me as particularly receptive. It would be a shame to see you hitting your head against a wall with them."

"I don't need ten studios that want to take me on, just one. And I'm sure I'll be able to find that," said Mimi. She wasn't about to start off with the kind of preconceptions about the Hanoverians that Josef seemed to have.

Josef embraced her and whispered in her ear, "You have Traudel's address now. When I'm not with her, she and I are in touch all the time. If worse comes to worst, come and find me, all right? And if you need any advice, just write."

"All right," said Mimi, and tears suddenly filled her eyes. She'd never been good at saying goodbye, especially to her beloved uncle.

As Josef's train, wheels screeching and motor roaring, pulled into the station, she was almost relieved to see it come. Josef seemed to feel the same. Still nimble despite the signs of age, he leaped up the two iron steps and into the wagon. A moment later, his head appeared at a window. He waved to Mimi and called, "Good luck, my dear!"

Mimi smiled. Luck? Yes, she needed luck, and soon.

"Good afternoon. My name is Mimi Reventlow. I'm a traveling photographer from Swabia. I specialize in naturalistic photographs. I'd like to ask if you would take me on as a guest photographer in your studio for a little while." Mimi spoke and smiled at the same time, in the hope that she might be especially well received. Her first studio. *In for a penny, in for a pound,* she'd thought to herself, and had chosen a studio in the center of Hanover as her first stop. It was large and brightly lit and must surely have been among the best in town.

"Naturalistic photographs—my passion, too." The man's gaze drifted at a snail's pace from the top of Mimi's head down over her breasts and body to her feet.

Mimi shuddered. She hated being ogled like that.

"I don't need a photographer, but I've recently devoted myself to nude photography, and I'm always on the lookout for willing models." The photographer licked his bottom lip.

Mimi inhaled sharply. Had she heard the man correctly? "Thank you, no," she said indignantly, and she hurried out of the shop.

"Good afternoon. My name is Mimi Reventlow. Is the owner of the studio here?" Mimi smiled uncertainly at the well-dressed woman who stood behind the counter wearily turning the pages of a newspaper.

"My husband's out buying cigars. You're more than welcome to make an appointment with me." The woman reached for her calendar. "Was it a portrait you wanted?"

Mimi smiled. "I'm a photographer myself—a traveling photographer. I'm looking for a studio in Hanover that will employ me for a while as a guest photographer. With me, you and your husband could offer your customers something fresh and special."

The well-dressed woman raised her eyebrows mockingly. "We really have no use for anything like that. My husband is very popular, and our clientele would be disappointed if it were not him behind the camera, and instead some"—she waved her hand as if she were trying to snatch the words like flies from the air—"itinerant photographer."

"Good afternoon. My name is Mimi Reventlow. I'm a traveling photographer from Swabia, and I specialize in taking naturalistic pictures. I'd like to ask if you would take me on as a guest photographer in your studio for a short time."

"Naturalistic pictures? Revolting! We run a reputable house. A bare neck is the most skin you'll see here."

"Forgive me," said Mimi with an embarrassed laugh. "You've misunderstood. What I meant was—"

The man interrupted her and pushed her back through the door. "Out! I don't want to hear your explanations!"

Half-amused, half-horrified, Mimi found herself back on the street. What the devil had just happened? Had her mention of "naturalistic photographs" been somehow ambiguous? First the man with his nude photographs, and now this misunderstanding. Maybe she should rethink her wording. She glanced a final time at the shop. Misunderstanding aside, she would never have wanted to take pictures in such a dusty old parlor, thank you very much!

"*What* do you want?" asked the man in the next studio, once she had introduced herself.

"I wanted to ask you whether . . ." Mimi struggled to find the right words. She felt she'd expressed herself clearly enough, or was the man hard of hearing? "Whether I might work with you for a time, as a guest photographer."

The man, like the one in the previous shop, was not young. He eyed her condescendingly.

"With a specialty of your own, you say? The only specialty a woman should have is the kind she cooks in the kitchen. Women belong in the home, nowhere else."

"Thank God not all men are as prehistoric as you," Mimi hissed. On her way out, she slammed the door of the studio so hard that the glass rang.

The next place she tried was almost worse.

The proprietor—Mimi guessed he was not much older than she was—said, "I know exactly what you have in mind."

"You do?" Mimi's expression brightened. Finally, someone who understood her.

Then he jabbed an index finger at her aggressively. "You plan to flatter me, make yourself at home, then steal my customers from under my nose. Tell me, which one of my competitors sent you here?"

"Excuse me? I——" Mimi was so flabbergasted that she could barely speak.

"Tell whoever it was that others might swallow that kind of nonsense, but not me! Now get out before I call the police."

That evening, as Mimi sat in her simple guesthouse eating an equally simple meal that consisted of an apple, a hard-boiled egg, and a slice of dry bread, she didn't know whether to laugh or cry. She had been prepared that establishing herself as a traveling photographer wouldn't be easy. What she had not counted on at all, however, was running into a brick wall of rejection and mistrust.

Tomorrow is another day, she assured herself before she fell asleep, physically and emotionally drained.

But the second day was no better than the first.

On the third day, Mimi decided she had had enough of the Hanoverians. Frustrated, she took the train to Hildesheim, smaller than Hanover, where the half-timbered houses and the pretty market square reminded her of Esslingen. New town, new luck—she'd find success here, she felt, as she made her way along Bahnhofsallee in search of the first studio.

But fortune did not smile on her in Hildesheim, either. The owner of one studio wanted a lackey, an offer that Mimi politely declined. It was the only one she got.

In Brunswick, her next destination, she could, in fact, have worked as a traveling photographer. The resident photographer, however, demanded an 80 percent commission for every picture she sold, and she would have to pay for the dry silver plates herself. Mimi had laughed in the man's face and walked out.

Five days later, she found herself on a train bound for Frankfurt. She did not know where she was supposed to go from there, but she *did* know that she had to put the north behind her and get back to southern Germany again.

If she was frugal, the money her mother had put aside would keep her above water for a few more weeks. *And thank God for that,* she thought as the train rumbled through seemingly endless, uninhabited landscapes. Still, something had to happen soon, otherwise . . .

Mimi looked pessimistically at her leather bag. She had not taken the camera out even once.

Jealous wives, pathologically suspicious business owners, woman haters, cutthroats, and nude photographers—she'd met them all! But so far, she hadn't been given the chance to take a single picture. *Is Uncle Josef doing it the right way after all, traveling the country year in, year out in his Sun Coach?* she wondered. She was quite certain that, in all the years he'd been on the road, Josef had not had to suffer as much unpleasantness as she had encountered in a single week. Even though she tried not to take it personally, her self-confidence had suffered a serious blow.

She would have loved to go home to her mother and father, to hide away there for a while and lick her wounds. Maybe she could think of a new plan in the sanctuary of the parish house, or she would see what she had done wrong in her first attempts. But that would be openly admitting defeat, and she could not do that. *Touchy about your pride, too, aren't you?* she thought with self-contempt.

In Frankfurt, she spent the night in a cheap guesthouse close to a factory that seemed to produce mostly stinking fumes from its smokestacks. She had planned to do the rounds of the photo studios along the city's striking boulevards the next morning, but as she lay coughing in her bed, all she could think was *Anywhere but here!*

CHAPTER 9

The next morning, Mimi was back at the train station by seven thirty. She'd eaten no breakfast, but despite her downcast mood, she readied herself for the day. She pinned up her hair, made sure her clothes were neat, and dusted her coat. *At least Aunt Elsa would be proud of me,* she thought in a moment of black humor.

The man at the ticket counter was young, with red hair and countless freckles, and he yawned hugely as Mimi approached. "Pardon me," she said. "Can you please tell me how I can get to Baden-Baden as quickly as possible?"

The man raised his eyebrows appreciatively. "Visiting the casino? That's my dream! But I can't get any farther than the horse races on the weekend. Watch out, ma'am: gambling'll make a poor woman of you."

Mimi laughed. She'd never given a thought to the casino in her life. For her, Baden-Baden was a wine-growing region, with tourists and fancy shops and gardens in full bloom. It was where the rich went for spas and cures, and now she wanted to try her luck there, too—in the *"beautiful landscapes along the Rhine valley,"* as her uncle Josef had described the region. If things didn't improve there, at least she wasn't far from home.

"The next train to Mannheim leaves in half an hour. From there, you have to change . . ." As he spoke, the young man scribbled the connections on a small notepad. Finally, he grinned and handed the note to Mimi. "If all goes well, you can put your first mark on red this evening."

She found a small guesthouse close to the center of Baden-Baden easily enough. The room was quiet, with a view over a small park. Mimi slept deeply, and after a good breakfast the next morning, she was ready to tackle the world again.

The woman who ran the guesthouse assumed Mimi was a tourist and pressed a small town map into her hand, recommending that she try one of the many restaurants along the Oos River for lunch. And Mimi should keep her eyes open, the woman whispered conspiratorially. There were rumors going around that some very important people were visiting Baden-Baden. With a little luck, she might even cross paths with Queen Charlotte of Württemberg!

Mimi almost told the woman that she was going out to look for photo studios, but then thought better of it. It was such a lovely day, and she was in a far better mood than she had been for days, so why not take a stroll through town? No doubt she'd run across a studio or two just by walking around, and if she didn't, then her search for work could wait until after lunch.

Everything in Hanover had been gray and grim, but Baden-Baden was abloom everywhere she looked. Mimi could not get enough of the exotic blossoms of winter jasmine, cornelian cherry, and pussy willow growing in the gardens of elegant villas and luxury hotels. The meadows along Lichtentaler Allee were a sea of spring snowflake flowers, and daffodils and violets in beautifully laid-out flower beds competed for the attention of visitors. And there were more than enough of those! One woman after another, all dressed so elegantly—Mimi found it hard not to stare.

She sensed that she had come to the right place. At the same time, a quiet voice in her ear whispered: *And those same senses have led you astray more than once.* Mimi shook her head grumpily, as if that might shake out the uninvited voice.

The Trinkhalle with its colonnade, the Kurhaus with its pillars, the theater and the Europäischer Hof—wherever Mimi looked, she was amazed. It was all so lovely! If only she could find a place at a photo studio—that would make her happiness complete. She walked toward a café to eat something that would fortify her for the search ahead.

The moment she opened the door to the café, she heard bright laughter and the clinking of champagne glasses—the people around her seemed to lead carefree lives.

Little did she know that dread and distress had made themselves at home just a few doors down the street.

"Mr. Marquardt! Please, wake up!"

"Otwin, if you don't wake up this instant, I'll kill you!"

The two young women shook desperately at their employer, the photographer Otwin Marquardt. Since early that morning, he'd been lying on the chaise longue in the back room of Photo Studio Marquardt, snoring like a train and refusing to wake up.

"Now what?" Sibylle Kraus, the older of the two employees, asked her younger colleague.

Instead of replying, Olga Moskovskaya stood up, went to the wash-basin in the corner of the room, and filled a cup with water. Without batting an eyelid, she sloshed the water onto her boss's face. Otwin Marquardt let out an extra-loud snore—but that was all.

Olga spat a few words in Russian that would have made a working man blush. Luckily, she thought, her older colleague could not speak Russian. "Now . . . we have a problem," she said in a strained voice, wondering whether she should go upstairs to her room and pack her bag now or in five minutes. Oh, she could pick her men!

The previous autumn, when Olga had decided not to return to Saint Petersburg as part of the retinue of her previous employer, a Russian nobleman, she did so with the conviction that Otwin Marquardt would provide her with a better life. But their affair had not lasted long. Otwin loved women too much, and Olga was too hot blooded and jealous to look the other way. In the end, in an almost amiable discussion, they had agreed that Otwin would keep her on as his employee until she found another situation. Privately, however, they went their separate ways.

It was a good solution, she'd believed. Members of high society were daily visitors to the elegant photo studio set among the colonnades. She was certain that it would not be long before she found a new patron.

Olga had been unaware that her former lover and present employer was as fond of wine and the casino as he was of women. Before they separated, he had spent his nights with her. But now, Otwin regularly gambled or drank the night away, and the following morning he was in no condition to practice his profession. Both Olga and Sibylle—his loyal employee for years—had become experts in coming up with new excuses to appease their esteemed clientele. Today, though, no amount of excuses was going to be enough. That much was clear.

"Olga, say something," Sibylle implored, dragging the younger woman out of her gloomy thoughts. "What in heaven's name are we going to do?"

Even Olga Moskovskaya, for all her experience, was at a loss. "I—" she began, when the sudden jangle of the bell over the door made her jump.

"Good afternoon. My name is Mimi Reventlow. I'm a traveling photographer, and I would like to ask if you could perhaps use my services? I have my own camera." Mimi patted the bag slung from her shoulder and gave the two women who had emerged from the back room a restrained smile.

She had discovered the studio while strolling through the colonnades. With its mirrored windows, the shop made such an elegant impression that she had been almost afraid to step inside. *They will never, ever take you on!* she'd thought, but then had summoned up all her courage and opened the door. She had everything to win, nothing to lose.

"You're a photographer?" the two women asked at once as they gaped at her.

Mimi nodded uncertainly. "Perhaps I could have a word with the owner?"

"That won't be necessary. You're hired!" Olga grabbed Mimi by the arm. "Come with me, quickly!" she cried in a Russian accent as she pulled Mimi into the room where the actual studio was located. Still halfway through the door, she turned to Mimi. "I'm Olga Moskovskaya and this is Sibylle Kraus. We're Otwin Marquardt's assistants."

"Mimi Reventlow," said Mimi for the second time, confused. Her uncle had certainly prophesied that she would have an easier time of it in the south of Germany, but he would never believe this.

"There's the platform, here's the props, and Sibylle will help you with the lamps." The attractive Russian woman pointed from right to left, and at the same time gave off such a strong scent of perfume that it made Mimi dizzy. "Mr. Marquardt, unfortunately, is indisposed today, and we are expecting an important customer in a few minutes. Do you think you could fill in for him for this appointment?" The expression on the assistant's face was melodramatically anxious.

"Of course," Mimi replied. "I'm ready for any challenge!"

The pretty Russian raised a finely plucked eyebrow. "I hope you're still ready when I tell you *who* we're expecting."

"So you know from the start—the only reason I'm here is that the rules of etiquette demand that I grace with my presence a number of the businesses in every town in which I stay. Visits to the hairdresser take forever, and because I've already been to the flower shop, I've decided to come to your studio." Queen Charlotte of Württemberg glared at the three young women. "Where is the photographer?"

Mimi stepped forward, curtsied, and said, "I will be taking your photograph, Your Majesty."

"A woman. Well, why not?" Charlotte of Württemberg stated drily. "But please hurry it up with your picture. I'd like to devote at least a little time today to something meaningful. My visit to the local children's home, for example."

Just like my mother when she's planning something important, thought Mimi, who felt as if she'd landed in some kind of strange dream. She scrutinized the woman opposite her. The forceful, jutting chin; the light-blue, intelligent eyes; the slight hostility she radiated—Mimi's very first customer was not going to make her work easy, but she decided to bank everything on one card.

"Forgive me, Your Majesty. I am not familiar with the etiquette," she said. "I want my customers to be happy with their photographs, so may I make a suggestion?" She heard Olga Moskovskaya beside her inhale sharply.

The queen impatiently gestured as if to say: *If you must!*

Mimi smiled in a way she hoped was both respectful and encouraging. "If Your Majesty would like, I could accompany you to the children's home. A photograph of Your Majesty surrounded by the children would certainly be a nice memory, don't you think?" Now it was Mimi's turn to hold her breath.

"Would that even be possible? I mean, all the equipment, the effort . . ." The queen looked around Otwin Marquardt's studio suspiciously.

"None of that will be any problem at all," Mimi said hurriedly, while a sound that was clearly a snore emanated from the back room.

That evening, when Mimi returned to her guesthouse, she was exhausted but happy—happier than she had ever been in her life!

"Did you have a pleasant day?" asked the proprietress. "And were you able to catch a glimpse of the queen?"

"You could say that," Mimi replied.

CHAPTER 10

March 1911, Meersburg, Lake Constance

"The head a little higher. Not that high. Tilt the chin a little . . . very good. Now, please don't move." Julius Bauer, owner of the photo studio that bore his name in Meersburg, raised his hand with the authority of a conductor leading a royal chamber orchestra.

The subject, a petite, attractive middle-aged woman, froze like Sleeping Beauty in the fairy tale. Though, in the blazing light from the photographer's lamps, her eyelids flickered slightly.

No surprise there, thought Mimi, who was watching from a bench on the far side of the studio. After all, the woman had been enduring the glare of the lamps for a solid hour, and all for just two portraits.

Mimi held her breath. *Now!* Now Julius Bauer would finally take his photograph and let the woman go. She was a Meersburg business-woman, the photographer had told Mimi earlier, a woman named Clara Berg, but the people of the town respectfully called her the Queen of Beauty. Mimi didn't know what to make of that, but she did know one thing: a woman like Clara Berg would certainly not like to have her time wasted.

Instead of tripping the shutter, the photographer began fumbling at the back of his camera, pushing around for the umpteenth time the cassette that held the dry plate that would later be used to create the picture.

Mimi rolled her eyes inwardly. It went without saying that a photographer should get the best they could out of every image. As a photographer, you owed it to your customer. But that included good preparation. Mimi glanced sympathetically at the woman, and they exchanged faint smiles.

Julius Bauer mumbled something to himself while he fiddled with the camera lens. The leather bellows creaked, the knobs squeaked.

Bored, Mimi looked around the studio. There wasn't that much to see: A little platform on which the customers sat in a small armchair, leaned against a pole, or stood in front of a balustrade. To the left of the platform was a shelf that held the typical props—top hats for the men, fans and bouquets of silk flowers for the women. The studio was as old fashioned as its owner, Mimi thought. In the six years that she had been traveling the country as a photographer, she'd been in dozens of studios like this one. Some days, and today was one, she got so sick of them. *Such a beautiful day for taking pictures outside,* she thought, and her gaze drifted longingly out through the window. And while the Queen of Beauty insisted on having her picture taken in the studio, Mimi would have arranged the scene very differently. Mimi's reputation was excellent, and most of the photographers from whom she rented space let her do whatever she wanted. Some even secretly hoped to pick up a trick or two from her. In other studios, however—Mr. Bauer's studio among them—she had to use a little cunning to work freely.

After what felt like an eternity, she heard the magical click.

"Done!" With a satisfied smile, the photographer appeared from behind his enormous camera. "I'll get to work on the portraits right away, Mrs. Berg. They will be ready in a week." Without even bothering to shake his customer's hand again, the photographer was about to disappear into the darkroom when Mimi cleared her throat discreetly.

Bauer, confused, furrowed his brow. He seemed to have temporarily forgotten that Mimi was in the room. "Oh, yes! My dear Mrs. Berg, may I introduce Mimi Reventlow? She is a well-known traveling photographer and is working in my studio as a guest until the end of March. Miss Reventlow works in a very modern style, and as you yourself are also of a modern mind-set, perhaps you might like to have a bit of fun and allow her to take a picture or two of you, now that the images for the cover of your new mail-order catalog are done?" He smiled patronizingly at Mimi.

Mimi grimaced very slightly. It was rare for her host to introduce her in this way—jovial, condescending, as if doing her a favor. When it did occasionally happen, as now, she tried to overlook it, but deep inside she felt her annoyance growing. *"Bit of fun"* indeed! If they were going to compare her work with anything, then it should be with art!

"I had no idea that women also practiced this profession. It would certainly be an interesting experience to be photographed by you." Clara Berg's smile carried both recognition and regret. "But I'm afraid I have to get back to the offices urgently." She was already wrapping her scarf around her neck.

"I could come with you," said Mimi hurriedly. "It is a personal interest of mine to photograph my subjects in their day-to-day environment. You in your offices—that would certainly be something special. What do you think? Should we give it a try?" She held her breath, hoping that her customer would offer her a little respite from the stuffy studio.

Clara Berg looked skeptically from Bauer's large camera to Mimi. "But all the trouble . . . I really don't have any time."

"It wouldn't be any trouble. I have my own camera, a portable one," said Mimi, and she held up the leather bag that was beside her on the bench. "And if we don't manage to find a good arrangement quickly, then we'll just drop the whole thing, all right?" Mimi quickly slipped into her coat.

"Fine, then. Come along. But it's some distance. My factory is on the outskirts of town." Clara Berg produced beauty products for women—creams, tinctures, and fine soaps.

"I need new photographs for our mail-order catalog," she explained to Mimi as they made their way on Unterstadtstrasse, the busy street they were walking along. "My assistants and my *parfumeur* seem to think my likeness ought to grace the cover." The businesswoman sounded a little embarrassed.

"It's a good idea," said Mimi. "But what do you think of me photographing you while you stir a cream? A picture like that would certainly come across well in your catalog. Your customers would see that even the boss is willing to roll up her sleeves."

Clara laughed. "In the eyes of my employees, I roll up my sleeves far too often. Some of them would prefer it if I were *less* involved in the production. Up this way." She turned onto a narrow lane on their right. Mimi followed. Picking up the thread of their conversation, the businesswoman said, "It's not as if I don't trust my employees. It's just crucial to me that every product that leaves our house carries my signature."

"I'm the same when it comes to my photographs. Like you, I want to give people the gift of beauty," said Mimi. "Which is why I love my profession so much."

"Oh, I believe you," said Clara wholeheartedly. "Still, I imagine it must be hard, constantly moving around, always having to adjust to new customers."

"I always find meeting new people quite marvelous. But all beginnings are difficult, and what I really had trouble with at the start was finding even a single photo studio willing to take me on as a guest photographer. I can't count how many rejections I got." Mimi shook her head. "It was horrible. But then I found myself in Baden-Baden, where the rich and beautiful go." She laughed. "Now hold on to your hat—in Baden-Baden, I got to photograph Queen Charlotte of Württemberg!"

"And that was your breakthrough, was it?"

Mimi looked at her in surprise. "Yes, it was. The queen was captivated by the naturalness of my pictures, and word got around. After that, I was suddenly in such demand that I was turning down invitations to work as a guest photographer. How did you know—"

Clara let out a laugh. "If you want to be successful, you always need a bit of luck on top of your own talent. That's been my experience, anyway. By the way, I have a shop in Baden-Baden. Maybe we'll bump into each other there one day?" She pointed to a plain-looking building across the street. "We're here."

When Clara opened the door, they were met by a captivating floral scent. A woman wearing a white apron came hurrying to meet them.

"Mrs. Berg, it's good you're here. There's a problem with the fill system for the bottles, and . . ."

"Business as usual." Clara smiled apologetically at Mimi, then followed the woman in the apron deeper into the manufactory.

Clara Berg, stirring a cream. Clara Berg sampling a scent. Clara Berg inspecting a bottle of facial toner against the light, checking for cloudiness. Mimi was in her element. Instead of glaring lamps, she used the pale winter sun falling through the high windows, encompassing everything in a diffuse veil of light. Mimi's heart beat faster and her fingers grew cold as she unpacked one glass plate after another and slotted them into her Linhof camera.

When Valentin Linhof, the camera's maker, invited a large group of photographers to Munich in January to present them with his latest product, Mimi had spontaneously accepted the invitation. She had felt honored that Linhof had actually invited *her*. She had not really intended to buy the camera; her Rüdenberg model had served her well so far and had never let her down. But with the first demonstration of the Linhof camera, her heart had begun to pound, and Mimi knew she had to have it! The price had cut a deep hole in her savings, but Mimi had not regretted the purchase for even a single moment. On the contrary: the camera offered her a level of flexibility in her work that she had never known before and could do far more than her first camera was able to.

"What exactly are you doing?" Clara asked at one point and laughed. "Do you really think I should have day-to-day things like this in my catalog?"

"Why not?" Mimi asked in turn. "As I understand it, the natural composition of your products matters a great deal to you. It's the same for me when I take pictures."

Clara looked at her thoughtfully. "Maybe you're right. Maybe pictures like this suit our creams and tinctures better than all the posed images do." She eyed Mimi critically. "You're a very beautiful woman, if I may say so. Your hair is such a rich brown and so shiny, you have exceptionally fine pores, you're slim, and you seem very strong and full of energy. I know I'm overly curious, but can you tell me what the secret of your beauty is? I always like to learn."

"My secret?" Mimi, somewhat abashed, ran her fingers over her slightly disheveled hair, then smiled. "I don't use anything in particular. Could it be that the secret is liberty? The liberty to do what you love? A face always mirrors the state of one's disposition."

Clara Berg's eyes shone. "How right you are!" she said and squeezed Mimi's arm amiably. "Let's hope that this kind of happiness is available to many more women in the future."

"A letter's come for you," said the proprietress of the small guesthouse where Mimi had been living for two weeks. "And there's something else. My friend Ursula and her husband are celebrating their anniversary, and I thought perhaps . . ."

After securing the job to photograph the couple and with the letter in her hand, Mimi went up to her room just after five o'clock. It was not very well lit and was always cold, and to Mimi's chagrin, it did not look out over the lake but toward grim old Meersburg Castle. A room with a lake view would have cost a third as much again as she was already paying, an amount that Mimi—in good times, when the money poured in—would have been glad to invest. But during winter, she tried to save whenever she could. The alternative would have been not to travel at all during the winter months and to spend the time at home in Esslingen with her parents, who always kept a room for her. But her former employer, Mr. Semmer, had told her long ago and in no uncertain terms that she should never again set foot in his studio, and there were no other photographers in Esslingen. Mimi could not bear the thought of doing nothing for the entire winter.

She sat at the small table in front of the window. Outside, the sky was darkening as a storm closed in. Mimi pulled her shawl closer around her neck. What an unpleasant evening! She would ask the landlady later for a hot-water bottle, she thought. Then she opened the letter, noting that it had been mailed from Esslingen the day before.

It was from her mother, who wrote regularly. The first thing Mimi did when she was in a new town was send her parents her address so that they always knew where she was. She also wanted to keep up to date on what was going on in the parish. There was never much personal in her mother's letters. Sometimes it seemed to Mimi that her mother, so preoccupied with all her important duties, had no life of her own anymore.

But this letter was different.

> I would like to ask you if you could pay a visit to your uncle Josef in Laichingen in Swabia before your next job, just to check on him. You won't have as much to do now that it's winter.
>
> I'm worried about him. I haven't had a reply to my letters for a long time, but Josef's neighbor wrote. His health is not good, it seems. Since he came down with a lung infection last year, he hasn't been the same . . .

Mimi lowered the letter. Uncle Josef had had a lung infection? Why hadn't her mother mentioned that in one of her previous letters? And shouldn't she have checked on him long ago? She was his sister, after all, and here it was already the end of March!

But then she felt a pang of self-reproach: instead of berating her mother, she would do better to look in the mirror. In her first year as a traveling photographer, she and her uncle had seen quite a lot of each other—once in Munich, where Josef was buying supplies for his studio, and once in Esslingen for her father's sixtieth birthday. To the disappointment of the family, he had come alone, without his new wife. "Traudel is a village girl," Josef had said. "She isn't one for outings like this." They had met a third time, too, in Pforzheim, at the funeral of another photographer, a friend of Josef's and a man whose studio Mimi had run for a short time. Her uncle had indeed invited her to visit him in the high country often, and she had had good intentions of visiting him many times. But all these years, she hadn't.

When Traudel suddenly died—it had happened in midwinter two years ago—heavy snow had kept Mimi trapped in Tessin. She had felt terrible about it at the time, and since then they had not been in contact.

Can it really be that we haven't seen each other for nearly five years? she wondered now in horror. Josef was one of the people dearest to her, and even if they had fallen out of touch, she thought of him almost every day, with gratitude and affection. It was impossible to imagine what would have become of her without him.

The wind had grown stronger and rattled the window with such force that it suddenly flew open and banged painfully into Mimi's shoulder, distracting her from her thoughts. She closed the window, then picked up the previous day's newspaper and stuffed it between the window handle and the jamb, hoping to keep the cold draft at bay.

There was another piece of unfinished business, too: an inquiry from Isny, in the Upper Swabian region, to which she had not yet responded. The mayor wanted some promotional photographs to bring in summer holidaymakers and travelers.

Ever since Baden-Baden, word spread quickly about which part of the country Mimi was in. The photography world was small, after all, and potential customers had little trouble finding her and sending inquiries about work, just as the mayor of Isny had done. He wanted Mimi to visit in a few weeks, as soon as the first flowers of spring were blooming.

Mimi flipped open her Baedeker travel guide.

How far was Isny from Laichingen and the Swabian Jura?

CHAPTER 11

Laichingen, Swabian Jura

It was one of those late March days that made it seem as if winter might never end. A storm thundered, and the icy winds snapped at the shutters and made people shiver in their houses.

Although it was half past seven in the morning, semidarkness cloaked the street. There was little activity, and only occasionally did one see a shadow flit by. Men on their way to the mill. Children on their way to school. Women were seldom seen. At the end of winter, the weaver families didn't have much money for shopping, so they made do with what they had and used the time to work from home.

Eveline sat at the dining table, in the somber glimmer of a single candle. She should already have been at work: a mountain of decorative pillow covers stood waiting to be embroidered with tendrils of flowers and leaves. Instead, she sat and rocked, humming softly to herself, her infant in her arms. The child was four weeks old. And so beautiful. Tiny hands, translucent cheeks, blond silky hair. Eveline's three other children—seven-year-old Erika, Marianne a year older at eight, and her son, fifteen-year-old Alexander—were also sitting at the table. They looked wide-eyed at their mother. *Do something! Say something!* those eyes pleaded. Eveline acted as if she noticed none of it. Much earlier she should have made sure all three were getting ready for school, but Eveline was unable to say a word or to get up and prepare breakfast.

The door opened. Eveline lifted her gaze slightly. Her husband, Klaus, brought in a few chunks of firewood, along with snow and a gust of icy wind. Eveline instinctively clutched the child closer.

"She's dead," she said softly to her husband.

He grasped her shoulder, a token of affection, but far too brief, and said, "The Lord giveth and the Lord taketh away. Life is a hard road. Who's to know what she's been spared?"

Eveline let out a tear-choked sob.

"Nothing hot to eat? And why aren't the children in school already?" Klaus, perplexed, looked from the empty pot on the stove to each of his children.

"We finished the rest of last night's *Schwarzer Brei*," said Alexander softly. Only with difficulty was Eveline able to suppress another sob. He was so brave, her boy.

"Then get going! It's nearly eight. If the teacher punishes you for being late, tell her what's happened." Klaus nodded in the direction of the dead infant, whom Eveline still held tightly to her breast, then looked in annoyance at the empty pot on the stove one last time and said, "I'll be off to the factory, then."

She would make soup for the evening and would throw in a few extra potatoes, Eveline thought to herself, feeling guilty. No need for the living to starve because she was so weighed down by grief that she couldn't even make it to the stove.

Without a word of protest, the children pulled on their jackets and shoes and took their writing slates from the shelf behind the table. *Like little machines,* Eveline thought.

With his cap pulled low over his eyes, Alexander handed her a sheet of paper. "This is for you. To remember."

Touched, Eveline looked at the pencil drawing. The fine hair, the too-pale cheeks—had he sketched his little sister in life or in death? She didn't know.

"Thank you," she whispered. "Go now."

When the children had left, Eveline rose to her feet, her movements as weary as those of an old woman. She laid the dead infant gently in the crib, the same crib her other children had lain in. Then she pulled up the chair, sat down again, and looked at the child. She wanted to memorize every line, every feature. The wispy eyelashes, the tiny half moons of the fingernails.

She had not even given the baby a name. The midwife had recommended against it. "Wait and see," she had said. "If it's still alive in three months, find a good name for it then," old Elfriede had said after the birth.

"It" . . . as if her daughter were an object. Or a farm animal.

Her name's Michaela, she should have said, then and there. Or Kirsten. Or Caroline. But no, she had only nodded. The midwife's advice had been well intentioned. Eveline had already laid three children to rest, after all. She knew others who'd lost more—so many children in the Jura never had the strength to live.

Her gaze drifted across to the washbasin. As usual, the *Schwarzer Brei*—"black porridge"—had left an unappetizing dry crust in the pot. It would take hard work and a stiff brush to loosen it.

The *Schwarzer Brei.*

Sometimes Eveline thought that the traditional dish was to blame for everything. It was made with spelt flour and boiled with a little salt until it formed a thick porridge.

"Why do they call this dish *Schwarzer Brei*? It's light gray, not black at all," Eveline had asked Klaus when she first arrived in Laichingen as a young bride. She knew about Swabian dishes like semolina pudding, which was made with butter and cream, and the rice porridge they served with hot cherries and cinnamon. But until that day, she had never heard of *Schwarzer Brei.*

Klaus had laughed brightly at her question. Back then he had still been able to laugh.

"Because the grains of spelt burn easily when you roast them too long in the oven. Then they turn black, and the porridge will be not only black, but also bitter, so watch out!"

From then on, Eveline had made a point of being careful with it. For her palate, the dish was bland at the best of times—even adding a few spoons of milk or a few onions slow fried in butter didn't make much difference. But she wanted to be a good wife to Klaus, her weaver husband, and if he wanted his favorite dish on the table occasionally, then she should learn how to cook it properly, she thought. How naive and romantic she'd been.

It had not taken long for Eveline to realize that *Schwarzer Brei* had little to do with sentimental memories of childhood but was a staple of the Laichingen weavers only because they didn't have the money for anything better. The deeper this realization sank home, the blacker the grains in the oven became.

Adults might be able to stomach the stuff, more or less, but infants? Toddlers? More than once Eveline had wondered whether, in the end, their crude diet had killed the children. *Death porridge,* she called it, if only to herself. What point was there in actually saying the words aloud? No one would have understood her. In the eyes of the people in Laichingen, even after more than fifteen years, she was still an "outsider," and someone with strange ideas in her head. That you ought to wash children and brush their hair every day, for example. Or that you politely said "please" and "thank you" when someone handed you the soup pot.

She laughed bitterly and stood up. If the people only knew! Politeness in the Schubert household was a thing of the past. With so much work around the house and in the fields, and all the embroidery on top, she had no time for that kind of nonsense.

She had no time to grieve, either. She looked at the lifeless child one final time, then covered the body with a cloth. "Farewell," she whispered. When she looked up, her gaze fell on the only picture that decorated the kitchen wall.

It was a cheap print behind glass in a cheap frame. *The Broad and Narrow Way* was a devotional picture, and Klaus had once told her that it hung on the walls of many houses in the area. The priests liked to see the picture in the homes of their flock, calling on people, as it did, to stay on the good Lord's path.

On the right side of the picture, a narrow, steep, and difficult path led past a church and onward to heaven. A black-clad priest with outstretched hands showed the way, making sure those on the path did not stray. The left side of the picture depicted a wide road, beside which stood an inn, a theater, and other stately buildings. As pleasant as it might be to follow, the end of the road led to a city swallowed by eternal fire. *This is what happens if you enjoy yourself too much in life!* the picture warned its observer.

Eveline stared at the picture with disgust. She hated it, just as she hated her life. She would have liked nothing more than to tear the picture from the wall and smash it to pieces. But instead, she pulled on her coat and set off for the church. She had to talk to the priest about the burial. Where she was supposed to find the money for that, however, was a mystery.

CHAPTER 12

Deep in thought, Mimi gazed out over the lake while she waited for the ferry that would take her to Friedrichshafen. From there, she would catch the train to Ulm, and from Ulm she would find her way to Uncle Josef in the Swabian Jura.

I'm very happy that you're able to take this weight off my shoulders and see to Josef. I will write to Josef's neighbor Luise immediately and let her know that you will be visiting. I am looking forward to hearing from you, her mother had written in reply to Mimi's letter. Once Mimi had made up her mind to visit her uncle, she could hardly wait to see him again after so much time apart.

Yet, as so often in recent times, when the day came for her to leave Meersburg, she felt a touch of despondency. She was the only traveler waiting at the pier, too, and that only made the feeling stronger. She had always hated goodbyes, and the older she got, the harder they became.

The evening before had brought a fierce storm, but now the lake was still and glittering in the morning sunshine. The storm had thrown driftwood ashore, knotted and polished, all along the narrow strip of gravel beach. Mimi stepped down from the pier and picked up one of the pieces of wood. *Isn't it the same for me?* she thought as she examined the smooth, wet chunk of wood in her hand. *Don't I let myself drift through life just like this wood does?* The questions confronted her so suddenly that she shook her head. What made her think of something like that now?

Yes, she was a free woman. She could go where she wanted without having to adjust her schedule to suit anyone. She had no husband governing her. There were no children to look after. She had no employer strapping her into a corset of regulations, duties, prohibitions. Even her parents had long since given up dispensing advice on how to live her life. She was as free as any bird . . . just as she had always wanted to be.

But one day, somewhere—between Hunsrück and Allgäu, between the spa season in summer and the quiet of winter—she became aware that the freedom she had could also make her lonely. Almost achingly so. To have someone beside her now, someone to put their arm around her, would be nice . . .

She tossed the piece of wood away abruptly. It immediately fell among the other driftwood, finding its place as if Mimi had never picked it up at all.

The next moment, she heard a woman's voice behind her. "Miss Reventlow, thank God! I was afraid I'd missed you." Clara Berg was nearly running, her overcoat billowing. Her cheeks were red, and it was obvious that she had too little time for all the many things that mattered to her.

And yet she came to say goodbye, thought Mimi, moved. How must it feel to have a woman like Clara Berg as a friend?

It was a gift, Mimi knew, to be able to meet so many wonderful people on her travels. Yet she had also learned that it was better to maintain a certain distance, or when it came to saying goodbye, she'd find herself trapped in feelings of melancholy.

"I've come to say thank you once again for your marvelous photographs," the businesswoman said. "My employees are as thrilled with them as I am. We've decided to print the last three pages of the catalog only using your pictures and a little text. The customer can take a peek behind the scenes—and I think that's an exceptionally good idea." Clara

Berg rummaged in her purse before handing Clara a small package wrapped in lavender-colored paper. "For you. A cream. It's made with witch hazel. If you happen to find yourself in harsher climes, the harmonizing qualities of the witch hazel will do your skin good."

"Then I'll probably have to use it today," Mimi said, and smiled. "I'm traveling up to the Swabian Jura to visit my uncle. He lives in a small town called Laichingen."

"Laichingen . . ." Clara Berg frowned. "Isn't that where they do the beautiful linen work? Laichingen linens, yes! An indispensable part of every good trousseau, my mother used to say. If I remember correctly, she had some sent from Laichingen for me."

Mimi smiled. "*My* trousseau was a camera—I never had much time for linen and cooking pots."

In the late afternoon, the main station in Ulm was a bustling, lively place. The air was filled with machine fumes and the noise from a nearby construction site. Although it was no more than twenty-five miles from Ulm to Laichingen, the complicated train schedule made an overnight stay in Ulm unavoidable. The next train up to the Jura was the following morning. Just a little longer to wait until she and Uncle Josef saw each other again.

She located a guesthouse close to the station quickly enough, and once her luggage was in her room, Mimi walked in the direction of Ulm's famous cathedral, the steeple of which loomed high above every building for miles around. She made it her habit to visit a house of God in every new town, and in Ulm, the cathedral was the natural choice. A little chat with God, a prayer of thanks to the guardian angel who watched over her on all her travels—this always made Mimi feel at ease.

When she left the church, she saw a small gathering of people in front of a makeshift podium. But there was no sign of a speaker anywhere. Were they waiting for a traveling theater group, perhaps? A street musician or roving preacher? A mime or magician? Mimi wondered who might appear, but without much interest, she hurried on.

All the shops! The historical half-timbered houses and small towers. Ulm was a pretty town. She stopped at a bakery and bought a bag of *Olgabrezeln*—the sweet puff-pastry pretzels, baked in honor of beloved Queen Olga of Württemberg, had always been a favorite of her uncle's. Mimi was determined to do something nice for herself, as well. She had spotted a café on the plaza in front of the cathedral. With the good weather, there were already a few cast-iron tables and chairs out, and a cup of coffee and some sunshine would do her good after the long journey.

Mimi drank her coffee in small, luxuriant sips. It was strong and invigorating. No wonder the café was so well patronized. She was considering whether she should order herself something to eat when she heard loud shouting from the crowd gathered at the podium.

"He's here! At last!"

"Hurray!"

"It's about to start!"

Excitement filled the air. People elbowed each other and craned their necks to get a better view. It was mostly men who had gathered, Mimi noted. There was probably going to be a knife thrower or an arm-wrestling competition, she thought, still without interest.

But the next moment, the question of whether to eat was forgotten completely. Instead, Mimi stared at the podium as if spellbound.

A man with unruly dark-brown hair, broad shoulders, and an unusually upright gait strode toward the podium. He was a big man, tall enough to tower over everyone around him, but he looked unshaven and dusty, as if he'd had a long ride on a bicycle or atop an open cart. Over his left shoulder, he carried a large shapeless linen sack, probably his travel bag. He casually dropped the sack on the ground—there was something almost arrogant in the gesture.

The stranger's face and his brown locks were lit by the sun in such a way that Mimi was reminded of images of Jesus at the center of a golden aura.

And, in fact, the men standing around the podium cheered as if the stranger were the Messiah.

What presence! thought Mimi, fascinated. Like a magnet attracts iron, the man seemed to draw in people from all sides. Mimi, too, instinctively stretched to see him better.

Those eyes, his shapely mouth . . . As a photographer, expressive faces had always fascinated her. For her work, it was vital to be able to read—or rather, decipher—faces. But this time, she knew deep down that the attraction the stranger held for her could not be attributed entirely to her profession.

"Would madam like something else?" asked the waiter as he stepped up to her table.

Mimi wanted to push him aside: he was blocking her view of the podium.

"Do you know what's going on over there?" she asked instead.

"Some fellow wants to hold a speech, but don't ask me what about. Everyone seems to have something to say these days." The waiter grimaced. "I pray that madam will not be excessively unnerved."

"Not at all," Mimi murmured. From the corner of her eye, she noticed an attractive woman with three children settle down at the next table. The waiter's expression brightened, and he hurried across to the newcomers to take their order. Mimi overheard the woman order four cups of hot chocolate, and cake for all of them.

Pretty and well off, apparently, thought Mimi, and was reminded of Clara Berg. But the next moment, her attention was once again captured by the handsome man at the podium, whose speech had begun to pick up steam.

"The days in which workers had to swallow whatever was handed to them are gone. Gone are the days of the moral cowards! In New York, in London—all over the world, workers are rising up against outdated and intolerable conditions. And I can tell you here and now that they are achieving great things! Things that are also possible here, in our land. The social democrat unions are proud to count more than two million members. The German Metal Workers' Union alone numbers more than half a million men. So today, I appeal to you, you who work for Magirus, Kässbohrer, and for all the other factories in and around Ulm—join us! Be part of the ever-growing mass of . . ."

A unionist, thought Mimi, disappointed. In the large towns, union representatives were making more and more frequent appearances. Sometimes, she saw posters announcing upcoming rallies. Mimi was always careful to avoid the public squares where such events took place: more than once, she had read in the newspaper about such assemblies turning violent, with fistfights or even worse breaking out.

Mimi startled when she heard a throat being cleared beside her. It was the woman from the next table. "Excuse me, but may I ask a favor of you? I have to go . . . into the café for a moment. Would you be so kind as to keep an eye on my boys? Not that they'll get up to any mischief." She smiled apologetically.

How tired the woman looked, Mimi thought. She smiled and said, "Of course. No need to rush." Then she turned to the three children. "All looking forward to hot chocolate?" Mimi guessed that the children were eight to ten years old.

They nodded shyly. Mimi could not drag her attention away from the speaker in the midst of the gathering.

"It is not right for our dear Mr. Industrialist to earn himself a bucket of gold on the back of your labor, while you, the workers, go home empty handed. Fair pay for fair work—that goes for a maid just as much as it does for a skilled metalworker. Fair pay for fair work—for the boy in the stable, for the weaver at his loom, and for the sailor on the Danube!"

The assembly cheered. *The man can talk, I have to give him that,* Mimi thought. And how his eyes glowed, as if he were burning with an inner fire. She was close to being kindled herself. Mimi grinned inwardly, then she glanced at the three boys at the next table. The oldest rolled his eyes.

"You don't agree with what he said?" Mimi asked, although even as she spoke, she realized that something was wrong with the boy. She pushed her chair back and stood up in shock. The next moment, the boy's head began to move from side to side, and he stretched his neck backward unnaturally. Then he fell off his chair. Mimi, horrified, took a step toward him. His body reared up, his right arm lashed out, hitting the leg of a chair, and his legs spasmed, kicking the table uncontrollably.

"Mother of God," Mimi heard someone beside her gasp. "The child's possessed!"

"Get back. It's probably contagious!" cried a woman, and she pulled her husband away by the wrist.

"The falling sickness! The boy's got the falling sickness!" shouted another.

The elderly waiter stood by helplessly.

For a moment, even Mimi was frozen. A seizure! In her father's congregation, there had once been a young girl with epilepsy. On several occasions, she had suffered a seizure during the service and had been as cramped and twisted as this boy now, so for Mimi the situation was not entirely unfamiliar. But she wasn't sure of exactly what to do. Wasn't the boy at risk of biting his tongue? Or of breaking bones?

While the boy's brothers pushed their chairs aside and stepped out of the way, Mimi kneeled beside the boy and tried to hold him. But the child, in his convulsions, was as strong as a bear. His head struck hard against the cobblestones, and he began to bleed from the resulting gash. His eyes were rolled back so that only the whites were visible.

Oh God! Why wasn't anyone helping? Mimi looked around angrily at the gawking crowd. "Go into the café. Get your mother," she snapped at the boy's brothers, but they simply stood as if rooted to the spot. *Dear God, don't let the boy suffocate,* she prayed silently as she tried to turn him onto his side to give him air.

"Let me through! Stand aside! Move!"

Mimi looked up and her eyes widened. The speaker pushed his way through the crowd toward them. He shoved the table aside roughly, wrapped his strong arms around the boy, and gently sat him up. "Take a spoon and try to get it between his teeth. He's bit his tongue."

Her knees trembling, Mimi got to her feet. One of the younger brothers handed her a spoon from the table. "Easier said than done," she said, trying with one finger to pry the child's jaws apart from the side.

"Good heavens, Erich! No! Not here!" Mimi heard the mother's panicked voice. *Finally, she's back,* Mimi thought. Just then, the boy's body went slack in the man's arms.

The boy blinked, then seemed to return to consciousness. "Mama?" He looked around, disoriented. His chest rose and fell quickly, as if he'd been running fast.

"It's all right. It's over," said his mother in a strained voice, while she wiped his bloody, spittle-smeared mouth with a handkerchief. She seemed unaware of the wound on the back of his head. "I'm terribly sorry," she said to Mimi and the speaker. "Erich has epilepsy. He had a seizure last night, and I didn't sleep a wink. Normally, there's more time in between. I didn't think he'd have another so soon, or I wouldn't have dared leave the house." She swallowed hard, and Mimi could see that she was doing everything she could not to cry.

She stroked the woman's arm. "It's all right now."

"This disease is the devil himself," the woman whispered, her voice choked with tears. "It holds you prisoner. It kills every bit of joy you have. It makes you live in mortal fear every minute and—" The woman broke off midsentence and shook her head. Mimi and the speaker helped the boy stand, and the woman put one arm around her son, who swayed slightly. Together they started to walk away. Her other two sons followed, their eyes on the ground.

"But . . . what about the hot chocolate for the children? Don't you want to rest a little?" Mimi called after her. She looked to the speaker, standing beside her. "Shouldn't we stop her? Or go with her to a doctor?"

The imposing stranger watched the departing family. "It isn't the first time his mother has been through this. She knows what's best. I have to go back. People are waiting." He nodded toward the crowd jostling impatiently at the podium. Some clearly felt they'd been waiting too long and were already leaving.

"Of course. Thank you for helping. One feels so powerless in a situation like that." Mimi laughed, feeling a little embarrassed.

But the man looked at her appreciatively. "Maybe so, but you acted bravely. What would you say to having a drink with me when I'm done, something to settle the nerves?"

CHAPTER 13

She hadn't actually said yes to his invitation, Mimi thought as she ordered another cup of coffee, but she sat and waited for him regardless. Instead of picking up with his speech, the man distributed some papers to his listeners. Union registration forms? Information leaflets? Whatever they were, Mimi didn't care.

The April sun was already setting, and Mimi was shivering by the time the man finally returned. He had his linen sack slung over his shoulder again.

"Thank you for waiting. There's another gathering taking place tomorrow and I had to let the people who were here know about it." He seemed satisfied with his day's work.

"You're a unionist by profession?" Mimi asked. "I didn't know they existed."

He laughed. "I prefer to be called an ambassador. That's closer to the mark. Come, it's too cold to be sitting here. There's a wine bar down by the Danube that's always got a fire going in the fireplace." He offered her his arm.

"But . . ." Mimi laughed, feeling slightly confused. "I don't even know your name."

Nevertheless, she went with him.

His name was Hannes, and, like her, he was constantly on the move. Years earlier, he'd emigrated to America and worked in the cotton trade for a while. On a trip to Baltimore, he'd come into contact with the trade union movement for the first time—the men who advocated for an eight-hour working day had fascinated him. In the so-called cotton belt, the cotton fields of the south, the workers could only dream of conditions like that, so Hannes had joined forces with the unionists and had learned from them.

Mimi was only half listening, but not because she found his story uninteresting. It was his eyes that were so distracting. Hannes had the most beautiful eyes of any man she had ever seen. Brown black, like coal, warm, filled with expressiveness and soul.

"You seem to lead an exciting life," she finally said, her voice raw. They had dropped all formality within a few minutes. It felt right, like everything about this encounter.

He gestured dismissively. "It sounds more exciting than it is," he said.

The fact that she was a woman traveling alone did not seem especially impressive to him, and Mimi found it refreshing not to have to answer all the usual questions for a change—the one she hated most was: "With no man to protect you, don't you get scared?" Hannes's easy manner had encouraged her to open up about herself. She had told him so much already: about her childhood and the time she'd fallen into the poacher's trap; about her parents, who were so involved in their parochial work that they completely lost sight of those closest to them; and about the melancholy she had felt recently every time she had to say goodbye to a place and its people.

So far, however, she had said nothing about her visit to her uncle Josef in the mountains. Something held her back, although she could not say what it was.

"And now you've come back to Germany?" she said. Their hands lay on the red-and-white checked tablecloth, less than half an inch separating them.

Hannes shrugged. "In the empire, like the rest of Europe, industrialization has been following a course that no one with any common sense could think is right. I want to make something happen *here*! I want to change things for the better."

Mimi nodded, impressed. *He's like Heinrich,* she instinctively thought. Her former beau had also been possessed of a missionary zeal, and had talked all the time about the things he wanted to achieve. But while she had always seen Heinrich's fervor as overbearing, even disquieting, with Hannes it was different.

"And now you're on your way back to your hometown?" She held her breath. Would he tell her where he was heading next? Maybe then she would tell him about her trip to Laichingen the following day.

A shadow crossed his face, but disappeared again as quickly as it came. "They say a prophet has no honor in his own land." His laugh had a bitter undercurrent. "I'm finished with my hometown. A dozen horses couldn't drag me back there. My family . . . at home, we . . ." He faltered. "Forget it."

Mimi wrinkled her brow. "I'm sorry. I guess you don't have good memories."

"You could say that." Hannes twisted his mouth into a wry smile. "But tell me more about yourself. The photographic profession is a little unusual for a woman, isn't it?"

Mimi laughed. "And *you* could say that. But I've learned to stand up for myself in a man's world."

He looked at her with evident admiration. "I believe you. And I suspect you're a master of your trade. And beautiful besides . . ."

"And *I* suspect that you're a flatterer," she replied impishly. Then, more seriously, she said, "I love to show people in their best light. That family earlier, for instance. If I had them in front of my camera,

I would ensure that everyone could forget the boy's epilepsy for a moment. I'd come up with a composition that looked natural, add some props—things a boy would like, maybe even use a canvas with a special background—I can already see the photograph in my mind's eye." Mimi smiled. She noticed that the wine bar was slowly emptying of customers. The proprietor, polishing glasses behind the bar, glanced grumpily in their direction every few minutes—he clearly wanted to close for the night.

And what then? Mimi wondered. The thought of having to part from this charismatic man was strangely painful, but it was getting very late. The guesthouse landlady hadn't given her a key for the house, nor had she asked for one. She had only gone out for a short stroll through town, after all, and now she would probably have to rap on a window in the middle of the night. *Well, who cares!*

Hannes abruptly pulled her out of her thoughts. "So you take *that* kind of picture." He took his hands off the table. The esteem was gone from his eyes, replaced by a look more of disappointment.

Mimi frowned. "What did you think? That I was a landscape photographer? No." She shook her head. "It's people that fascinate me."

"Then why do you lead people to accept some pretty make-believe?" His eyes were shining now, as they had when he'd been delivering his speech earlier.

Mimi could hardly believe her ears. "I don't!" she said indignantly. "I want to give them a gift, and that gift is beauty."

"Beauty, where none exists?"

The proprietor stepped up to their table, but Hannes waved him away harshly. Then he leaned across the table to Mimi. "That mother— would a picture of yours change her life one little bit?"

"Of course not. But no one expects that, either." Mimi looked at him in confusion. "Do you think I should have just let the boy writhe on the ground? Should I have pulled out my camera instead?" she snapped.

"No. No, you did the right thing," Hannes said, and Mimi calmed down a little. "Although," he continued after a momentary silence, "if people were stirred by pictures of a seizure like that, then perhaps our scientists would make more of an effort to research conditions like epilepsy."

Mimi looked at him in disbelief. "Scaring people with pictures like that wouldn't help anybody. I know there's a shift in photography these days toward—"

But that was as far as she got, because the proprietor suddenly reappeared at their table, his arms crossed over his chest, and said, "I beg your pardon, but I really must ask you to leave. Closing time was ten minutes ago!"

CHAPTER 14

Laichingen, Swabian Jura

"Next we have a half slip with broderie anglaise. It can also be worn as a petticoat, of course. Wholesale price . . ." Herrmann Gehringer leafed through his price list while his assistant, Paul Merkle, diligently held the linen slip aloft.

The air in Gehringer's office was stuffy and suffocating, as it always was when he turned the heat on. He despised the heat and would have preferred to throw open the window, but he could not let their esteemed clientele freeze.

Martin Scheurebe, buyer for a large department store in Hamburg, examined his fingernails while he waited. He was bored and did not give the slip a second glance.

"Four marks, thirty-five pfennigs. No! I beg your pardon. That's the price for model 349." Gehringer looked up apologetically from his lists. "I'll have it in a moment. With such a range, one can get quite muddled."

Why hadn't Merkle marked the prices for this year's collection with an *X*? Or written them on a separate list? He glanced angrily at his assistant.

Across the desk, Scheurebe took a deep breath. "Forgive me, Mr. Gehringer, for being so frank, but I don't like having my time wasted. If I go to the trouble of coming all the way down to the Swabian Jura, then it is surely not too much to expect for you to prepare for our business meeting accordingly."

Gehringer's ears burned. The impertinence! But he managed to pull himself together and, with feigned obsequiousness, said, "You're absolutely right, Mr. Scheurebe. My sincere apologies. Here, model 350. Three marks, fifty-four pfennigs."

"Three marks, fifty-four pfennigs for a plain little rag like that?" Martin Scheurebe laughed.

"Hand embroidered, as always with us." Herrmann Gehringer raised his eyebrows. "Laichingen linen is the highest quality. The price is very fair."

"*You* may see it that way, my dear Mr. Gehringer," said the Hamburg buyer. "But you seem to be a little out of touch with what your competition is providing for that price. Quality is only one attribute, originality quite another. Your entire collection strikes me as a little outdated. These are the same pieces you showed me last fall. I might as well have saved myself the trouble of coming here." He gestured toward the table where Merkle had laid the sample slip. "Thread buttons everywhere! For today's young women, polished tortoiseshell buttons are the fashion. And don't get me started on the broderie anglaise." He picked up the camisole that Merkle had displayed earlier and which made a set with the half slip. "Our customers want to see flowing floral patterns and playful embroidery—new, fresh designs. And if it *must* be broderie anglaise, then why not on the shoulders?"

Gehringer could not believe his ears. How dare he! Herrmann Gehringer had built up Gehringer Weaving here in Laichingen by himself, by the sweat of his own brow. Day and night he'd slaved away, he and his family making sacrifices, for decades! Scheurebe hadn't broken a sweat in his life.

Snorting angrily, he said, "And who's going to pay me for these new fashions? Everyone wants lace and frills, and modern designs to boot, but they won't pay for more than a plain old smock!"

Scheurebe smoothed his black jacket. "Believe it or not, I'm certainly prepared to pay more for my goods. But what would I be getting for my money if I did pay more? This?" He made a sweeping gesture that took in Gehringer's walnut-paneled office, the small iron stove, and Merkle with all the samples. "Year after year, I find myself in this airless office and have to put up with that horrible noise. I get a headache every time." He nodded toward the window, through which the clacking of looms penetrated into the office.

Gehringer smiled. "You happen to be in a weaving mill, sir."

Scheurebe waved it off. "The customer does not have to see the day-to-day operations. Look around, Mr. Gehringer. See how they do it elsewhere. Other manufacturers have properly equipped showrooms, quiet places with the sun shining in through large windows. The clothes are lined up neatly on hangers, and attractive models demonstrate the undergarments. They have sample catalogs, too, with interesting photographs, not just lists of article numbers." Martin Scheurebe stood up, shaking his head. "For the sake of loyalty, I'll take seventy percent of my last order. But I genuinely hope that things are different on my next visit, or I will have to start looking for a new supplier. I will certainly not miss this office."

"For the sake of loyalty!" Herrmann Gehringer glared through narrowed eyes at the order sheet that Merkle had hastily filled out while Martin Scheurebe was preparing to leave. Was he supposed to be thankful for this? Should he bow and scrape?

He sniffed disparagingly. "So the fellow wants modern designs? Then tell me: What are we supposed to reinvent when it comes to flower patterns?" he said to Merkle, who was busy folding their sample garments. True, they worked mostly with their old motifs, but so far no one had complained.

"Wouldn't it perhaps be advisable to look for a pattern designer?" said Merkle cautiously.

"Oh yes. As if people like that grew on trees here in the Jura! I'm happy just to have good people for my looms." Gehringer waved his hand dismissively. "And a showroom? Models for the undergarments? Does he think we're in Paris?"

Merkle shook his head energetically to underscore his incomprehension.

"At least our looms are the most modern money can buy," Gehringer said. He'd put a lot of money into better hardware in recent years. But add the wages for more than fifty weavers and just as many women to do the embroidery, plus the spiraling costs of raw materials . . . There had been nights when he could not sleep for all his worries. No one, of course, ever wanted to hear a word of that. He rearranged the writing implements on his desk nervously.

Merkle, who was standing in the doorway, cleared his throat. "Didn't Arno Birnbichler, that buyer from Ellenrieder's in Munich, say just last week that such showrooms were becoming commonplace in other towns?"

Gehringer shuddered at the mention of Birnbichler's name. "Another one who's full of himself. Even if half the world has showrooms, where do you think I'm going to find one?" Now Merkle was starting to sing the same tune as the rest of them!

"Perhaps a new building on the factory grounds? A pavilion with big windows for the light? We certainly have the space." Merkle looked as eager as a schoolboy who thinks he's solved a tricky math problem.

But Gehringer shook his head brusquely. "My office is as far from the looms as I can make it, and you can hear for yourself how loud it is. Anything we build would be closer to the mill and even more exposed."

"I don't find it so loud in here," Merkle said. "What if you were to rent a suitable room in the village?"

"In Laichingen? In a weaver's house, d'you think? With its roof covered in straw like the stable at Bethlehem? I'm sure that Scheurebe and the other buyers would feel right at home," Gehringer said sarcastically. "The only decently lit shop in town is Helene's store, and she is *not* going to rent me her holy of holies."

Merkle chewed thoughtfully at his bottom lip.

Gehringer narrowed his eyes. "D'you have something else in mind?" He knew Paul Merkle well enough to know that he hadn't given up yet.

"It's just an idea . . . ," Merkle said slowly. "There's that shop, the one at the end of the square. It belongs to old Josef Stöckle."

"Who?" Gehringer frowned. What was the man on about?

Merkle smiled. "It's been closed for quite a while, so I'm not surprised you didn't think of it yourself. The windows are covered so you can't see in. But if memory serves, it's actually very bright inside."

"You mean the old photographer's shop? Is he even still alive?"

"'Still' is certainly the right word. They say Mr. Stöckle is very ill." Merkle smiled knowingly.

Gehringer narrowed his eyes until they were almost shut, as he always did when he pondered a new idea. The place was close to the church, across the square from The Oxen. He had never used the photographer's services. When his wife was still alive, she had always insisted on having her photograph taken in Ulm.

Gehringer nodded thoughtfully. "Not a bad idea at all. The building's still in relatively good shape. A bit of sweep and polish . . ." As he spoke, he jumped up from his desk. "I think I'll go and take a look at it. If I like the place, I'll make the old man an offer. He'll probably be overjoyed just to bring in a few marks rent."

Merkle diligently handed the weaving mill owner his top hat and walking stick. But Gehringer stopped midstride. "I've just had another idea. Why don't we draw up a contract right now. I want Stöckle to promise to sell me the building after he's gone. Sit, Paul!" Gehringer waved his assistant back to the desk. "Get writing!"

CHAPTER 15

When Mimi awoke the next morning, the first thing she pictured before opening her eyes was Hannes's face. Had she no more than dreamed the previous evening they had spent together? She blinked. With every flick of her eyelids, more and more memories of the previous day returned.

Hannes. She didn't even know his last name. She didn't know where he came from or where he was going. Hadn't he mentioned at some point that he wanted to visit Munich? As spirited as their conversation had been, he had guarded his personal life closely. Unlike her! She had practically worn her heart on her sleeve, which was not like her at all—something about the man earned her trust. They were kindred souls, he'd said. *Kindred souls,* she thought. *A beautiful notion.*

Mimi closed her eyes and buried herself beneath the thin blanket of her guesthouse bed.

After the proprietor had locked the door behind them at the wine bar, Hannes had linked arms with her. They had strolled side by side along the Danube, and Hannes had walked her back to her guesthouse later. When they said goodbye, he kissed her and said that he had never met a woman like her and hinted that they might travel together. His own guesthouse, he said, was nearby.

Mimi had pretended not to hear either suggestion. She had to check on her uncle Josef's well-being, as she had promised her mother.

One night of love? She had tried that a couple of times and decided she wasn't that kind of woman. Besides, what sense would it make to fall in love with him? Hannes had rattled at the window of her heart too much as it was, and so she had said, as lightheartedly as she could, "Everyone meets twice in life. Maybe I'll pass through Ulm again in a few days," when they parted. Back in her room, she had shed a few tears, but she also told herself it was for the best.

Perhaps, in different circumstances, Hannes would have been the man for her.

With new resolve, she opened her eyes. Enough dreaming. She should be grateful for having had such an ardent encounter at all instead of mourning something that had no place in her life. Hannes had his commitments, and she had hers. In a few hours, she would be seeing Josef again. It was time to prepare for that. She did her best to ignore the ache she felt in her heart when she thought of all this.

When Mimi climbed aboard the train that would take her up to the Swabian Jura, the only other occupant of the compartment was an elderly man so engrossed in a book that he didn't even look up when Mimi joined him. The train stopped at practically every town along the route, but no one joined them in their compartment, which was not a bad thing, because it allowed her to think back on her memories of the evening before with Hannes.

She had had too little sleep. Soon, her eyelids drooped of their own accord, and eventually she dozed off, although she did not miss very much—the landscape grew more barren with each passing mile.

When Mimi awoke and looked out the window, she could hardly believe it. "What in the . . . Everything's white!" she cried. Appalled, she turned to her fellow passenger. "Isn't it strange? It's like a second coming of winter."

The man looked up from his book. "Second coming of winter?" he said, and grinned. "Three-quarters of the year is winter here in the Jura. Snow is exactly what I'd expect at this time of year."

Still stunned, Mimi stared out at the world around them. Just yesterday, in Ulm, it had been warm enough for a cardigan. Now she'd have to dig her thick coat out of her luggage. "The only place with this much snow now should be the Black Forest," she grumbled to herself, then abruptly stood up. "Where are we? I haven't missed Laichingen, have I?"

The man, who had returned to his book, just shook his head.

The Laichingen train station was situated at the edge of town, Mimi realized as she waited for the train to come to a standstill. The first thing she saw, while they were still some distance out of town, was a prominent church tower. It was always the church tower that she noticed first when she came to a new place. She was a priest's daughter, after all, Mimi thought with a smile.

A long street led in the direction of the church tower, but there was little else of interest. In every other direction, all she saw was trees and wilderness, all of it under snow.

An icy wind met her as she disembarked. Tiny ice crystals—neither snow nor rain, but more like a frozen fog—glittered in the air. Shivering, she turned up the collar of her overcoat. The Laichingen station was almost as lively as the station in Ulm. Upper-class gentlemen in black suits looked to be on their way to business appointments. Tradesmen unloaded materials from the train. Mimi was surprised she didn't see many women.

She slung her camera over her right shoulder, picked up her suitcase in her right hand, and carried no more than her small photo bag in her left. It was an old superstition. If she rearranged her heavy luggage, she would certainly have been able to carry it more easily, but Mimi always left some space on her left—for her guardian angel. After a few steps, she began to feel a rumbling in her belly. Was it hunger or nerves? Not much longer, and she would see her beloved uncle again. She wondered how he was feeling, and whether he would reproach her for so rarely even sending him a letter, let alone visiting.

Hopeful and a little troubled, Mimi marched into town. Josef lived close to the market square, her mother had written in her letter. Because churches and market squares were almost always close together, Mimi was sure she would have no trouble finding him.

The long street from the station to the village was busy. Carts and carriages of every description rolled out toward the station, and Mimi had to get off to the side several times to make room for a passing vehicle. She even saw a few automobiles. In cities like Stuttgart and tourist towns like Meersburg, cars had become part of the daily scenery, but Mimi had never expected to find them fouling the air of the Swabian Jura, too. The fumes from the exhaust pipes mixed with the icy fog to form a gray cloud that hurt her throat when she inhaled. The drivers were wrapped up in coats, caps, and scarves, and Mimi caught no more than a glimpse of their faces. *Protecting themselves from their own stench,* she thought as she coughed.

Factory buildings, large and small, lined both sides of the street, and Mimi could hear the rhythmic clacking of machinery from inside them. Müller Table Linen, Morlock Linen Weaving, Best Bed Linen by Hirrler—she could see by the factory signs that everything was tied to the linen trade. People seemed to live well from it, too, if the big houses of the factory owners were any indication. In front of some of the houses were automobiles, and well-tended gardens with boxtree hedges and wrought-iron gates also stood as signs of wealth. But it was a mystery to Mimi how the inhabitants of those beautiful houses could live with the constant clack-clack-clacking from the factory buildings right next door. She walked faster, wanting to escape the disagreeable noise.

It was barely five minutes before she passed a small power station. The facility still looked quite new. Mimi guessed that it had been the factory owners who'd pushed for the construction of the power station. Had they laid cables directly into the houses? There were streetlamps, too, she noted, and they were already lit, although it was only just after midday. *That must surely be because of this fog,* Mimi thought.

She stopped for a moment to readjust her camera bag. She screwed up her face: one day she'd be bent and buckled from all this carrying.

After another ten minutes, the main road disappeared into a confusion of small alleys. There were no villas anymore. The houses here were low and pressed close together. The roofs were covered not with shingles but with straw—through the frozen fog, it looked like the fur of polar bears. *This will be where the poorer people live.*

She walked on, looking up continually to keep the church tower in view. There were no cars to see anymore, and fewer adults were out on the streets. *Probably all at work in the factories.* But she saw children on their way home from school. They wore plain linen smocks and shoes of woven straw. Weren't they freezing? Mimi shuddered at the sight.

So far, she had passed a shoemaker, a blacksmith, and a wagonmaker. But were there any actual shops? Or did you have to go to the next town to buy food? Mimi hoped she would find at least a bakery. The bag of *Olgabrezeln* she'd bought the day before had gotten crushed in the incident at the café, and after that she'd been with Hannes, so she hadn't thought to buy more.

A door opened on Mimi's right, and a woman stepped out and hurled a bucket of wash water into the road so forcefully that Mimi was barely able to jump clear in time. "Excuse me, could you tell me—" Mimi began, but the woman didn't even dignify her with a glance and disappeared back into the house.

They're not very chatty around here, Mimi thought, tromping onward. The narrow street she was walking along took a sharp left turn, and the next moment, Mimi found herself standing in a large, open market square. To her left was the church with the tower Mimi had used to navigate by. It had undecorated brown windows and did not look particularly inviting. In front of it was a frozen pond; she decided it was one of the reservoirs typical of the dry region, as mentioned in her Baedeker travel guide. Such a pond was called a *Hüle*, she had read. The surface was like a mirror, and she was sure the ice was thick enough to skate on.

Mimi turned away from the pond and let her eyes sweep across the market square. There was no photo studio to be seen, but a welcoming half-timbered building opposite the church housed an inn called The Oxen. To her relief, a few buildings beyond that she saw a general store. She would ask directions there, and surely she could buy some pastries for her uncle as well.

Did every inn like The Oxen stink of stale beer, male sweat, and over-used cooking oil? And damp dishrags . . . Disgusted, Anton stared at the rag with which he was wiping down the tables that were still sticky and dirty from the night before.

Clean in the morning. Shop for the day's cooking. Cook, serve, clear away. Scrub the kitchen. Late at night, lift all the chairs and sweep. Then start all over again. The thought that this cycle might continue for the rest of his life was so unbearable to Anton that he could not hold back a groan of pain. Damn it, he was only eighteen. He was tall and strong, not one of those weaklings like his former schoolmates, who went hungry in their weavers' houses all the time. He was good look-ing, or at least he thought he was, and never at a loss for words. What was it they said: fortune favors the bold? He knew it to be true from countless books. Alexander the Great was still a young man when he left little Macedonia to conquer the world. Nearly two thousand years later, Columbus discovered America. And three hundred years after that, Alexander von Humboldt, tutored at home, set off on the first of his marvelous expeditions.

Not one of them ever even considered following in his parents' footsteps. And here he was, dishrag in hand.

He groaned again.

"Something not to Mr. High and Mighty's liking?" his mother snapped. As she did every morning, Karolina Schaufler was polishing the beer and cider glasses. She was proud of the fact that they had real glasses in The Oxen, not just the usual tankards. *Although no one but her appreciates it,* thought Anton sullenly. "When you're done with the tables, go out back. Someone threw up out there last night. Men!" she muttered.

"Why should I be the one who—" Anton began.

"If you can dig up that useless father of yours and get him to clean the mess, be my guest," Karolina snapped. "But knowing him, he's snuck off to the forest. He's sitting in a blind somewhere while I'm here breaking my back."

Anton rolled his eyes. His mother was probably right. The game his father hunted was a nice addition to their menu, as his father was only too happy to explain. But he went off to the woods outside hunting season, too—someone had to look after the forest, he said. His father could always find an excuse to escape The Oxen and his wife.

Anton slapped the cleaning rag onto the table angrily. "What do I care if you two fight all the time? Why do I have to work here? Why can't I do an apprenticeship, like some of my old schoolmates? As a businessman, or as . . ."

"What, then?" Karolina asked. Hands set on her hips, she glared at him from her close-set eyes. "What great plans does sir have lined up today? Last week, you wanted to be an agent for Epple's Brewery." She jutted her chin toward the cellar where the beer barrels were stored. "The week before that, you were off to join the navy. In between, if I remember right, you wanted to be a train conductor."

"So what? Is it a crime to plan for the future? Not everyone wants to go to seed in the Jura like you two." Anton spoke with more conviction than he actually felt. Why lie to himself? He'd started going to seed long ago. While his schoolmates were learning a trade in the weaving and linen mills, he was fated to mop up vomit.

"Plan for the future?" His mother sniffed. "Dreaming's what it is. What makes you think the world's waiting for *you*? There's people out there that's been to college, folks with brains. Why would the likes of you ever need that?"

"I could've studied, too. Easily!" he shouted at her. "I had the best grades of all my schoolmates our final year."

"What does that count for in a village school?" Karolina shook her head and turned away.

Anton's shoulders slumped, and his gut felt as raw and sore as if he'd just been socked in the belly. His mother's disparaging words should mean nothing by now. For Karolina, every man in the world was an idler, an idiot, or a good-for-nothing.

But he was her son, damn it! Couldn't she spare him her loathing for men? Couldn't she say, just once, *If you're so unhappy here, go follow your own path. With God's blessing and mine.* Maybe then he would have found the courage to break the ties that bound him.

"I'll clean up out back," said his mother in her most martyred voice, and she held out a shopping list. "You go to Helene's."

CHAPTER 16

Absorbing every ounce of warmth the stove radiated, Eveline stood and stirred the *Schwarzer Brei*. The smell of the spelt, musty from the long winter, filled her nose, and she turned her head from it in disgust. There were days when she could hardly swallow a mouthful of the stuff. But she had to eat to stay strong. Repulsed, she put the pot aside to cool.

Edelgard Merkle sat at Eveline's table. She had brought her sewing machine along on a handcart and was working on a jacket for Eve's son, Alexander. The sewing machine had been a gift from Paul, Edelgard's younger son, which she liked to tell people, whether they wanted to hear it or not, and she had been earning her living ever since with the kind of sewing work she was doing now. She did very well for herself, too, because she was the only woman in the entire village with her own sewing machine.

Eveline sat and began to sort the fabric remnants left over from cutting out the jacket. She put every piece larger than the palm of her hand aside for later use. Looking up, she caught Edelgard's approving glance: thrift was a virtue here in the village.

Eveline looked at her two youngest children, who were sitting on the floor doing their homework. Alexander, her oldest, sat on the windowsill, sketching. His cheeks glowed, and he seemed engrossed in his work. A wave of maternal love swept over her.

Edelgard looked up, following Eveline's gaze.

"Boy, you'll hunch your back with all your drawing," Edelgard said. "How do you think this jacket will fit then?"

The old seamstress laughed, but the remark cut Eveline deeply. She knew that Edelgard had meant no harm, but why couldn't anyone ever say how lovely Alexander's drawings were, even once? A bit of praise for a change, just one encouraging word—was it asking too much?

"Alexander's very artistically minded. I think it's important for children to have the chance to develop their talents," she said.

Edelgard laughed. "No need to tell me. Look at my sons. One's worked his way up to be Mr. Gehringer's assistant. And Johann . . ." Her smile turned melancholy. "You know."

Eveline pressed her lips together tightly. *The grass is always greener somewhere else,* she thought bitterly.

"Once I've edged everything and tacked it together, Alexander has to try it on. If he'll let me disturb him," said Edelgard with affectionate irony.

The boy looked uncertainly from one woman to the other.

"Keep doing what you're doing. I'll tell you when we need you," said Eveline gently, then she picked up the embroidery work she'd begun the day before. While Edelgard's machine whirred and she pushed her own needle with the polished embroidery yarn through the fabric, her thoughts fluttered away like small birds.

Her mother had also owned a sewing machine, the latest Singer model. As a businessman's wife, however, she had all her clothes tailored for her in the finest fashion houses in Chemnitz, and only took up sewing for the fun of it—lace curtains, tablecloths, and elaborate decorative cushions. She had, though, taught Eveline to sew.

If her mother could see Eveline now, so poor that a sewing machine was forever out of reach . . . The very thought was unimaginable, and so humiliating that Eve squeezed her eyes closed, as if she could escape her misery like that.

When she opened her eyes, she glanced around the room, and she felt distant from all of it, as if she could not believe, even after so many years, that this was where she had ended up.

The long room in which they sat occupied the entire ground floor. At the back wall was the stove, where Eveline prepared all their meals. The dining table was on the right, and aside from meals, it was also where Eve embroidered Herrmann Gehringer's decorative pillow covers; and if she wasn't working at the table, the children were doing their homework or Klaus was fixing some damaged piece of farm equipment there.

On one wall, a tin basin was attached with leather straps. Every Saturday, Eveline took the basin from the wall and boiled pots of water for their baths. It was a lot of work, but those hours, for Eveline, were the best of the week. When her children were bathing, Eveline devoted herself to them without an ounce of guilt. They sang and laughed together without anyone calling it a waste of time, and she could show them small gestures of affection, too, which were often impossible with all her daily work. When, in the end, she got to take a bath herself, she put two extra pots of water on to boil to make the dirty tepid broth a little warmer and more agreeable. When she lay in the water with her legs pulled up tightly against her body and her eyes closed, she could almost imagine that it was as it once had been, when the servants had drawn a pleasant-smelling bath for her whenever she wanted one. As the daughter of the industrialist Karl-Otto Hoffmeister and his wife, Margarethe, all she had to do was snap her fingers for any wish to come true.

Eveline blinked and, as so often, wondered whether "once had been" was something she had only ever dreamed? Or was it really that her present life was a bad dream? Maybe she would wake up one day to discover that everything was different after all? She shook her head angrily to rid herself of these confusing thoughts.

Her eyes shifted to the shelf to the left of the stove, where she kept her food supplies. Every shelf was glaringly empty. They didn't have a pantry, not even a cellar where they could store cabbages and turnips, although there was a trapdoor in the floor on the left side of the room. It opened onto a wooden ladder that led down into the so-called *Dunk*—"the heart of every weaver's house," as Klaus had proudly told Eveline after carrying her over the threshold of her new home as his fledgling bride. The name, Eveline thought, derived from how dark—or *dunkel*—it was down there. In the *Dunk* stood a huge old loom that had last been used by Klaus's father, who'd been dead for twenty years. Eveline had asked her husband more often than she could remember if she could use the *Dunk* to store food and anything else she needed to put away. But Klaus did not want to upset "the old order." It did not bother him that, because space was so tight, the house was in disarray.

Eveline sighed audibly. From behind her sewing machine, Edelgard gave her a knowing look. The children did not react. They would have been more surprised to hear their mother laugh.

A narrow, uneven stairway led to the upper floor, where the bedrooms were. Even after all these years, Eve was still afraid of the stairs. Often, she or one of the children missed a step and slipped. Just the week before, little Erika had fallen down and sprained her ankle.

Eveline stopped mid-stitch and closed her eyes. To lie down, pull a blanket over her head, and forget all her cares . . . how lovely that would be. Instead, she was plagued by questions of how she was supposed to fill her family's bellies now that they were nearly out of food after the long winter. And she could not ignore the work she had to catch up on because she hadn't been able to do much in the days after the death of her baby. The decorative cushions she had to embroider were piled higher than they had ever been. And on top of it all was the feeling of unease that came when she thought of her husband.

"How is Klaus?" asked Edelgard just then, as if she had read her mind.

"Klaus . . . is how he is," Eve said evasively. There was little point in telling the world that Klaus was becoming more depressed with each passing week. There were days when he hardly said a word, days when she had to shake him as hard as she could to wake him up and get him out of bed. A kiss? A caress? Nights in which two bodies merged into one? Rare, too rare, these days.

"It's time for winter to finally admit it's over," said Edelgard emphatically. "Melancholy has found its way into many a house this year."

But it wasn't just winter that brought Klaus down. His melancholy had started years earlier with the death of their first son, and that had been on a hot August day. If he were still alive, he would be just a year older than Alexander. She had been young, then, and to her own surprise she had recovered from the loss reasonably well. A stillbirth happened sometimes. In her old circles, too, people whispered privately about such things. She was young, and she would be sure to carry her next child to term.

Klaus, however, had never gotten over his son's death. "The devil's dancing in this house," he'd said, again and again. "My own mother lost children here. I wish I'd never brought you. What have I done?" He'd gone on for weeks like that, tearing himself apart. Never once did it occur to him that she, too, might have wanted a little consolation. The devil in the house? Eveline had found it hard not to let him scare her with all his talk, and had been deeply relieved when Alexander arrived just over a year later. But Klaus's strangeness had remained. Sometimes he looked around as if inwardly asking himself, *What am I doing here?* In that, at least, his suffering was not very different from her own.

Eveline inhaled deeply. All these thoughts were making her throat tight. "The late snow gives a little room to breathe, at least," she said. "When it's gone, I'll have to juggle a dozen things at once: the embroidery, the housework, plus all the work in the fields . . ." The overflowing basket of linen caught her eye again. Would she be able to manage it if she got up an hour earlier each day? They needed the money so urgently now that Alexander's confirmation was looming, and she didn't even have what she needed to pay Edelgard.

Edelgard, in the meantime, had called Alexander over and dressed him carefully in the pinned-together jacket. She stood back with her hands on her hips and looked the boy up and down. "It's as I feared: the fabric from Klaus's old vest wasn't enough. The sleeves are too short. I'll have to add a trim from those checked remnants. You had to shoot up in the last six months, didn't you?" Half-amused, half-annoyed, Edelgard rapped Alexander gently on the head with her knuckles.

Checked trim on a black jacket? Well, isn't that going to look good! Eveline fumed. She yearned for something that looked decent. Was a little bit of style too much to ask?

"I'd like to know why the priest insists on the boys wearing a dark suit. We're drowning in linen here, but who's got any black fabric lying around?" Eve said angrily.

Edelgard laughed. "You get some ideas," she said. She rummaged in her bag and produced a tin box. "Come, children. Who'd like a nice cookie? You've been so diligent with your schoolwork, you deserve a treat, right, Marianne?" She stroked the eight-year-old's head fondly and whispered something in her ear that made both of them laugh.

Eveline winced. Edelgard smiled all the time these days, ever since she'd become a widow. It was as if she'd been given a new lease on life. *I wouldn't mind a new lease on life myself,* thought Eveline, watching enviously as the seamstress used a scrap of cloth to tie a bow in Marianne's hair. Then she, too, could hand out cookies and love instead of sitting hunched over her embroidery. And if *she* had tied the bow in Marianne's hair, she would have done a far better job of it!

"In winter, the cold and the dark make our lives a misery, and in spring it's the stones we have to pick from the fields," said Edelgard. "I often think my Johann was right when he went to America seven years ago."

Johann Merkle. Eveline felt a small, sharp pang strike her heart, as she always did when she heard Johann's name or thought of him.

She could see him, now. A man's face, but so different from most. Finer, softer, and yet radiating an inner strength. Brown eyes that actually looked at you instead of looking past you. And then his dark-brown, unruly hair . . . When she closed her eyes, she could feel the touch of his hair against her skin. Johann. Had he also been just a dream?

Eveline abruptly stood up and went to the window. If Johann were to come around the corner now . . . but instead of Edelgard's son, Eveline saw a woman she didn't know, bent with the weight of the luggage she carried. A salesperson? No, she was far too well dressed for that, like a real lady. The stranger looked around uncertainly, as if she couldn't quite believe where she'd ended up—Eve knew the feeling all too well.

The elegant winter coat, the leather traveling case, the artfully coiffed hair—Eveline suddenly had the feeling that she was seeing herself back when she had first come to Laichingen. And she sensed in the woman, as she had then, her bewilderment at the poverty and plainness of the village.

Go! Run as fast as you can! Take the next train and get out! Eveline wanted to call to the stranger. *You don't belong here any more than I do.*

"What are you gawking at out there?" asked Edelgard, joining her.

Eveline pointed in the direction of the stranger. "Do you know who that is?"

"Josef Stöckle is supposed to have a relative coming. It could be her. Luise said she wrote to Josef's sister in Esslingen, and that someone was finally going to come and sort things out for the old man."

Indeed, the woman turned and left the narrow street again, heading back toward the market square where the photographer had his house.

And Eveline knew instinctively that for this woman, too, there would be no escape.

CHAPTER 17

The sign outside the small general store told Mimi that it belonged to a woman named Helene, and when she pushed open the door, she walked into a patchwork of odors: the warmth of fresh bread, the tang of pickled cucumbers, the spice of smoked ham. Mimi's stomach growled louder. The evening before, in the wine bar with Hannes, she had been so fluttery that she'd been unable to eat a thing, and during the night, her mind had been so preoccupied with what might have been that her appetite still hadn't returned by morning.

The shop was full, with at least half a dozen women waiting for Helene to serve them. Linen aprons peeked from beneath their overcoats, and all the women wore headscarves. When Mimi entered, the buzz of conversation fell silent. The women's glances carried curiosity, some also suspicion. *Don't worry, I don't bite,* Mimi thought, but she didn't say it out loud. She just greeted the women politely, then took her place at the back of the line. The women went back to their talking. Mimi, unable to follow the Swabian dialect very well, looked around. Sacks of flour, sugar, and salt. Baskets of eggs and potatoes. And on a shelf, turnips, wrinkled heads of cabbage, and parsnips. There wasn't much to be had at Helene's, and some of it looked as if it had been there for a long time. She probably wouldn't find any *Olgabrezeln* here, she was thinking, when the door opened and a young man with broad shoulders stepped inside. The women stopped speaking again and nodded to the new arrival as he joined the line behind Mimi. She smiled at the young man, but he didn't respond.

Some customers left, others came. After a quarter of an hour, it was finally Mimi's turn. "Hello. I'd like some pastries, please," she said.

The shop owner—Mimi assumed that she was dealing with Helene in person—reached for an old tin box that stood with others on a shelf. "I've got some sugar loaf and a batch of almond crescents."

While Mimi was still considering her choice, the door suddenly flew open. A chilly wind gusted in, and with it came a well-dressed man in a suit, overcoat, and top hat. All conversation ceased once again.

"Good morning, ladies," the man greeted those present in a sonorous voice. He seemed not to notice the presence of the young man.

The women standing behind Mimi quickly stepped aside to let the older man pass.

Helene, who a moment earlier had been proudly presenting Mimi with her tin of baked goods, now ignored her completely. "Good morning, Mr. Gehringer," she said. "A rare honor! What can I do for you?" She smiled at the man.

"Chocolate! Your finest dark chocolate, if you please."

What the . . . ? Mimi was dumbstruck. She cleared her throat loudly. "Excuse me, but it's my turn. The end of the line is back there," she said, and pointed behind her.

Disquiet spread among the women, and she heard indignant whispers. Someone inhaled sharply.

"Not to worry, young lady," said the man, doffing his top hat. "I'll be very quick."

Mimi felt her cheeks turn red. "Pushing in like that—how ill mannered." She watched angrily as the man, unperturbed, chose three bars of chocolate.

"That's Mr. Gehringer," the young man whispered in her ear, as if that would explain everything.

"Oh, so he doesn't have to wait his turn? It's common courtesy," Mimi whispered back.

There were men like Gehringer everywhere, Mimi thought grimly, while she waited until it was her turn again. Mayors, schoolmasters, factory owners. Men who believed they could push others around because of their position and their power, men who believed that everything belonged to them. They never gave a thought to others and did everything to suit themselves. The hard lines in the faces of such men—the embittered creases around their mouths, the deep grooves between their eyes—were rooted in the liberty they took as their due. With such men in front of the camera, posed grandly, of course, Mimi rarely went to any trouble to remove those hard lines when she retouched the pictures. Anyway, most of them were blind to the hardness and coldness in their faces, or were proud of the "power" that, in their opinion, they radiated.

As the man left the store, Mimi gave him a final furious glare. For her, the way the Gehringers of the world believed their time was somehow more valuable than others' was an outrage.

Anton had followed their exchange of words with fascination. Who was this woman? And what was she doing here in Helene's little store? A woman of the world did not stray into Laichingen by accident. In The Oxen, they had certainly never hosted anyone as elegant. The wives of the linen mill owners tried to play the role of gentlewomen, but they handled their knives and forks as if they were in the field with rakes and shovels.

When the stranger, a short time later, left the shop with the cookies she'd chosen, Anton went after her. He could buy the potatoes for his mother later. The newcomer was probably just passing through and could hardly wait to be out of Laichingen again. If he didn't manage a few words with her now, he'd never have another chance. And Anton

Schaufler was not one to miss an opportunity to breathe in the air of the wider world.

The woman, meanwhile, was standing in the market square with her luggage, looking around as if she was lost.

"Can I help you?" he asked, coming up beside her. He was instantly surrounded by her scent, which he'd already noticed in Helene's shop. Was it a perfume? Or some kind of hair cream? Her hair certainly glistened, thought Anton. And how neatly she'd pinned it all in place. Not a strand dared to come loose. She wore an elegantly curved silver hair clip as an ornament. Anton had to resist an impulse to reach out and touch it. It must have been worth quite a lot.

"I'm looking for my uncle's house. Josef Stöckle. My mother said he lived by the market square, but I don't know where."

Anton smiled. "No problem at all, ma'am. You're standing right in front of it." With a flourish, he pointed to the house behind her.

Frowning, the woman turned around, and froze.

Anton instinctively tried to see the house through her eyes. It was solidly built from irregular gray tuff, its roof covered with clay shingles, not straw like the rest of the houses in the area. It was also considerably larger than the other houses. Over the years, the soot from surrounding chimneys had settled on the facade, which made the house look rather run down, and the front windows were covered with old newspapers, which did nothing to change that impression. The house looked abandoned, even lifeless, he thought, and Anton almost felt a little ashamed about that.

"I'm sorry, there must be some confusion." The woman let out a small bewildered laugh. "I mean Josef Stöckle, the photographer. He has a big studio here in Laichingen."

"The studio is in the garden behind the house, and the main door is also around the back. You can't go in from this side. The business has been closed for a while."

The stranger looked first at the barricaded house, then at him. "But . . . I don't understand."

It seemed she had expected something very different. In a spontaneous gesture, he offered the woman his arm. "Come with me. I'll show you around to the back. It's very nice inside," he said encouragingly.

She placed one hand lightly on his right arm, and Anton suddenly felt quite gentlemanly. Together, they turned into the narrow alley that went down the right side of the house.

"I'm Anton Schaufler, by the way. I'm the son of the owner at The Oxen. When your uncle was still in good health, he often came to our inn." They reached the door too quickly for his liking. "I'm sure he'll be very happy to see you. If you need anything, you can almost always find me at The Oxen."

"When your uncle was still in good health . . ." The handsome, friendly young man was long gone, but his words still rang in Mimi's ears. *And how is my uncle today?* she'd wanted to ask, but a question like that would only show how little the family had taken care of Josef.

Instead of knocking, Mimi looked around. Most of the other houses she'd seen had a small garden in front, but Uncle Josef's had a large garden in the back. At the far end she saw several more buildings. Neighbors' houses? Was one of them Josef's studio? A narrow track in the snow showed that someone had walked through the garden not long ago. Josef? A neighbor?

Mimi took a deep breath and knocked.

Nothing stirred.

"Uncle Josef? It's me, Mimi!" she called loudly as she banged on the door again. What if he wasn't home?

Mimi was just wondering which house might belong to his neighbor Luise when she heard shuffling noises from inside.

"Yes?" A pale face peered suspiciously through the door, opened only a crack.

"I don't mean to startle you, showing up out of the blue after so long. It's me, Mimi. I've brought something to eat." She held up the paper bag from Helene's shop invitingly.

The thin face frowned. "I'm not buying anything."

"Uncle Josef! It's me, Mimi!" Mimi's smile felt frozen on her face. Surely her mother had told him she was coming? Or didn't he recognize her anymore?

After a long moment, the door opened.

"Mimi! Child, what are you doing here?" Josef's face lit up in disbelief and amazement. "How wonderful to see you!" He staggered a little and had to support himself against the wall.

"Oh, I didn't mean to give you a shock," said Mimi in dismay. "Didn't Mother write to you that I was coming?"

Josef looked at her uncertainly. "Yes . . . no. Oh, I don't know. Probably." He shook his head. "Come inside!"

A little apprehensively, Mimi followed her uncle into the house.

"I don't know what to say. You've caught me completely unawares. Not that I'm unhappy to see you, but it's rather awkward just at the moment. I have company, you see," said Josef, as he shuffled along the hallway.

Company? That's nice, Mimi thought, encouraged. "I'm actually just passing through and wanted to see how you are." *He's so stooped,* she thought. And his hair, once dark brown, was now as white as the snow outside. "I don't want to be any trouble. You know I'm not complicated," she added, with an exaggerated lightness in her voice.

Her uncle glanced back at her doubtfully. "Everyone says that."

"Well, I'm sure you can manage a cup of tea for me." With a smile, Mimi followed him into the kitchen. The next moment, she stopped dead in her tracks.

"You?" It was the man that had pushed ahead of her so brazenly in Helene's shop, now sitting at Josef's kitchen table and looking very out of place. On the table lay the chocolate he had purchased in such a hurry.

Josef looked from one to the other.

"Are you already acquainted?"

Mimi, taken aback, shook her head.

"Then may I introduce my niece, Mimi Reventlow. She is a photographer. This is Mr. Gehringer, and he has just made me an interesting offer."

"Has he?" said Mimi cautiously. She felt an automatic and deep distrust stir inside her. It made no difference what the offer was; she knew in her heart that this man would shortchange her uncle at the drop of a hat.

The man gave her a venomous glance, then turned his attention back to Josef. His expression instantly turned to charm as he said, "Your shop is exactly what I'm looking for, and I'm sure the rent comes at just the right time for you." He pulled his scarf a little closer around his neck and shivered a little too dramatically.

Mimi, herself freezing, glowered at him. The man was acting as if her uncle were on the brink of starvation.

But Josef's eyes sparkled. "When exactly would you like to start renting it?"

"As soon as possible," the man said. "You only have to sign here." He hovered a gold quill over a sheet of paper.

Mimi, who had followed their conversation in silence, cleared her throat. "Forgive me for interrupting your business dealings, but my uncle, I'm sure, would like to read through the contract before he signs it. Wouldn't you, Josef?" She smiled at Gehringer with exaggerated goodwill. "And maybe I can help him with a little advice." *Now we're even,* she thought with satisfaction when she saw the blood rise in the man's face.

CHAPTER 18

"Child, have you lost your mind? What was that all about?" Josef asked her the moment they were alone.

Mimi grimaced. "Sorry. That was a little rash of me." *What got into me?* she wondered. What right did she have to stick her nose into someone else's business? If Josef's visitor had been anyone else, she probably wouldn't have done anything of the sort.

Josef sat down and frowned across the table at her. "Unheard of," he muttered.

Off to a wonderful start, Mimi, she thought to herself. Remorseful, she explained the encounter earlier in Helene's shop, and to her relief, a smile appeared on Josef's face.

"So you felt you had to chime in now? You know, I really could use the rent that Gehringer's offering."

"Then let me read the contract through first, carefully. You can still sign it tomorrow if you want. All right?" said Mimi.

"So you're a lawyer now?" he said, teasing her. Then he looked curiously into the bag of treats that Mimi had put on the table.

"Help yourself. They're all for you," she said. "I know just as little about contracts as you do, but my gut tells me you have to watch out around a man like Gehringer. Besides, I can't stand people who cut in line."

As she talked, she looked around as unobtrusively as possible, hoping to spy a teapot somewhere. She wanted something to drink and was still feeling chilled, so a cup of tea would be wonderful. But her uncle made no move to offer her anything, and after her performance just now, she didn't have the courage to ask.

"Herrmann Gehringer's a businessman and doesn't have time to stand in line. Everybody here knows it, and they accommodate it. Gehringer owns one of the biggest weaving mills in Laichingen. He employs more than fifty people at his factory, and the weavers' wives also work for him, doing embroidery at home."

"And that's supposed to make him special?"

"What's special is that, even in bad times, Gehringer doesn't turn his back on his people. A few years ago, sales of linenware suddenly slumped, and nobody knew exactly why. Gehringer cut people's hours, but he didn't let anyone go. When business picked up, there was more work for everyone again. The people here count that to his credit. No one in the village has to fear being unemployed. If the father works for Gehringer, then the son will also find work there," Josef said. "You know yourself what industrialization and all its machines are doing in other places. Unemployment everywhere, because soulless machines are taking over the work done by human beings. But in Laichingen, things have changed for the better. In the past, when people worked on a loom at home, they were at the mercy of so-called 'putting-out' merchants who bought what they made. Now those gentlemen, I know from several reliable sources, were real crooks."

"That may be so, but does that give Gehringer the right to run around acting like a little Napoleon?" Mimi snorted angrily. "Oh, forget it," she said, wanting to talk about something else. "Why do you want to rent out your shop at all? It looks as if it's been closed for quite a while."

"Ah, the shop." Josef waved it aside. "Anyone who wants something from me knows where to find me: out in the studio."

Mimi relaxed a little. Few photographers granted themselves the luxury of a shop of their own. Most sold their photographs, postcards, and, if they produced any, lithographic prints directly out of their studios.

"Could I make a cup of tea?" she suddenly blurted. The kitchen was roomy and had a large stove for cooking, but no heater to keep the room warm. Pots and pans hung from the wall on iron hooks, and the stone sink had a faucet. So he had running water—a luxury that was unlikely to exist in the straw-roofed houses. Certainly, Josef would have made the house comfortable for his wife when she was still alive.

"Of course! Would you light the fire in the stove?" Josef said. With trembling fingers, he plucked an almond crescent from the plate where Mimi had arranged them.

How can he slide a dry plate into a camera with a tremor like that? Mimi wondered. Suddenly, she felt close to tears. Despite his opposition to her butting in, her once strong uncle now seemed extremely fragile. And old.

"I'll get this place nice and warm," she said, putting on a happy front, struggling against the lump in her throat. Kindling and a few pieces of wood lay in a basket on the floor, and Mimi also found matches there. A little unsure of herself, she opened the hatch of the stove and began to place the kindling inside, carefully angling it into a cone shape. She thought she'd seen someone do it that way once, although she hadn't paid much attention at the time. She couldn't actually remember ever lighting a fire in her life. Still, with a little effort, she managed to get the stove lit. Then she opened one kitchen cupboard after another until she finally found a jar containing some unidentifiable gray-green herbs—she hoped it wasn't wormwood for the Christmas turkey—and put them in the teapot. She spent longer preparing the water and tea than was really necessary, but as she did so, a strange feeling crept over her, something she had never previously felt in regard to her uncle: that she had to protect him.

"So tell me," she began when they were finally sitting with the tea, "how have you been? Mother wrote that you'd been very ill."

Josef raised one hand dismissively. "Old news. I caught pneumonia last November, but now I'm fit as a fiddle again. Don't tell me you came here because you were worried about me."

"Of course we're worried," said Mimi. She took his hand and squeezed it.

"Don't be. You can't kill a weed." Josef pushed the crumbled almond crescent back and forth nervously on his plate. He'd eaten almost none of it, yet he was practically skin and bone. The way he sat, shoulders slumped, he looked shrunken. Though he'd always been such an imposing figure.

The uneasy feeling in Mimi's stomach grew stronger. Josef was definitely not "fit as a fiddle." But what exactly was wrong with him? She'd have to speak to his neighbor Luise as soon as possible. And with the doctor, too, of course. Both could probably tell her more about the state of Josef's health than he would himself.

Mimi rose to put another piece of wood on the fire.

"Child, go easy with that. My winter wood is nearly spent," said her uncle uneasily.

"But I'm cold . . ."

"Up here, they say it's always a cardigan colder than anywhere else. You'd do best to get back on the road again tomorrow. That's where you belong. You've got customers to visit and you won't earn a pfennig if you stay here with me." He handed her a blanket as he spoke.

He seems in a hurry to get rid of me, Mimi thought as she spread the blanket over her lap. She took his hand in hers again.

"Oh, Josef, it's terrible that we've been out of touch so long. To be honest, I don't even know how it happened. The five years or so since we saw each other last have been hard work. Since my breakthrough in Baden-Baden, I've been booked almost constantly. Sometimes I was wanted in two places at once! But God knows, that's no excuse. I really know nothing about your life here in Laichingen. Tell me, how did the people here take to you? A widely traveled photographer in a little place like this . . ."

A shelf on the wall caught her eye. It was filled with all kinds of souvenirs from her uncle's wandering years. A wide-brimmed hat piled high with large red pom-poms—a *Bollenhut* from the Black Forest. A sword that looked as if it came from a medieval castle. A tankard from the Hofbräuhaus in Munich. Italian faience ware. An Altrichter violin varnished the color of honey.

The old photographer shrugged. "When I first started here, they came out of sheer curiosity. They'd never seen so much glass in one place as the load I had delivered for my studio. Traudel was kept busy, too. Sundays, believe it or not, were our busiest days!"

"Sundays?"

"During the week, people were too busy to have their picture taken, so I made a pact with the local priest. Those were good times . . ." Her uncle shook his head with a sad smile. "But the first rush passed quickly. Money in most households is tight. There isn't much left to pay for a photograph. Oh yes, they come to me if there's a wedding or a christening, but not otherwise. And the wealthier people here, the businessmen and their clerks, travel to bigger towns if they need anything."

Mimi frowned. Was that why he'd closed the shop? "What's keeping you here? Mother would be more than happy if you moved in with them, I'm sure of it," she said, with more conviction than she felt. "The parish house is big enough."

"Your mother has more important things to do than look after her old brother," Josef replied, his tone mildly ironic. "No, no, I'll spend the autumn of my life here. Laichingen folk are a peculiar lot, but I've taken to them, and my neighbor Luise looks after me well. Please tell your mother that I want for nothing. And aside from that, well, here in the house I'm still close to my Traudel. I hear her voice. I sense her presence.

Sometimes, when I open the cupboard that holds her linenware, I can even smell her." Josef's eyes shone.

Mimi felt a sharp stab in her heart. A love that crossed time and space, lovers who remained close even when separated. In her mind's eye, unbidden, appeared the image of a man with wild hair and a fearless expression. *Where is Hannes right now?* she wondered. *Still in Ulm?* Why hadn't she told him that she was planning to travel to Laichingen? She had even mentioned the village to Clara Berg, so why not to him? She had cut whatever bond had briefly joined them. Afraid of her own emotions?

"Now it's your turn," said her uncle. "Tell me, my child, is there love in your life? Do you still not regret leaving your fiancé behind back then?"

Mimi laughed. "Heinrich? Oh, no. I haven't thought about him in years. My freedom is more important to me than anything. Besides, my profession and a husband? How would that work?"

Josef looked at her intently. "Child, if you love someone with all your heart, you can move mountains."

"I'm satisfied with my life," she said as lightheartedly as she could.

"Satisfied . . . Is satisfied enough?" Josef smiled. "Is business good? Where have you been recently?"

Mimi was relieved by the change of subject. She said, "I spent the winter at Lake Constance. It's much milder there. Last fall I was in Bad Kissingen. There are so many spa visitors that there are days when you can hardly move in the street. I asked the local photographer there— Mr. Stöckmayer, you remember him, at the spa garden next to the Rákóczi Spring—if I could offer my services. Not only did I take some beautiful photographs, but I also turned a very tidy profit."

"Of which you had to give at least twenty percent to Stöckmayer," Josef said. "That was one good thing about my little studio wagon: I didn't have to share my income with anyone." He sighed. "I'll never forget the days on the road with Grete and the Sun Coach. Who didn't I have in front of my camera? There's only one thing I never managed: to photograph royalty. You've got that one over me, child, but *that* would have been my dream."

"I thought your studio here in Laichingen was your dream?" Mimi said.

"Would you like to see it?" Her uncle stood up so abruptly that he banged his legs on the edge of the table.

"Tomorrow, certainly. Let's talk for now," Mimi said. The last thing she wanted was to go back out into the cold. She picked up their thread: "Traveling as lightly as I do has advantages, even if I have to come to terms with resident photographers."

"And where are you going to have to 'come to terms' next?" said Josef with affectionate irony as he took his seat again.

Mimi straightened her shoulders. "Isny." In the rolling Alpine foothills, new grass would already be sprouting and the first flowers blooming. She could hardly wait to get back down to spring!

"Will you be adding church towers and bridges to pictures where none exist?"

"If that's what the customer wants," she replied with a laugh. "I've become quite an expert in retouching. I had the world's best teacher, didn't I?" She shivered involuntarily. The longer she stayed here in the house, the colder it got, and the little fire in the stove didn't seem to make any difference at all.

"If I were as young as you, I wouldn't take studio photographs of people or photograph landscapes. I'd dedicate myself to the new trend in our métier. So much has been achieved there in the last few years. Jacob Riis in America, for example, has been looking very realistically at people's everyday lives in his work. It's exciting stuff."

"Riis? Isn't he the one who takes pictures of filthy coal miners and half-starved children in the poor quarters?" asked Mimi, surprised. "How do you know *him*?"

"I don't *know* him, but I've certainly heard of him." Josef laughed, but the laughter turned into a coughing fit. Flecks of spittle flew, and Mimi automatically put her hand over the plate of cookies.

When his coughing had settled again, Josef said, "I may be old and I may, in your eyes, live at the end of the world, but I still have a few contacts in the photography trade. We write letters back and forth, and sometimes I get Alfred Stieglitz's photography magazine *Camera Work* in the mail. In one of the last issues, there was an article about Riis and one about the Berlin photographer Heinrich Zille. He also takes pictures among the working class."

"Then why do you lead people to accept some pretty make-believe?" In her ear, Mimi suddenly heard Hannes's voice. Blast it, why did she spend so much time thinking about him? It was a chance encounter between travelers, nothing more!

"Taking pictures of people in their misery wouldn't do anything for me," she said vehemently. "I think of a carefully composed picture as a work of art, like a painting or an opera. Do you know the ones they call light painters? Photographers who work with retouching but also with the play of light and shadow to create a painterly effect? They do some amazing work, and their photos really do look like paintings. It's an area of photography I'd love to try, but most of the time customers only . . ." Mimi was just warming up to her subject, in fact, when she had to stop. Her uncle had nodded off. He breathed softly in his sleep, his chin sunken against his chest. Mimi affectionately placed the blanket he'd handed her over his knees.

"If you love someone with all your heart, you can move mountains . . ." Deep in thought, Mimi dunked a teacup in the tepid dishwater after Josef had gone to bed for a short nap.

A knock at the door interrupted Mimi's thoughts. She hurriedly dried her hands and went to see who it was. An elderly woman wearing a black dress and a headscarf over her gray hair was standing there. She held out a deep bowl in which a pale-brown soup sloshed.

"I'm Luise Neumann, the neighbor, and this here is Josef's dinner. I've only brought enough for one."

"That's all right. I'll just have a bit of bread," said Mimi with a friendly smile. She held the bowl in one hand and extended the other to the woman in greeting. "I'm Mimi, Josef's niece."

"About time someone came to see to the old man," the neighbor said gruffly. "Your uncle needs his hot porridge in the morning and soup for lunch. If he doesn't eat it all, you can warm it up again in the evening and add a slice of bread or a few potatoes. Even the mice are starving to death in his pantry, so you'll need to go and buy some food, and the sooner the better. I've done his laundry for him, but now that someone from the family's here, that's sorted itself out. Good evening to you!"

Before Mimi could get a word out about her uncle's health, Luise Neumann was gone. Mimi stared after the neighbor's departing figure, completely at a loss. She had so many questions she wanted to ask.

CHAPTER 19

Anton was sweeping the steps of The Oxen when Herrmann Gehringer appeared. At his side, as usual, was his lackey, Paul Merkle. *He's like his shadow,* thought Anton contemptuously.

The businessman looked grim. Was he still annoyed at the comments made by Josef Stöckle's niece in Helene's store? Served him right to have someone stand up to him.

If anyone had asked Anton whether he detested Gehringer or Merkle more, he would have been hard put to answer.

For Anton, Gehringer was a self-righteous man who loved to make others dance to his tune. And Paul Merkle was the father of Christel, Anton's sweetheart. Because of him, Christel and Anton were forced to meet in secret, although she was already nineteen years old and should have been able to decide for herself who she went out with. But she listened to what her father told her, and he obviously thought a pub owner's son wasn't good enough for his daughter. He probably wanted to marry Christel off to some businessman, maybe even to Gehringer himself! The mere thought made Anton so furious that he ground his teeth together until his jaws hurt.

Without greeting the two men or so much as glancing at them, Anton held open the door to the inn, but he did so only because his mother had an eye on him. As they entered, he overheard Gehringer tell his assistant, "Just then, when Josef Stöckle was about to sign my contract, his niece turned up. Mimi Reventlow is her name—quite a presumptuous young woman. At Helene's, just before that, she scolded me like a schoolboy."

Mimi Reventlow. Now he had her name! Anton grinned. But what had Gehringer wanted with old Stöckle, and what contract was he talking about?

"Find out what the woman is doing here and how long she plans to stay. She's the last thing we need!" Gehringer said to Merkle as if Anton did not exist. "I do not intend to put my plans for a showroom on ice because of her."

Anton cleared his throat.

"Yes?"

"Well . . . it's like this . . ." What he had in mind was actually repugnant to him. But he only had so many chances to make something of his life, and he intended to exploit every one of them, so he pushed on. "I've been wanting to ask you for a long time whether you might have some work for me. Perhaps as a guard at the factory? Or as a linen salesman, or maybe a buyer for raw materials. I can write well and I'm good with numbers. Everything else I can learn. I'll spare no effort."

Gehringer patted Anton's shoulder patronizingly. "My boy, I have no time for childishness today, by God. Bring us two beers and a bowl of soup, and make it fast!"

His lackey smirked.

When Mimi awoke the next morning, it took her a moment to realize where she was. She had trouble opening her eyes, which were sticky with sleep. Her limbs were stiff with the cold, and when she looked down, she saw that the cardigan she had pulled on in the night had wrapped itself around her body like a straitjacket. With cramped fingers, she tugged her nightdress and the cardigan straight. Her stomach was rumbling, and she could not remember the last time she'd been so hungry. A boiled egg and a little ham and bread would be just the thing.

She recalled with longing her guesthouse by Lake Constance, where the landlady had gone to such trouble with breakfast every morning. But Luise Neumann had not been exaggerating about Josef's pantry— there was absolutely nothing edible in the house. Mimi had been so ravenous the night before that she had eaten two of the cookies that she had brought as a present for Josef.

With a groan, she swung her legs over the side of the bed. Even though the last thing she wanted was to venture out into the cold, before anything else, she had to buy some food at Helene's store.

The water bowl atop the chest of drawers caught her eye. A quick splash? In this cold? No thank you! Instead, she pulled on every bit of clothing she'd brought with her.

Her uncle was still asleep when she peeked into his room. No wonder, she thought, after he'd spent half the night coughing. So much for his pneumonia being "old news"! It was high time that Josef's doctor paid him a visit and prescribed him some proper medicine. Maybe then he could finally get back on his feet.

She finished the shopping quickly enough. Back in the kitchen, her hands numb with cold, she did her best to stoke the fire from the coals in the stove so she could make Josef a cup of tea and, later, some soup. She had to bring more wood inside, and then maybe run an errand or two. And she still wanted to read Gehringer's contract. Josef's doctor was also high on her list, after which she would write a letter to her mother about the current state of affairs so that her mother could arrange everything else that was needed. Finally, she had to get on her way to Isny. Mimi smiled at the idea, her thoughts wandering. Maybe she'd stop in Ulm again along the way? If she were in luck, Hannes would still be there—the thought alone made her heart beat faster. *No time to lose,* she thought as she worked on the fire in the stove.

The next moment, she nearly jumped out of her skin when she heard a noise behind her. She whirled around to find Luise Neumann standing in the kitchen. "Morning. I've still got this, but I won't be needing it anymore," she said as she put a key on the table. Then she took the matches out of Mimi's hands and rearranged the wood in the stove. "Family is long overdue here," she said. Before Mimi's eyes, a flame flickered over the coals. "I first wrote to your mother when your uncle had pneumonia. That was November, but all I got in reply was a few kind words. I wrote again at Christmas—Josef was still bedridden then—and again in the new year. But instead of coming, she just kept putting me off. Seems a very busy woman, your mother." Luise looked at her as if it were Mimi's fault her mother never came. Then she filled a pot with water and put it on the stovetop.

"I don't know anything about that. I thought . . ." But Mimi was too upset to finish her sentence. In her letter it sounded as if her mother had only recently found out about Josef's illness. "I guess you're the only one who's looked after my uncle," she said with a pang of guilt. "I hope so much that he'll be better again soon. Would it help if his doctor simply changed his medication?"

"That would be a miracle medicine!" Luise said, and she laughed loudly.

"What do you mean?" Mimi was putting some of the tea she'd purchased in the teapot and paused in the middle of the process.

Luise shrugged. "Your uncle's an old man. There are more and more days when he can't get up and has to take all his meals in bed. Other days, I'll come and find him at the table with a newspaper, and he'll tell me all about the world out there. Then I'll come back to find him coughing and coughing and not wanting to eat a thing. We all thought the pneumonia would kill him. It's a miracle he's still alive, especially now that our good doctor can't check in on him or—"

"What?" said Mimi, her brow suddenly furrowed.

"Dr. Ludwig's off on an extended trip. Portugal, Spain, God knows where else he's been. And his nurse, Sister Elke, is also away, visiting family on Amrum. You didn't know?"

Mimi shook her head. "Where do sick people go?"

"Most here in the village can't afford to be sick," Luise said flatly. "Everyone has to work. If someone gets sick, they cure themselves. The finer folk in the villas go off to Ulm or Blaubeuren if they come down with something, and I've heard there are a few businessmen's wives who go as far as Stuttgart." She said the last sentences quietly, as if afraid of being overheard.

This gets better and better, Mimi thought. "Do you know when the doctor's coming back?"

"At the beginning of May, thank God."

"But . . . that's still a month away!" Mimi cried, horrified. She needed to hear what a doctor had to say *now.* Josef needed medical attention *now.*

"You'll manage," said Luise. "An old man doesn't need much. Fresh clothes, something warm to eat, a bit of a chat . . ."

"*I'm* supposed to look after Josef? But I—" Mimi stopped short and ran her fingers over her hair nervously. "Of course, I want to help him, but it's not as simple as that. I've got business appointments. I'm expected in the Allgäu any day." She bit her lip, then went on, "Couldn't you continue taking care of him?"

Luise folded her arms across her chest, then narrowed her eyes and peered at Mimi. "Young lady, listen to me. Traudel was my best friend. When she died two years ago, it went without saying that I'd tend to Josef. Bring him food, do a little work around the house—men aren't big on cleaning. Back then, no one had any idea he'd suddenly need so much attention. Don't get me wrong. I've looked after your uncle gladly until now, if only because Traudel and I went back so far. When he really got sick, I didn't have any choice." She shrugged. "But looking after your uncle for the rest of his life . . . not with all the goodwill in the world. In the last few years, I've cared for both my parents all the way to the grave, so I know what to expect. That aside, there's also the expense. Just the food I bring him—"

"It shouldn't be a matter of money," Mimi interrupted. "It's ridiculous that you haven't been paid anything for all you've done. I can only ask your forgiveness for that. From now on, we'll be glad to pay you. I'll talk it over with my uncle. We'll work out an agreement that will give you security." *And us, too,* she added silently.

"Things can't go on like this. You'll have to start paying Luise for her services," Mimi said to Josef when they were sitting together at lunch.

"I need no one," Josef said sharply. "Luise poking around all the time bothers me."

"It doesn't necessarily have to be Luise. We could find a young woman to look after the household for you."

"And I suppose she'll work for free?"

Mimi rolled her eyes. She'd forgotten how stubborn her uncle could be. "Of course she isn't going to work for free."

Her uncle glared defiantly out the window, as if to say: *Well, that's that!*

"What will happen if you're bedridden again?" Mimi asked, her tone now more gentle. "And even if you're well . . . do you plan to start doing your own laundry? Or stand at the stove and cook every bowl of porridge and soup yourself? You should be able to enjoy your retirement."

"And who's going to pay for it?"

Mimi laughed. "Has old age turned you into a cheapskate? Neither Luise nor a local girl would cost you very much. And if you do rent the shop, you'll have an income from that. Forget that Mr. Gehringer, though. The rent he's proposed is a pittance and won't help much at all. You should try to find another tenant." Mimi had only skimmed through the contract before they sat down to eat—the low rent was bad enough! Who knew what other snares it contained?

"You make it sound like there are people lining up to rent my shop. So far, no one else has shown any interest. Gehringer's offer is my salvation, so do me a favor and don't say another word about the matter," said Josef.

"Your salvation?" Mimi looked at him in confusion. "What do you mean?"

"I mean just what I say. I need every mark I can get. My savings are gone. I'm bankrupt." Josef Stöckle scratched at a candle-wax stain as if there were nothing more important in the world. "Now don't go looking so horrified. It never occurred to me, either, that some chest infection would stop me from working for so long. I did have a bit of money put aside for a rainy day, but it's gone, too. Right now, I have to work out how to get by until the end of April, when the confirmation ceremony takes place. The photos for that will bring in a bit of money again."

"It's not easy to photograph young people. You have to be well and truly back on your feet for that."

"With the money from Gehringer, it will work out one way or another. If worse comes to worst, Luise won't let me starve."

Mimi felt as if someone had punched her in the gut. Rarely had she felt as helpless as she did now. Uncle Josef was penniless and in need of care—she'd been prepared for anything, but not that. Where in the world were things supposed to go from here?

CHAPTER 20

"Do you remember when we met back in Chemnitz?" Klaus stopped whetting the scythe and looked at his wife.

Eveline frowned and looked up from her embroidery.

It was nine in the evening. The children were upstairs asleep. It had been a long, hard day, and Eve was so tired that all she could think about was going to bed herself, but she had at least two more hours of work.

"Of course I remember. How could I ever forget? What made you think of that?" Her eyes drifted toward the stove, where a small fire still burned. A hot cup of tea would do her good, but she was too tired to get up and put the water on.

"It was a mistake to bring you here," said Klaus. He turned away and went back to his sharpening.

Eve sighed. "Couldn't you say something to make me feel a little better?" she said, annoyed. "Something to make me forget all of this?" She jutted her chin toward the overflowing basket of pillow covers. "Work, work, and more work."

How pale he was. His face was as white as a linen handkerchief. She thought about going to him and putting her arms around him, but he probably would have just pushed her away. Instead, she said, "Let's sing something, like we used to. Something to make us happy." More forcefully than necessary, she thrust the needle through the pure-white fabric.

"Sing!" Klaus said, and he snorted. "How can I be happy when I'm to blame for all the misery here. I've made you unhappy, and the children, and . . ."

"Klaus, please," said Eveline. "No one is unhappy here except you. The children are sleeping peacefully in their beds. They have full bellies and they're dry and warm. That's more than people can say in some other houses."

Franka Klein had complained in Helene's just that day that her roof was leaking and that her husband, Benno, had no time to fix it.

"It's a credit to you to say that." Klaus laughed sadly. "But I saw how much water you had to add to the soup to feed all our hungry mouths, and I also saw that you only had half a bowl yourself. And then I think of our little one lying in the cold graveyard instead of here in a warm crib . . ." He turned away as if to hide tears from her.

Eveline pressed her lips together. What did he expect from her? That she console him? She, too, cried every night in her bed when she thought of her lost daughter. She had been looking forward to the child's arrival so much. New life in the house would bring new happiness, she'd hoped.

Long ago, when one or both of them was feeling down, they had held each other in their arms, had comforted one another the best they could, had even laughed together. Gallows humor—sometimes it was better than nothing. These days, she drowned in her anguish, he in his.

"How could I have ever believed I'd be able to make you happy?" The whetstone slid along the blade with an unpleasant swish. "I was cocky. Young and stupid. Now you all have to suffer for my stupidity. You could have had everything so good."

Eveline's expression darkened further. "If all you can do is whine, then keep your thoughts to yourself. I've got too much work to do to start thinking about what could or should or must have been. Things are what they are!"

Mimi stared at her traveling case, at a loss about what to do. A quick visit to see her uncle to make sure everything was all right with him—that had been her plan. But suddenly she could not imagine walking out the door the following morning with her luggage and a cheerful goodbye to Josef. Her uncle assumed that he'd be able to work again in a few weeks' time, but what if he couldn't? Even if he accepted Gehringer's offer, the money wouldn't be enough—not to live on, and not to hire help.

Of course she could assist financially. After the good winter at Lake Constance, she wasn't short of funds, and she had money in the bank that would help with her uncle's care, at least temporarily. But if Luise was right and he didn't get back on his feet, what then?

Wasn't it only proper for someone from the family to look after him at the end of his life?

Mimi placed both hands to her temples. The questions buzzed in her head like a swarm of bees, but she could not find an answer to even one of them. *If only there was someone to talk to about these things,* she thought, and the next moment, angrily: *Why isn't Mother here?* It wasn't as if Esslingen were a world away.

Resigned, Mimi began to unpack her suitcase. She felt like crying, but could think of no other solution than to stay until the start of May, when the doctor returned. She would be firm with the doctor and tell him that money was no object when it came to Josef's treatment. If necessary, she was prepared to put all her savings into it. The most important thing was to get Josef fit and well again.

The thought that everything would be sorted out by four weeks from then, at the latest, cheered her a little.

When she had put her few possessions away, she took out her stationery and, with a heavy heart, began a letter.

Mayor Schönleben, Isny

Sir,
A personal matter has come up and I am afraid that my
leaving for Isny must be delayed. I estimate my arrival
for mid-May at the earliest. This could, however, be of
advantage for the photographs you would like me to take.
At that time of year, the weather is almost invariably
pleasant, and I can present your region in its very best
light . . .

Ulm, adieu! She would never see Hannes again, and the tears she had held back until now ran wet and salty down her cheeks.

When she awoke the next morning, the first thing she heard was a strange monotonous sound. Pling. Pling. Pling. And there was something else. A feeling of warmth and light and . . . Mimi rubbed the sleep from her eyes and looked toward the window. The snow had begun to melt and was falling in fat drops from the roof onto the windowsill. The sun shone on her face, and even managed to warm the room a little. How lovely! Mimi climbed out of bed and went to the window. The first thing she saw was the impressive glass roof of the studio in the garden. With the snow melted away, it sparkled in the sunshine like a diamond.

Suddenly, Mimi was in a hurry to get dressed. She wanted to look at the studio and the shop. If she was going to stay, she might as well work and see to it that a little money came in!

It was still quiet in the house when she went downstairs. No fire in the stove, no tea brewing, no newspaper brought inside. As she had the day before, Mimi set to work lighting the fire. When she was finished, she went back upstairs and gingerly opened Josef's bedroom door.

"Mimi . . . what time is it? I'll get up in a minute." A coughing attack followed, and Mimi gave Josef a handkerchief that he pressed to his mouth, but she felt useless.

"Stay in bed a little longer. You're not missing anything. I'm here. I'll take care of you and everything else, and that's not about to change anytime soon. I'll be staying awhile," said Mimi in as light a tone of voice as she could manage. God, if she'd been standing there now with packed bags . . . inconceivable.

He nodded weakly.

Concerned, she went down again to the kitchen and made tea and put together a tray with bread and butter and brought it all upstairs. "Breakfast in bed—now if that isn't luxury!" she said, and to her relief Josef managed to sit upright and reach out a shaky hand for a teacup. But he didn't drink anything, nor did he want to eat.

"Can I look at your studio and the shop after breakfast?" Mimi asked.

"Oh, child . . ." Tears appeared in Josef's eyes. "I would so dearly love to show you everything in person, but I'm not well today," he said, and he closed his eyes. "Go and look. The key is hanging on a board in the kitchen."

The studio looked more like an oversized woodshed or storage shed and not like a home of the photographic arts, Mimi thought dispiritedly as she followed the narrow path most likely created by Luise's frequent visits. Josef had mentioned the day before that, to get to her house, one went through the garden, past the studio, and out through the back gate.

The building was made of wood, though at least it had a stone foundation. Mimi guessed it was a little over thirty feet long. The side visible from the house didn't have a single tiny window. *How could anyone take pictures in such a dark space?* Mimi wondered. Oh, there was the glass roof, certainly, and that would let in a lot of light. But was it enough? The narrow end of the building was about twelve or thirteen feet wide and also windowless. Almost with trepidation, Mimi went around the corner . . . and nearly fell over backward. What was she thinking about it being too dark? The opposite long wall of the studio was almost completely made of glass. Only toward the front was there a five-foot wood section where the entrance door was located. Mimi looked in amazement at the long glazed surface: it was built with many narrow panes of glass that overlapped like fish scales. Mimi knew immediately why the panes were arranged as they were. Depending on the direction of the light, individual panes could be turned to create different daylight conditions. The long glass wall faced eastward, and at both ends there were dark curtains that could be opened or closed as needed to prevent sunlight falling directly on a subject. In most of the studios Mimi had visited, the limited daylight that found its way inside had to be supplemented with smelly gas lamps—in Josef's studio, that was unnecessary. She could hardly wait to take a look inside. The thought of working in her uncle's studio was suddenly thrilling.

She was just about to open the door when she saw someone waving to her over the fence at the end of the garden. It was Luise. She was with another woman and two boys who Mimi guessed were about twelve and fourteen years old.

"Is your uncle feeling any better?" Luise asked as Mimi came closer.

Mimi shook her head. "No, unfortunately. He didn't even want to get out of bed this morning. I've postponed my appointments for now to take care of him, at least for the next few weeks. I'm also planning to reopen the studio. I'm a photographer, too, as it happens," she added, grinning.

"Well, you've certainly got some plans!" Luise raised her eyebrows appreciatively. "By the way, this is my daughter, Sonja," she said, introducing the pregnant woman beside her.

Mimi stepped up to the fence and shook hands with Luise's daughter. "It's a pleasure to meet you—"

"I should say Sonja is one of my daughters," Luise interrupted before Mimi could get in another word. "I have my Berta, too, but you'll be lucky to catch a glimpse of her. She lives at home, but even I rarely see her! She works long days at Gehringer's mill, and with the rest of her time, she is busy planning her wedding and visiting with her fiancé."

"Goodness, she does sound quite busy," Mimi said. Then, hoping to resume their introduction, she smiled directly at Sonja.

"It's nice to meet you, too. And those are my sons." Sonja pointed at the boys who were running around in a game of tag. *What a photogenic face she has,* Mimi thought.

"Good to know you'll be opening the studio again. Your uncle once took some very nice photographs of my husband and me," Luise said. "I could choose any hat I wanted, and even got to hold a lace umbrella. I felt like quite the fine lady, I can tell you." Luise's eyes shone with pleasure. "It was so nice to get away from all the day-to-day chores for a moment."

"You're welcome to visit anytime," said Mimi amiably. She was surprised by Luise's friendliness, considering how surly she'd seemed at the start, but maybe she was relieved to finally have responsibility for Josef off her shoulders.

The neighbor shook her head regretfully. "We'll only treat ourselves to something like that again for our fortieth anniversary." The sudden chiming of the clock from the nearby church tower startled Luise. "So late already? The work isn't about to do itself. I've got to be off," she said, then turned and hurried away.

Her daughter Sonja sighed. "It's always like that here. You'll notice it for yourself before long. No one in Laichingen has any time. The work is going to swallow all of us one day."

"Time is something you have to take for yourself," Mimi said. "How would you like to be my first guest in the studio?"

"Me? As pregnant as I am? Paul, my husband, would think I'd gone mad. Justus"—she pointed to the elder of the two boys—"has his confirmation at the end of the month. We'll come to you for a photo then. And when this child is born," she said, laying one hand protectively over the swell of her belly, "we'd love to have a picture of the christening."

Mimi smiled. She'd be long gone by then, but she kept that to herself.

When Sonja went off after her mother, Mimi took out the key, opened the door, and found herself in a small entry area, the vestibule, which was separated from the actual studio by a wooden wall. An upholstered bench, a mirror on the wall, a small tray with a comb and brush—this was where customers could take off their coats and arrange their hair and clothing. There was also a glass case beside the mirror, in which several photographs were on display.

Mimi stepped inside the studio proper. To the right, by the window, stood an ornate desk on which a wooden apparatus had been set up. The apparatus, a retouching desk, was used to hold a processed glass plate in place, which was then worked on with a variety of styluses and pencils. Waistlines were slimmed, sparse growth on a top lip became an imperial mustache, and wrinkles were eliminated. Her uncle had been a true master of the art of making people better looking. The thought that he might never stand behind a camera again filled Mimi with sadness.

The elongated room was otherwise set up like most studios. Against the wall at the back was a platform on which the photographer could position various items of furniture, usually chairs and small tables. Josef had set up a small wrought-iron bench decorated with roses. On the bench was a dusty bouquet of flowers, no doubt there since the previous autumn. One of Josef's painted backdrops—a typical landscape scene with a pale-blue sky and feathery white clouds—hung on the back wall.

In a tall, narrow cupboard to the left of the platform, Mimi discovered more than a dozen rolled backdrops. Josef's treasure trove! Almost reverently, Mimi unrolled one canvas after another. A mountain landscape with a medieval castle in the background. A stony, vaguely Romanesque assembly of pillars on which Josef had carefully considered the fall of light and consequent shadows. An elegant salon with windows, curtains, and pictures on the wall, all so lifelike and three dimensional that Mimi could only shake her head in admiration. Josef Stöckle could easily have been a successful painter. Mimi carefully rolled up the backdrops and put them away.

The platform was wide enough for even a sizable group of people to stand, she was happy to note. If a family or a small wedding party or the staff of a workshop wanted their picture taken, the platform would be ideal.

Mimi tried opening one of the windows, and found that it moved without squeaking or jamming. Very good. Then she pulled one of the curtains across. It moved smoothly on its rod, but also sent a cloud of dust flying.

About six feet from the platform, Uncle Josef's enormous wooden bellows camera was mounted on a large tripod on wheels. Mimi still remembered from her apprentice days how to use one of the big, old-fashioned beasts, but she knew she would prefer to work with her smaller and considerably more flexible Linhof.

On the wooden wall on the left were various hooks on which hung accoutrements of all kinds: top hats for the men and pretty straw hats for the women, walking sticks, and umbrellas, including a lace one—perhaps the very umbrella Luise had mentioned. Her neighbor's eyes had positively glowed at the memory of the sitting.

There were various accessories on several small tables: vases and bouquets of silk flowers, a Bible, and toys—a rocking horse, a porcelain doll, a spinning top.

Against the wooden wall there was also a large wardrobe, and when Mimi opened it, she was struck by the smell of mothballs. Clothes of various sorts and sizes hung inside, packed tightly. Mimi recognized a few outfits she knew from her own childhood. Her uncle certainly had not kept up with fashion!

There was no darkroom, however. While her uncle certainly did his retouching in the studio, he must have developed the plates themselves back at the shop or the house.

When she was done looking around, Mimi sat on the wrought-iron bench on the platform. Josef's studio was certainly a little dusty and aged, but it had everything she would need. The room was set up to transform a simple farmer into a country gentleman with his top hat and cigar. The weaver's boy could put on a snappy sailor's outfit and suddenly be the scion of a well-to-do household. The maid could become a lady, the lady a can-can dancer. The hobbling farmhand, who would have loved to join the army, could pull on a uniform and finally be the soldier he dreamed of being. Long-held dreams came true. Thanks to the conjurer with the camera, the glass plates, and the photographic techniques, people could live out their desires, for once in their lives, to be someone else. What a magical thing that was . . .

But did that magic also work in Laichingen? Her uncle had told her that business was slow and irregular. She only wanted to stay for four weeks, and if everyone here was as hesitant as Luise and her daughter, then she might as well give up now. Quite apart from that—she was a traveling photographer. Of course, there were things that she had silently faulted in the studios where she had worked as a guest, and she often had thought about what she would do differently or would improve. But that was a far cry from being able to singlehandedly run a shop and studio. She had not learned to run the business side during her apprenticeship in Esslingen, either, so how was she supposed to manage the feat here, in such unfavorable circumstances?

CHAPTER 21

"Where's the second basket?" Paul Merkle seemed puzzled when Eveline handed over only one basket of finished pillow covers.

Eveline lowered her eyes. "I've only managed the first half. I fell down the stairs and hurt my hand. I had to stop doing the finer work . . ." Embarrassed, she looked up again.

"That's no good," said Merkle, with no sympathy at all.

"I know. I'm terribly sorry," said Eve, feeling guilty. She limped to the table to sit down—her hip had also suffered in the fall. The left side of her body hurt so much that she was afraid she'd broken something. She glanced angrily at the steep stairs.

Alexander was sitting at the table with his sisters. He said, "I've drawn some flowers. Look! Would they do for a new pattern?" He pushed a sheet of paper across the table to Paul Merkle. Eveline smiled gratefully: what a decent young man Alexander was.

In fact, his attempt at distraction seemed to work. Paul Merkle inspected the finely sketched intertwining tendrils with interest. Flowers small and large flowed across the entire sheet of paper in a skillful sweep, and yet Alexander had drawn them with no more than the nub of a pencil. Eveline imagined how lovely his drawings would be if he had the chance to use some quality Faber pencils, like the ones she had had in her childhood.

"You really drew these?" Merkle furrowed his brow.

Alexander reddened.

"My son is artistically gifted," said Eveline proudly. Merkle probably thought that because they were poor, they lacked talent.

But he only looked from the drawing to Alexander. "Don't bank on your scribbling yet. You'd do better to focus on school." Without another word, he folded the sheet of paper and slipped it into his pocket.

The disappointment in her son's eyes cut Eveline deeply. She lowered her head, a gesture that Merkle no doubt interpreted as humility. But in truth, Eveline only wanted to prevent him from seeing the hatred in her eyes.

Merkle pointed to an array of rakes, shovels, and other tools leaning against the wall by the kitchen table. "Careful the children don't cut themselves on a scythe. One cripple in a house is enough." He laughed as if he'd said something very funny indeed.

"Klaus sharpened the scythes and rakes last night. We'll be working in the fields again soon," said Eveline.

"Best not to count on your husband for that. He'll be home late for the next few days," said Merkle.

"Again?"

Paul shrugged. "After the maintenance work on the looms a few days ago, three of them still didn't work properly. We've fallen behind."

"But that's not my husband's fault!"

"The orders have to be filled, and there's no discussion about it. Why don't you send your young artist out into the field with a shovel and rake"—Merkle nodded toward the tools—"while you stay here and do the embroidery. I'll be back at the end of the week." He picked up the basket of unfinished linen pillow covers from the floor and threw it on the table. Then he counted out a few coins and tossed them onto the table before he picked up the basket of finished work.

Eve swallowed. All her sleepless nights were worth so little. The money would never be enough to pay Edelgard for her sewing work and to buy a candle for Alexander's confirmation. And they had little enough to eat as it was.

"I don't like to ask," she said, her voice pained, "but could I have an advance for the other basket?"

Merkle hesitated for a moment, then tossed a few more coins down. "But for that I expect it to be done the day after tomorrow."

No one took any notice of the boy, standing there with his hands in fists, fighting back the rising tears.

"You should have heard how that woman visiting Stöckle stood up to Gehringer! She pointed him to the end of the line at Helene's." Anton laughed and shook his head. "Her eyes were damn near on fire! She's not afraid of a man like Gehringer. I don't think she's afraid of anything at all," he said with admiration. "It looks like she's setting up old Stöckle's shop. She's torn down the newspapers and cleaned the windows, at least. I saw her at it earlier, when I was sweeping out the front of the inn. Hey, are you even listening?" Alexander said nothing but just stood looking miserable, staring off into the distance. Anton gave him a push. He started, then nodded, although in his mind he was still far away.

As they had done many times before, they had met for a few minutes behind the inn, at the alcove where the steps led down to the cellar, stolen minutes that their respective mothers weren't supposed to find out about. Anton liked to smoke a cigarette filched from a guest when they met like this, and Alexander just stood with him. They told each other about the events of the day, complained about this or laughed about that. Sometimes Anton babbled on about Christel. Then each went his own way. Sometimes, Alexander felt that those few minutes with his friend were all that stopped him from going mad.

Now Alexander felt Anton's appraising gaze on him. "Your eyes look glassy. Haven't been crying, have you?"

Alexander quickly rubbed his face. "Crap! I'm just angry." He clenched his hands into fists. "Paul Merkle was at our house earlier. He gave my mother such a scolding because she didn't get all the embroidery finished on time. He doesn't care at all that she fell down the stairs and can hardly walk." He felt his gut compressing into a hard ball.

"Merkle!" Anton's face darkened, too. "He's just Gehringer's flunky, but he puffs himself up like he's the one who says what goes."

"What do you think?" Alexander asked Anton. "Should I offer to help her with the embroidery? She'll never finish that big basket by the day after tomorrow."

"A boy embroidering pillows?" Anton frowned. "Don't do it. If anyone finds out, you'll be a laughingstock."

Alexander forced himself to nod. "You're probably right. But something's got to be done. The way Merkle treats my mother . . . He treats all the women who work from home the same. He'll threaten to fire you in a second if you don't hand over good work on time." Then they'd have even less money than they did now, and his belly ached with hunger often enough as it was. Alexander thought of the drawing he'd handed over to Merkle. He'd been naive, hoping to earn a few pfennigs for it, but Merkle had simply walked off with it. Could he just do that? Alexander wondered whether he should tell Anton about it, but decided not to. His friend would only get angrier than he already was, and maybe at him, too, because he hadn't taken the drawing back from Merkle.

"That's plain intimidation, that is—good embroiderers don't grow on trees! The women have to figure out how to stand up to Gehringer. They'd have him over a barrel, and he'd be left looking stupid. But no, they take it, just like their husbands. Yesterday I heard the men saying they had to do overtime again for a while. I'd like to know if Gehringer even pays them for it." In frustration, Anton kicked at the gravel so hard with the tip of his shoe that stones sprayed up.

"Anton! Where are you hiding? Anton!" they heard Karolina Schaufler shouting. "When I get my hands on you!" His mother's voice sounded as irate as ever.

Instinctively, they ducked deeper down the cellar steps.

"She doesn't even give a guy five minutes," Anton murmured.

"Merkle said my father had to work longer now, too," said Alexander, and as usual when he thought of his father, he felt a little queasy. Klaus Schubert wasn't a big man, but Alexander had never seen his father as thin as he was these days, with his sunken eyes and the dark shadows under them, and his thin, bloodless lips. He moved around the house so much like a ghost that it was spooky. It would be different if his father at least spoke to him, but Alexander couldn't remember the last time Klaus had said a word to him directly, unless he was shouting. "The boy should get out in the field with you today," he'd say to Eveline, or "The kindling's running out. The boy should fetch you more." And that was how Alexander found out what chores he had to do. That was their way of communicating. Was it the same in other places? Anton's father wasn't home much, either. Hunting kept him busy.

"The way everyone here grovels to Gehringer is a disgrace," Anton continued, when Alexander said nothing more.

"Your mother doesn't grovel."

"No, but she tears into everyone else, and that's no better," said Anton harshly.

For a moment, they both fell silent, heads bowed, each with his own thoughts.

Anton looked up first. He grinned. "I've got an idea. Let's go pay a visit to that woman at Josef Stöckle's place. Her name is Mimi Reventlow, and she's Stöckle's niece. I heard Gehringer tell Merkle who she is. But I want to know what she's up to here in Laichingen."

That took Alexander by surprise. "You want us to go visit a complete stranger? Just like that?"

"So what?" Anton said. "I'd like to get to know her."

He said it so casually! "What about your mother?"

"She can wait."

"I don't know. We can't just show up at the door, can we?"

"You go to Josef Stöckle's all the time, right? To help with the wood chopping? We can say we want to help with something, and we'll just happen to pay her a visit, too."

"But I have to go home. We're going out to the field soon." At the thought of trying to work the soil, still so heavy with snow and in which every step was torture, Alexander felt himself slump a little more.

"Forget the field. You might only get one chance in your life to meet a woman as fantastic as her."

Anton was practically in raptures, and Alexander looked at him intently. "You haven't fallen for her, have you? I thought you liked Christel."

Anton laughed out loud. "Don't be a dunce. The woman is ancient. But that's beside the point. If you ask me, she's got more guts in her than ten men put together."

"You're not short on courage, either. You don't put up with anything, not from anyone," said Alexander with a trace of envy. Anton certainly wouldn't have stood there with his head hanging like a sacrificial lamb, watching his mother beg Merkle for an advance. And all because of Alexander's own confirmation. He could not hold back a sob of despair any longer. Then he felt Anton's hand on his right arm. The touch felt invigorating and startling, a bit like an electric shock.

"We won't let them bring us down. I don't know how, not yet, but somehow we'll find our own happiness, one day. Then no one can hurt us, not Gehringer, not anyone else," Anton said, his voice suddenly raw.

And Alexander believed him.

CHAPTER 22

A cup of coffee, the Ulm daily paper—the half hour from seven thirty to eight, before his assistant appeared and the work began, was pure bliss for Herrmann Gehringer. At that time of the morning, the looms had not yet started, nor was there a warehouseman, a machinist, or Paul Merkle in sight. For a little while, no one wanted anything from him.

But on that particular sunny April morning, Gehringer's reading pleasure was short lived. He stared in disbelief at the newspaper in his hands. An entire double-page spread was devoted to the opening of a branch of "Egon Morlock's respected Laichingen weaving mill." *"Respected"*—what an affront! Morlock's operation was no more respected than any other mill in Laichingen.

"Egon Morlock has opened a branch in Ulm! A big corner place with three floors," he blurted, even before Paul Merkle had closed the door behind him. "It says right here: 'The Laichingen businessman's new rooms are as elegant as they are bright and inviting. Mr. Morlock will use the new premises to welcome not only the esteemed women of Ulm but also business contacts from around the world. Morlock Linen Weaving is thus helping to make our beautiful city better known internationally than our famous Ulm cathedral has already done.'"

Merkle, who had taken his seat in front of Gehringer's desk and now sat with pen and pad in hand, let out a laugh. "Squeezing Old

Morlock and the Ulm cathedral into one sentence—hats off to the writer for that!"

"I have no interest in ironic flair just at the moment," Gehringer reprimanded his assistant. "Not when I have to sit here and read the daily paper like every other Tom, Dick, and Harry just to find out what my competition is up to. Why didn't I know about Morlock's plans in advance? Something like that would normally get around in a place like this. This can't go on, Merkle. I expect you to have your finger on the pulse a little better than it is." Gehringer banged his fist on the desk so hard that his inkwell jumped.

Merkle, rarely intimidated by his boss's outbursts, put his pen and paper aside. "I do have some news for you, as it happens. I'm afraid, however, that it is not particularly pleasant . . ."

Gehringer narrowed his eyes and glowered at his assistant. Was he mistaken, or did he hear a slightly malicious undertone in Merkle's words? "I don't have time to waste. Out with it."

"Mimi Reventlow has reopened the photo studio and the shop. I walked past Stöckle's shop yesterday, and the newspapers on the windows had already been taken down. She'd also polished the floor and was standing inside—" His words were swallowed by the thunderous tremor triggered every morning at that time when thirty looms started at once.

Gehringer used the momentary interruption to think. This was really the last thing he needed this morning. The day before, he'd spoken to the carpenter about building some shelves he would need when he rented the shop, and the man had been ready to start after the coming Easter weekend. Gehringer would now have to put the job on hold for an indeterminate time, and he was not happy about that. He hadn't counted on the woman putting down roots in the town.

Still, as indifferently as possible, he said, "In God's name, good luck to her. Doing business here in Laichingen isn't as easy as some might think. When I take over the shop in a few weeks, she'll have already set it up nicely, I'm sure. Less work for me."

Paul Merkle stared at him in surprise. "One could look at it like that."

"One *must* look at it like that," Gehringer shot back. He rose to his feet. "Now take a letter. The competition never sleeps, clearly. There's a lot to do."

Merkle zealously picked up his pen and writing pad. At the same moment, a folded piece of paper slipped from his trouser pocket.

"The wastebasket is in the corner," said Gehringer gruffly.

Merkle picked up the sheet of paper, but instead of tossing it in the basket, he unfolded it and laid it out on the desk in front of Gehringer.

"These flowers were drawn by Alexander Schubert, Klaus Schubert's son," said Merkle. "Not bad, eh?"

Gehringer straightened his glasses on his nose. Not bad? The drawing was damned good, and his assistant knew it, too. The flowers and leaves were beautifully drawn with bold lines . . . Something about the spiraling tendrils looked far more modern than the embroidery patterns he currently used. And then there were the curved ovals of the leaves, like a paisley pattern. Wasn't that pattern often stitched into Indian silk? How in the world did a weaver's son know about an Indian pattern like that? If this were used as a border around the neckline of a woman's blouse, it would look very modern indeed. Herrmann Gehringer could already picture the blouse. Excellent.

"Klaus Schubert's son drew this?" he asked, and he felt the inner twitch that always came when he found himself on the trail of a good business idea. He'd remember that young man. He could certainly use him.

Paul Merkle nodded eagerly.

Gehringer crumpled up the drawing and threw it forcefully into the wastepaper basket. "Then it looks like the son is as much a day-dreamer as his father. The day before yesterday, there were two delays on Schubert's loom, and by the end of the day, he was an hour behind on his production. What do they say? Like father, like son. I'll wager the boy is always sketching away in school and has bad grades as a result."

"But I thought . . . because you were looking for a new pattern designer . . ."

Gehringer let out a guffaw. "As if I could use a weaver's son for that! If anything, the boy will work at a loom, like his father. No point putting ideas into the boy's head." *And the same goes for you, Merkle,* he added silently. If he wasn't careful, Paul Merkle would start thinking he was smarter than Gehringer himself. He was pleased to note that Merkle could not hide his disappointment.

"I've changed my mind. Pack your pen and paper away," he said, and he nodded toward the door. "Go and find out how good that woman is as a photographer. I can't imagine a woman would understand a profession like that, and Laichingen folk certainly won't be played for fools. I'll probably be able to take over Stöckle's shop sooner than we think."

There was so much work at The Oxen over Easter that Anton wasn't able to sneak away to visit Stöckle's niece with Alexander until the following Tuesday.

When the two of them finally made it to Josef Stöckle's shop, the woman was just locking up.

"We've come at a bad time. Let's go," Alexander muttered.

"No way. Who knows when I'll be able to get away again!" Anton hissed in a low whisper. He turned and looked across the square, hoping that his mother wouldn't look out the window at that moment. "Am I mistaken, or are you opening up Mr. Stöckle's shop again?" Anton said cheerfully as they came up to the woman.

"Anton, isn't it? That's the plan. I'm a photographer, too, actually. I'm Mimi Reventlow." Her expression brightened when she saw Alexander. "Are you perhaps the first confirmand?"

Before Alexander could reply, Anton said, "This is my friend Alexander Schubert. He helps your uncle, chopping wood. We wanted to ask you if you also needed some help." He nodded toward the shop.

Just as she had the first time Anton had seen her, Mimi Reventlow looked like she'd stepped out of the pages of a fashion magazine. And yet here she was, cleaning the shop. There wasn't a single speck of dirt on her dark-blue outfit, and the small lace collar was starched and pure white. She had tied her hair in a single long braid and she smelled as good as she had the first time, too—of spring and flowers. She was a vision!

Mimi thought for a moment. "I'd like to move the retouching desk from the studio to the shop. It would be very nice of you to help me with that."

"Your wish is our command," said Anton, with a subtle jab to Alexander's ribs: this was how you got to know interesting people.

They walked around the house and through the garden to the studio. "My uncle's asleep," said Mimi, looking back at the house. "I'm worried about him, the state he's in."

"When it's warmer and everything starts growing again, I'm sure your uncle will do better. Then you can come to The Oxen with him on Sundays, like he always used to."

At that, Mimi smiled, and Anton was thrilled to see it.

The ornate desk was not particularly heavy, and Anton was able to move it by himself. Alexander carried the wooden apparatus and a chair, and Mimi brought a case that held various tools and bottles. Together, they marched back to the shop.

"The table goes right in front of the window, so anyone passing can watch me while I work. Maybe that will get people to come inside," the photographer said, which Anton thought was not a bad idea.

"How's business been?"

Mimi grimaced. "I've spent the whole week cleaning, clearing away and rearranging things, and so far not a single customer's stopped in."

At a loss, she sat down on the chair. "Normally, having a traveling photographer in town is like a minor sensation, but no one here seems very interested at all."

"People around here just don't appreciate special things," said Anton. Damn! If no one came to her shop, wouldn't she just pack up and leave again? He wanted to get to know her a little better. He was sure she had a lot of stories to tell.

"After the long winter, money's tight for everyone," said Alexander, speaking up for the first time. "Most people here are happy if they don't have to buy on credit from Helene's. No one's going to think about visiting a photographer. Our parents have to work extra just to get enough money for our confirmation photos." As he spoke, his face turned bright red.

Why's he saying stuff like that if he's so embarrassed by it? thought Anton in annoyance. "Laichingen isn't just poor weavers. We've also got a few wealthy people here," he added quickly. "What do you do in other places to get customers in?"

Mimi raised her finely formed eyebrows. "Good question. In other places, I'd put an advertisement in the local paper, but I doubt that the Ulm paper will do me any good up here. Usually, word of mouth is enough, though. When I was in Helene's store yesterday, I told the other women there that I'd taken over running Josef's business, but none of them was particularly interested." She lifted her arms helplessly and let them drop.

"Maybe Gehringer's got something to do with the people not coming? Having him against you isn't good," Alexander whispered to Anton, who replied with a warning jab. Too late. The photographer had heard every word.

Frowning, she looked from one to the other. "You think Mr. Gehringer's to blame for people staying away? What do you mean?"

Alexander really had a talent for putting the woman off. "Men like Herrmann Gehringer can get unpleasant if they don't get what they want, and apparently what he wanted was to rent this shop," Anton said in Alexander's place. "It's possible he's trying to stir up the people against you. But that doesn't mean he'll get away with it. People here can still decide for themselves what they want to do."

"But . . . how . . . how in the world did people find out that Gehringer wanted to rent the shop?"

Anton laughed scornfully. "Everyone hears everything in the village." He straightened his shoulders and said, "What would you think if Alexander painted you a nice sign to tell people you're open for business?" *Strange,* he thought as he spoke. He'd actually been hoping vaguely that the widely traveled woman would come up with an idea for him, something that would help him make good on his plan to break free of The Oxen in the foreseeable future. But now he and Alexander were helping her.

"You can paint?" Mimi said to Alexander. "So can I. Or rather, I can retouch. Should I show you how that works?"

Alexander nodded eagerly.

The photographer sat at the desk, on top of which she had set the wooden apparatus. She now fixed a glass plate to the frame. From above, the frame was shaded, and it was fitted with a mirror in its base. The construction allowed the user to reflect light onto the glass plate perfectly.

Anton looked at the glass plate, where he saw a woman's face. "She's beautiful," he said. He picked up a slightly pungent odor, which he ascribed to the chemical layer on the glass plate. "Who is she?"

The photographer looked up and smiled. "Her name is Clara Berg, and she's a very successful businesswoman. I took pictures of her at Lake Constance. She makes beauty products for women. Creams, lotions, that kind of thing. And you're right, she really is beautiful."

Beauty products for women? What was that all about? Still, Anton nodded as if he dealt with such things every day. Then he stepped aside so that Alexander could more easily watch the photographer at work.

Mimi picked up another glass plate. The woman pictured was not nearly as beautiful as Clara Berg, Anton thought. He watched with interest as the photographer chose a fine brush from a glass. Then she screwed the lid off a bottle of ink and dipped the brush into it. With a light touch and fine brushstrokes, she delicately removed a wart on the woman's left cheek, which Anton thought already improved her looks.

What would Mimi do with a picture of Christel? he wondered. Christel was beautiful, as Anton had overheard guests at The Oxen say often enough. Usually, they added words to the effect that beauty would fade, but faith would not, or that one shouldn't let one's beauty go to one's head, and that Christel Merkle was a little conceited, even stuck up. Some actually seemed to think that beauty was somehow dishonorable. On such occasions, Anton felt like telling them they were just jealous. No, Christel's picture would certainly need no retouching. A picture of her father, Paul Merkle, on the other hand . . . as far as Anton was concerned, Mimi Reventlow could give him a hooked nose or paint on a big black mole. Anton smiled at the thought.

"Why are the shadows on the picture bright and the sky dark?" Alexander asked, pointing to another glass plate with interest.

"These are just the negatives," said Mimi. "Later, when I produce the actual pictures on paper, the photograph will look just as it should." She looked up at Alexander. "In my darkroom, I can do far more than just touching up little bits like this with a brush or stylus. I can make a montage and put a hat on the woman's head, for instance. Or I could put her in front of a church tower or some other background, as I please. Or rather, as the customer pleases."

The idea left Anton aghast. "But that's . . . that means you could"— he waved one hand in the air, trying to come up with a suitable example—"you could put a mountain range behind our inn? Or a forest?" But wasn't that a deception?

The photographer laughed. "I certainly could! Illusions, looking good—people love it." She held out the brush to Alexander. "Do you want to try?" As she spoke, she stood up and made room for him.

"Didn't you want to paint a sign for the shop?" Anton asked, somewhat annoyed. He wasn't used to Alexander being the center of attention.

"Soon," Alexander murmured without looking up from his work. The photographer watched over his shoulder.

"I see you're using many tiny points. That's very interesting, and yes, you can retouch like that, too. Painters have a name for that kind of work. They call it pointillism."

Anton furrowed his brow and Alexander also looked up uncertainly. What was the woman talking about? Enough retouching, Anton thought, and said brusquely, "I could tell our customers at The Oxen that you've reopened. Or even better—I can go to the owners of the weaving mills, door to door, and do some publicity for you."

Mimi laughed. "And then I pay you a commission for each new customer you bring in, right?"

"I wouldn't say no to that." Anton grinned. "If you want to be a real businessman, you can't start early enough!"

"You may be right," said Mimi, "although I'm afraid I can't afford your services." She sighed deeply. While it was true she had some money put away, now that she was helping with Josef's bills and supporting herself, she needed to be cautious until she started working again. "At the end of April, the confirmands will be coming for their portraits, or at least that's what my uncle says. But I hope very much that people here will take an interest before that. A sign for the shop would really help. Look, the side of this box would be just the thing," she said, extracting a large cardboard box from behind a cupboard.

Alexander's eyes lit up. "A valuable box like that? You'd really let me paint it?"

The photographer shrugged. "If you think you can. I've got pens and different colored inks in this case." Mimi handed him a wooden case. "Just be careful not to spill any. The ink is expensive."

As reverently as if he were holding a royal crown, Alexander picked up the wooden case and the cardboard box.

Anton knew Alexander would be working on the sign for a while, but he had an idea. "Would it help you if the confirmands came in, let's say, a week early?" Maybe he'd also manage to get Christel to the shop. "And what if the prettiest girl in the village lets you photograph her? That would have to be good publicity, wouldn't it?"

Mimi looked at him with surprise and respect. "That would help me very much."

Anton thought for a moment. Then he held his right hand out to Mimi. "I'll get you the confirmands a week earlier than usual, deal?" He wasn't so sure about Christel, however.

She hesitated. "I really can't pay you anything for your help."

"I'll do it for free. A favor for a friend, you can call it," he said, while the gears in his brain turned over, searching for an argument that would get customers through the door sooner. The Laichingers were stuck in their ways, and nobody knew that better than he did.

"Nothing is ever free," said Mimi, still reluctant to shake on the deal.

Anton smiled. "Who knows? Maybe you'll be able to return the favor one day."

When she finally took his hand, it felt to Anton like a small victory.

CHAPTER 23

"Guess who came by earlier," said Mimi to her uncle as she plumped the pillow behind his back. It was one of his good days, and he had made it out of bed and onto the sofa. Mimi had put the newspaper, a pitcher of water, and a few cookies within reach, trying to make him as comfortable as possible.

For the first time in days, she was feeling a little more lively, and it had a lot to do with her youthful visitors. Until she met Anton and Alexander, she had only encountered older people in the village, and then mostly when she went shopping at Helene's. The storekeeper was not particularly friendly toward Mimi, and Mimi suspected she bore a grudge against her because of the run-in with Gehringer, so she'd enjoyed the time with Anton and Alexander all the more.

The pub owner's son was an uncommonly good-looking young man, she thought with a private smile. His dark hair, parted sternly on the right, his sultry mouth, intense eyes, assertiveness, and then his broad chest and shoulders—Anton Schaufler would certainly be breaking girls' hearts soon, if he wasn't already. And there was something else about the young man, a restlessness in those eyes. He seemed like a man with great things ahead of him.

"Your first customer, perhaps? It would be about time," said her uncle. "I still don't know whether I should welcome your waltzing in and taking over everything. It would have been much easier all around if I'd just accepted Gehringer's offer."

"The few marks he was offering were never going to make you rich. Aren't you at all happy that I'm going to be taking pictures of the confirmands? It will bring in quite a lot of money, you know." It hurt Mimi that her uncle resisted her attempts to help, but she tried not to let it show.

"Let's wait and see," Josef grumbled. "All right then, who stopped by?"

"Young Anton Schaufler and a friend of his, Alexander." How pale Josef looked, she thought as she sat down in an armchair. She saw that he'd eaten none of the cookies.

"Anton and Alexander. They spend every free moment together, although they couldn't be more different. They're fire and water, those two," said Josef. "What did they want? Not pictures, I guess?"

"I think they were just a little curious." Mimi laughed. "But then Alexander painted a sign for the shop to let people know that the studio is open again, and we hung it in the window right away. A few people have already stopped to look."

"I always planned to make a sign but never found the time," said Josef softly. "When Traudel was still well, we enjoyed our life together, and when I had to look after her, I didn't really have any room in my head for the studio anymore."

No wonder everything was looking a little run down, Mimi thought sadly. Josef's wife had suffered from a tumor in her belly, and that was presumably also what had killed her.

"Never fear. I'll get everything up and running again," she said as happily as she could. "Anton promised he'd do some publicity for me, which I think was very nice of him."

Josef looked at her warily. "You have to watch yourself around Anton. He's a bit of a wild one, that boy."

Mimi laughed. "You might be right! He's older than Alexander, isn't he?"

Her uncle nodded. "He finished school two years ago and he's been working at The Oxen ever since. His mother, Karolina, really needs the help. Her husband isn't exactly the hardest working fellow in town."

"It looks as if Anton doesn't want to stay at The Oxen forever, though. He actually said that he wants to be a businessman one day," Mimi said. "His friend Alexander struck me as much more modest."

"He's a good kid," said Josef, nodding and smiling. "Alexander visits me quite a lot. He cuts wood for me and does some other little jobs. In return, he can stay here and draw whenever he wants. He's so incredibly happy every time I get out the good sketch pad and a few colored pencils for him. Both seem to be in short supply in his home."

"Does he like to paint and draw?" Mimi had been very surprised to see the neat, expressive letters Alexander had created for her sign earlier. When he was done with the basic information, he decorated the sign with a flowing stem of flowers. A professional sign painter couldn't have done a better job. But when she tried to pay him two marks for his work, he refused to take it.

Josef pointed toward the dining table. "Go and look in the drawer. The sketch pad is in there."

Mimi found the pad quickly enough. She sat next to Josef with the pad on her lap, and together they went through it page by page. A dragonfly, rendered in exacting detail, various butterflies, a raven. Two squirrels playing in a tree.

Mimi was amazed. "The precision! And everything is so three dimensional. He's gotten the proportions exactly right. Alexander did all this without any instruction at all?"

"Well, I showed him a trick or two: how to develop a perspective, and how to add light and shadow to make something look more realistic. But they don't teach art in the local school."

"He really has talent." Mimi went through the illustrations excitedly a second time. "The boy's gifted. You know, someone like him belongs at an art school. Do you think it would be all right if I sent these to Mother? She has good contacts at the Stuttgart Art School. The director—"

"Don't go putting ideas into Alexander's head!" Josef interrupted her sharply. "The Schuberts are among the poorest weaver families in the village. Klaus Schubert is often depressed, and his wife has her hands more than full looking after house and home and feeding all their hungry mouths. The last thing she could afford right now is to have her son go off to study." He spoke as if he was expecting Mimi's rebuttal any second. "The boy *has* to go to work at the mill, like his father. There's no other way."

Mimi said nothing, but she saw things very differently.

Laichingen, April 18, 1911

Dearest Mother,
Now that I have been with Uncle Josef for several days, I
can report a little about the present state of affairs.

Mimi stopped and stared at her first sentence. Didn't it sound rather stilted?

It was eight thirty in the evening, and Josef was already asleep. He'd eaten nothing of the dinner she'd prepared. The bread was too hard and the sausage she'd bought at Helene's was too salty, he'd said. A little sheepishly, he then asked her if she could perhaps cook a little *Schwarzer Brei* for him, as Luise had often brought over. That would also fill him up.

Mimi, who had no idea at all about the dish with the strange-sounding name, had assured him that she would. "As soon as I can, I'll go to Luise and have her show me how to make it." She would do anything to make him a little happier.

Now she was sitting at Josef's small desk, writing the long overdue letter to her mother.

She was, in fact, exhausted and wanted to go to bed herself, but since she had been in Laichingen, it had felt as if there were not enough hours in the day to take care of all that needed to be done.

Dishes were piled in the kitchen sink and a mountain of laundry sat in a basket on the floor beside it. It was amazing how much dirty laundry an old man could produce.

On her travels, Mimi had always spent her nights in decent guesthouses, or had been the guest of the local mayor or priest. She would find a slice of cake waiting for her in her room or a hot-water bottle waiting in her bed. She washed her own clothes discreetly in a washbasin and then asked the housemaid where she was staying to iron them for her. She had never learned how to manage a household herself, and now she didn't have the time. She had to make sure to get the photo studio back on its feet. *Maybe a miracle will happen and the washing will do itself?* she thought with disdain, then she returned her focus to the letter in front of her.

> *Unfortunately, Josef's doctor is away on an extended trip abroad and will only be returning at the beginning of May. I am afraid I can only give you my own impression of the state of Josef's health and not a professional opinion.*

She briefly described Josef's condition, his precarious financial situation, and her plan to stay in Laichingen until the doctor returned.

> *I am very glad to provide what care I can for Uncle Josef. However, there is no getting around the fact that you will have to give some thought to how things will continue for him when I am no longer here.*

Didn't that sound a little arrogant? And what if it did? Her mother should feel Mimi's annoyance at her lack of involvement in her brother's situation. Then the sketch block with Alexander's drawings caught her eye; she had nabbed it from the drawer in a quiet moment.

Can I ask you for a favor while I hold the fort here with Uncle Josef? There's a young man here by the name of Alexander Schubert, who, to my eye, seems exceptionally talented. I am including a few of his drawings, all completed with no art instruction at all. Unfortunately, I have not been able to come up with more of his work at short notice. I would be very interested to know what an educated eye makes of them. There is no one here to whom I can show these pictures, but I know you are acquainted with the director of the Stuttgart Art School. I would like to ask . . .

A few minutes later, satisfied with her work, Mimi put her pen aside. It was only fair for her busy mother to take the trouble to go to Stuttgart on her and Alexander's behalf. If it happened to upset her mother's oh-so-important plans, then it served her right.

The next morning, when Mimi went to the small post office and stood waiting with the letter in her hand, she no longer felt so sure of her ground. Was she doing the right thing? Her uncle had insisted that she keep her nose out of it, and shouldn't she at least speak with Alexander or his parents first? On the other hand, there was no telling if she would even get a response, let alone a positive one. Art people were an odd lot, she thought, and Mimi had no idea whether the naturalistic style of Alexander's drawings was of any contemporary interest at all. Chances were she would get no more than a curt rejection.

"Next, please."

Mimi pulled herself together. "I'd like to send this letter. To Esslingen."

CHAPTER 24

"You are so beautiful." Anton found it hard to take his eyes off Christel. "Your hair shines like spun gold in the sun."

Paul Merkle's daughter laughed. "I'm not some princess in a Grimm fairy tale." She sounded defensive, but Anton saw her cheeks blush red with pleasure.

"You're a princess to me," he said firmly.

The pub owner's son and the young woman had managed to sneak away for one of their rare rendezvous outside the village, where they could hold hands and walk along a rarely used path, always cautious that no one saw them. Anton's mother believed he was at the mechanic's, and Christel's mother thought her daughter was visiting a girlfriend.

Anton kept an eye out for somewhere dry under the trees, someplace where they could sit. Then he would have been able to put his arm around Christel, and maybe she would have let him, and they would be one step closer to their first kiss. He knew exactly how her lips would feel and taste—warm and soft and sweet. But the grass, through which an occasional daisy already battled to raise its head, was soaked from recent rain and snow, and Christel would never have agreed to sit on it.

Anton forced himself not to think about Christel's lips. As casually as possible, he asked, "Has your brother already had his confirmation photo taken?"

"No. Why? Confirmation is still two weeks away."

"That's true," he said slowly. "But I've heard that the studio has a shortage of the glass plates they need for the pictures. Josef Stöckle's niece has had to order new ones, and she doesn't know when they're coming. It's bad luck, but she might not be able to take pictures of all the confirmands."

"Mother would be horrified if there were no confirmation picture of Justus." Christel looked at Anton, appalled at the thought.

"If I were you, I'd visit the studio as quickly as I could, or your brother will have to go empty handed."

"What about all the others in his class?"

"If he really has to, then he should tell his best pals, too," said Anton generously. "But you didn't hear it from me, right?"

"Thank you," said Christel with relief.

Anton put his arm around her as an experiment, and she let him. A little awkwardly, but nestled side by side, they walked on. It felt wonderful to hold Christel so close. She smelled almost as good as Josef Stöckle's niece.

"The photographer also said she keeps an eye open for pretty young women who'll sit for her."

As expected, Christel stopped in her tracks. "Why would she do that?" she asked with as much indifference as she could feign, but Anton saw the excitement in her eyes.

"She's in touch with a businesswoman who makes beauty products and often needs good-looking models for her catalog." Anton looked at Christel with exaggerated pensiveness. "Now that I think about it, no one but you would even come close, would they?"

She gave him a little shove. "You flatterer! You know perfectly well you're not supposed to say things like that."

"Well, if it's the truth," he said, and laughed. "I've seen some pictures that Mimi Reventlow took of other women. They look like film stars."

"What do you know about film stars?" Christel mocked. "Or have you been to a theater since the last time I saw you? And without me?"

A cloud crossed Anton's face. "With all the work I have these days? There's so much to get ready for the *Maienfest*, and after that there's the Pentecost market." For a long time, he and Christel had dreamed of seeing a movie together. He simply could not imagine what the "moving pictures" he'd read about in the newspaper actually looked like.

Christel relaxed a little. "No need to tell me. Now that my mother is pregnant again, she's got me working harder than ever. I don't think there's a maid in the world more slave driven than I am. I spent all day yesterday doing laundry, and look at my skin!" She thrust her hands toward him. They were red and chapped all over. The skin around her fingernails was raw and broken. "I couldn't do any embroidery yesterday evening because I would have made a mess of the fine pillow covers. Of course, that just made Father angry, and he shouted at me that I should have done a better job of looking after my hands. But how was I supposed to do that?"

Anton swallowed hard. Paul Merkle. How he hated the man. With great tenderness, Anton took Christel's hands in his and kissed her fingers one by one. "One day, I promise you, you won't have to lift a finger again. You'll have the finest creams and lotions and your hands will look like Queen Cleopatra's. They say she was very beautiful, or at least that's what I read in a book I got from the priest. But I'm sure she was no more beautiful than you, queen or not."

Christel's giggling was not exactly the reaction that Anton had been hoping for, but he was glad he'd at least been able to cheer her up.

"If only that 'one day' wasn't so far away," said Christel. She nodded toward the few knotty damson plum and apple trees that grew alongside the path. They were still just bare sticks, although it was already mid-April. "Not a bit of color anywhere, everything just gray. Sometimes I can hardly stand all the poverty and barrenness up here."

Anton held her and believed he could feel her heartbeat through his jacket. "There was a story about Italy in the newspaper. It said that the almond trees were already in full flower in the south. The tulips are out, too, and the lemons on the lemon trees are already ripe," he said dreamily.

Christel sighed. "The likes of us will never get to see something like that. But it's not as cold as it was a few weeks ago, at least, and listen to the birdsong."

"I don't care about the birds. I'd like to be able to give you a bright bouquet one day, or take you out to a café, but we've got nothing like that here. But even if there was a bar or a nice restaurant, it would still be impossible. Your father refuses to accept me, so all we can do is meet in secret." How could he ever court Christel properly?

"Stop it!" said Christel, and she twisted free of his embrace.

"Stop what?" Anton was genuinely baffled.

"Blooming almond trees and taking me to a café! You always go on like that, and it makes me dream, but afterward I feel even worse than I did before. Maybe we'll never get to see a film, and what then? In my entire life, I might not even make it as far as Ulm. What if I never have the chance to visit a hairdresser, or nice shops with dresses and hats and flowers?" Her voice had grown hoarse, as if speaking hurt. "When you go on like that, my longing just gets stronger, and it's harder than ever to be a good, loving daughter." Tears of despair flowed down her cheeks. "If the dear Lord or my father knew what was going on in my head . . ."

Anton had never heard Christel speak like this before. "Why make do with everything here if you have this longing inside you? Let's go away together! We still have our whole lives ahead of us, so why stay here and waste away? We'll get by somehow, and—"

"Anton, honestly, that's enough!" Christel snapped with a severity in her voice that contrasted strangely with her youth and beauty. She wiped the tears from her face, smoothed her braids, and, with more composure, said, "I'll never leave here. God put me in this place, after all. People in other places may well have more opportunities than us, but are they any better off for that? I doubt it. When you see a lot of pretty things in a shop window, you want to have them all, too. But God values modesty, not greed."

"Now you sound like the whole world's some den of iniquity and Laichingen alone is the village of the blessed. Has God chained you here? Has he put shackles on your legs? Where do you get ideas like that?"

"It's reality. And you, you're nothing but a dreamer. If Father knew how you talk . . ." Furious, Christel turned and ran away.

Anton, understanding nothing, could only watch her go. All he'd said was that he'd like to take her to a café one day. What was so bad about that?

CHAPTER 25

"Your hand on the arm of the chair, yes, just so. The Bible in your other hand. Very good, Vincent." The boy's jacket was wrinkled, and Mimi smoothed it as best she could. The boy, like the one before him, stood as stiff as if he'd swallowed a broom handle. His expression was aloof, and his angular chin was thrust awkwardly forward. Mimi, annoyed, thought that wooden marionettes showed more life. She chatted away, trying to draw him out. "So what do you want to be when you leave school?"

Vincent Klein looked at her in surprise. "I'm going to be a weaver, of course."

Mimi laughed. "You're the third confirmand I've met today who's said that. Now, I know that being a weaver is everyone's first choice here in Laichingen, but tell me the truth: What else would you like to be?"

The boy shrugged and his expression reverted to its previous stiffness.

"Don't you have a hobby? Something you like to do in your free time?"

The boy looked at her as if she were an idiot. "What do you mean?"

"Well, do you go skating on the *Hüle* in winter, for example? Or sledding on the hills? Or maybe you're one of these modern cyclists, or in the shooting club?" As she focused the camera, Mimi ran through every kind of youthful pastime she could think of.

Vincent shook his head. "I don't have time for things like that. After school, I help at home or out in the fields."

"That's right, and after we're done here we still have to go out to the field to gather stones," his mother, Franka Klein, piped up from where she sat on a chair behind the camera. "This photograph would really have been better left to next week, but because of the shortage, we wanted to make sure we didn't miss out."

"We're almost done," said Mimi, looking through the viewfinder. What stones did the woman want to gather? What shortage? Miss out on what? What in the world had Anton told everyone?

"All right . . . now smile!"

The boy didn't move a muscle.

Mimi sighed inwardly, then put her camera aside. "You can relax," she said to Vincent. To his mother she said, "I'll be right back."

She left the studio and ran up to the house. Was she mistaken, or did it smell stuffy inside, like unwashed laundry and dust? She threw open a window in passing, then she went to the shelf where Josef's souvenirs were on display. She searched through them quickly: she could use the sword and the *Bollenhut*, and she took a globe of the world, an eighteenth-century atlas, the violin, and an artfully designed map of the German Empire.

"What are you doing there, child?" asked her uncle, appearing just then in the kitchen with an empty teacup in his trembling hand.

"I'm trying to coax the youth of Laichingen out of their shells," she replied with as much good cheer as she could muster. "What are you doing up and about? I thought you were resting on the sofa." She looked at him with concern.

The previous night, Josef had spat blood. Ashamed, he had hidden the soiled handkerchief in the laundry basket. Mimi had seen it, however, and it had scared her out of her wits. More than once in recent days, she'd urged him to let her call in a doctor from one of the nearby villages, but Josef had resisted the idea emphatically, so she was left with no choice but to look after him as well as she could. She cooked vegetable soup—the only thing she knew how to cook—and cored and sliced shriveled apples. She plumped his quilt and pillow and read to him when he was too weak to read by himself.

She stroked the old man's cheek affectionately. "Go lie down. When I stop for lunch, I'll make a fresh pot of tea and there'll be hot soup, too."

"Child!" he called after her when she was almost out the door.

"Yes?" Mimi turned back.

"You're really in your element today." Josef wore a smile of both pride and melancholy.

Mimi nodded. Ignoring the lump in her throat, she ran back to the studio.

"If you don't mind, I'd like to make Vincent's confirmation photograph a little more modern," she said to Franka Klein. As she spoke, she placed Josef's travel keepsakes along the edge of the platform.

"What about the Bible?" said Franka Klein, appalled.

"That will be in the picture, too, of course. We can put it here on the little table, in the foreground, and your son can choose some other object to be in the picture with him."

"Isn't that sacrilegious?"

"Why would you think that?" asked Mimi in surprise. "I rather think that God finds it pleasing—the Lord, after all, does appreciate the good things in life."

Franka Klein thought it over for a moment longer, then said, "All right. As long as it doesn't cost extra."

"Look what I've brought," Mimi said to Vincent. "Anything in particular you like?"

Vincent pointed cautiously to the globe.

Mimi smiled. "An excellent choice. The globe stands for the big, wide world. Who knows what you'll get to see in the years ahead? Africa, India, maybe even China?"

And the boy actually smiled a little.

The next confirmand was Justus Merkle, one of Luise's grandchildren. The boy had a pimply face and came with his mother, Sonja, and a younger brother. The two boys pushed each other around and giggled excitedly.

"So lovely to see you again," said Mimi to Sonja. Only then did she notice that Sonja had a young woman with her along with her sons. The young woman was so alarmingly beautiful that, for a moment, she took Mimi's breath away—and Mimi had seen many, many beautiful women.

"We really hurried to get here," said Sonja. "Because of the glass plates." She gave Mimi a conspiratorial wink.

Mimi frowned. Was this Anton's doing? Had his "publicity" involved telling people that she didn't have enough supplies for her photography?

"The early bird catches the worm," Mimi said.

"Just what I say! And now for the best part." Sonja looked at Mimi with delight. "My husband, Paul, has given his permission for you to photograph our daughter, Christel. Isn't that wonderful?" She pushed the girl forward.

Mimi's expression brightened even more. Now addressing the young woman, she said, "I promise you, I will make you look like a princess." She could hardly wait to get the beautiful girl in front of her camera.

Mother and daughter laughed bashfully.

"You know, my husband is Mr. Gehringer's right-hand man," said Sonja as Mimi led Sonja's son onto the platform. "We can afford an occasional luxury like a photograph. But Paul isn't usually so generous, so I was surprised when he said that Christel should also have her picture taken."

Mimi nodded. What was she supposed to say to that?

Justus didn't want any of Josef's props, but only wanted to hold the Bible. In reply to her question of what profession he wanted to learn, all he said was "weaving at Gehringer's." His confirmation photo was done in record time, and the boy leaped from the platform only to start squabbling immediately with his younger brother. He flat refused to have a second picture taken. A pity, thought Mimi. She would have liked to arrange a different scene with the boy, but this gave her more time to devote to Christel.

"Would you like to sit over there?" Mimi asked, indicating a plaster-and-stone half wall. The young woman didn't answer, but she sat where Mimi suggested.

With her sculptural features, milk-and-honey skin, and gold-blond hair, Christel was an extraordinarily attractive girl, Mimi thought as she slid a new glass plate into her camera. The diffuse light of the rainy day would bring out Christel's shimmering skin to wonderful advantage. Mimi adjusted one of the windows, throwing a little more light onto the girl's left side. Perfect! From the corner of her eye, she watched as the two boys pushed each other around and worried they'd go through a window or break something.

Like the confirmands before her, Christel was also dressed in black, which suited neither her youth and grace nor her inherent beauty.

"And what do you do?" asked Mimi as she considered how she might bring a little lightness to the picture despite Christel's black dress.

"Our daughter doesn't have to work. She will make someone a good wife before long," Sonja answered for her daughter. "Until then, she helps in the house and works at home as a needlewoman, of course, like me. If you look at it like that, the whole family works for Gehringer." Sonja Merkle's dark-brown eyes shone with pride.

Mimi glanced at Sonja, but said nothing. She had been thinking for some time that Mr. Gehringer would come by in person, because she had written him a brief message telling him that her uncle, for now, would not rent out his shop. But the businessman had neither replied nor made a visit. *I guess he couldn't have been too serious about the shop after all,* Mimi concluded as she pulled over a ladder so she could hang a canvas backdrop of a blue sky dappled with a few bright white clouds. The stone wall and the sky—the beautiful young woman needed no more than that.

Mimi had just climbed onto the bottom rung when Sonja doubled over on her chair and cried out in pain. Shocked, Mimi stepped off the ladder again. "Is everything all right, Mrs. Merkle?"

"I guess I . . . did too much lifting yesterday. It wasn't good for me or the child," the pregnant woman said, pain still on her face. "You two settle down!" she snapped at the boys. "Or you'll get a whack!" But the two boys kept up their mischief, and she shooed them outside.

"Boys are always more work than girls," said Mimi with a smile.

"You are right about that. I've got another two, as well. They're with my mother at the moment. And now a real latecomer!" she said and then abruptly changed the subject. "Why aren't you married, if I may ask?"

Mimi frowned. The woman was getting very curious! "If my parents had had any say, I would have been married long ago. I had a boyfriend who actually proposed to me, back then." She laughed softly. "But I felt that being married, and everything being married involves, was not the life for me. I was so eager to find out what was out there in the big, wide world!" How grandiose that sounded. She laughed, abashed.

"And you turned down a marriage proposal for that?" Sonja looked at her in disbelief.

Christel, still sitting on the plaster wall, listened breathlessly.

Mimi nodded. "My mother was not particularly pleased, not at first, as I'm sure you can imagine. But you can't make everyone around you happy if you want to be happy yourself. In the end, my mother gave me her support."

Sonja shook her head. "I've never heard anything like it. Here in Laichingen, every daughter lives the life of her mother and grandmother, as tradition dictates. I, for one, don't know a single woman who's turned down or broken off an engagement." She looked sternly at her daughter. "That would never occur to you, would it, Christel?"

The young woman shook her head, but her expression was inscrutable. Although Mimi felt she usually had a good understanding of people, she could not tell what was going on in Christel's mind.

"Traditions can be wonderful, but one can't let them become a prison," Mimi said adamantly. "I'm well aware that not everyone can take—or wants to take—the kind of chances that I have. But I think you must take your personal inclinations into account, whether deciding who to marry or which profession to choose, don't you?" As she spoke, she directed Christel to turn her left shoulder a little toward the windows. The girl did as she was asked, with natural grace.

"Absolutely!" Sonja Merkle said, nodding wholeheartedly. "It's no different for us. Linen is our life. And that's exactly how we want it to be and no different. Right, Christel?"

A shadow crossed the girl's face just as Mimi released the shutter. *Blast! I can throw that plate away,* she thought. She wouldn't even bother developing it. Mimi was annoyed: that's what you get from too much talk.

Sonja Merkle, however, was just getting started. "You and I will *have* to sit down for a chat one day. I'm sure you've seen so much and have so many exciting stories to tell. Nothing new ever happens here in the village. I said that to my husband just the other day, and he said it was because people here had their hands so full with the old. Which is also true, isn't it?" Sonja laughed.

Mimi wasn't quite sure what the woman meant. "Then you have no other choice than to try something new yourself," she said. "Women especially can be exceptionally inventive. In Meersburg, where I spent the winter, they have what they call a kindergarten. The children spend the day playing, they get a hot lunch, and they're well looked after while their mothers go to work." Mimi looked through the viewfinder again, studying the arrangement. The daylight conjured a golden shimmer on Christel's hair, and her profile, turned slightly to the right, looked noble and classical. If only she weren't wearing black!

"We don't need anything like that. Around here, the little ones just come along with us. My mother also helps me quite a lot, and I take the children to my mother-in-law sometimes, too. Have you already met her? Edelgard Merkle. She sews for almost everybody in the village. She uses a sewing machine!"

"That's good to know," said Mimi. "I've got a hem coming loose on a skirt. Maybe your mother-in-law could fix that for me."

"No doubt," said Sonja. "Tell me: Isn't it nice here in Laichingen?"

"I've been so swamped with work that I've seen almost nothing of the town, unfortunately. All I really know is how to get from Uncle Josef's house to Helene's shop and back. But Josef and the business come first," Mimi said. Her gaze drifted through the windows. As much as she liked being there for her uncle, she dearly wanted to be out on the road again. To feel her freedom, discover new landscapes, meet interesting people, negotiate with mayors and hoteliers—she genuinely missed all of it very much. And somewhere out there, making his way in the world, was Hannes . . . Would she ever see him again?

Mimi pulled herself together and focused on her subject. "Now smile, please!"

"If Father Hildebrand allows, I'll put the photos out in the church foyer after the confirmation service. I'll bring Christel's photographs with me, too, and you can choose which one you like most," she said, and she pointed to the three glass plates she'd used for Christel, which were now wrapped in lightproof paper. She made a mental note to go and find the priest the following day at the latest. The idea of selling the pictures at the church had come to her the previous evening, when her uncle had told her a little about him—an amiable and honorable man, it seemed. If the confirmands' parents picked up the photographs at the church, then Mimi wouldn't leave her uncle with anything he needed to do with them when she departed.

CHAPTER 26

The next confirmand was a boy named Fritz Braun, who flipped eagerly through Josef's old atlas. Mimi, with joy in her heart, tripped the shutter when Fritz was engrossed in a map.

A girl named Gisela wanted to wear the *Bollenhut*, but her mother didn't think much of the idea at all. With an encouraging smile, Mimi photographed the despondent young woman with the Bible in her hand. Gisela's best friend, Ida, was next, and, as a budding musician, she chose to pose with the violin.

After a brief lunch break, Mimi sorted the glass plates, which would make it easier when she started developing them. She was satisfied with her morning's work and could hardly wait to get down to the cellar and try out Josef's darkroom. She knew for certain that the images of Christel were among the best she'd ever taken.

It was four in the afternoon when Eveline arrived at the studio with Alexander and her two daughters. The woman behind the camera momentarily confused Eveline. Where was Josef Stöckle? But then she recalled that the old photographer's niece was visiting him and running his studio—at least for now. *You're so exhausted, you're getting forgetful,* she chided herself.

"I'll be with you in just a minute. Please have a seat by the entrance," the photographer called over her shoulder.

Eveline sat down on the small bench, and her daughters did the same. Alexander was too on edge to sit, so he stood just inside the door. Eve was happy the photographer was busy with another customer. It gave her a momentary break from everything. Marianne and Erika had spent half the night coughing, and they were tired, which made them whiny, but Eveline couldn't hold it against them. They should have been in bed with a hot-water bottle, but for as much as she hadn't wanted to leave them home alone, she also didn't want Alexander to be the only boy without a photographic memento of his days as a confirmand.

She looked fondly at her son, who was fidgeting nervously. *He's such a good, unassuming boy,* she thought. The evening before, he had claimed again that he'd already eaten with Anton at the inn, so that she would eat his portion at dinner. She had, too. Every time he glanced surreptitiously at her plate was like a stab to her heart, but was she supposed to accuse her son of lying? This morning, she'd given him a thick slice of bread with his bowl of *Schwarzer Brei,* and he'd wolfed it down.

Eveline stroked the velvet upholstery of the bench. Velvet. It had been a long time since she'd felt that texture beneath her fingertips. Her eyes moved to the curtains, which hung in generous folds. Brocade. Not crumpled linen. Velvet and silk, fine satin . . .

Eveline closed her eyes for a moment. There had been a time in her life when her own clothes had been made of such beautiful fabrics. Back then, her skirt had been as full as the photographer's, and the outfits she wore during the day had been adorned with fine trim and lace. She had been well turned out every moment of the day, just like the woman at the camera. Her skin had been as delicate as the skin of a peach, and her dark-brown hair had been glossy and thick. And it was not just because she'd been nearly twenty years younger—no, she had lived a completely different life.

A whiff of the scent of violets drew Eveline out of her daydream. Perfume? At this time of day? Her mother would have frowned on that. Perfume was something to be used from the early evening onward, or not at all. Eveline sniffed covertly at her armpit. If she hadn't been working out in the field that morning, and if she had more to clean herself with than a chunk of hard brown soap, then she might also smell of roses or violets and not of acrid sweat. But not everyone had it as good as her ladyship there.

Eveline shook her head, annoyed at herself. Why was she being so horrible? The photographer was not to blame for Eveline's lot in life.

"Here. Wipe your nose." Eveline handed her older daughter, Marianne, who was sniffling away, a handkerchief. The long wall of glass caught her eye: so much light! What a change from the tiny windows they had at home. She'd completely forgotten how bright it was in the studio. The last time she'd been there must have been for Erika's christening seven years earlier.

Erika had been so tiny then, lying on her embroidered christening pillow, as beautiful as a sleeping angel. She hadn't cried once during the ceremony, and Eve had been proud of that.

The memory hurt. Tomorrow, if Death had not snatched her away, her unnamed daughter would be two months old. If she'd lived, she could have cried the whole church to the ground! Eveline wouldn't have given a damn. She would have let the little girl howl her heart out.

Would have, could have, if . . . What good did it do to waste time thinking about everything that might have, should have, must have been? Things were as they were. Most of the time, Eve was able to live by that motto. But sometimes, the memories came back by themselves, and she couldn't help but think of all that might have been if she hadn't been quite so naive and romantic. If she hadn't followed Klaus . . . if, instead, she'd done what her parents wanted.

Would have, could have, if . . .

She'd been nineteen years old, and one of the most desired young women in all Chemnitz. Her mother, Margarethe Hoffmeister, had placed great hopes in her. "Money marries nobility. Or power"— her mother's favorite saying. She had chaperoned Eveline several times a week: a reception here, a soiree there, an evening of dance at Lichtenwalde Castle. Margarethe also entertained at home, inviting carefully chosen guests to dinner or to a picnic in their garden, which was on the scale of a park. And Eveline had been the centerpiece of every party. Young men—the sons of diplomats and businessmen—had swarmed around the young beauty with the lustrous dark-brown hair. She had enjoyed their attentions, had laughed and chatted along. But none of them had touched her heart. She found them all too superficial, too smooth, too . . . uninteresting, without exception. Their paths in life were already mapped, to the final fork in the road. The diplomat's son would be a diplomat like his father. The entrepreneur's heir would go into the family business. *Where is the adventure?* she asked herself. *Where is the passion? For what would they sacrifice themselves?* The young men and their concepts of life hadn't interested Eveline. But the realization that, fundamentally, she was in the same situation as them—her own path in life preordained by her parents' wish that she marry well—only served to magnify the feeling. At nineteen, she had had a deep yearning for the unknown, the unpredictable.

And one day, the very thing she had been longing for appeared.

It was on one of her rare visits to her father's factory. She had something to give him, perhaps a letter or invitation. She no longer remembered exactly what it was. Her father had not been in his office, and his secretary didn't know where to find him. Eveline had wanted to surprise her father with her impromptu visit, so she went in search of him.

Her father's plant was among the largest loom-making factories in all Germany, with almost seven hundred employees. Her father, Karl-Otto Hoffmeister, was a pioneer in the industrial production of looms, and Hoffmeister looms were considered the best available and were sold around the world. But none of that interested Eveline, and she was glad it was her brother, Alois, who would one day take over their father's business.

She finally had caught up with her father in the training hall, where demonstrations were held to present the company's latest models and buyers were educated in the newest technological advances. Her father had two certified experts for that purpose, but when Eveline entered the hall, she found her father in shirtsleeves, surrounded by some twenty young men, proudly demonstrating his latest technical refinements. He was so deeply in his element that he didn't notice his daughter's arrival. Eveline didn't like to interrupt him, so she stopped in the doorway.

While she waited for her father to finish his presentation, she happened to notice a young man with precisely parted blond hair. He was slender, almost skinny, and wore a simple dark suit. His hands were as fine as a pianist's, and he had trouble standing still, as if he could hardly wait to sit at the loom himself and turn the knobs and shift the levers that her father was just explaining. His eyes were the deepest blue she had ever seen, and he watched each of her father's movements intently.

It was this concentration that captivated Eveline. His interest in new things, his desire for something out of the ordinary—she read these feelings in the stranger's eyes. Such intensity! The young men in the circles in which she moved usually acted as if they were bored and above everything and everyone. How must it feel to dedicate oneself to something so wholeheartedly? Eveline was fascinated. Of course, the other young men around her father were also listening, but only half-heartedly, that was clear. One stifled yawns, another sneaked a look at his pocket watch, another gazed out the window at the fresh spring day.

Eveline knew that she had to meet the young man. But how? Training on a new machine lasted a week, and after that they would all travel back to their homes. If she heard correctly, her father was going through an introductory presentation of the loom, which meant that the young men had only just arrived. That gave her a few days, but she still had no time to lose. Eveline took a deep breath and began making plans for how and where she could "bump into" the young weaver.

The next afternoon, she had waited in front of the factory door until those taking part in the training were leaving. Considering how interested he was, he would certainly not be the first to go, she had speculated. And, in fact, he was the very last to come out.

An awkward stumble on her part, a helpful young man who got her back on her feet and escorted her to a bench on the perimeter of the factory grounds—that was all it had taken. A shy, hesitant conversation. Glances from beneath lowered eyelids, eyes meeting.

Klaus Schubert was his name, and he was twenty-three years old. He came from Württemberg, where he worked for a man named Herrmann Gehringer, a well-known linen manufacturer. Klaus considered it a great honor that he, of all people, had been allowed to take part in the training. He told her that his colleagues back home were thoroughly envious.

She, the businessman's nineteen-year-old daughter, and he, the serious young weaver. It was love at first sight. But no one could be allowed to find out about it.

"Let's go away together," she had said to him a few days later. "Somewhere where no one knows us, where we can start a new life."

"That's not possible. Mr. Gehringer paid for me to come here," he'd replied, and had told her about Laichingen, a small town in the Swabian Jura where the winters were harsh and the summers hot and dry. Württemberg—wasn't that the kingdom where paradise was real? Her father had his most affluent customers in Württemberg, Eveline knew, and as a foreman in the Gehringer factory, Klaus would certainly be able to offer her a good life. Yet her parents would never—never in her life!—agree to their liaison, Eveline knew only too well. A good marriage necessarily entailed a respectable livelihood. Power. A good name. A position in society. If she'd fallen in love with Mr. Gehringer himself, things would be different, but her affections belonged to the young weaver.

Sure of her feelings, she had packed only the most necessary things into one small suitcase she hid under her bed. She had walked through each room in her parents' house, looking over all the things she had known all her life. She had met with her girlfriends, gossiping and laughing and acting as if everything were completely normal. But in truth, she had been saying goodbye. She would see none of it, none of them, ever again. The thought had felt strange, but had not caused her any pain, not then. She had a new life waiting for her.

When Klaus's training was over, she left with him. In the middle of the night. For love—

"I'm sorry you had to wait. I'm Mimi Reventlow, and I'm standing in for Josef Stöckle here in the studio. Welcome!"

Eveline jumped, and her reverie popped like a soap bubble. She reached for the photographer's perfect hand, more painfully aware than usual of the roughness and chapping of her own.

"Eveline Schubert."

"Hello, Alexander. How nice to see you again." The woman shook Alexander's hand, too.

Eveline looked from one to the other in confusion. Where did they know each other from?

As if she had heard Eveline's unspoken question, Mimi Reventlow said, "Your son and Anton Schaufler were here a few days ago to chop some wood for my uncle. Alexander painted a sign for the shop to let people know that the studio was open again. It's hanging in the window. You must have seen it?" She smiled conspiratorially at Alexander. "I do believe it's already helping," she whispered. "I've had my hands full all day."

Alexander beamed, but Eveline's expression soured proportionately. Anton! She couldn't say why, but she didn't like the fact that, of all the people Alexander could have chosen, he had made friends with the pub owner's son. It wasn't as if Anton exercised some kind of bad influence on Alexander, but Anton was as loud as Alexander was quiet. Eve thought of her son as cultivated, but Anton was coarse and unsophisticated, not to mention three years older. For Eveline, their friendship simply didn't make sense.

Don't be such a hypocrite, she again berated herself.

"We're here for Alexander's confirmation photo," she said.

Miss Reventlow nodded. "I'd like to compensate him, and you, for the sign he painted. I'll do this one for free."

Eveline was taken aback. "This is the first time your talent has actually paid for something," she said to her son. One less thing to worry about, thank God!

Miss Reventlow laughed. "If you like, you can choose one of the props, like your classmates have already done. What would you like to have in your photograph besides the Bible? The atlas, perhaps? Or the globe or sword?" Mimi pointed from one object to the other.

"Alexander should have been confirmed last year," said Eveline as her son looked through the various props, "but he was in bed for weeks with an illness. A strange fever . . ." She shook her head as if trying to rid herself of the memory as quickly as possible. Night after night, she'd sat at her son's sickbed, praying and fretting. "So I'm even happier that he could take part this year." She glanced lovingly at her son.

"I can certainly understand that," Miss Reventlow said warmly. Just then, Erika began to cough, and Marianne joined her.

"Oh, the poor things. Sage tea is good for coughs. And cough drops, of course, but I'm afraid I don't have either of those here. I can offer them a glass of water." She looked sympathetically at the girls, then poured a glass of water from a carafe that stood on a small table and handed it to Eveline.

Eve pulled Erika's shawl tighter around her neck. She didn't need that kind of advice. The sage she'd gone to such trouble to gather and dry the previous summer had rotted in December when rain leaked through the roof. She had no money for cough drops.

"Can I hold this?" Alexander asked, and he pointed to a small oil painting that hung a little askew on the left wall of the studio.

While Eveline made sure that Marianne and Erika took turns drinking the water, Miss Reventlow had Alexander sit in an elegant armchair. She placed the painting in his hands to make it look as if he were mesmerized by it. Nothing about her composition looked artificial or posed. On the contrary, in fact: Alexander really did gaze at the painting with great interest. The sight of him like that made Eveline smile. Her son, a connoisseur of the finer arts. Still, she said, "I don't know much about these things, but shouldn't the Bible really be the main thing? Doesn't it look a little too much like decoration? Shouldn't Alexander be looking at that instead? It's his confirmation picture, after all."

Miss Reventlow thought it over for a moment, then said, "You're absolutely right. We can certainly make the photograph more realistic." Resolutely, she took the picture out of Alexander's hands and set out a fountain pen, an inkwell, and an old sketch pad for him. "We'll stand the Bible in the foreground. If you draw something now, then the picture will look like it's taken from real life."

Alexander beamed.

Eveline, however, leaned back on the bench, feeling a little put out. *This isn't what I had in mind at all,* she thought, while Mimi Reventlow began adjusting her camera.

Klaus already fought with the boy enough about his painting. "Why are you lounging around here like a good-for-nothing with a pencil in your hand? Would sir perhaps like to sit back and sketch a little while the rest of us break our backs?" It almost seemed to Eve as if it made Klaus angry that Alexander found joy in anything at all. Or worse: that he had an interest in something that was forever closed off to his own father. Klaus didn't need to know that she was proud of her son and gave him the paper wrapped around her purchases at Helene's store to draw on, or he'd rail at her about spoiling the children. Spoil—he didn't know the meaning of the word! Eveline pinched her lips together tightly in disapproval.

When she thought back to her childhood, when every wish and whim she'd had came true . . .

"Child, you'd like a watercolor set?" "You'd like to try to learn piano? But of course, darling, we'll get you your own little piano!" "Ah, the violin is more your instrument? Then Father will find out who the best violin maker is."

Her parents, in their good-natured way, had given in to her every whim. And when, after a short time, she lost interest in the piano and violin, there had been no drama. "The child just likes a change now and then," her father had said with a chuckle. Her mother had nodded and said the serious side of life would begin for her daughter soon enough.

The serious side of life! As if she wanted to protect her own daughters from just that, Eve laid one arm around each of them.

For a moment, the only sound was the scratch of the fountain pen on the paper.

How well he handled the unfamiliar pen! She would dearly love to be able to give him one of his own, Eveline thought. With a silver shaft, finely engraved, just as she had had at his age. Alexander had spent his school years scratching away with a pencil, and not even now, near the end of his schooling, did it look as if he'd ever own a writing implement as fine as Miss Reventlow's prop. *What a life,* Eveline thought, filled with loathing.

The camera clicked several times while Alexander, oblivious to everything around him, concentrated on his drawing. *How grown up he suddenly looks,* Eve thought. But was it any wonder? In summer, he'd be sixteen. Time was passing, and they were all being swept along with it . . .

"He's very talented. You must be proud of him," Miss Reventlow whispered to Eveline, and smiled.

"He can certainly draw," said Eveline, dragged out of her gloomy thoughts. "But where will it get him?"

"Where will it get him?" Mimi frowned. "A talent like that is a gift from God. Others would be grateful to be so artistically endowed. My uncle showed me a few drawings that Alexander did for him, and I can well imagine that your son's talent could be fostered at an art college."

Eve's inner hackles rose. An art college! What kind of nonsense was this?

"You should let us decide for ourselves what our children do," she snapped. "Alexander will be a weaver like his father." *If Gehringer takes him on,* she added silently.

"But I—" Miss Reventlow began.

Eveline looked at her with anger. What business was it of hers, what her son did?

"The weaver's profession is naturally an honorable profession, especially here in Laichingen." The woman gave Eveline a conciliatory smile, then she pointed to Marianne and Erika, who had fallen asleep on the bench. "What about a picture of your pretty daughters? Childhood passes by so quickly. It would be nice to have something to remember it by."

"Something to remember it by . . ." With every passing day, the face of her dead daughter faded in her memory a little more. Before Eve knew it, tears flooded her eyes and she sobbed loudly.

"Heavens, have I said something wrong?"

Eveline said nothing. She woke her daughters and fled with her three children.

CHAPTER 27

In the last week of April, something happened that the inhabitants of Laichingen had all but given up on: spring found its way to the Swabian Jura. The endless hollows and hills of the Jura highlands suddenly turned green. As if from nowhere, new shoots appeared, the forests dressed themselves in emeralds, and even on the stony, dry fields, the first green sprouts pushed through the ground.

Gardens in front of houses flourished. The trees in front of the church gently shook their branches of tiny flowers, and swallows turned in sweeping curves against the sky. If they looked down into the village, they would have seen a sizable crowd, all dressed in black, all streaming stone faced toward the church for the confirmation service. Only among the village youth was there any sense of excitement.

Mimi was also among the churchgoers and her uncle was with her. Supporting himself on Mimi's right arm, Josef stopped and gazed at a slender fir tree, its trunk stripped of bark. The tree lay in the center of the market square, waiting to be raised upright for the next weekend. "Our May tree . . . Ah, the good times Traudel and I shared at the spring festival, the *Maienfest*, each year. Those were the days."

"Why don't you pay a visit to the festival this year?" said Mimi, but her mind was elsewhere. Did she have enough wrapping paper for the photographs? If need be, she could always run back and get more.

"Oh, I'm much too old for a festival like that," Josef said, waving it off. "But maybe you'll join in this year? The choir will be there, and they'll be pouring the first *Maienbier* in The Oxen, too."

"We'll see," said Mimi vaguely. As a single woman, she made it a general rule to avoid festivals. For one thing, the sight of couples dancing was always a little painful—on such occasions, she felt her own loneliness more keenly than ever. And for another, there were always a few men who, after a beer or three, became disagreeable, and that was not going to be any different in Laichingen. Besides, she would probably be gone in a week. But she didn't want to speak with her uncle about any of it.

They only had to cross the market square to get to the church, but those few steps felt to Mimi like an endless trek. When Josef had insisted on going to church with her, she'd seen it as a good sign. But he moved at a leaden pace. They had to stop several times for him to catch his breath, and she worried that he would have been better off resting at home. All the while, she pulled a little cart containing the photographs with her free hand, and it rumbled so loudly over the cobblestones that she drew admonishing looks from other churchgoers.

Josef shook his head. "You've gone to a lot of trouble, you know. Couldn't the people have picked up their photographs at the shop? I thought that was why you'd reopened it."

"That's true. But you'll never get as many people in one place as you do in church. If I display the photographs there, it's the best advertising I could ever get for the studio. That's why I'm so happy that Father Hildebrand let me put them out in the church foyer," Mimi said.

The best advertising for the studio? How long did she want to go on fooling herself that Josef would one day be strong enough to take up photography again? In the three weeks Mimi had been here, his condition had not visibly improved. There were more bad days than good. Yet still she hoped the doctor would tell her that things weren't so bad after all.

"For lunch today, when we've got some money in our pockets, we'll go and eat at The Oxen, just like you did before." Mimi nodded as she spoke, as if to lend weight to her words.

"And think not to say within yourselves, We have Abraham to our father: for I say unto you, that God is able of these stones to raise up children unto Abraham. And now also the ax is laid unto the root of the trees: therefore every tree which bringeth not forth good fruit is hewn down, and cast into the fire. I indeed baptize you with water unto repentance; but he that cometh after me is mightier than I, whose shoes I am not worthy to bear: he shall baptize you with the Holy Ghost, and with fire . . ."

Of all the passages in the Bible, what made the priest choose this *for a confirmation?* Mimi wondered, her brow furrowed. Wouldn't it have been better to offer the confirmands, standing as they were on the threshold of adulthood, God's goodness and mercy to take with them wherever their paths might lead? But the priest was intimidating them with divine judgment. Weren't the young men and women allowed to experience the world for themselves? Were they supposed to conclude from the sermon that it was useless to develop one's own will because the road ahead was predetermined by their roots?

"I indeed baptize you with water unto repentance . . ."

When she thought of her father's sermons . . . in her mind, she saw him standing in the pulpit, his eyes shining and his heart overflowing. His sermons were always so positive and intense. When the *General Slocum* sank in New York's East River in 1904 and almost a thousand German immigrants died, Franziskus Reventlow cried to his flock: "Give thanks to the Lord that he has spared those in your own families who emigrated!" And when, in Finland, women were given the right to vote, he used the opportunity to quote several passages from the Bible that ordained that man should make woman his subject. Not because he shared that opinion, but because he vehemently did not! "Faith itself is at a historical turning point. Who knows? One day, the Bible itself might have to be reinterpreted. Not for nothing did God give us the gift of being able to think for ourselves," Father Reventlow called to the faithful. Those particular words had caused an uproar in the church. Somehow, word of the sermon even reached the ear of the bishop, and her father had found himself in some trouble. Not that Father Reventlow was the kind to let that intimidate him. Her wonderful, beloved papa! A wave of homesickness engulfed Mimi, so powerful that it hurt.

"Whose fan is in his hand, and he will thoroughly purge his floor, and gather his wheat into the garner; but he will burn up the chaff with unquenchable fire . . ."

Mimi, head bowed, glanced forward to where the confirmands sitting in the front row pulled their heads deeper between their shoulders. Shy Vincent. Alexander the artist. Fidgety Justus. Quiet Gisela. Musical Ida. *Who is the chaff? Who is the wheat?* they seemed to be wondering anxiously.

Grow and thrive, she wanted to shout to them. *However you want. You can be a flower or a prickly fern. You can be wheat if you want, or something completely different.* But she'd probably be fooling them as much as the priest was, because their futures were predetermined.

It took some effort, but Mimi suppressed a snort of disgust. Here, in Laichingen, the children were expected to become weavers and embroiderers. Because—just as in other places she'd traveled through—"tradition demanded." In the Thuringian Forest, the sons of glassblowers became glassblowers. And in Gönningen, one had little choice but to become a seed trader. The professions were normally passed down the male line, but Mimi knew there were exceptions. Wasn't she an exception herself?

Tradition was something tangible and secure to hold on to. But it could just as easily become a prison cell. Mimi hoped that at least one or two of these young people could turn their dreams into reality. Alexander, especially . . . it would be a terrible shame if his talent withered away here before it even fully bloomed.

Mimi's thoughts drifted to the letter she had sent her mother. So far, she had heard nothing, either about Uncle Josef or about her request that her mother make inquiries at the art college. Had her letter gone missing in the mail? What if her mother's reply arrived when Mimi had already left? *Then it would be too late for Alexander,* she thought, feeling numb.

It was a pity she would never see Alexander or the other young people again. She would like to know if one or two ended up as something other than a weaver.

Mimi blinked. What state of mind was this? Smile, click, a picture, and then goodbye? That was her life—she had never felt any wistfulness, let alone the real pain of separation. Quite the opposite, in fact. Her joy and curiosity at what lay ahead had always won out. To be free as a bird had, so far, been the most important thing of all. *Could it be that freedom is slowly meaning less than it used to?* Mimi wondered, while the congregation launched into a hymn.

Jesus Christ, our true Salvation,
Mocked by scorn and reprobation,
Gave us, to recall His dying,
This oblation sanctifying

The first stanza had just finished when Josef began to cough. He hurriedly took out a handkerchief and held it over his mouth. The cough worsened. Mimi looked at her uncle, who was doubled over in pain. She saw the handkerchief turn dark over Josef's mouth. Blood! Suppressing a sob, Mimi took Josef's arm and led him out of the church.

The church foyer was cold, and the thin blade of sunlight falling through the slightly open door did nothing to make it warmer. Mimi quickly pulled over a stool for him, and he sat, keeping the handkerchief over his mouth. He stared at the floor, but still Mimi could see in his eyes the exhaustion that the coughing fit had brought with it.

If only she could do something for him! As much as she had been looking forward to the return of Laichingen's doctor, she was becoming afraid of what he would say.

Nervously, she rearranged the confirmation photographs on the stand that usually held the hymnals. She put the pictures of the girls at the top, the boys beneath, arranging the photographs in orderly rows. But Mimi could take no pleasure in their presentation. She was too concerned about her uncle, hunched over on the stool. "You need to get straight back to bed," she said softly. "When the doctor comes back tomorrow, I'll bring him home to see you right away, even if I have to kidnap him at the train station! He needs to examine you properly and write you a prescription for better medicine. The cough syrup isn't helping."

"Child, let the poor man find his feet first. I don't want to denigrate your efforts, but I've known for a long time what's wrong with me." He looked up, and for a moment his glassy eyes seemed almost defiant. "I have consumption," he said bitterly.

"You have . . . what?" Mimi laughed, suddenly disoriented.

Josef calmly folded his blood-smeared handkerchief. "You heard me right, my child. I have the weaver's disease, though I've never spent a day in a *Dunk* in my life. The last time I visited the doctor, he told me my inner organs had already been affected. He was afraid I wouldn't survive the winter. Well, good Dr. Ludwig is in for a surprise when he sees I'm still kicking. I've survived the winter, but the summer . . ." He shook his head. "No. I can feel it. The end is very near."

Tuberculosis! She looked at her uncle in disbelief. The unnatural gleam in his eyes, the greenish-white sputum and blood he coughed up and spat—and only sometimes into his handkerchief. Why hadn't she realized it before? She'd encountered people infected with tuberculosis on her travels. Death marked them with the same symptoms as Josef.

With tuberculosis, not even a "miracle medicine," as Luise had put it, would help.

From inside the church, a sad hymn reached them. Mimi swallowed hard against her rising tears.

Josef squeezed her hand. "Don't be sad, child. I've had a good life, and death doesn't scare me. I'm looking forward to seeing Traudel. And who knows who else I'll see again . . ." Then tears sprang to his eyes, and before Mimi knew it, they were both crying.

CHAPTER 28

Mimi was relieved when ringing bells announced the end of the service. She wiped the tears from her eyes, banished the feeling of hopelessness that had overcome her, and took her position beside her photographs. When the first churchgoers entered the foyer, she forced herself to smile. A little distraction was exactly what she needed just now. It was the Klein family, whose son Vincent Mimi had photographed with the globe.

"Do you like Vincent's photo?"

Vincent's parents stepped up very close to the wooden stand. While Vincent's mother smiled proudly, her husband said, "Could be worse, the picture."

Mimi felt her smile slipping. *"Could be worse?"* What—

Josef beckoned her close and whispered in her ear, "If a Swabian tells you something 'could be worse,' it's the highest praise." The old man laughed, which instantly triggered a new coughing fit.

And, in fact, Vincent's father handed Mimi payment. "Do you have a frame for it?"

"Unfortunately, I don't." Damn it, why hadn't she ordered any frames?

"Look at our Justus! He looks so good and so grown up with the Bible in his hand!" cried Sonja Merkle, whose pregnant belly led the way as she pushed into the foyer with her husband, their sons, and their daughter, Christel. As she had at the studio, the young woman stayed in the background.

"Paul Merkle." Sonja's husband held out his hand to Mimi in greeting. "We haven't had the pleasure yet." His small eyes scrutinized her strangely, and his excessively pointed chin thrust toward her.

The girl certainly inherited her beauty from her mother, Mimi thought as she tried to extricate herself from Merkle's painful handshake. "I also have the photographs of Christel with me," she said, and she took the three images from her bag and passed them to Sonja.

"I didn't even notice that you'd taken three pictures of Christel! We only agreed on one," said Sonja. "Do we have to take all three?"

"Of course not. You can choose which one you like the most, and I'll only charge for that. But take your time and look through them first," Mimi said.

Mother and daughter turned eagerly to the photographs. "They look like expensive painted portraits! So artistic, and she looks so noble . . ." Sonja Merkle shook her head, perplexed. "How did you do that?"

Mimi's smile widened. "With the right light, one can lend an overall painterly aspect even to a photograph. I'm glad you like my compositions."

Paul Merkle looked around as if to see who would notice the purchases he was about to make. "We'll take all three," he said importantly, and whipped out his wallet.

Mimi decided to take advantage of the moment. "I would very much like to photograph your daughter outdoors. Perhaps beside a tree or in front of the *Hüle*. I'm certain I could capture her beauty even better in nature."

"I'd like that," said Sonja. "Paul?"

"Why is our son looking at an atlas? Shouldn't he be reading the Bible?" Mimi heard just then from a man standing behind Christel's family. He was pointing to the confirmation picture of Fritz, in which the boy pored over Josef's old atlas.

"The atlas and the Bible—could there be a more pious image than those two books together?" said Josef to the man, who nodded uncertainly.

"He looks like a scholar, our Fritz, but we're just simple people," said Fritz's mother, running her fingers reverently over the photograph. She took Mimi's right hand in hers and squeezed it affectionately. "Thank you," she said.

"The picture of Fritz is really very lovely. You certainly know your craft," Sonja Merkle added with honest respect.

So the magic of photography also works in Laichingen, Mimi thought. But Sonja's voice brought her moment of joy to an abrupt end. "If only you'd let her take *your* picture with the atlas!" Sonja railed at Justus. "The props didn't cost any extra. Even Alexander Schubert's got something in his hand. Just . . . what *is* that?" Sonja stepped so close to the stand that her pregnant belly pressed against the wood.

"Alexander is holding a pen and a sketch pad. He loves to draw," said Mimi.

"Alexander can draw?" Fritz's mother repeated, surprised. She had her purse in her hand.

"Since when have you had an artist in the family?" said Sonja to Eveline Schubert, approaching just then with her family.

Confused, Eveline looked from Mimi to Sonja. "Excuse me?"

"Alexander's confirmation photograph. He's drawing!" Sonja Merkle laughed as if she'd come out with a particularly funny joke.

"What of it?" said Eveline unblinking. "My son happens to be very talented. Maybe I could take a look at the picture?" She elbowed her way forward. "This is how one imagines a real artist should look," she said, gazing almost rapturously at the photograph. Filled with affection, she squeezed her son's arm. Alexander looked up expectantly at his father.

"Mr. Schubert? Would you like to take a look at the photograph, too?" said Mimi.

"What does it cost?" the man asked coldly, without responding to her question.

Mimi frowned. Unfriendly fellow! Didn't he see that his son was practically begging for a little recognition?

"You can be very proud of his talent. Being able to paint and draw is special," said Mimi, louder than necessary, her last words directed to Alexander. Let them all hear it!

"Well, for that, you first need to have the time," said Sonja.

"And money for paper and pencils," Fritz's mother added.

"Some have their purse strings tied a little looser than others," Paul Merkle added.

As if by some secret agreement, all eyes suddenly fell on Alexander. But instead of admiration, all Mimi saw was distrust and censure, as if the young man were suddenly an alien among them. Mimi blinked in confusion. It was almost as if they held Alexander's extraordinary talent against him.

Alexander stared at the floor. Eveline, sensing his pain, positioned herself protectively in front of him.

Then the restlessness among the confirmands and their parents abruptly grew. Mimi followed their eyes and saw Father Hildebrand coming toward them. Beside him was Herrmann Gehringer. *The businessman . . . wonderful,* thought Mimi grimly. It was the first time she'd seen him since their encounter at Josef's, and her heart began to beat faster. *Have you gone mad?* she chided herself. Had she reached the point where she was actually afraid of the man?

"A salesroom in the church?" Gehringer remarked, raising his eyebrows.

Father Hildebrand began to respond, but Gehringer cut him off with an impatient wave of his hand. "What an excellent idea to put the confirmation photographs on display here! No one has to go to the trouble of returning to the studio. May I take a look?"

The people standing around him hesitantly handed over their pictures.

"Young Vincent with the globe in his hand, as if he's already got the big, wide world in his sights! And Fritz eagerly looking over the maps in the atlas. Planning his next journey, no doubt. And Ida with a violin? Now all that's missing is a youngster with a mortarboard. The things you see!" Gehringer laughed and shook his head. "Is this the new custom? Looks like we old dogs haven't learned the new tricks, right, Benno?" he said jovially to Vincent's father, who—like the other parents—seemed extremely ill at ease. A moment before, they had been admiring Mimi's exceptional photographs. Suddenly, they seemed far less sure of their ground.

Without waiting for an answer from Vincent's father, Gehringer continued, "And what do we have here? Alexander Schubert practicing to be the next Vincent van Gogh?" He laughed again. "How very original!" His eyes sparkled with amusement, as if he were looking at a well-crafted caricature.

Mimi started to tremble with anger. What right did the man think he had, making fun of the boy like that? "Where is it written that all confirmation photographs have to look the same?" she asked him.

Instead of answering, Gehringer looked at those around him, especially the youngsters who had just been confirmed. "Judging by these photographs, you all seem to be called to higher things," he said ironically. "If that's the case, I guess I'll be manning a loom myself before long. That's good to know. It means I can save myself an apprentice contract or two." He clapped Fritz on the shoulder, scuffed Vincent lightly on the head with his knuckles, then marched off.

"Those props were not such a good idea, I'd say," said Fritz's mother, looking reproachfully at Mimi. "I was against it from the start."

"The Lord likes the humble," said Eveline's husband. "Vanity is no virtue."

Mimi looked at him in incomprehension. "My photographs are art! Tell me what that has to do with vanity?"

"Are we in trouble?" one of the boys asked anxiously. "What if Mr. Gehringer doesn't take us on at the factory?"

For a moment, there was a dismayed, even helpless, silence. Eveline Schubert was the first to break it. "Nonsense!" she said. "You can have your photographs taken how you want, each one of you. It's a private matter, and nobody else's business." She wrapped one arm protectively around Alexander's shoulders—the boy looked as if he was about to burst into tears.

"Time will tell. None of you have done yourself any favors with these pictures," said Paul Merkle ominously to the crowd. Then he stepped closer to Mimi. "You shouldn't have picked a fight with Mr. Gehringer. You'll see where it gets you," he whispered in her ear before turning to leave. The look he gave Mimi over his shoulder carried both contempt and malicious pleasure.

CHAPTER 29

"I'm sorry I can't give you any better news, but tuberculosis at this stage can no longer be cured. Your uncle was spitting blood before I left town. Given that, I'm happy to see that he's still among us." Dr. Otmar Ludwig, himself the picture of vitality after his extended travels, looked earnestly at Mimi across his desk.

"But Uncle Josef has never spent a day in a mine in his life, nor down in a *Dunk*. How did he catch tuberculosis?" Mimi asked in despair. The doctor was still a young man, Mimi guessed in his midthirties. Maybe he lacked experience? Maybe he was mistaken? He hadn't believed that Josef would make it through the winter, after all.

It was one in the afternoon, Monday, the day after the confirmation service. The doctor had arrived in Laichingen that morning, and his suitcase was still in the hallway when Mimi found him at his office. After the confirmation, Josef's cough had left him in peace for a few hours, and he had slept soundly. But Mimi, in her grief and worry, had been awake half the night.

"You're more than welcome to get a second opinion from one of my colleagues," said the doctor. "But it will be no different, I assure you. It is a widespread misconception that tuberculosis is a disease of the poor. Certainly, in a mine, in a cold, damp atmosphere that attacks the lungs, or in a dusty factory, or with a lot of people crammed into a small area, like you find in the poorer quarters of the cities . . . bacteria spread easily in those conditions and in weakened bodies. But keep in mind that your uncle came into contact with many people in his work, every day. It would take only one person with the disease to cough on him. Some scientists even claim there's a risk of infection if you cross a plaza where an infected person has just spat. It's not possible to say exactly when your uncle was infected—it might have been years ago. But the fact is, he has advanced tuberculosis."

A young woman in a white apron entered and placed a pile of letters on the doctor's desk.

"Allow me to introduce Sister Elke," said the doctor.

Mimi nodded to the nurse. "How do you explain that my uncle is sometimes much better? There are days when he spends hours watching me work in the studio. A dying man couldn't do that," she said hopelessly.

The doctor, however, remained steadfast. "The bacteria that cause tuberculosis are not always active to the same degree. Sometimes they lie dormant in the cells. When the weather is fine, as it is now, or when the patient eats good, nourishing food, or gets out in fresh air, then his immune system is able, for a time, to hold the bacteria in check."

Mimi's expression brightened. "But if that's all it is, good food can be arranged. And if necessary, Josef will simply have to move somewhere warmer. To Italy, for instance, where the winters are milder. Or to a sanatorium in Switzerland for people with lung diseases—" She broke off when she saw the look of sympathy on the doctor's face.

"If I know Josef Stöckle, he'll turn down all of it. You can't move an old tree, they say." The doctor folded his hands as if praying. "I'm sorry, but you have to accept that your uncle will soon die."

"Sometimes everything turns out differently than you think," Mimi murmured.

"Quite soon, your uncle will probably be unable to leave his bed at all. He will need constant care. Sister Elke will be able to show you what's needed, because there are a number of things you will need to watch. You will have to make sure you don't get too close to your uncle, for example. It's best for you to be especially careful since you're with him so much. Of course, he will naturally do his best not to infect anyone, and you should be certain he has handkerchiefs with him at all times and that he covers his mouth and nose anytime he coughs, particularly if he's among people in town." The doctor began to sort through the pile of mail that lay on his desk. It seemed their conversation was over.

Mimi pressed her hand over her mouth to stifle a wail. Her beloved uncle was really dying?

"How long does he have?" she asked when she had herself more or less under control, her voice still heavy with emotion.

The doctor looked up from a letter. "That's hard to say. I've underestimated his strength once already. Maybe six months?"

Mimi, feeling numb, started back to Josef's. The May tree was still in the middle of the square; they were supposed to set it upright the following weekend. At the sight of it, Mimi could no longer hold back her tears. Josef might see the *Maienfest*, but certainly not another Christmas. Half-blind with tears, she stumbled toward the bench beneath the lime trees in front of the church.

Where are things supposed to go from here? she wondered. How would the last months of Josef's life be? Would he be in pain? Would he finally just suffocate?

He could still wash and change himself, and could still make it to the toilet and back, but what would happen when he couldn't do those things for himself anymore? If she decided to look after him, she would have to wash him in his bed. She would have to take him a bedpan and feed him like a child. And when he lay dying, he would need someone to cool his feverish brow with a damp cloth. The thought of everything she would soon have to face frightened her. Would she be able to do it? Even if Sister Elke showed her what to do ten times over, Mimi was no nurse. She had never taken care of anyone in her life. She would probably have no time for the photo studio, either, and what were she and Josef supposed to live on then? Would she be able to ask her parents for money?

But could she leave him alone? Bring someone in to take care of him and go off traveling again, as she'd originally planned? That seemed just as wrong as every other option. Mimi felt more lost than she had in a long time. She looked up to the sky, where a few swallows arced against the blue. God was always close by, she felt. But how good it would be to have someone dear to her sitting there with her just then. Someone she could share her fears with, someone who listened, who asked good questions or found an answer when Mimi did not know where to turn. Like Hannes had done, that evening in Ulm.

But she was on her own—as usual.

With heavy steps and a heavier heart, she made her way home.

When she arrived, she found Josef sitting in the parlor, flicking through a photography magazine that an old colleague had sent him a few days before. Mimi was relieved: he had had a good day.

Strange, she thought bitterly as she went to the kitchen to butter some bread for sandwiches—the magazines Josef's friends sent him never went astray, but her mother's letters apparently did! The sight of the overflowing laundry basket and the sink full of dirty dishes brought Mimi to the edge of tears again. She couldn't even keep a household under control. How was she supposed to look after a dying man?

"Well, what important things did you learn from our Dr. Ludwig?" Josef asked when they sat together to eat.

Mimi, for whom every morsel was already hard to swallow, abruptly put down her bread. "How can you be so flippant? This is your life we're talking about!" Before she knew it, her tears were flowing again.

"Mimi, child . . . don't be sad." Josef patted her arm awkwardly. "Having you visit has been such a joy for me. I never expected anyone to look after me again the way you have. I'm eternally grateful for that."

Mimi blinked. It sounded as if her uncle was already saying good-bye. "What did I do that was so wonderful? If Luise knew how I've let your household go to ruin, she'd throw her hands up in horror. But somehow there aren't enough hours in the day to do everything I want to. I haven't even managed to cook you the *Schwarzer Brei* you love so much, and I keep meaning to ask Luise for the recipe. I feel so useless!" she sobbed.

Josef smiled. "You're simply not a housewife, child. You belong behind the camera. Your profession happens out in the great, wide world, not here in this little corner of it. That's why you should get out there again. I insist. Tomorrow, why not?"

"What . . . you want me to go?" What had she done wrong?

"I don't want you to watch me die. I would like you to remember me in a more or less tolerable state," Josef said as soberly as if he were talking about the weather. "Didn't you tell me yourself that you've got a job waiting for you in Isny?"

"Isny! As if I could take pretty pictures of a town hall now. I want to be here for you."

"Child, don't make this so hard for me. You're a young woman, and you're my niece. The thought of you having to clean my rear because I can no longer do it myself makes me terribly uncomfortable. You see that, don't you? Besides, everything that happens does so for a reason. I'm ready."

"Then who's going to look after you?" Mimi asked quietly. As much as it hurt her to have him send her away, she could understand why he was doing it. Shame . . . it could take a toll on a person.

"Luise," he said, with exaggerated confidence. "When things get very bad, the doctor and Sister Elke are here. The most you could do . . ." He hesitated. "Maybe it would help if you could make some small contribution toward my care. Or your mother."

When Josef returned to his bed, Mimi went out to the studio. Somehow, she had the feeling that writing another letter to her mother would be easier in the consoling presence of Josef's photographic props.

It smelled of old dust inside, and Mimi opened a few of the windows. Sweet spring air immediately flooded in, but it contrasted strangely with the gloominess of Mimi's thoughts. She sat on the platform, where just a few days earlier the Laichingen confirmands had posed for her—those sittings in Josef's studio had been special. She frowned when she recalled the events of the previous day in the foyer of the church. She still did not understand why the churchgoers had been swayed by Gehringer's stupid commentary and then reacted so negatively to the talented Alexander. Did they envy his gift? No, it seemed that they found the boy . . . weird.

She sighed. Then she stood and went to the table. Enough brooding. She needed facts.

Laichingen, May 1, 1911

Dearest Mother,
Either your letter has gone astray or you have not yet had the chance to write back to me, although I need your assistance and advice so urgently.

Mimi paused, the fountain pen in midair. She'd made up her mind, and she wiped her eyes with her free hand. No more crying now! Josef had done everything he could to make her feel better. She needed to make a little effort.

In brief: Uncle Josef is suffering from advanced tuber-culosis. Today I spoke with his doctor, and he says that Josef does not have much time left. In his last weeks or months, he will need constant care and assistance. The idea that he would have no family nearby during that time is unbearable to me. I am sure you see the matter just as I do. Dearest Mother, I have done everything I can for Josef in these last few weeks. But now I am passing the baton to you, his sister. I am more than happy to stay with him a few more days until you have made all the necessary arrangements and can come.

She paused again. Somehow, she couldn't really picture Amelie Reventlow looking after her brother in his final days.

CHAPTER 30

As he did at the beginning of every month, Herrmann Gehringer was poring over the incoming order list—a customer in Mannheim wanted five hundred nightshirts for a stand at the *Maienfest* in Mannheim, and the sooner the better—when his assistant entered the office and stopped expectantly before his desk.

"What is it, Merkle?" Gehringer asked.

Good Lord! Surely the man in Mannheim didn't discover the *Maienfest* just yesterday, did he? It was true that it came later than the festival in Laichingen, but how in all the world were they supposed to fit an order that large into their existing schedule? And besides, plain nightshirts were in the lowest price range and wouldn't bring him much more than a sleepless night.

Paul Merkle cleared his throat. "It's about the photographer. You were able to see her 'art' for yourself yesterday. But you tasked me with finding out how good she really is in her field, so I don't feel it would be proper of me to withhold the pictures that Mimi Reventlow took of my daughter." Like a card player revealing an excellent hand, he placed the three pictures on Gehringer's desk one at a time. "As you can see, the woman is truly a master of her trade."

Damn, Merkle's daughter was beautiful! "Making your daughter look good doesn't exactly take talent," he said dismissively. Why didn't he have Christel working for him at the factory? Piecework from home was something for old women and mothers! *The beauty of youth,* he thought, and at the same moment was struck by another thought. "What would you say to Christel modeling garments for our esteemed clientele?"

Paul Merkle frowned. "Surely you don't want Christel to take off her clothes in front of strangers?"

Gehringer laughed. "Good God, man, I'm not suggesting that at all. She wouldn't be showing off our nightdresses or petticoats, of course. Just aprons, blouses, smocks—all very decent and proper." He might have guessed that Merkle would need coaxing for this kind of thing. "I don't make this kind of offer to just anyone, you know. This is an honor! You could show a little gratitude," he said sternly.

"Of course," Merkle replied quickly. "But a fashion show, with Christel, here in the office?" He swept his hand in a gesture that took in the stove, the dark-paneled walls, and the high stacks of files. "Forgive me for saying this, Mr. Gehringer, but that would really be casting pearls before swine."

Instead of getting angrier, Gehringer let out a laugh. His assistant was no shrinking violet, and he liked that. "You know, Merkle, when you're right, you're right!" He stood up energetically. "Come, let's go."

"Have I forgotten an appointment?" Merkle whipped out his note-pad and leafed through it frantically.

Gehringer laughed even louder. "Take it easy! Spontaneity is as much a part of entrepreneurship as good planning, my friend. So is a bit of oomph! If you want to get anywhere in this world, you have to attack like a terrier at an ankle—sink your teeth in and don't let go!"

The weather was lovely, so instead of taking the car, Gehringer decided to treat himself to a walk through the village. Work was already underway in the surrounding fields, the women going out with their rakes and shovels over their shoulders, swarms of children in tow. Gehringer greeted all of them. No one could accuse him of snobbery!

Besides, these were his people. And Laichingen was his village. He'd once read the motto "Better a shark in a pond than a mackerel in the sea" and had found it particularly fitting. His Laichingen was indeed a small place tucked away in the Swabian Jura, but thanks to his linenware, he was known across Europe and beyond, and that applied to Gehringer Weaving, too. And he had plans to spread his fame even further.

With his walking stick in his hand and Merkle at his side, Gehringer strolled past his competitors' factories as if he didn't have the slightest care in the world. All around him, he could hear the rhythmic knocking of the looms. Did Hirrler, Morlock, and the others have to put up with customers like that fellow from Mannheim? Hirrler, very likely, but Morlock, with his first-rate showroom in Ulm, probably not. Buyers of quality linenware knew that excellence required a certain lead time and that nothing happened overnight!

Josef Stöckle's shop was closed. "So much for Miss Reventlow's diligence," Gehringer crowed.

Merkle knocked at the door a second time. "Maybe she did so well from the confirmation that she's already left town," he said derisively.

What a wonderful notion, thought Gehringer. Standing in front of the shop, he could see just how ideal it would be as a showroom. The large windows, all the light, and right on the market square. And from there it was just a short hop to The Oxen. He'd be able to invite his customers to dine as soon as the order forms were signed. "Let's find out," he said, and he went around the side of the house toward the studio.

They found Mimi bent over a sheet of paper, writing. Whatever she was working on seemed to demand all her attention. She didn't notice the two men standing in the doorway.

He cleared his throat loudly.

Startled, Mimi looked up. "Yes? How can I help you?"

By leaving, Gehringer thought. "Glorious day, isn't it?" he said instead, as if they were old acquaintances who met regularly. "Spring is just gorgeous up here in the Jura, don't you think?" He pointed outside with his walking stick.

"I can't claim to have seen much of the countryside around here. I've had my hands full with work and looking after my uncle," said Mimi Reventlow, her voice cool. She put her pen and paper aside and stood up. "Is there anything else?" she asked, smoothing her silk blouse.

No linen for the lady, Gehringer noted. Velvet and silk it had to be. He was curious to know why an attractive woman like her had to work at all. Hadn't she been able to find a husband? It wouldn't surprise him. What man would want to put up with a willful female like this one? He smiled broadly. "I've actually just come to wish you all the best on the next leg of your travels."

"How do you know—" The photographer broke off in midsentence and looked at him with distrust.

So she really was planning to go! Gehringer rejoiced inwardly. "Well, a successful woman like you can't sit around forever in a little place like this. You must have a hundred other engagements to get to," he said. Now that he knew she'd be leaving, he could afford to be generous and pay her a compliment. "Springtime is the ideal time to travel. And, if you're worried about your uncle, no need. In Laichingen, people look after each other. We take responsibility very seriously here." He looked pointedly at the letter, where the pen she had hurriedly set aside was creating a large ink stain. "My offer to rent your uncle's shop still stands, by the way." He looked around with interest. "And now that I think about it, I could actually rent Josef's studio, too. The backdrops, the platform . . . they'd be perfect for presenting my linenware. A fashion show in the glasshouse—my customers would enjoy that, I'm sure. Of course, I'd increase the rent by, let's say, ten marks. If you'd allow my assistant to sit at your table for a moment . . . Merkle! The contract! Amend it accordingly, please."

"Now hold on. I haven't said yes yet," the photographer said.

She acts so surprised, Gehringer thought. Arrogant creature. Probably trying to drive the rent higher. Well, not with him!

"But you will, young lady. Your uncle needs the income, and you know it as well as I do," he replied. "It was nice of you to pay him a visit. Nothing's more important than familial bonds. But it is also good that you are leaving again. You would not be happy here in Laichingen. Take my word for it. Around here, a centuries-old system prevails. People appreciate the traditional, and everything else is nonsense. I mean, really: Photographing a confirmand with a globe of the world? Or an atlas? It's not as if we were in Munich or Berlin, where fashions come and go every week." He chuckled at the thought. Then he wagged his forefinger sternly. "I know exactly what you're up to, young lady. Putting ideas into the boys' heads, aren't you? And yet you know that our boys will spend their entire lives in this place." He pointed the tip of his walking stick at her reproachfully. "But what of it? If need be, we'll straighten their heads out again, won't we, Merkle?"

His assistant nodded obediently.

Mimi Reventlow sighed loudly, as if he'd said something she was struggling to comprehend. "You certainly won't have to straighten anyone's head out just because of my photographs. And as for your centuries-old system—neither you nor I know what the future holds," she said vehemently.

Now that's enough, thought Gehringer angrily. "That's where you're mistaken. I know very well what the future holds for us here in Laichingen." His jovial tone was gone, and his voice was hard edged. "Our lives here might seem to you to be modest or even backward, but believe me, nobody here wants it any other way. We live in our own little world. I look after the people here, and they are appreciative of that."

The photographer let out a laugh. "Have I understood you correctly? Are you trying to tell me how I'm supposed to take my photographs?" Her hands pressed to her hips, she glared furiously at him.

"I wouldn't dream of it." He raised his hands placatingly. The conversation was starting to wear on his nerves. He snatched the amended contract out of Merkle's hands and held it out to her. "Here. For me, your signature is just as good as your uncle's."

But the photographer was not finished. "For *me*, it sounded very much like interference in my work. And another thing: the disparaging way you talked about the confirmation photos yesterday was ridiculous! Art is and remains a matter of personal taste, and you'd do well to remember it."

"I agree entirely, and I regret that you mistook my intention," he said mildly. Then he tapped on the contract again. "Bottom right, if you please."

Mimi looked first at the contract, then sharply at him. "I think you are the one who is mistaken, Mr. Gehringer," she said slowly. "You will have to look for a showroom elsewhere. Neither the studio nor the shop is for rent, nor do I have any plans to leave Laichingen in the near future. My uncle needs the support of family, which is why I'm staying and taking over his studio, and everything that goes with it."

It was rare for Herrmann Gehringer to be at a loss for words, but when he stepped out of the studio, he was silent.

"I'm sorry," said Paul Merkle in a low voice, which did absolutely nothing to improve matters.

"There's nothing to be sorry about," Gehringer muttered through his teeth. "That woman will find no success here. I will make her life harder than she can imagine."

Mimi, a smile on her lips, watched the businessman storm off. She'd gotten his hackles up and she knew it. The self-righteousness of the man, trying to tell her the ways of the world!

But her good cheer vanished as quickly as it had come. Whatever she'd told Gehringer made no difference: she could still leave if she wanted. But did she want to? Suddenly, she realized that her response just now had been more than just stubborn defiance, and she also realized that, deep inside, she had long ago made up her mind to stay. It was only her doubt about whether she would be able to cope with the tasks ahead that had made her hesitate. It didn't help that Josef had told her unequivocally that he didn't want her to look after him. Of course she understood his sense of shame—she would feel exactly the same. But would it really be any easier for him to have a total stranger help him through his days? For money?

The letter to her mother caught her eye. She read through it a final time. Then she tore it to pieces.

Slowly, she stood and went back to the house.

Josef, in the meantime, had woken from his afternoon nap and was sitting red-cheeked at the table, poring over the daily paper.

"I'm staying," Mimi said the moment she came through the door. She joined her uncle at the table.

Josef opened his mouth to reply, but she raised her hand to stop him. It was her turn. "You're probably right. The time ahead of us won't be easy. Not for you, not for me. There'll likely be times when you think I'm an idiot. But I promise you that I'll do my best. We'll fight, and we'll certainly not always agree on things. But whatever happens, whatever effect this disease has on you—you will always be the wonderful traveling photographer Josef Stöckle. You are, and you will forever be, my hero and my role model."

The old photographer looked at her, and Mimi saw his tired eyes shimmering with tears. "But why would you do this to yourself, child? Why?" he whispered.

"Because I love you" was all Mimi said.

CHAPTER 31

"Where the devil is the driver from Schlössle's brewery?" Karolina Schaufler checked the clock on the kitchen wall opposite the stove for the hundredth time. "If we don't get the beer into the cellar to cool soon, we'll be serving it lukewarm."

It was only two days until the big festival weekend. Then the May tree would be set up. Although it was only the start of May, the temperature was already summery—just three weeks earlier, it had still been snowing. Everyone was looking forward to the *Maienfest* and being able to dance around the May tree without thick socks or warm coats.

"With this heat wave, he won't be killing his horse to get here. The road from Ulm will take longer than usual, that's all," said Anton listlessly. Since early that morning, he'd been hard at work chopping vegetables and bones and browning all of it in large iron pans. Later, they would add water to make a gravy: served with the usual sausages, the bone gravy was a specialty of The Oxen, and reserved for festivals.

"So suddenly you're a horse expert?" his mother said. "And where, pray tell, is your father wasting his time right now?"

"He's setting up the tables outside." Anton gestured toward the window that opened onto the square, where his father was just then chatting with the blacksmith.

"Then he's making himself useful for a change," Karolina grumbled. She was taking cutlery out of a drawer and putting it in large baskets. With weather this good, all the guests would want to sit and eat outside, so it made sense to keep the cutlery and crockery handy on a side table.

If only we could do the cooking outside, too, Anton thought, and not for the first time. He looked at the large pans in disgust. They would simmer away for hours, and the air in the kitchen would soon be so thick you could practically cut it with a knife.

"Why do we always have sausages and gravy at every festival here in the village? Let's roast a pig on a spit over an open fire for a change. We've got enough room outside for that, and the smell of roast meat would spread across the square and bring in even more guests, I'm sure of it."

Karolina waved off the suggestion. "Cooking's done in the kitchen, or why do we even have a kitchen? Besides the fact that people look forward to our gravy, not everyone can afford roast pork."

"We could offer larger and smaller portions. Add a slice of black bread and a bit of salted radish—that doesn't cost all that much, and people would love it," said Anton. "Something new for a change," he added, and felt a moment of hope stir inside him, because Karolina didn't belittle the idea instantly, as she usually would.

But after a brief pause, she said, "The idea itself isn't bad. But to make sure a pig's really cooked through, we'd need a proper spit you could turn on its own iron frame. We'd only use it once or twice a year, and that wouldn't warrant the cost."

"Who says we couldn't use it more often? If people in the big towns around here knew how pretty our inn is, right on the market square and next to the *Hüle*, and that we served up roast pig, I'm sure a lot of them would enjoy a little trip out to the Swabian Jura. A bit of advertising, that's all we'd need! The photographer could take a picture of The Oxen, we'd put an ad in the Ulm paper and bring day trippers out to Laichingen on Sundays. Picture it: we'd have as many people here every

Sunday as we're expecting this weekend!" Anton felt his inner restlessness grow at the thought. Festival days, when the market square and the plaza in front of The Oxen filled with the residents of the village, were among his favorite of the year—something was actually happening!

"Then tell me, smart aleck: Who's supposed to do all the work? We'd need twice as many people working here to do all this," said his mother with a laugh. She pointed out the window. "Finally, here comes the beer! Go and help them unload." She took the cooking spoon out of Anton's hand and went on stirring the bones and vegetables herself. "And another thing: don't go getting mixed up with that photographer. Last night I overheard some of the regulars saying that Gehringer was talking bad about her. Seems he didn't like the idea of her selling the confirmation photos in the church like she did. He's of the opinion that no one ought to be doing business with someone as 'irreverent' as her."

Anton laughed. "*Gehringer* is saying that? As if Sundays are sacred to him! How many times has he had his workers at the looms on a Sunday?"

His mother made a face. "Maybe you're right. It still doesn't mean we have to do business with the woman. We'd be finished if Gehringer went somewhere else. Everyone would follow."

"Where? There's nothing here besides The Oxen. Or do you really think they'd travel down to Ulm or Blaubeuren for a beer and a bit of gossip?"

"That might be true for the regulars, but Gehringer comes here all the time with his customers, too. And then there's the Christmas party at his house every year, and his birthday, and we cater for both of those, if you recall. And what if other factory owners decide to stay away? Or their foremen or clerks? We couldn't live from the weavers who sit and nurse one beer all night, I'll tell you that. I don't care how beautiful her pictures are, we're not having any taken of The Oxen, and that's the end of it."

Anton knew he'd been a fool to think anything might change. He stomped outside.

He was in the process of rolling one of the big beer barrels around the house to the cellar steps when Alexander walked by, his head hanging.

"Not exactly your day today, either?" asked Anton.

"Today? The whole week's been horrible," Alexander replied. "My parents fight almost all the time. Father is furious about the confirmation photo. Gehringer didn't like it, he says. If I don't get into the factory because of it, then good night."

"Crap," Anton muttered. "The way I heard it, Gehringer was making fun of all the confirmation photos, so everyone must be worried about whether they'll get an apprenticeship."

"They are!"

"Eh, Gehringer is always glad to have new slaves for his looms." Anton stopped speaking and groaned as he used all his strength to keep the beer barrel from tumbling down the cellar steps. Over the years, the slope on the ground above the first step had become steeper and slipperier, and he had to be extremely careful.

"Think you'll finish back there sometime today?" they heard the wagon driver call from the front of the house.

Alexander grabbed hold, too, and together they maneuvered the barrel carefully, step by step, to the bottom. "This is really heavy. Be sure it doesn't land on your foot," he said through gritted teeth.

"I could live with a permanent limp," said Anton, and laughed. "There's one consolation: they're a lot lighter when you carry 'em back up."

"Then maybe I should see if your beer deliverer will hire me," said Alexander, also feeling a little better. "I won't have to worry about Gehringer giving me a job or not."

"Gehringer, Gehringer! I can't hear that name anymore." Anton grabbed hold of Alexander's arm and shook him hard. "He needs you.

Get that into your head. Good weavers don't grow on trees. Even if he finds some excuse not to give you a job, then you'll just do something else. There are other factories. Maybe someone needs a pattern designer or sign painter? You've got the talent for it."

Alexander shook his head. "Those jobs don't grow on trees either. No, Father's right. It would be best if Gehringer took me. At least you make regular money as a weaver." A shudder seemed to pass through Alexander just then, as if the thought of having to stand at a loom chilled him to the bone.

Anton knew only too well how his friend felt. "Why does everyone have to follow in their parents' footsteps? It's not like it's a law."

"Look who's talking," said Alexander, and he looked sadly at the beer barrel that Anton was heaving onto a stand.

CHAPTER 32

Mimi, feeling ill at ease, walked to Luise's house. After years of traveling alone, Mimi was used to handling things by herself, and she rarely asked for help, so going to Luise for just that made her uncomfortable. But she had no choice. Without Luise, her plan to stay in Laichingen didn't stand a chance.

From inside the house, she heard pots rattling and Luise singing. Josef's neighbor was obviously busy, and there was Mimi, coming to disturb her. Hesitantly, Mimi knocked. A heartbeat later, the door swung open and Luise Neumann was standing in front of her.

"Mimi Reventlow! Well, now, what did the doctor say?"

Luise's friendly face made Mimi relax a little. Briefly, she told Luise about the devastating diagnosis. She finished by saying, "I've decided to stay awhile and look after my uncle."

Luise nodded. "People need to stand by one another. You're doing the right thing."

Mimi smiled. Yes, staying did feel "right." "There's just one problem . . . ," Mimi said slowly. "Now that I'm going to be staying, I must learn how to manage the house. But I have no experience in that at all. I don't know how to cook or do laundry or store food properly." Josef's pantry was still as empty as it had been when she'd arrived. She simply did not know what would keep for how long. Instead, she'd gone to

Helene's store practically every day to buy a few things she knew they would eat. She had, however, realized how quickly that practice was using up her savings. If she kept on like that, the money she'd brought from Meersburg would be gone before she knew it. Of course, she could still go down to the bank in Ulm and get more from her account, but her plan was to make Josef's studio profitable, not just to spend, spend, spend.

"And you want me to teach you?" Luise's brow furrowed. "Young lady, I'll be glad to help you, but all that is what young women normally learn over *years* from their mothers. Or at a home economics school."

Mimi frowned. "I know. But I've never been to a home economics school, and my mother never had the time to teach me anything practical." She wrung her hands almost pleadingly. "Couldn't you at least teach me how to cook? Josef has been missing the *Schwarzer Brei* you cooked for him for so long, but I don't even know what it is." Mimi shrugged. "Since I've been here, we've been eating bread and drippings from sausage, or vegetable soup, which is the only thing I do know how to cook. I think you'd agree that a sick man should eat something more nutritious than that."

Luise nodded. "I am about to make lunch. You can watch and learn if you like."

Mimi, whose mouth started watering at the mention of lunch, nodded eagerly. A warm meal had never been more tempting than now.

"First and most important: set everything up," said Luise when they were standing in the dark hallway. She pointed to a small side table where various bowls of grain and potatoes sat. Above the table was a shelf that held a range of foodstuffs, and beside the table was the stove.

"You cook out here in the hallway? Don't you have a kitchen?" Mimi asked.

Luise only laughed. "This is an old weaver's house, not a hotel. Come with me. I'll show you something." She went into a sparsely furnished parlor and opened a trapdoor in the floor. "Take a look."

Mimi, with a mixture of surprise and trepidation, peered down into a cold, dark room in which a huge loom stood. "What is that?" she asked.

"That's the *Dunk*. Before they went to work in the factories, our men worked down there. Everyone around here has a *Dunk* in the house." There was pride in Luise's voice. "You can go down if you like."

Mimi had no great desire to climb down into the dark hole. But when she looked into Luise's expectant eyes, she knew she couldn't turn her neighbor down.

One step at a time, doing her best not to lose her grip on the rungs worn smooth over decades, Mimi climbed down into the depths.

It was so cold down here! And so dark. One small window set high on a wall allowed a little daylight to penetrate. Mimi saw the feet of someone passing by outside, but that was all. Her throat constricted, an icy shudder ran down her spine, and she began to shiver. It was like being buried alive. Just like when she'd fallen into the poacher's trap all those years ago. Mimi could not imagine how the men had ever managed to work for hours at a time down there, day in, day out.

"I'll bet you've never seen anything like that on your travels, have you?" Luise called down.

"I can't say I have," said Mimi shakily, climbing back up the steep ladder. Upstairs again, she rubbed herself vigorously to warm up. "It's freezing down there. Didn't the weavers at least have some sort of stove?"

"Oh, no," said Luise. "The *Dunk* had to be cold and damp, or it was no good for the flax during the weaving. My Georg also sat down there, winter after winter, until he was thirty. I'd make him hot tea or broth to warm him up a bit. But when he came up in the evening, his limbs were as stiff as an old man's. No wonder his bones hurt him the way they do these days." She sighed. "Compared to that, the men in the factories have got it easy today. The mechanical looms all but run themselves, and the weavers only have to make sure nothing breaks."

"I'm glad to hear no one has to sit in a *Dunk* anymore," said Mimi, relieved.

"Believe it or not, there are still a few weavers who do. Not we women, of course!" she added quickly. "We work at home. Once or twice a week, someone comes and brings us things to embroider, and a week later they come back for the finished work. It's a good system."

Mimi, who hated all forms of needlework, nodded vaguely. "How long have the factories been around?"

Luise leaned on the table. "I'd have to think . . . Georg hadn't yet proposed to me when Morlock's opened, and a few years after that, Hirrler started up. But both of them only had a few men on the books, mostly relatives. We'd just married when Mr. Gehringer opened his factory, and it was just after that that Georg started with him, thank God." While she was speaking, she went to a cupboard. "Look here: all of it Laichingen linen." Almost devoutly, she unfolded tablecloths and bedsheets, and presented pillowcases and nightshirts. "All finest quality and beautifully embroidered. This is our treasure!" she said, and she ran her fingers lovingly over a nightshirt that no one had ever worn.

Mimi was genuinely impressed. "It's rare to see fabric so fine. And the embroidery is really all done by hand?"

"On all of this, certainly," Luise said. "These days they have embroidery machines, but they can't do what we women do by hand. Laichingen is another word for quality when it comes to linen, you know. The linen we make here used to go as far afield as Italy and Spain. Oh, what am I saying? We used to send them all the way to Central and South America, although that doesn't happen much these days! Every girl here in the empire dreams about having Laichingen linen in her trousseau, and there are some old women, too, who occasionally treat themselves." She smiled as she took out another tablecloth. "Look: my latest acquisition! I saved a long time to afford this."

"It's very beautiful. Haven't you ever used it?" She pointed to the crisp folds in the fabric.

"Oh, I'd never put it out. It's far too good for me!" Luise admitted with a laugh. She took a pillowcase out of the cupboard. It was smaller than the others and embroidered with countless flowers and stalks of grass. "Traudel was gifted with an embroidery needle. This was one of hers. Can you see the special stitching she used?"

For Mimi, the embroidery looked just like all the rest, but she was fascinated by the passion Luise invested in the subject. Laichingen suddenly seemed to be a very special place, after all.

But there was one thing she didn't understand. "If your linen is so sought after, how is it that the weavers' work is so badly paid? At least, that's what I've heard," she added.

"Well, times are changing," Luise said. "These days, a lot of people prefer nightshirts and bedclothes made of cotton, because it's easier to iron." She shrugged. "And there's another reason. Local flax is no good for the mechanical looms, so the men who run the factories bring in raw materials from abroad. If they also paid their workers a handsome wage, the linen would be so expensive no one would buy it anymore." Luise sighed. "Oh yes, times have changed, that much is clear. But we all get by. God makes sure of that. And linen is our constant companion, from birth to our last breath, and that will always be so." Luise clapped her hands together resolutely. "Right! Let's get cooking!"

An hour later, Mimi was beginning to think that cooking wasn't as difficult as she'd imagined. Some of what Luise did wasn't all that different from how Mimi prepared her vegetable soup, but with the addition of flour or semolina, eggs or bread, she could make four different kinds of soup. And, of course, Luise had shown her how to make Josef's favorite *Schwarzer Brei*.

"You can get all the ingredients you need at Helene's, and they're much cheaper than sausage and bread." In a slightly critical tone, Luise added, "Those are things you really don't need to be spending money on."

It seemed Mimi's purchases had become the talk of the village. She smiled to herself.

"Thank you very much. You've really been a great help. Maybe I can take your picture sometime in return? Perhaps a portrait of you and your husband together?"

"If we must . . . Our fortieth wedding anniversary is coming up." Luise smiled uncomfortably, but Mimi could see that she liked the idea. Her neighbor put her hands on her hips. "Right, on to the clothes! I've never seen you do laundry at all—do you really not know how to wash clothes?"

Mimi laughed in embarrassment. "Maybe you could enlighten me. How do people do it here in Laichingen? Is there a laundry?"

Luise shook her head, half-smiling, half-shocked. "I can see you need to start at the beginning. Lucky for you today is also my laundry day." She pointed to a huge pot simmering on the stove, and without waiting for Mimi to respond, she tramped outside with a basket of laundry and a washboard. Mimi followed.

"The laundry is always done in front of the house," said Luise, and pointed to the wall, where a collection of wooden tubs hung.

"But everyone will see you out here," said Mimi uncertainly. Her underwear was nobody's business but hers.

"People are meant to see that you work hard," Luise replied flatly. She threw an armful of laundry into a tub of ice-cold water.

"We let the laundry soak for a while, and then it goes into the hot water. Then you take your curd soap and scrub out all the stains. Like this." Luise went to work on the shirt in her hands. "Your turn."

Mimi dipped her own hands tentatively into the tub, hoping she wouldn't grab hold of any of Luise's husband's underwear. She came up with a linen bedsheet. After a few minutes, Mimi's hands were stiff and her skin had begun to crinkle uncomfortably. Her upper arms ached as if she'd been holding her camera overhead for an hour.

"Very good," Luise praised. "Now comes the wringing . . ."

"Well, young lady, enough for today, I'd say," Luise said an hour later, when they had hung the last of the undershirts on a long cord strung from one side of Luise's garden to the other. She gave Mimi a friendly wink. "Now you're ready to go!"

Mimi sat down on a low wall. She didn't feel ready to go at all, but rather utterly exhausted. "As a photographer, traveling around the country, it always made me happy to see women washing clothes at a spring or on the shore of a lake, but I never gave a thought to how much effort goes into it. But there's one thing you still need to tell me: the washing, the cooking, the whole household—how in the world am I supposed to get all of it done on top of the work in the studio?"

"The same way we do. Once we're done with our day's labor, we take care of the housework. So after a day in your studio, you start on the house," said Luise, and she laughed. "That won't be a problem for you, will it?"

CHAPTER 33

It was a glorious Saturday, the air suffused with a light sweetness and the sun agreeably warm—the Laichingers could not have asked for better weather for their *Maienfest*. Now that she had decided to stay, Mimi was determined to make the most of it, and the day was perfect for taking some pictures of her own. She even managed to convince her uncle to go out with her.

Around eleven in the morning, Mimi picked up her Linhof camera and took Uncle Josef with her—he was having one of his good days. Even if he only stayed for an hour or two at the festival, Mimi believed he should experience nice things as long as he was still able to.

Josef found a place on the bench beneath the lime trees, where he sat with a couple of other older men and told anyone who came by that Mimi was going to be staying for the summer and how happy that made him.

People nodded and acted as if they were happy for the old man. But word had gotten around in the village that Herrmann Gehringer had mocked Mimi Reventlow's photographs after the confirmation service. Someone had heard the businessman say that one ought to steer clear of the photo studio, and that the woman was not pleasing to God. Another claimed that there had been some kind of incident in Josef Stöckle's old shop, but didn't know any details. Still, there was something not right about a woman who got on the bad side of Mr. Gehringer the moment she arrived in town.

Looking through the viewfinder of her camera, Mimi took a step to the right to put the May tree precisely in the center of her picture, but the result was too static. Concentrating, she took another step. Using the May tree as a central axis was fine as far as it went, but the picture just had no dynamism. She squinted and shifted her frame. Now, the tree was just left of center, its streamers blowing slightly in the breeze, and to the right were the chestnut trees in full bloom, and behind those the high church tower . . . A painter could not have arranged things better. Perfect! Mimi snapped the shutter and looked up with satisfaction. She stowed the plate in her bag and disappeared under her black cloth for a moment to slot a new one into the camera. Then she unscrewed the Zeiss lens she'd been using and replaced it with a Plaubel wide-angle lens: she needed the wider angle to capture the festivalgoers.

She squinted up at the sky. Against the bright May light, a few wispy clouds drifted in front of the sun, and the shadows cast by the chestnut trees didn't look as hard anymore, but softer and more diffuse—the best light for what she had in mind. Her beloved Linhof would take care of the rest, she thought, while she looked around for the right place to take her next picture.

Men raising their mugs of beer. Women chatting. Young men and women exchanging covert glances. Through the viewfinder of Mimi's camera, the scene as a whole suddenly came to her like an Impressionist painting. As so often happened just before she took a good picture, Mimi felt a warm current pass through her.

"You're not getting me with my fat belly in there, I hope?" she heard Sonja Merkle say. On her husband's arm, Luise's daughter approached ponderously. Her sons ran among the rows of tables, yelling loudly.

"Don't worry, everything will be a little blurred, like a Renoir painting. It's a sort of artistic effect," Mimi hurried to say, but her reassurance only seemed to disappoint Sonja a little. Her husband, Paul, gave Mimi an unfriendly, even hostile look, before they found their seats at one of the beer tables, where Luise and her husband were already sitting.

"Join us!" said Sonja.

"Gladly, but just for a minute, then I'll have to get back to work." With her camera on her lap, Mimi squeezed onto the bench with the others. "I want to breathe a bit of fresh life into the studio with some new, modern photos, lots of light, all in my very own style."

"We already know about your very own style," said Paul Merkle derisively. "But what if we here in Laichingen prefer the old style? One can't object to tradition, or do you disagree?" He looked around the table for support, garnering nods.

"Didn't you like the portraits I took of your daughter? I mean, you bought all three of them," said Mimi innocently. Turning to the others, she said, "Weddings, christenings, your children finishing school—with today's equipment, we have marvelous opportunities to preserve life's best moments photographically. Imagine how wonderful it will be to show your children and grandchildren pictures of what life was like before." She turned back to Paul Merkle for a moment and challenged him with her glance.

"An album of photographs is something I'd like very much," said Sonja admiringly. "I don't know why, but when you talk, I could listen for hours. You make everything sound so lovely and modern." She stroked her prominent belly. "Not much longer now, then we'll get christening photos made, won't we, Paul?"

"We'll see," her husband said. "Maybe we'll go down to Ulm for them."

"To Ulm? But why . . ." Sonja frowned.

"I love to take pictures of infants," said Mimi quickly. "They have such an innocence about them, and no wonder: they're a gift from God, after all. When the child comes in summer, perhaps we could set up the cradle beneath a wild rose bush." Her voice sounded dreamy. She'd been wanting to try a picture like that for a long time, but the photographers where she'd been a guest had always insisted on the classic "baby on the christening pillow."

Sonja Merkle beamed. "I don't think you're a photographer at all—I think you're an enchantress! When I think about how you photographed our Christel, like a fairy in a fairy tale."

"Fairy tale, enchantress—enough with all that nonsense. A photograph is a photograph, no more and no less," said Luise. "Josef Stöckle also knew how to do his job, you know."

Mimi nodded in agreement. "My uncle was my very best teacher. He would also be very happy if you came by as a customer again before too long."

"That's going to be difficult in the next few months," said a woman beside Luise. "On top of everything else, we're out working in the fields. No one has time for unnecessary stuff." The woman was around Sonja's age, perhaps forty, but Mimi had never met her before.

"What do you mean . . . ," Mimi began, but the talk at the end of the table had already moved to the Pentecost market at the beginning of June.

Paul Merkle stared at her with a spiteful smile.

No one had ever called her photographs "unnecessary stuff," Mimi thought grumpily as she stood up.

"Leaving already? The festival's just begun," she heard a male voice say behind her. It was Anton, just rounding the corner with a tray laden with beer glasses. "Can I treat you to a glass?"

"That's very nice of you, but no, thank you. I still want to take a few photographs of the *Hüle*. After that, when I've taken my uncle home again, I might go for a short hike out to the escarpment or somewhere." She shrugged. "If I'm going to be here for a while, I'd like to get to know the village, the people, and the region as well as I can."

Anton's expression brightened. "If you like, I could show you a few trails on my day off."

"Well, the people you run into!" said a woman who suddenly appeared behind Anton. She was carrying a tray of food, and she looked surly and smelled of sweat. "Is that beer supposed to get any warmer? Go and take it where it belongs."

"This is my mother, Karolina Schaufler," said Anton to Mimi, before he quickly left to obey his mother's orders.

"And I'm Mimi Reventlow. I'm Josef Stöckle's niece. Nice to meet you!" Mimi smiled at the proprietress of The Oxen.

"I'd be obliged if you didn't keep my son from his work," said the woman.

Mimi, surprised, could only watch as the woman turned and walked away.

Alexander Schubert stared glumly at the bare table before him. Most of his classmates had a glass of cider in front of them, but not Alexander. Before they left home for the festival, his mother had warned him and his sisters to only drink water. "So soon after confirmation, we don't have any money for anything special."

But there's money for Father's beer and schnapps, Alexander thought, looking at one of the nearby tables from the corner of his eye. His father had called the waitress over at least three times, and certainly not to make small talk. Why did he drink so much? No one knew better than he how tight money was. And there was Mother, sitting beside him, her lips pressed to a thin line. It seemed to Alexander that he could read her mind: next week, the soup would be even more watery than usual.

Alexander felt a light jab in the ribs. Vincent Klein, sitting beside him, pointed at Josef Stöckle's shop on the other side of the square. "Did you really make that sign?"

Alexander followed his classmate's gaze. From this distance, the letters were almost impossible to read, but the decorative curlicues in each corner were clearly visible. Maybe he should go over the letters one more time and make them a little darker.

"Yes, I did," he said proudly, and saying so made him feel a little better. He'd never had such a large piece of cardboard to work with in his life, and as relaxed as he'd made himself out to be in front of the photographer, he'd been trembling on the inside. What if he'd messed it up by making one letter bigger than the others or gone outside the lines he'd drawn? But his hand had been steady, and the pens he'd used had glided easily over the smooth surface.

"Wow! I wish I had a talent like that," said Vincent. "Maybe you could do a sign for old Helene, too? Or one of the factory owners?"

Alexander's classmate Fritz Braun, sitting across the table, chuckled. "They'd have to pay you really well!"

Alexander shook his head dismissively. "There are sign painters for that kind of thing, and I think they use a special kind of paint." Soon, he worried, the sun would probably fade Stöckle's shop sign.

Vincent let out a long, low hum, and Alexander had to grin. His classmate had done that as long as Alexander could remember, whenever he thought deeply about something. "If being a sign painter is a profession, then why don't you do something like that?"

"Or be a mapmaker," said Fritz. "In the atlas I was allowed to have in my confirmation photograph, each map was so detailed you could see every little creek and every twist and turn of the Danube. I could have looked at it for hours."

For a moment, the three boys fell silent.

Mapmaker, sign painter, designer—he'd take any one of them, Alexander thought. The idea of working with pens and ink and brushes and paint as a profession . . . He wrapped both arms around his body as if, like that, he could save himself from the ache of his unstilled hunger.

Anton suddenly appeared at their table, and he set a glass of cider in front of Alexander. "On the house," he said.

"Thank you!" Alexander looked up happily at his friend. He sipped the cider as devoutly as if it were communion wine, and immediately felt a little more grown up.

"I can carve pretty well," said Fritz abruptly.

"Since when can you do anything *well*?" said Anton, poking fun. Fritz pretended he was going to throw his glass at Anton, who walked away laughing.

"Actually, I love everything to do with wood," Fritz said.

Alexander looked at him. "So what do you carve?"

Fritz's cheeks turned red, and his admission suddenly seemed to embarrass him. "Believe it or not, *I* carved all the figures in our Christmas nativity scene, not my father." Alexander did not doubt him. Walter Braun, Fritz's father, was as depressive as his own. He probably spent hours staring off into nothing, too.

Fritz's eyes widened. "Mouths, noses, eyes. I carved all of 'em and did a fine job of it, if you ask me. And I even carved baby Jesus with curls. My mother whispered to me that our nativity was nicer than the one in the church."

Alexander raised his glass of cider when he saw Mimi Reventlow walking across the market square. She waved cheerfully to him and the others.

"That woman's really something," Fritz murmured.

Alexander laughed. "Something good or something bad?"

His classmate shrugged. "I don't know. At least she's not as boring as everyone else. I think the pictures she took of us were terrific."

"My father says that for our graduation photographs, they won't let her do any tricks like that," said Vincent unhappily.

"And my father says I'm not going to get a picture at all to save the money," said Alexander bitterly. "All because old Gehringer made fun of my picture. What business is it of his, anyway?" he asked, and he realized that, for a moment, he sounded just like Anton.

His two classmates nodded vigorously.

"Anyway," said Vincent. "Maybe it's better not to get any deeper into Gehringer's bad graces. If I don't get an apprenticeship there, all hell is going to break loose at our place."

That thought had already occurred to Alexander, but he kept it to himself.

"Don't worry so much," said Fritz. He stood up, walked around the table, and squeezed in between Alexander and Vincent, laying one arm across each of their shoulders. "What do you think? I'll look for a carpentry apprenticeship, Alexander will be a sign painter, and we'll find something for Vincent, too. Then Gehringer can go jump in the lake."

As Mimi crossed the square to the *Hüle*, she waved to the newly confirmed boys. Alexander looked worried, too worried for a boy his age. Would a positive response from the art school in Stuttgart cheer him up?

The day before, finally, a letter had arrived from her mother, although one could hardly call the short note a letter. Amelie Reventlow had all but written a telegram.

> *It has been absolutely hectic here! Forgive me for not writing sooner. A thousand thanks for your help. I'll write more in the next few days.*
>   *Mother*
> PS: *I will see to your request on behalf of the weaver's son, of course.*

Based on the note, Mimi believed that her more recent letter, in which she had written about her talk with the doctor and her decision to stay, had not yet reached her mother. If it had, then her mother would surely have written more than a few brief sentences, wouldn't she?

Mother's next letter will be interesting, she thought as she picked up her camera again. Photographs that reflected the sky or the surroundings in the water were often remarkably lovely.

Carpets of duckweed partially covered the surface of the old reservoir, and moss and grasses grew on the banks. It was good that the *Hüle* was no longer used for drinking water: it didn't look very appetizing at all, Mimi thought with a smile. From a photographer's perspective, however, the different shades of green had an appeal that translated even in black and white. Maybe she'd paint in a stork delivering a baby. Pictures like that made people smile and sold very well. Of course, she could also—

"Child, what are you taking a picture of there?" Uncle Josef called out. He shuffled from the bench in her direction. "You don't really think anyone's going to buy a picture of the old *Hüle*, do you? Or the church? We're not in the big city here. People don't have albums and collect pictures of everything from Bismarck to the Brandenburg Gate."

Mimi looked at him and smiled. "Maybe not yet, but things change. Besides, I don't want to sell photographs. I'm going to choose the best images and have *postcards* printed. Everyone loves postcards, and if the locals here in Laichingen don't like seeing their village at its very best, they would be the first. I'm going down to Ulm next week to look for a good printer."

"Postcards. I see."

"Trust me. Would you like a glass of beer? Anton was going to treat me to one earlier. Or are you hungry?" She looked at her uncle. The skin beneath his eyes was so translucent and his shoulders so slumped. It seemed coming to the festival had been too much for him.

"No, no. I'm a little tired." Josef smiled apologetically.

Mimi put one arm around her uncle's shoulders, and they strolled back to the house.

"I don't like to be a naysayer, but if you want to sell your postcards, you're going to have to get people into the shop. No one here in Laichingen has leisure time, certainly not in spring," Josef said.

Mimi heard again the woman's remark about "unnecessary stuff."

"I know it isn't easy to do business in Laichingen," she said, screwing up her nose. "But just the other day someone mentioned the Pentecost market, and I've decided to rent a stand and sell my postcards there."

"You've got an answer for everything, haven't you?" Her uncle laughed. "Although, your idea's not exactly new. I used to go to markets all the time. I took pictures and did fairly good business, all in all. Some of the people who come to the markets have deep pockets, and I can tell you this: the Laichingen Pentecost market is famous well beyond the village borders. You get dozens of hawkers coming in, selling all kinds of things. The local linen makers are also out in force. Shirts and blouses, aprons, table linens, bed linens—it's unbelievable how much they put out. Some young women come to buy their entire trousseaus." He stopped to catch his breath before going on, "There's many a weaver who's met the love of his life at the Pentecost market, and it's really no surprise: people come in from the villages all around. After the long winter, the market is the first big outing of the year for a lot of folk. Still . . . don't set your hopes too high, or your disappointment will be all the greater if your plans don't turn out how you'd like. People here are poor. Not everyone can afford the luxury of writing postcards."

Mimi raised her hands defensively. "Wait and see—they'll love my cards so much, they'll *have* to buy them!"

CHAPTER 34

While Josef napped, Mimi developed the glass plates. The festivalgoers. The *Hüle*. The church. The long street leading out of town to the train station.

The results were good, as she'd expected. But for her postcards, she would need more than just pretty pictures, so for the next two hours, Mimi ran back and forth between the darkroom in the cellar and the retouching desk in the shop, refining the pictures with all the tools and skill she had.

The first image she developed in the darkroom was the *Hüle*. She scrapped the idea of the stork and the baby: she suspected that jokey postcards like that would not go over as well out here in the country as they did in bigger places. Instead, with a little work, she soon had a family of swans drifting sedately on the surface of the pond—mother, father, and three little cygnets. She inserted the swan image using a kind of photo montage with a different glass plate in her collection, but to an observer, the birds looked as if they belonged right where they were.

Mimi scrutinized her work at arm's length. Proportions and outlines were so true to life that even a practiced eye would find it almost impossible to see that the swans had been added afterward.

Next, she attached the plate with the image of the May tree to Josef's retouching desk. *Greetings from Laichingen,* she wrote on it in sinuous black letters—when printed on paper, the letters would appear white. Writing on glass plates like that was a task Alexander would enjoy, Mimi thought, smiling to herself.

On a whim, Mimi took the glass plate and went back to the darkroom with it. She used another glass plate from her collection to add a border around the image. The finished product looked almost like an embroidered selvage. Then she had another idea. She quickly searched through the stack of new plates until she found the one showing the street that led from the edge of the village out to the station. Back at the retouching desk, she took a stylus and began to scratch letters onto the glass plate: *Laichingen: The Linen-Weaving Town!* The technique would result in black letters when the picture was printed on paper.

Finally, she went to work on the picture of the people enjoying themselves at the festival. She didn't want to fabricate anything for this image, but she gave Luise a more slender waistline, and her husband, Georg, a thicker beard. For the woman sitting beside Luise, who had a very high hairline, she drew in a few strands of hair over her forehead, and the woman immediately looked younger and less stern.

In two hours, her work was done. Her neck ached and she was hungry, but she was able to forget all of that when she looked at the four plates she'd worked on. They would make wonderful postcards, and she would take them down to Ulm on Monday and find a shop to print them for her.

"When you finish with that, you're done for the day."

Anton, who was putting away the washed and dried cutlery, turned to his mother in surprise. She was sitting at a table counting the money they'd taken in during the *Maienfest*. The stacks of coins were impressive.

Without looking up from her work, Karolina Schaufler went on, "You heard me. The inn's closed for the day. I have to go to the doctor, and hardly anyone comes in the day after the festival weekend, anyway."

"Are you sick?" His mother looked no different than she always did, Anton thought, and he was already wondering what he could do with all that time on his hands. There were not many options.

Instead of answering his question, his mother waved him over. She picked up one of the piles of coins. "Here, for you. You worked hard this weekend."

She must be very sick, Anton thought, and he quickly put the money away in his pocket.

"Let's go somewhere. We could spend the day in Blaubeuren, for example. There's a lake there that's bluer than the sky. It's called Blautopf, and there are all kinds of legends surrounding it. I read about it in a book I borrowed from Father Hildebrand. It's—"

"Are you crazy? Do you think I can just sneak away from home?" Christel interrupted him. She looked around frantically, then, with a wave, she signaled to him to follow her back to the chicken run, where they would be out of sight of her mother.

After he'd found himself unexpectedly free for the day, Anton had immediately gone to the Merkles' house. He knew exactly what he wanted to do with his time. He'd picked up a few small stones and had tossed them at Christel's window—their secret signal. Shortly afterward, Christel had come outside, a cleaning cloth in her hand.

"Mother wants me to clean all the winter dirt off the windows today," she said.

"We can go in the afternoon, then, when you're finished." Anton was disappointed. The idea of getting out of Laichingen for an entire day had been too wonderful. Maybe he had to make their little excursion more enticing? "One of the legends says there's a fairy that lives in the Blautopf. She's named Schöner Lau. Maybe she'll show herself to us? Though I'm sure you're a thousand times prettier than she is." He moved his hand delicately in the air as if he were stroking her golden hair and her cheeks as smooth and fine as porcelain.

Christel smiled. She liked it when Anton paid her compliments. She took his hand in hers for a moment.

"Guess what Susanne and Hilde said when I showed them my photograph." Her eyes sparkled expectantly.

Anton shrugged. "I have no clue." He didn't give a damn about her girlfriends' opinions. "But what about our little outing? Tell your mother you're going out with Susanne or Hilde!"

"Thank you for that sterling suggestion, but she'd see through that particular lie in two seconds. They both work in the factory, and my mother knows that only too well," said Christel reproachfully, but the next moment her eyes lit up again. "Susanne said I was beautiful enough to be a seamstress's model. And Hilde actually said I could be an actress in a movie! Me, in a film at the theater! Imagine it." She giggled excitedly.

"You'd be the best and most beautiful actress of them all." Anton's heart was beating so hard it hurt. "You're finally starting to dream of a better life. We should just leave, today! Why not?" he said, his voice filled with emotion. "I'll help you become an actress. We just have to get to know the right people. I've got one contact already, at Lake Constance—a woman who makes beauty products. I'm sure she could help us." He held his breath and looked at Christel. He'd do anything for her, anything and everything. In his mind he pictured the two of them, strolling arm in arm beside Lake Constance, on their way to important meetings . . .

"Wouldn't that be something," said Christel dreamily.

"We could go and visit her. Look! I've got money. We'd get a long way on this." Proudly, he held out the handful of coins his mother had given him.

"Christel!" Sonja Merkle's shrill voice destroyed the moment. "Where are you? Christel!"

The blissful expression on Christel's face vanished. "Enough dreaming," she said firmly. "But who knows? Maybe I'll get to be a model for Mr. Gehringer. My father hinted at that just the other day. Mr. Gehringer's always going to Stuttgart to have pictures of his nightshirts, aprons, and blouses taken. He's got two models who work for him there, but maybe he'll use me for his pictures instead?" An unusually brazen look appeared on her face as she spoke.

Anton was stunned. From film star to nightshirt model—could a career dream dissolve any faster than that?

"Forget Gehringer! Why do you want to stay a caterpillar when you can turn into a butterfly?"

He moved toward her as if he wanted to shake her awake, but Christel stepped back from him, aghast. "You're comparing me to a caterpillar?"

"It's just a figure of speech. I wanted to say—"

"I know perfectly well what you wanted to say. I'm not an idiot," Christel cut him off. "You think people have to go somewhere else to turn into a butterfly, that the people here are doomed to be ugly caterpillars for the rest of their lives. Thank you for making that clear to me." The look in her eyes had turned hostile, and the air between them was suddenly pure ice.

For a moment, Anton was afraid that, in his anger and dismay, tears would come to his eyes. Why did she twist his words like that? Couldn't she see that all he could think of was what was best for her?

"Then stay here and rot with your parents," he said angrily. "Be their slave and nanny. It's not the life for me."

"That's as clear as glass," Christel spat back.

CHAPTER 35

Mimi had mixed feelings as the train pulled into the main station in Ulm. She'd been looking forward to the trip very much, and to the kind of melancholic nostalgia she knew would come with it.

While there was business to do finding a printer, if she were honest with herself, Mimi also wanted to feel closer to Hannes. She had even considered a sentimental side trip to the wine bar on the banks of the Danube. To sit at the same table where they had sat together just over four weeks before, to dream about what might have been . . . and yes, she might have gone so far as to ask one or two discreet questions about where he might be now. The waiter at the café in front of the cathedral, for example, would certainly have known whether the unionist had held more speeches on the plaza, and perhaps the proprietor of the wine bar could have told her something about Hannes's whereabouts, too.

To do any of that, however, she would have to be alone. And Mimi was not alone. Anton Schaufler was at her side.

She had just left for the Laichingen station when she ran into Anton. "You look miserable," she'd said.

"That's how I feel," he'd replied. Then he'd told her about his free day and, in broad strokes, about the argument he'd had with Christel.

Mimi had only half listened before interrupting him. "I'm sorry, but I've got to get to the station. I've got some urgent business in Ulm."

"Ulm?" Anton's expression had brightened immediately. "Would you mind if I came with you?"

Mimi had hesitated. He didn't expect her to pay for his ticket, did he?

Reading her mind, Anton produced a handful of coins from his trouser pocket. "Don't worry. I've got enough money for a ticket and lunch."

Mimi had found no other reason to turn him down.

"Busy place!" said Anton the moment they disembarked. He rolled up the sleeves of his jacket in anticipation—he could hardly wait to throw himself into the commotion.

Mimi, on the other hand, needed a moment to adjust to all the hustle and bustle after quiet Laichingen. So many people! All in a hurry, all pushing and jostling to get out of the station as quickly as they could. Heads high, the women swinging their bags and the men brandishing their walking sticks—everything about them seemed to say: *Out of the way, and be quick about it!* Every one of them seemed to take themselves terribly seriously, Mimi thought with silent scorn, only to suffer a painful push in the back the very next moment.

"Watch where you're going!" Anton shouted after the man who'd barged past.

"He's probably got somewhere he has to be," said Mimi, then she made a beeline for the counter where the stationmaster stood. "Excuse me, but could you tell me where I can find a printer's shop in Ulm?"

"You'll find two or three down along the Danube," said the man, head down and scribbling frantically in a black book.

Along the Danube! Mimi's heart stumbled for a moment. It had to be a sign. Maybe she'd meet Hannes down there? *Don't be a fool,* she immediately told herself. The chances of bumping into the good-looking unionist a second time were slim at best.

She thanked the man for the information, but he didn't even bother to look up. "I'd completely forgotten how charming city folk can be," she murmured to herself wryly as she and Anton exited the station.

Once outside, and with as much conviction as possible, she said, "It's best if we each go our own way. You'd only get bored with me. There are two trains going back to Laichingen today. The second leaves before four, but you'll have to ask that friendly guy back there for the exact time." She had to be alone. On the final stretch, it had occurred to her to revisit the guesthouse where she'd spent her last night in Ulm four weeks earlier. Hannes had walked her to the door late that night. Maybe he'd gone back the following day and left an address for her?

But Anton was not about to be shaken off. "I don't think anything you do could be boring. If you don't mind, I'd like to come with you," he said brightly. He pointed toward the center of the city. "The sign says the Danube's that way."

Mimi didn't seem to have a choice. Besides, she realized Anton might have been a little uneasy in the city, since it was unlikely he visited Ulm very often. She glanced at various advertisements as they passed. There was a circus visiting the city, a charity holding a general meeting, and a furniture store promoting walnut cabinets. She saw nothing about any union-related events, though. *Then focus on your own business,* she chided herself.

Should she have the postcards printed on glossy card? Or was a matte finish better? She needed picture frames, too, and she hoped a printer might be able to send her to a good shop for them. It hadn't been very professional to have none available for the confirmation.

Mimi was so caught up in her thoughts that she ignored the many shops and lovely houses they passed. She'd almost forgotten Anton's presence, too, but in the middle of the plaza in front of the cathedral, he pulled at her sleeve and stopped them.

"Are we late? Do you have an appointment somewhere?" Anton looked at her curiously.

"No."

"Do you have to get home to your uncle on the first train back?"

"Not at all. Why do you ask?" Mimi frowned. Everything was taken care of. Luise had promised to look in on Josef and bring him a bowl of soup for lunch, and Mimi had hung a "Closed" sign on the door of the shop—not that she'd miss anyone by not being there.

Anton grinned at her. "Then why are you racing along as if the devil's at your heels?"

"Was I? I hadn't even noticed. You're absolutely right, I do have time." Mimi laughed. "I'll try to keep to a more leisurely pace, all right?"

Anton pointed to the window of a bookshop. "Jules Verne's *Around the World in Eighty Days*. I've read that. Father Hildebrand lends me one of his books now and then. He usually gives me ones that are supposed to be 'edifying'—you know, how to live a virtuous life, conversion stories, lives of the saints . . ." He screwed up his nose. "Not many exciting novels."

Mimi stepped closer to the window to see the display better. "That's a beautiful edition. Do you think my uncle would enjoy it?" It made her happy every time she saw Josef reading. As long as he could still do that, all was not lost.

"I'm sure he would," Anton said with conviction, holding open the door of the shop for her.

"I can already see how far I'm going to get with you," said Mimi with a laugh, but she stepped inside willingly.

They emerged a few minutes later, Mimi with the book for Josef in a paper bag, and continued on. A few shops farther, Anton stopped at the window of a fashionable boutique. "Pants for women?" he said in disbelief. "The women I know wouldn't even dare to say the word."

Mimi smiled when she saw a pair of black pants draped over a chair. "Believe it or not, there have always been women who've ventured to wear pants. But I *am* surprised to see them becoming fashionable for women. I think I'd like to try something like that on . . ."

"Would you like to know what I think?" asked Anton. "First, I can't imagine how you could look any better in trousers than in what you're wearing right now. And second, you already stand out enough in Laichingen without fashion like that."

Mimi laughed out loud. "Then let's forget it. I don't want to make anyone in Laichingen faint!"

The shop next door to the boutique advertised a phonograph "equipped with all the latest improvements."

"In the past, we heard music coming from your uncle's house all the time, but after his wife died, he stopped playing his records," Anton said. "It's a shame. The one man in the village with a phonograph and he doesn't use it. If I had something like that, I think I'd play it day and night."

Mimi looked at Anton thoughtfully. "Now that you mention it, the phonograph is sitting on the floor behind an armoire in my room, and it's been sorely neglected. I hadn't actually given it a thought."

They went into the shop, and Mimi bought a recording of operatic arias by Enrico Caruso. The salesman gave her a small pamphlet advertising various recent recordings, and also offered to send new records by mail. Mimi thanked the man and told him that if her uncle enjoyed the Caruso songs, she'd be more than happy to take him up on the offer.

"Books, records, beautiful cafés . . . I think I could get used to living in the city," said Anton, his face flushed, as he looked at the display in the window of the café on the banks of the Danube. "Everything looks so delicious!"

Small cakes, chocolate hearts, *Olgabrezeln* . . . Mimi's mouth was watering. It had been a long time since she'd eaten anything sweet.

"Shall we?" Anton asked, nodding toward the entrance. "A cup of coffee? My treat." He clinked the coins in his pocket.

Mimi raised her eyebrows in surprise. For an eighteen-year-old, Anton was very forward! She shook her head. "Work first, then we'll see."

Anton sighed dramatically. "I'm not going to say that you sound like my mother."

Mimi grinned, and they walked on. "There, that sign up ahead: Brauneisen Printing," she said. Two buildings beyond Brauneisen Printing, she saw another sign: "Printing, Engraving, Rubber Stamps." "Two printers so close together? That certainly makes things easy."

Anton nodded with satisfaction, as if he were personally responsible for that circumstance. Mimi enjoyed exploring the city with him. He was so excited by everything new that she also felt as if she were seeing it for the first time. Or was it more that she'd forgotten how invigorating a visit to a city could be? In contrast to Ulm, Laichingen felt cut off from everything. *We live in our own little world,* Gehringer had said, and his description was not far from the truth. The only question was whether Laichingen could ever be *her* world.

"Mimi Reventlow. Are you, by chance, the noted photographer they commissioned last year in Oberammergau? The official photographer for the Passion play?" With Mimi's pictures in one hand and a pencil in the other, the printing-shop owner looked up from his order book.

A real gentleman, thought Anton, admiring Otto Brauneisen's twirling imperial mustache. The man's jacket was tailored from a fine dark fabric that looked as if it would keep its wearer cool even on a warm day like today. Anton looked down at his own old jacket and suddenly felt very shabby.

"That was me, yes. But how do you know about that?" said Mimi with a surprised laugh. The Passion play in Oberammergau was performed only once every ten years and was a huge event, drawing visitors from around the empire and abroad.

"I have relatives in Ammergau," Brauneisen replied. "I always make a point to visit when the Passion play *is* being performed. They agree that no one has ever captured the crucifixion scene as powerfully as you and that you photographed the new stage perfectly, just marvelous." He made a small bow. "Madam, I am honored to take your order."

Mimi returned the gesture with a slightly forced smile. "I'd need the postcards a couple of weeks before Pentecost. Perhaps by May twenty-second or twenty-third at the very latest. Would that be possible?"

"No problem at all. I will have them to you sooner than that. Fifty each of four cards. You're in Laichingen at the moment, you said?"

Mimi nodded. "Yes, I am. And that's a relief. I plan to sell the post-cards at the Pentecost market in Laichingen. I've heard it's very popular and draws people in from everywhere."

"Not to worry, madam." Brauneisen consulted his calendar. "We'll deliver them to you on the nineteenth. I would suggest that we . . ."

Anton drank in every word of their discussion. For both Mimi Reventlow and the owner, problems seemed to exist for no other reason than to be solved. There were no complaints, no hesitation or dither-ing. He wanted to be as professional as that, to feel like a real business-man, to act without waiting for someone else to make a move. How he wished that for himself . . .

And how good it smelled in here. Of paper and printer's ink. Of good business and high society. Of the big, wide world.

"Oh, one more thing," Mimi said when Brauneisen had finished writing down her order. "I also need picture frames and photo albums. Would you know where I can find those in Ulm?"

The man smiled and indicated the door behind him. "I happen to have a very good selection in the next room, and in case we don't find anything to your liking, we could pay a visit to my printing facility in Münsingen on the other side of Laichingen. I have an even wider range there, and you could also see how your postcards will be printed—we don't do the actual printing here, you see, but there in the Swabian Jura."

Lucky she didn't know that ahead of time, thought Anton. If she had, she probably would have gone straight to Münsingen, and there wasn't much in Münsingen besides sheep. It was doubtful he would have gone there with her.

"Maybe I'll take you up on that another day," Mimi said. "I don't have the time right now." She raised her eyebrows and looked at the door behind the man for emphasis.

"Just let me turn the light on," said Brauneisen, opening the door with an effort. "After you!"

"That could not have gone any better," said Mimi when they left the printer's shop half an hour later. "Such a nice man, and so obliging. I can hardly wait to get my postcards, frames, and albums."

"You're really famous," said Anton, and there was more than a little awe in his voice. "Next to you, I feel like a village idiot with no idea about anything."

"Don't be too hard on yourself," Mimi said with a laugh. "If you hadn't sent the confirmands to me in advance, I might still be printing their photographs now instead of being here in Ulm. That was very helpful of you."

"I'll make sure everyone in Laichingen knows how famous you are," he said importantly.

"Just don't go telling any more stories about shortages or a lack of raw materials," Mimi said, jabbing him in the ribs. "Right, task number two: I need a few new props and accessories for the studio." Full of energy, and to Anton's delight, she headed toward the large department store he'd noticed on their way to the printer's. "Goods of Every Kind," read a large sign that filled two entire shop windows.

So many different things! Stationery. Tobacco and pipes. Toiletries for ladies and men. Anton didn't know which way to turn. If it had been up to him, they would have spent the rest of the afternoon in there.

He would look for a present for Christel, he decided on the spur of the moment, fingering the coins in his pocket, and go without lunch if he had to. He could always say he wasn't hungry. His stomach growled in protest at the thought, though. Maybe he'd just choose whatever was cheapest on the menu.

With the help of a young shop assistant, Mimi picked out a silver-plated hand mirror and matching hairbrush, hair ribbons in different colors, and several silk scarves with various patterns.

Anton surreptitiously made his own choice for Christel.

"For the next photographs I take, I want the women of Laichingen to feel extra beautiful," Mimi whispered to him while they were waiting to pay.

"That's a good idea," Anton whispered back. "But I can't honestly imagine my mother with a ribbon like that in her hair."

"Then who's that ribbon for, if not your mother?" With a sly smile, Mimi touched the pink ribbon in his hand.

"My girl!" said Anton brashly, and it felt good to say it.

With their shopping done, Mimi and Anton went to the café on the plaza in front of the cathedral.

"It is *so* nice to be able to sit at a table with a real tablecloth." Mimi was content with the day's work, and more at ease than she had been for a long time. Her buying spree had eaten a sizable hole in her funds, but right now that was the last thing she wanted to think about. Instead, she looked around the plaza, but saw neither a podium set up in front of the cathedral nor anyone preparing to deliver a speech.

"What made you decide to stay in Laichingen?" Anton asked.

"My uncle," Mimi said plainly. "I want to be there for him, as long as . . ." Her words trailed off.

"And afterward?" Anton asked, as if she'd finished her sentence. "Will you leave Laichingen again?"

Bet on it, Mimi thought, but she said, "Here and now, my uncle Josef is my first priority. I want to make sure that he is comfortable during his last days and weeks. I don't just want to feed him *Schwarzer Brei,* but something better now and then, something special. And if he has a good day, I'd like to bring him to The Oxen, too. But a good life costs money, so I urgently need to earn some."

Anton nodded knowingly. *What are your plans for the future?* Mimi wondered, but she kept the question to herself. Anton's mother hadn't left her with the impression that she'd give her son much freedom.

"I can hardly wait to see what women think of my new props," she said, changing the subject.

"It won't be easy to drag the Laichingers out of their shells," Anton said cautiously.

"You sound like my uncle," Mimi said with a giggle as the waiter arrived with their coffees.

"Your uncle knows how things work in Laichingen. I can't tell you how many ideas I've had for The Oxen. Maybe not all of them were good, but some certainly were. But no, my mother wants everything to stay old and dusty. In cities like Ulm or Munich or Stuttgart, there would be music playing and people dancing, but at The Oxen, it's like time's stopped. And it's always going to be that way." The young man's expression, so bright just a few moments before, had soured.

"You paint a very dark picture," said Mimi, her brow furrowed. "Maybe you can't turn your ideas into reality just yet, but what about when you start running The Oxen yourself?"

"I'll be an old man by then," Anton said, shaking his head.

Mimi said nothing. The waiter brought her apple strudel with cream, but the pastry had suddenly lost all its sweetness. Looking around the busy café brought home more than ever the contrast between the well-to-do city dwellers and the simple, hardworking weaver families.

Was she chasing an illusion when she thought she could earn a living with her photographs in a remote little village like Laichingen? So far, hardly anyone had actually visited her studio. What if all her ideas turned out to be a fantasy? If even the rebellious Anton was so skeptical about his hometown.

When Mimi thought of the expensive postcards she'd just arranged to have printed, the strudel suddenly sat as heavy as a log in her stomach. Would she be stuck with them in the end?

They still had an hour until the train back to Laichingen. Should she or shouldn't she? She thought it over for no more than a moment. "I've got one more thing to take care of. Let's meet at the station, OK?" she said. Before Anton could reply, she was already on her feet.

The proprietress of the guesthouse was sweeping the pavement outside when Mimi arrived. The woman's face brightened instantly when she saw Mimi. "The traveling photographer! How lovely to see you! Do you need a room?"

"Thank you, no. I'm still at my uncle's house in Laichingen," said Mimi. "It's just . . . I wanted to ask if by any chance a man came by after I left last time and left an address for me?" She held her breath.

The woman's brow creased as she thought for a moment. "Not that I know of . . ."

"All right. I just thought I should check. Thank you." Mimi struggled to hide her disappointment. *You and your delusions,* she thought sadly as she walked away, her shoulders slumped.

A short time later, the proprietress's husband appeared from inside the house. "Wasn't that the photographer who stayed here a few weeks ago?"

His wife nodded. "She wanted to know if a man had left an address for her. Probably some business matter. But there wasn't anyone, was there?"

"Actually, yes," said the man, to his wife's surprise. "Let me think . . . The photographer had just left when a man came by. He looked rather unkempt and carried a linen sack on his back. Was he a business-man? He didn't leave an address, but he did ask where the photographer was traveling next."

"And?" the landlady asked eagerly.

Her husband shrugged. "I thought about it for a moment. I wasn't sure if I should tell the man anything, you know. But in the end, I said that Miss Reventlow was on her way to Laichingen. It wasn't meant to be a secret, was it? Or was it?"

CHAPTER 36

Eveline cracked eggs into a cast-iron pan. An unpleasant smell rose from the pan. Rancid fat? She didn't want to think about the possibility that one of the eggs was bad. She couldn't throw away a whole pan of scrambled eggs.

"We have to get the turnips and cabbage seedlings into the ground. But instead of helping us get the soil ready, you're working twelve hours a day at the factory instead of the usual ten. How much longer is this going to go on?"

Klaus stuffed the last piece of bread into his mouth and shrugged at his wife. "Paul Merkle says we've got big orders coming in every day, and we'll only meet them if we work overtime. I have to get back. The second shift starts soon." Already at the door, he looked intently at her, as if to say, *Don't you start on me now, too.*

"You're always leaving. If only we'd left for somewhere different, like I begged you to back then, in Chemnitz," said Eveline bitterly.

Klaus crumpled as if she'd hit him, but then for a moment she saw something light up in his eyes, a spark of life and the question: *What if . . . ?*

"But we didn't. We came here," he said. "And we stayed. For love." Then he closed the door behind him.

For love! Eveline laughed spitefully. Love dies, hunger stays. If only someone had told her that back then.

Alexander came in with his sisters. He looked at the pan of scrambled eggs, then at Eveline. "Mother? Is everything all right?" he asked. "We just saw Father outside, but he didn't even look at us. Don't we have to go to work in the fields?"

"Not now. Sit and eat," said Eveline. She dished out the scrambled eggs and stroked her son's hair absently. In her mind, she was far away.

Yes, she'd stayed. For love.

She could still remember her arrival in Laichingen as if no time had passed at all. After a hard journey in packed train compartments, they'd arrived in the village. Eveline had been exhausted and chilled to the bone. All she could really think about was taking a hot bath. Filled with the pride of ownership, Klaus had carried her over the threshold of the tiny house, which was in the middle of a row of nearly identical houses separated from one another by just a few feet of land. Eveline had seen the straw roof and asked in confusion why they had to spend their first night in Laichingen not at his house but in a barn.

"This *is* our house," Klaus had said earnestly.

His parents had died when he was young, and none of his siblings had reached adulthood. Klaus was the only Schubert still alive. "There isn't anyone my age in the village who owns his own house," Klaus had told her proudly.

When he had called this shack a *house*, Eveline had been bowled over. And over and over and over. Even today, she hadn't managed to get back on her feet. That moment, then, on the threshold . . . that was when she should have turned around and set off for home again. She would have been able to explain to her parents somehow. A regrettable mistake, no more. But there were Klaus's blue eyes and the way he looked at her, his gaze so heartfelt that it went right through her, and she found the joy of love in his arms.

Soon after, her father's letter arrived. In a few words, Karl-Otto Hoffmeister had told her that, from that day forth, she was dead to him. The door to her old life had slammed shut. She never heard from her parents again, and she had never tried to contact them.

Eveline sighed deeply. This was all she had. "Why are you sitting there gawking?" she snapped at the children, who had emptied their plates and were waiting for her to tell them what to do. "Erika, come here. We're going to fix up your braids. We all want to look our prettiest today."

"Pretty?" The seven-year-old's face reflected her confusion.

Eveline almost burst into tears. "Yes, pretty," she said, her voice betraying her emotion. "When we're done with you, it's Marianne's turn."

In her old life, Eveline's mother had placed great store in the word "pretty." The big mansion had been *pretty* top to bottom: fabulous flower arrangements, embroidered proverbs in frames on the walls, crocheted blankets on the sofa.

Eveline would have liked a pretty house, too, but she had no time and no money for it. Maybe the most basic evil of all wasn't the lack of money or even all the work. No, it was the fact that she could never, even for a moment, do something she actually enjoyed.

But that was about to change, at least for today! Eveline dug into an old flowerpot in which she'd hidden a few coins for emergencies. When she saw how little money she actually had, she almost changed her mind, but she took a deep breath and said, "Girls, we're going to visit that nice woman at the photo studio, and we're each going to have our picture taken. Won't that be fun?" She looked at her girls with excitement.

"But we still have to finish the weeding." Alexander frowned.

"The weeds aren't going anywhere," Eveline said. Yes, she had a thousand other things to do, and maybe she was just being sentimental. Or foolish. But when Mimi had talked about pictures of her children to remember them by, she'd struck a chord with Eveline, one she hadn't heard in a very long time.

Love.

She loved her children, and she wanted a photograph of each of them as a memory. She'd been gifted Alexander's confirmation picture, so she could afford this extra expense, just this once, she thought, justifying her plan to herself.

"Mama, I don't feel good," said Marianne, her face suddenly chalk white. "I think I'm going to throw up."

Damn! One of the eggs had been bad after all. Eveline quickly pulled her daughter over to a bucket. The cheap print on the wall of *The Broad and Narrow Way* caught her eye. *Does God actually mean the path to be so narrow?* she wondered as Marianne gagged and vomited into the bucket. So narrow that you rubbed yourself raw on its narrowness? So narrow that you couldn't breathe? Or was it rather the devil himself who'd set her off along this road?

As Mimi swept the kitchen, the scent of spring and good cheer and soap wafted in. *How lovely it smells today,* she thought. She looked outside through the open window, where a line of freshly washed laundry hung. She smiled. It seemed, after all, that she could take care of a house and her uncle, too. She was just shaking out the blanket that her uncle wrapped himself in for his afternoon naps when the mailman pulled up in his horse-drawn wagon, and Mimi saw several cardboard boxes and crates on it. Mr. Brauneisen's shipment of frames, albums, and postcards! *Perfect!* she thought. *He promised it would arrive by today.* She hurried outside. "Put everything here in the shop, thank you!" she said.

Grumbling to himself, the mailman carried the boxes into the shop, and Mimi signed the delivery receipt.

The mailman was almost back on his seat again when he said, "I almost forgot. I've got a letter for you, too." Mimi's face brightened even more.

As the wagon rolled away, Mimi sat down on the steps in front of the shop and quickly tore open the envelope. The sun shone like a spotlight on the crackling letter paper.

> *Esslingen, May 13, 1911*
>
> *Dearest Mimi,*
> *It was with the deepest humility that I read your most recent letter. It is such a comfort to me that Josef is not alone in these difficult days. I thank you from the bottom of my heart for all you have done for him.*

Mimi frowned. That was well and good, but what else did her mother have to say about the matter? She read on.

> *I would so gladly be there to help you. I would cook a good soup for Josef or read to him. But God has once again burdened me with so many duties that I haven't even been able to write to you until today.*
> *The last few weeks in the Reventlow household have been so busy.*

Nothing new about that, Mimi thought.

> *I have had the honor to be elected to the committee of the state association that oversees provisioning of the poor. At the same time, the General German Women's Association has asked me if I would be able to write an essay on the need for adequate support of domestic servants. It is to*

*be published in a handbook that aims to be the standard
work for running a household. The book is supposed to
be printed this coming summer, so there is some urgency,
and I have said yes to both projects! It is so important for
someone to stand up for the weaker members of our society, a sentiment which I am certain you share. I promise
you one thing faithfully, however: as soon as my time
allows, I will come to Laichingen and take over from you.
Seeing Josef again lies close to my heart. There is so much
that binds us, after all. In the meantime, please give my
brother my love and best wishes.*

Mimi lowered the letter. For a moment, she didn't know whether
to laugh or cry. What had she really expected? That her mother would
drop everything and, overcoat billowing, come to Laichingen? The truth
was that Mimi was on her own—and she had known as much when
she wrote to her mother. She was about to put the letter back in the
envelope when she noticed a second sheet of paper inside.

*Dearest Mimi,
Now to your request, which I am answering separately in
case you wish to hand this letter on.
First, let me say how happy it makes me to see you
standing up for young Alexander Schubert. Helping those
who have no voice of their own . . . The apple doesn't fall
far from the tree.
As far as your talented protégé is concerned, I have
not been idle, and despite all my other obligations under-
took a trip to Stuttgart. The director of the Stuttgart Art
School, Wilhelm Hahnenkamm, is a very busy man, but
by pure coincidence I happen to know his cousin. She
and I . . .*

Will you get to the point! Mimi thought, while her mother explained the various charitable deeds she and the cousin had undertaken together.

> *It was possible for me to arrange an appointment with the gentleman at relatively short notice. I presented him with Alexander's drawings and what can I say? You were right in your estimation. The director sees great potential in Alexander's work.*

Mimi's mouth was growing drier and drier in her excitement. Alexander was to go to Stuttgart for an admissions examination! If he was accepted, a scholarship would not be out of the question. The school only needed the young man's address so that they could send him an official invitation to the admissions examination.

Dazed, Mimi looked up from the letter. Her heart was pounding, and for a moment Mimi did not know why. Was it the good news she had been hoping for so very much? Or was it because neither Alexander nor his parents had the slightest idea of her endeavors on his behalf?

CHAPTER 37

It was almost three in the afternoon when Eveline made her way toward the photo studio with her two daughters—Marianne felt much better once the egg was out of her system—and Alexander at her side. Eve did not know why he'd insisted on going with them, but she hadn't made him stay home. Did he perhaps hope that the photographer would give him another good sheet of paper to draw on?

Eveline had just stepped through the front gate of Josef Stöckle's garden when she saw Luise and Sonja waving to her.

"Come back for a minute!" Sonja called.

Mother and daughter were doing the laundry. Eveline walked through Josef Stöckle's garden and past the studio to exchange a few words with them.

"What brings you here? Have you come to complain about Alexander's confirmation picture after all?" said Luise, with a glance toward the studio.

"What would I have to complain about?" Eve asked. "I've actually come to have photographs of my girls taken."

"Oh, that's lovely," Sonja said as she looked at the two girls.

Eveline smiled. "Yes, I want to have a nice memory of their childhood days," she said.

"If you think it's worth it," said Luise uncertainly.

But Sonja exclaimed, "Photographs of your children as a keepsake—Miss Reventlow has some wonderful ideas."

Eveline nodded. "And she certainly understands her trade."

"She does indeed, but . . ." Sonja gestured to Eveline and her mother to come closer. "Imagine," she whispered, "yesterday afternoon, when I was on my way to Helene's store, Miss Reventlow was sitting on the steps in front of the house, her face in the sunshine—reading a letter! And I heard music playing on Traudel's old phonograph inside, too. Just let me try something like that—Paul would chew my head off! And he'd be right to do it, too. Hard work is the right hand of happiness, and thrift the left. The photographer should spend some time working on Josef's vegetable patch. It looks terrible."

Eveline smiled inwardly. She was starting to like Mimi more and more, and she decided to take her side. "Doesn't it say in the Bible: 'They sow not, neither do they reap, yet your heavenly Father feedeth them'? If I could, I think I'd live my life doing what I love, just like Miss Reventlow does."

"There's nothing wrong with Josef's niece," Luise said, shifting the subject a little. "She just never learned how to run a house. I trained my two girls well in *that*, at least." She looked at Sonja, who had gone back to scrubbing at the washboard. "When our Berta gets married in August, she'll be another hardworking wife."

Luise's second daughter would do better to rethink the whole thing, Eve thought.

"I have to go," she said, but just then Edelgard Merkle came around the corner of Luise's house. Eveline felt a flush of guilt at the sight of the seamstress: she still owed her payment for her work on Alexander's jacket.

Sonja looked at her mother-in-law in surprise. "What are you doing here? What's the matter with Paul?"

"There's nothing wrong with him," Edelgard said, calming her pregnant daughter-in-law. "But you'll never guess who wrote to me." She flapped a letter in the air excitedly.

"Johann?" all three women cried at once.

Edelgard nodded. Her eyes suddenly filled with tears as she said, "He's coming home. Forever, if I've read his letter right. Lord have mercy, he's sending me my child." She crossed herself. "I'm off to the church to light a candle in gratitude."

Eveline's heart was suddenly beating in her throat. Her cheeks flushed red, and she quickly kneeled and busily began to adjust Marianne's shoelaces—no one should see her response.

"The letter was mailed in Munich a few days ago. That must mean he'll be here in the next few days." Edelgard looked from one woman to the other excitedly.

"When Paul finds out . . . ," said Sonja, and she didn't look particularly happy at the thought.

Her mother raised her eyebrows. Everybody in Laichingen knew the two Merkle brothers did not see eye to eye.

While the other women talked about why Johann would be returning to Laichingen, Eve did her best to breathe normally.

Johann Merkle. For a time, she had seen him as a way out of her miserable marriage. She had never given much thought to how that would actually happen, however, and not much would have come of it if she had. But she had dreamed about him, and in her dreams anything was possible.

Johann Merkle . . .

Johann had had his eye on her, too. Eve had been well aware of that eight years ago. Marianne was just born, and Erika not yet conceived. The way he looked at her across the pews in church, when no one else could see, and the way he swept her across the makeshift stage when they danced together at the *Maienfest*, and the effort he had to make to hold back his unspoken words. *I understand you only too well,* Eveline would have murmured to him. *I feel just the same.*

She hadn't only dreamed of Johann at night. And recently, more and more often, he had been creeping into her thoughts during the day, too. How would it be to sit with him at the table instead of with Klaus and his melancholy? Johann's passion for her certainly would not die as quickly as her husband's had. Klaus preferred to cry in his sleep instead of taking her in his arms. Johann would talk with her, would pay attention to her and not look through her as if she were air most of the time. He'd kiss her, stroke her hair, speak words of encouragement when she needed them. They would get through their days *together,* not each for themselves. Dreams . . . some days, Eveline could not bear life without them.

What could never be would never be, however. She was a married woman, and Johann Merkle an honorable man. When he had left, Eveline was even a little relieved. But now he was coming back. And it had to be now, now when she felt as if the burden of making it from one day to the next was enough to break her. It was a sign. Providence. Eve would have liked nothing more than to light a candle in the church herself.

"I can hardly wait to see him again," said Edelgard, her voice choked with tears.

Neither can I, thought Eve.

"I don't believe it," Mimi said the moment Eveline stepped through the door. "I was just on my way to find you." The photographer, the key already in her hand, looked from Eveline to the children and back. "You must have read my mind."

Alexander saw the way his mother stiffened inwardly and retreated like a snail when you tap its shell too hard. She'd been acting strangely just now, too, talking with the neighbors. Did she suspect the worst, yet again? The photographer wasn't like other people. She didn't have a scrap of ill will in her, as he'd seen for himself the first time he visited her. She'd taken so much time to teach him a little about the techniques of retouching, and she'd had him make the sign for her shop. Alexander smiled at the memory. He could have sat and sketched in there for hours.

Ever since, he'd been hoping for another opportunity to visit the photographer, but he'd been unable to come up with a good enough reason, and after his father had been so upset about the confirmation photograph, it was probably for the best, he'd told himself. And yet . . . when Anton told him about the day he'd spent with her in Ulm, Alexander had been filled with envy.

"Do you want to be paid for the confirmation photo after all?" his mother asked cautiously.

Alexander's jaw tightened. God, couldn't she see how the photographer's eyes sparkled? How cheerful she looked?

"My goodness, no! What makes you think that?" Mimi said in confusion. "Come inside. We have to talk about something that we can't just in passing." She winked conspiratorially at Alexander. The day was getting stranger and stranger, he thought.

"I'd like to have my daughters' pictures taken, but I have to ask what it costs first," his mother said, once they were inside the studio.

"Children's pictures cost the same as adults'. The work is the same. But I have quite a selection of toys I can photograph the children with. Porcelain dolls, a spinning top, even a rocking horse." The photographer pointed to the platform. "Maybe your daughters would like to try them out? There's another matter we need to discuss, and it's urgent."

Marianne and Erika looked wide-eyed at their mother, and when she nodded they jumped onto the platform, where they were soon squealing with delight as they played with the dolls and other toys. Watching them, Alexander and the women had to smile.

"What do you have on your mind?" his mother said, more positive now.

Mimi Reventlow nervously tucked some loose strands of hair back into place. "I don't really know where to begin."

Alexander frowned. Suddenly, the photographer was acting more like an anxious schoolgirl than a woman of the world. His frown gave way to surprise when he saw his mother smile.

"Just come out and say whatever's on your mind."

The tension eased and both women laughed. Like he and Anton did, companionably. His mother seemed to like the newcomer. That was good.

"It's about you, Alexander," Mimi began.

"Do you want me to draw or paint something else for you? I'd love to." His heart beat faster.

"Oh, not now, but perhaps another time. It's like this: some time ago, my uncle showed me a few drawings that you did for him. Squirrels, birds, butterflies, that kind of thing. Nature studies, all exceptionally detailed. I was thrilled to see them."

Alexander saw the crease between his mother's eyes, and he was also wondering where the photographer was going.

Mimi chewed her lip for a moment, then said, "Acting on an impulse, I included the pictures in a letter to my mother. She lives in Esslingen and has contact with the director at the Stuttgart Art School."

A sudden humming in Alexander's ears was so loud that he was afraid he'd faint.

"And?" he croaked, as if his voice were still breaking.

"What can I say?" The photographer lifted her hands helplessly, then her mouth stretched into a broad grin. "He was very impressed by your illustrations. They want to invite you to take an admissions examination, and there might also be a scholarship involved. That would mean—"

"I know what a scholarship is," his mother interrupted. "My God, you've really done all that? I'm so excited I can hardly breathe!" She squeezed Alexander's hand so hard it hurt.

He was so dizzy himself that he had to hold on to the nearest piece of furniture, the prop closet, to stay on his feet. Him, in Stuttgart, for an admissions exam! And a scholarship! That would mean that he could finally learn how to paint. Wait until he told Anton—he'd be the one to damn near die with envy!

"When my mother's letter came a little while ago, I nearly jumped through the roof with joy. I'm so happy for you!" Mimi impulsively grasped his left hand while his mother still held on to his right.

The moment suddenly seemed so crazy to Alexander that he laughed out loud, but his laugh came out raw, as if it were rusty. "First of all, I have to pass the admissions exam. After that we'll have a reason to be happy," he said stiffly, but deep inside he sensed that this was the most wonderful moment of his life.

Mimi let go of his hand, turned, and hurried away, and when she came back, she had a sketch pad and a pencil in her hand. "All I need is your address so the art school can send you an official invitation." Mimi looked expectantly at his mother, but her distracted look had returned.

"Mother?" Why didn't she say anything?

"Is everything all right?" the photographer asked. "You're not angry at me, I hope. I know I should have talked to you about it first, but I really didn't want to get your hopes up."

To Alexander's relief, he saw a faint smile appear on his mother's lips. "What you've done is . . . a very good thing," she said softly. "In all these years, no one has had a kind word for Alexander's talent. I know I'm no expert, but I can well imagine he would have a good chance at an admissions test like that. I'm very proud of him . . ." She turned to face him then, and went on, "Believe me, I will do everything I possibly can so you can take this opportunity. But please don't be too hopeful." Her voice was a mere breath now, which perhaps would explain why her words thrummed in Alexander's ears like an approaching thunderstorm.

"Don't be so skeptical," Mimi said. "The professors in Stuttgart wouldn't invite just anyone, only those young people who show real talent."

"I'm not talking about Stuttgart," his mother said sharply. Alexander knew what was coming. "It's my husband. He won't like this at all. On the contrary, he'll . . . he'll be furious when I tell him." She blinked and swallowed hard.

Before his mother could stop him, Alexander snatched the pad from the photographer's hands and scribbled their address. "I'm not going to let Father ruin this for me!" he cried, feeling a lump forming in his throat. *Don't start bawling now,* he thought.

"Oh, my boy . . . most dreams in this world burst like soap bubbles. You still have to learn that," his mother said sadly. She turned to Mimi. "People here would call us lunatics if they knew what we were talking about. Look around. Since you've been here, have you seen a single person dare to follow their own desires? In Laichingen, the sons live like their fathers and the daughters like their mothers—that's all there is in God's great plan. They even preach it from the pulpit." Imitating Father Hildebrand's sonorous voice, she said, "'Verily, verily, I say unto you, The Son can do nothing of himself, but what he seeth the Father do: for what things soever he doeth, these also doeth the Son likewise.'" She snorted with derision. But her outburst of emotion, as powerful as it was, passed quickly. In a calm voice, she said, "If we're lucky, we'll see Alexander sitting at a loom at Gehringer's, like his father." Then she added bitterly, "But only if my husband and I continue to do our work and I am not constantly late with my embroidery."

Gehringer! Everything always comes back to him! Alexander thought. Why couldn't the man just drop dead? He, for one, wouldn't shed a tear.

Mimi furrowed her brow. "Don't lose heart yet. Who knows, maybe your husband won't react like you think he will at all. And if he does, well, I can think of a fitting passage from the Bible. Psalm 18, verse 29, says: 'By my God do I leap over a wall.'" She looked from Alexander to his mother. "Maybe it's time to try a giant leap?"

CHAPTER 38

Other than Eveline, no other customers appeared that Friday afternoon, so Mimi closed the studio at half past five. Instead of going straight into the house, she went around to the shop first and picked up a small stack of the new postcards. As she held the different designs in her hand, she breathed in the scent of printer's ink—for Mimi it smelled like the finest perfume. She beamed. It had been a thoroughly good day.

Her uncle had had a visitor, an elderly neighbor who dropped in for a chat and a glass of schnapps. Now Josef sat by himself at the kitchen table, his cheeks flushed pink and in a fine mood, and Mimi's smile only got broader. Had the doctor perhaps been mistaken after all? Would Josef get better?

As the previous day's soup warmed on the stove, she proudly presented her postcards to her uncle. "Look how lovely Laichingen can be," she said.

She had decided not to say anything to her uncle just yet about Alexander's big opportunity. He'd made it very clear to her that he thought getting mixed up in other people's business was a mistake. If he found out that she'd gone ahead and done it, he'd only get upset.

Josef laughed brightly. "Swans on the *Hüle*! Child, you have some ideas. Now the only question is: Will they sell, or gather dust?"

"They'll go like hotcakes," Mimi joked.

"It'll be fine," Josef said. "But don't think you're the only one with good ideas. Your old uncle has his moments, too."

"Oh yes?" Mimi raised her eyebrows cheerfully. It was so wonderful when he was feeling better and was so active. Just the day before, he'd gotten out the oil paints and worked over some of the clouds on one of his backdrops. His hand had been shaking so much that the clouds now looked like frayed scraps of linen, but Mimi didn't care. Josef could do whatever he liked if it made him happy.

"I already told you that I used to open the studio on Sundays. Maybe you should think about doing the same. In the spring and summer, everybody goes out after work and slogs in the fields until dark. Sunday is the only day they could possibly visit you in the studio. And after church, they're already dressed to the nines."

Mimi clapped her hands and threw her arms around her uncle. "Of course! I'll start the Sunday after the Pentecost market. But first I have to take care of my table at the market. You know what I was thinking? I'd love to have a wooden stand I could use to present each of the four different postcards. It would be something I could also put in the window of the shop later on. Do you know if there's someone in the village who could make something like that for me? I've already made a sketch of what I want." She held out the drawing to her uncle. It was a stand she'd once seen that she'd liked very much, and she had sketched it from memory.

Her uncle's smile faded. "Our carpenter passed away last autumn, and there's been no one to take over. Maybe our wagonmaker, Mr. Meindl, could help you. His workshop is on the street behind Helene's store. Say hello from me, he's a good fellow."

Mimi left the house in a better mood than she'd been in in a long time. Luise was hanging the wooden washtubs on the wall in front of her house, and the two women smiled and waved at each other before Mimi turned toward the front gate and the market square.

Farther down the street, Vincent Klein's mother sat in front of her house repairing a woven basket, Karolina Schaufler was briskly sweeping the entry of The Oxen, and a group of older men had gathered at the front of Helene's store to talk. Mimi exchanged a few words here and there. The village had seemed practically dead on her midwinter arrival, but was now full of life, though most seemed in a hurry to get home or get out to their fields. All but the so-called finer folk, as Luise liked to call the businessmen and their families—Mimi saw them sometimes driving through the village in a horse-drawn coach, but never encountered any of them on foot. Did they go down to Ulm to shop? Or did they have things delivered? Mimi hoped that they, too, would find the time to visit the Pentecost market in search of nice things, and she already pictured throngs of people crowding her stand.

"Sorry, ma'am," said the wagonmaker after a quick glance at Mimi's sketch. "I couldn't take on a job like that before autumn. I've got so many tools to fix right now, I'm dreaming about pitchforks, ladders, and handcarts in my sleep. Next please!" He waved the next customer forward.

Mimi stepped aside and promptly bumped into a washtub that had a hole in one side as big as the palm of her hand. The little workshop was so full of farm tools and other equipment that it was difficult even to turn around. What now? She looked down at the piece of paper in her hand, completely at a loss.

"Couldn't you perhaps make an exception? The Pentecost market is still a good two weeks away," she said hopefully.

The man only shook his head.

She left the workshop disappointed. Where was she supposed to find her postcard stand with so little time left? A frown on her face, she walked so quickly back in the direction of the market square that she almost ran into the horses pulling a wagon that came around the corner just then. One of the horses whinnied in fright.

"Watch out there, young lady!" the driver shouted.

Dazed, Mimi stopped in her tracks. An accident with a wagon—wouldn't that be the icing on the cake?

"Now it's *you* who looks miserable," said Anton, who'd just come out of The Oxen.

Mimi exhaled loudly and unhappily, then she told him what had happened.

Anton's expression clouded. "Typical Laichingen, again." He turned to where the wagon had just pulled up and shouted to the driver: "Start unloading. I'll be right there." The driver grumbled, but did as he was told.

"What about your gift from Ulm?" Mimi asked, not wanting to burden Anton with her bad mood. "Was it appreciated?"

"I think it was," said the young man with a grin. "Look, I've got an idea for you. Can I see the drawing?"

"Do you know someone who can help?"

Anton concentrated on the sketch for a moment. "There is someone who says he's good with wood. He's . . . ," he began, then paused. "Don't worry about it. Count on me: I'll come up with a display stand for you."

Baffled, Mimi watched Anton put her sketch in his pocket as he turned and went to help the driver unload.

Early in his career, Herrmann Gehringer had made it his habit to tour his factory twice a day. He would start at the warehouse, where the linen was packed and dispatched. The next door opened into the raw materials storage. He had a warehouse manager, of course, but Gehringer himself checked every day whether they had enough yarn to weave the linen for the orders they had to fill. Usually, they had plenty in stock, but better safe than sorry, he liked to tell himself. After that, he looked in on the seamstresses. There was rarely anything there to find fault with, and he occasionally allowed himself a joke with the women, who always laughed shyly. Sometimes he praised one or another of them about their work, but not too often—he didn't want anyone getting a big head. His last stop was always the hall where the looms rattled away. It was the heart of his operation, and keeping an eye on things in there was crucial.

He varied the times of his rounds every day—he was no fool. If his workers knew what time he would show up, they'd adapt. But like this, although his visits were not unexpected, their timing always came as a surprise. His people had to be on top of things at all times so that he found nothing to complain about. And there were, in fact, days on which he found nothing to complain about. And then there were Mondays like this one.

Gehringer had started his rounds in the shipping department, where everything looked to be in order until he noticed one package that was about to be mailed with torn wrapping paper around it. He should have known immediately that it was an omen.

"What are you doing?" he asked the warehouseman. *You idiot,* he felt like adding. But Gehringer prided himself on treating his employees well. They heard no angry expletives from him. "That must be repacked. If the customer returns the goods because they arrive soiled or damaged, it's more expensive for us than another sheet of wrapping paper now."

Shaking his head, Gehringer turned and left. *If I didn't watch every detail, every minute . . .*

He walked toward the sewing workshop. He loved the brisk hum of the sewing machines, of which he had twenty in all. But when he pushed open the door, he could hardly believe his eyes. Instead of sitting at their machines, the women were standing around and . . . eating cake!

Herrmann Gehringer let out a bewildered laugh. "Well, pardon me for disturbing your little coffee circle."

Some of the women tried to hide their pieces of cake behind their backs guiltily. A few stuffed a last piece into their mouths, which didn't improve matters at all.

"It's my birthday," said one of the women quietly. "I turned fifty today." Her cheeks had flushed a fiery red, like a schoolgirl caught copying someone else's work. "I brought cake for everybody."

"Oh, and none of you had anything better to do than eat it during work time?" Gehringer looked angrily from one woman to the other.

"But it's lunchtime," said the woman.

Gehringer whipped out his pocket watch. It was just before half past one. From one to half past one was, in fact, lunchtime. "You know perfectly well that it's forbidden to bring food into this room. It's a *sewing* room. You'll mess up the linen."

"Where are we supposed to go? The canteen is closed because of the rats," another seamstress said. "The rat catcher says we're not allowed back before next Monday because the poison is too dangerous, and we didn't want to stand outside."

"Did the rat catcher also tell you why the rats were there in the first place?" Gehringer snapped at the woman. "Because people are always leaving food scraps behind. Right, half past one." He clapped his hands. "Pack every crumb away this instant and get back to work, or I'll be forced to dock each of you a half hour's wages." After striking his walking stick against the floor to punctuate his point, he left. He could only hope that things were running better in the weaving mill.

But that hope, too, was soon shattered.

From the door, Gehringer immediately saw that three of his twenty looms weren't running.

Benno Klein was leaning over his machine, knotting threads. "A warp break," he said. "It's the shuttle. Sorry. It's one of those things." Gehringer took a deep breath and exhaled. What the man said was true. A flying shuttle breaking the warp threads was neither predictable nor preventable. Nevertheless, the repair, which involved knotting dozens of warp threads, would take a good hour of Klein's time. "Hurry it up," he said. "And do a clean job. I don't want to see any other errors come of it."

In the next row, Kurt Kleinmann was changing out several bolts. "One of them had too much play, but I'm not sure which," the man said, sweat running down his face.

"But you can *hear* something like that," Gehringer shouted. "Why do you have ears? So I can box them for you?" Before he said anything worse, he turned away, and saw immediately that the third loom out of commission was Klaus Schubert's. The weaver stood at the side of the machine, changing the shuttle for a new one. Gehringer clenched his teeth together so hard that his jaw ached. "Can you still not do that without stopping the machine?"

"Sorry, Mr. Gehringer. It's too dangerous to do when it's running."

"Dangerous!" Gehringer laughed mockingly. "Any weaver worth his salt would pass a little test of courage like that. Am I right?" He looked around for approval, but the other weavers acted as if his words were drowned out by the knocking and rattling of the looms.

"If you think I'm paying any of you to sit and watch the looms do nothing, you're sadly mistaken. There will be consequences!" Fuming, he stomped toward his office.

It took some time, but he eventually calmed down enough to attend to other matters. He stared at his calendar. They were currently ahead on their orders. Still, a glance at his order book did not impress him. Most were for the simplest ready-made clothes—orders that took time and labor, but which left little in the way of profits. Orders for more elaborate garments like embroidered blouses, nightdresses, or decorative aprons were lower than usual for this time of year. Worse: he had to offer them at unusually low prices. He'd heard from buyer after buyer that his patterns were outdated and there was nothing original—and they were not prepared to pay higher prices for that. "You have to modernize," one of the buyers had told him to his face.

Gehringer let his eyes roam across his wood-paneled office. Modern was not a word one would normally associate with his weaving mill.

Until now, he'd been happy to keep up the old traditions—traditions he was proud of. But what if traditions weren't enough?

So many problems for which solutions had to be found. Maybe he should hire a manager to keep an eye on operations. His regular rounds were taking a toll on his time and his nerves. Was Merkle the man for the job? He doubted it. And if his people already tried to fool him, what would they try with a manager? Some things simply had to be done by the boss.

"Paul!"

His assistant appeared in the room in an instant, as if he'd been waiting for his name to be called. *Doesn't the man have enough to keep him busy?* Gehringer wondered.

"Mr. Gehringer. How can I help?"

Gehringer tapped on the open newspaper in front of him.

"There's an architect with an ad here in the paper. Richard Rauner. He specializes in greenhouses. Write to him and set up a meeting."

"Greenhouses?" Paul Merkle turned and looked out the window, where the chestnut tree in the courtyard was in full bloom.

"I don't want him to build me a greenhouse. I want a glass pavilion here on the premises, somewhere I can receive visitors in the future. One has to move with the times, Merkle. He who does not embrace the modern gets left behind, I can promise you that."

"So you're doing it after all," said Merkle with a grin. "Putting my idea into practice, I mean. I'm glad to see it."

Gehringer frowned. He'd completely forgotten that the suggestion for a pavilion had originally come from Merkle.

"There's another thing," he said. "I've heard that your brother is coming back."

"Johann, yes. But how do you know about that?" His smile vanished.

Gehringer noted the change in Merkle's expression with satisfaction. "A good businessman has ears everywhere, as I told you not long ago. In this case, however, it was not particularly difficult, because your mother's been telling anyone who'll listen how happy she is about her prodigal son's return."

"I hope she isn't rejoicing too soon," said Merkle grimly. He looked at Gehringer now with his eyes narrowed. "You don't plan to hire him, do you? My brother was always headstrong, and I can't imagine that's changed much in the last few years. Johann is—"

Gehringer cut his assistant off with a gesture. "I'm not *planning* anything of the sort. But, as a good businessman, I am keeping my options open. If I remember correctly, your brother was one of the best and fastest weavers we'd ever seen. Of course, he also had a very big mouth . . ."

Johann Merkle was as hot headed as his and Paul's deceased father had been. Gehringer had had run-ins with Johann several times, and if he hadn't quit when he did, Gehringer would have fired him.

"You can, of course, hire whoever you want," said Paul. "But if you want my advice, forget about my brother. He'll probably come to town for a day or two to get money out of my mother before he heads off into the big, wide world again." His last words were filled with scorn.

Gehringer looked stonily at his assistant. "I appreciate your advice, Merkle. Even more so when I ask for it."

"Besides," Paul continued, chagrined, "the school year is almost over and many boys will be expecting apprenticeships, including my son Justus. You needn't worry about the next generation of workers in the mill."

"Now that you mention it, make a list of the weavers whose sons will be finishing school this year. Then I can think in advance about who I'm going to take on."

"Do you mean you won't be employing them all?" Merkle sounded incredulous.

"It means, at the very least, that I will think very hard about who I train and who not," said Gehringer pompously. "Today has given me a lot to consider. The work ethic of my employees is not what it should be. If the weavers won't stick to the unwritten rule that every man gives his very best, then I see no obligation on my part to stick to the custom of employing every son just because his father works for me. It's time I make a few examples. Oh, and add some notes after every name, whatever you can tell me about the boys. Maybe there's one or two with talents we can use."

"Useful talents? A man's ability to handle a loom only becomes clear with time. Or do you have in mind a talent like the Schubert boy's drawing? Do you want to take him on as a designer after all?" Merkle's expression brightened again. "I'm very happy to see my ideas falling on such fertile soil."

Gehringer smirked to himself. *Pride goeth before a fall, as they say.*

"If I employ him at all, it will be as a *weaver*," he said. Merkle didn't need to know that Gehringer had recognized the boy's talent very clearly indeed. A young man like Alexander Schubert would not shy away from the modern. No, young people wanted change, and he, Gehringer, would profit from that.

"As long as we fill our orders on schedule, the boy is welcome to try out a new pattern now and then. He can at least make up for some of his father's shortcomings as a weaver. The man can't even change out a shuttle without stopping his loom. When I think of all the money I once invested in Klaus Schubert . . . I even sent him to train in Chemnitz, you know. And how does he repay me?"

"A loom *is* a delicate piece of equipment," Merkle said.

Herrmann Gehringer sniffed. "In the past, a weaver pampered his loom like he'd pamper a woman. These days, I count myself lucky if they remember to oil and clean them. No, no, Schubert's mind is too often somewhere else. Every time I see his apathetic, absentminded face, it infuriates me!"

"I'll keep my eye on the man," said Merkle.

"Do that. In the meantime, I'm wondering if I shouldn't run a little cost-benefit calculation for every man I have. Improving your flock, Paul, means weeding out the sick before they infect the rest."

CHAPTER 39

"By my God do I leap over a wall . . ."

While Eveline prepared the family's dinner, the photographer's words from Friday suddenly reappeared in her mind. *Easy for her to talk about not losing heart and leaping walls,* she thought, *in her nice house with her glass studio and her own income. But what if God had forgotten all about you?*

A thousand thoughts swirled in Eveline's head. She could have spent the entire weekend just thinking about Johann's return. How would it be to stand face to face with him again? Would the old feelings flare? And what did it even mean that he was coming home now, now when her life was as hard as it had ever been?

Eveline banished the thoughts as best she could. She had to, because she felt Alexander's eyes watching her at every turn. Since their visit to the photographer, he'd been begging her to put in a good word for him with Klaus. She'd forbidden Alexander from saying anything. Couldn't he see how weary and despondent his father was? If she wanted to get anywhere with Klaus, she would have to pick a good moment.

But that moment hadn't come, and now it was Monday and she felt Alexander's dark eyes following her, filled with reproach at her silence. Didn't he know she would do anything for him? There was nothing she wanted more for her children than a chance at a better life: Alexander a famous artist, Marianne a teacher, and her youngest . . . maybe Erika would one day marry a rich man who would lavish her with care and attention. But what use was all her wishful thinking? There was always Klaus. And her husband saw things very differently. But with God or without him, she wanted to leap over walls, and if that meant bloodying her knees, so be it.

When Klaus got home from work, it was already dark. Without a word, he hung his jacket on the hook by the entrance, where Eveline had leaned the rake and shovels to make it look as if she and the children had just come back from the field. He didn't need to know that they had not been out to work in the field at all.

"I have to talk to you about something," she said to Klaus when they each had a bowl of soup in front of them. She couldn't put it off any longer, even if Klaus's face was as long as a winter's night. She looked at her children apologetically—she would much rather have spoken to Klaus when the children were asleep, but he often grabbed a bottle of schnapps and went off to bed by himself. No, she *had* to talk to him now, and could only hope that their discussion didn't turn into a fight.

"What is it? Has the shovel handle come loose again?"

Eveline felt her jaw tighten. Did he think she had nothing to say to him besides banalities?

"It's this," she began. "The photographer—"

"That woman? Didn't I tell you to stay away from her?" His eyes immediately turned to the drawer that held Alexander's confirmation picture. When Eveline had tried to put it out on display, he'd forbidden it, saying he couldn't stand the blasphemous sight of it. Eveline had been stricken, but had not found the courage to stand up to him.

"You did, but—"

"No buts! She's wicked, that one. She does not belong here. Bad enough that she uses the church as her showroom, but even worse that she abuses our young ones to live out her artistic life. No wonder she's turning everyone against her."

Everyone? Eveline held back a snort of contempt. Why didn't Klaus call "everyone" by name: his boss, Gehringer. That was who he meant, after all.

"Father Hildebrand saw nothing blasphemous in her selling the confirmation pictures at the church. In fact, he allowed it," she said calmly. "And other than you, everyone I know thought the photographs she made were lovely."

"Mother . . . ," Alexander said, a note of warning in his voice.

She glanced briefly at her son. How in the world was she supposed to raise the invitation to the admissions test now? She'd already made Klaus angry, and hadn't even gotten to the heart of the matter.

"Anyway, it's like this," she began again. "The photographer sent a few of Alexander's illustrations to an art college in Stuttgart, and now they want our boy to come to an admissions examination." She spoke the last words in such a rush that Klaus had no chance to interrupt her. She swallowed breathlessly, waiting for his reaction.

She didn't have to wait long.

"Alexander's illustrations?" Before she knew it, Klaus had reached across the table and slapped his son hard on the side of his head. "Have you been wasting your time drawing again? Didn't I forbid that?" He turned aggressively to Eveline. "And you had nothing better to do than run to that woman with the pictures and bow and scrape to her like a whore? Did you really think that was necessary?"

"I didn't know anything about it. The photographer took it on herself to—" But she got no further, because Klaus's fist slammed so hard on the table that everyone jumped. Erika began to cry softly. Beneath the table, Eveline quickly squeezed her daughter's hand. For now, she could do no more.

"Who does that woman think she is, sticking her nose into my family's business? She'll hear from me!" Klaus jumped to his feet.

"Klaus!" Eveline grabbed hold of his sleeve and held him back with all her strength.

"Father, think about what a huge chance this is," Alexander begged. "The Stuttgart Art School. It's a great honor."

"Aren't you proud of your son at all?" said Eveline gently. *Well done, Alexander,* she added silently. To her relief, Klaus sat down again. He looked from her to Alexander with something like revulsion in his eyes.

"What's to be proud of? All your scheming behind my back? A son who'd prefer to waste his days with pencil and paper than do a solid day's work in the field? So it's an honor, is it, that you've gotten yourself invited to some Stuttgart school? Isn't the school of life enough? Are you putting on your mother's airs now, Alexander? This is a weaver's house! Weavers have lived here for generations. I'm *proud* to be the son of a weaver. I see it as an *honor* to work for one of the biggest weaving mills in Laichingen. It's God's will that the sons of weavers also become weavers, and it's my job to see that the tradition goes on. No photographer who's wandered in off the street and who's probably never done an honest day's work in her life is going to change that!"

CHAPTER 40

Vegetables. Potted plants. Men's smocks and women's aprons. Underwear and socks. Wool cardigans. Washboards. Wooden shoes. Fried sausages and salty pretzels. Sour pickled fish and sweet gingerbread. Rabbits and chickens and even cows—all for sale at the Pentecost market. One stand after another lined the street from the train station into town. At the marketplace, too, the crowds on that Monday, June 5, made it hard to even move. Both Laichingen locals and those from elsewhere thronged not only the sales stands but also the tables set up outside The Oxen—browsing, haggling, and buying made them hungry and thirsty. A few among them looked up with yearning at the sky the color of violets, envious of the crows cruising overhead, undisturbed and with all the room in the world. The tumult down below was too much for the birds, but they would come back to earth the next morning to pick through what the people left behind.

Anton was in his element. As fast as his feet would carry him, he trotted from the inn to the courtyard in front of the plaza, his arms heavy with trays of foaming glasses of beer. He pushed his way between the crowded benches and tables, and if an elbow caught him in the ribs or someone stomped on his foot, he took it with good humor. Whether serving or being served, the Laichingen Pentecost market was no place for the faint of heart, so Anton, with cold beer and warm banter, was welcomed at the tables.

On his way back into The Oxen, Anton looked at the large blackboard set up beside the entrance, where the three dishes of the day were chalked in large letters: fried potatoes with ham, sauerkraut with sausages, and lentil stew. "We're down to three servings of the fried potatoes!" his mother had just called to him, so Anton took a piece of chalk from his pocket and struck out the first dish on the list. What a success the day had been! Even though it wasn't a roast pig they were serving, the blackboard and the choice of meals had been his ideas. The guests liked having alternatives to the obligatory sauerkraut and sausages. The ringing of the cash register was music to his ears.

Smiling broadly, Anton allowed himself a moment to catch his breath. He stood and surveyed the turmoil of the market.

Mimi had set up her stall on the opposite side of the square, in front of her shop. A large gathering there hid the actual stall from view, but he could see the photographer, her cheeks flushed red as she laughed and gesticulated wildly with her hands. She seemed to be having just as much fun in all the hustle and bustle as he was, thought Anton, grinning. No wonder: she was not only famous, she was also a good businesswoman.

But his grin disappeared when he saw who else was pushing his way through the bustling market: Christel's father, Paul Merkle, was waving his arms around importantly, clearing a path for his employer, Herrmann Gehringer. The businessman acted as if he were really interested in the stallholders' offerings, and greeted people left and right like some kind of feudal lord. Christel, her mother, and her brothers followed their father obediently in single file.

As the group came nearer, Anton noted with delight that Christel was wearing the hair ribbon he'd given her. He also saw how heads swung to follow her as she passed. *My girl!* thought Anton with pride. He tried to catch her attention with a covert wave. They hadn't been able to meet for several days, but perhaps they'd be able to sneak away for a moment in all the confusion? A stolen kiss, a secret embrace . . . When she did not react to his attempts to signal her, he tried a whistle. But it was no use. Whenever her father was around, Anton was as visible to her as air. He did not understand why their friendship had to stay such a secret. Did Christel, like her father, think a pub owner's son wasn't good enough for her?

He didn't have time to be angry, so Anton went inside to get the next round of beer. When he emerged, Gehringer and his entourage were steering toward the tables in front of The Oxen. What a pity: all the tables were full just then, Anton thought with a smirk. He didn't mind at all that the factory owner would have to wait. The next moment, someone grabbed him by the sleeve. "The next free table is ours!" Paul Merkle snarled.

"You'll have to sort that out for yourself. I'm busy," Anton replied, pulling free. As he spoke, he saw Gehringer peering across the square toward Mimi Reventlow's stand.

"What's going on over there?" Gehringer asked. "Something for free?"

"That's the photographer's stand. She's been in great demand lately," Anton said. "It's been like that the whole morning. She's practically drowning in customers."

He expected Gehringer's expression to cloud over, but the businessman only laughed and said, "Is that so?" Then he snapped at Christel's father: "Find out what's really going on over there."

Paul Merkle hurried off, and Anton went back to work.

By the time Anton returned, Gehringer and his party were sitting down at a newly vacated table. Sonja Merkle sat to Gehringer's right and Christel to his left. The very sight of her sitting beside that man made Anton furious—Gehringer had better not get too close to his sweetheart!

"What are you standing around gawking for?" his mother hissed in his ear as she passed by. "Mr. Gehringer is bound to be hungry. Go! And put out cloth napkins for them when you take their order."

"What'll it be?" Anton asked sullenly as he stood beside the table. Christel looked at him and smiled brightly, but she turned away quickly when she saw her father returning.

"It really is the photographer's stall," said Paul Merkle breathlessly. "She's selling postcards of Laichingen, and it looks like she'll be opening on Sundays in the future."

"So she wants to do business on the Sabbath? Push people around in front of her camera and rob them of their well-earned day of rest? Make them too tired to do a good day's work on Monday?" Gehringer shook his head as he looked across the plaza toward Mimi. "The nerve of the woman."

"Just like her uncle. He used to open on Sundays, too," Merkle said.

Mimi Reventlow and her uncle weren't as easily intimidated as the rest of them, Anton thought. As slowly as he dared, he distributed cutlery and napkins, trying not to miss a word of what the men said.

"Should I do something about it?" Merkle asked.

"Leave that to me. You know I've always got a plan up my sleeve," said Gehringer, looking even more smug than usual.

Merkle looked inquiringly at his boss, but Gehringer seemed to have no intention of letting his assistant in on anything. *Damn!* Anton thought. What did the man have in mind? Anton wanted to know more—perhaps he would be able to warn Mimi.

Twenty minutes later, Anton was bringing the food to Gehringer's table when excited shouts sounded from a side street by The Oxen. A woman let out a loud cry—something was obviously causing a stir.

"What the devil is going on now?" Gehringer said. "Can you see anything?" he asked Merkle.

"Isn't that your mother?" Sonja asked Paul. "Why is she in such a crush of people?"

Anton squinted to see better. Other than Edelgard Merkle, he recognized Helene and a few of his former schoolmates. Directly beside Edelgard there was a tall man with long, unruly hair.

"Misfortune seldom comes alone," said Christel's father, who recognized the man approaching with his mother.

Almost aggressively, Eveline pulled the hairpins out of her hair. Yellowish pollen, small leaves, and a little earth sprinkled the floor. She began to brush her hair with long, firm strokes. She was sweating and wanted to wash herself from head to foot, but it had only been two days since bath day. What a stupid idea it had been to go out to the field on Pentecost Monday, she thought angrily. If it had been up to her, she would have gone to the market when the stalls first opened in the morning. But no, Klaus had insisted they go out to the field first and water the seedlings. It had rained just the night before last—the plants weren't about to die of thirst. Eveline had said nothing, though. She didn't want to set Klaus against her any more than he already was. The atmosphere was bad enough.

"We're leaving soon, children," she said to Marianne and Erika, who sat waiting on the bench, dangling their feet. The market would be horribly full now, and the best of the traditional straw shoes would already be gone.

Would she be able to pin her hair up like Mimi Reventlow had done? Eveline examined herself critically in the small shard of mirror that hung on the wall. Wrap the braid around itself once, then a figure eight and . . .

The door opened and Klaus and Alexander came in. They'd been fixing a hole in the chicken pen. Alexander looked more distant than usual. Eveline quickly pushed the last of the hairpins into place.

"Klaus, before we go to the market . . . can we talk again, please?" She held out the letter from the Stuttgart Art School like an offering. The mailman had brought it on Saturday and had looked at Eveline in amazement when he handed it over. She had accepted the letter casually, as if she received envelopes sealed with the Stuttgart coat of arms every day, but her hands had betrayed her, trembling like never before. Thank God it had been she and not Klaus who had answered the door! He would probably have thrown the letter away on the spot.

She had wondered if she should wait until Alexander returned from the field before opening it, but impatience had gotten the better of her. It was only a few sentences, written in flowing letters in the blackest ink on heavy cream-colored paper. Alexander was invited to take the entrance examination at the end of June, and the school required confirmation by the middle of the month that Alexander would participate.

"Look at this letter. It's his invitation," she begged when Klaus still did not react.

"Will you throw that scrap of paper away? Art school. I don't believe it. Sodom and Gomorrah it should be called," Klaus finally said. "Making blasphemous drawings in the day and going from one pub to the next at night—how can you want our son to lead such a degenerate life?"

"A degenerate life? In Stuttgart?" Eveline let out a shrill laugh. Klaus didn't know the first thing about how people lived in Stuttgart. The town was a far cry from Paris or Berlin. "If Alexander is talented enough, he'll get a scholarship. He would have to prove how hard he can work. He'd spend so much time learning, he'd have no time left for other things."

Eveline noticed the dark shadows under Klaus's eyes. Was it any surprise? He'd spent half the night tossing and turning in bed instead of sleeping. He'd managed to wake her at least three times. What was robbing him of sleep? His own pigheadedness? His twisted imaginings?

"Klaus . . . ," she tried again, speaking gently. "Think about back when you took me with you from Chemnitz. Think about how brave you were, how you seized the chance you had. You wouldn't have let anyone hold you back, would you? This might be the only chance our son has to make more of his life."

"More of his life than his father's made . . . is that it?" His blue eyes looked as cold as a mountain lake. "Are you using the boy to get your revenge on me?"

"What?" Eveline laughed in confusion. "What are you saying?" From the corner of her eye, she saw Marianne and Erika edge closer together. "Go outside, girls," she said.

"Mother's right. This is my big chance. There's nothing I want more in my life than to learn to draw," Alexander pleaded the moment the door closed behind the two girls.

"I want, I want," said Klaus, imitating his son. "You sound like your mother. All she ever wants is more. But make do with the humble things we have? No, you can't do that. Is it so hard to lead a simple, godly life? I do. Every day, I sacrifice myself for all of you. Why can't you follow my example? The narrow path is the one God wants us to walk," he said, pointing to the picture on the wall. "But the devil is dancing in this house!"

Self-sacrifice. Pleasing God. Leading a humble life . . . *The only devil in this house is you!* thought Eveline, and she could have screamed as much in her fury and weariness.

"Alexander can lead a life in Stuttgart that God would find no complaint with. Besides, it isn't even certain they'll accept him. Why don't we at least let him take the admissions test? Then we'll know where we stand. If his talent doesn't turn out to be as great as we think, then—"

"Enough! I won't hear another word," Klaus shouted, cutting her off. "When you married me, you knew perfectly well my ancestors were weavers and that I was a weaver, too. Now Alexander will also be a weaver. Anything else is unthinkable. That's the end of it."

Eveline pressed her lips together so tightly she could hardly breathe. Yes, it was true—back then, as a young woman, she'd admired him for his passion for weaving and the loom. *Passion?* she thought bitterly. *When did Klaus's passion turn into narrow mindedness?*

"Maybe one of the girls will take an interest in working in the mill later on. Then—"

"Have you gone completely out of your mind?" Klaus interrupted her. "A girl working a loom? There hasn't been a girl at a loom in hundreds of years. Never say that if anyone else is around." His eyes were narrowed to slits and he glared at her. "In this house, what I say still goes. You can live out your nonsense all you like when I'm dead and gone."

"Then the sooner the better!" Eveline hissed. Then, startled, she took a step backward, as if to distance herself from her words. Had she really said that? She heard Alexander beside her inhale sharply.

"Now I know how I can finally make you happy," said Klaus, and he laughed sourly. He tossed her his old leather purse. "There. For the market. Get out of my sight." He stepped to the cabinet and took out the bottle of spirits he'd bought with his last wages. Without another glance at Eve or Alexander, he stomped up the stairs to the bedroom.

Eveline watched him go. Would he drink himself into a stupor again? He'd done that often enough lately, then followed it by crying in his sleep. Once, he'd wet the bed. Instead of saying anything to him, she'd simply changed the bed linen. Would the same happen tonight? She didn't like to think about the money he was pouring down his throat. He might have gone to The Oxen for a beer in the past, but he never used to buy schnapps by the bottle at Helene's—it made Helene give Eveline strange looks these days. Eve was close to tears, but who would it help if she spoiled her children's day, too?

"I'll try again tomorrow, once he's calmed down a little," she said to Alexander. "Maybe I'll be able to talk him into it."

"You don't believe that. Father is so terrible! How could you be so stupid to marry a man like that!" Her son's eyes were filled with disgust.

Before Eveline could stop herself, she slapped Alexander hard on his cheek. In a trembling voice, she said, "Don't you dare talk to me like that again. You are not the only one who wants a different life. I'm doing what I can for us. Don't you ever forget it."

CHAPTER 41

"Swans on the *Hüle*—what will they think of next?" The man at Mimi's stand actually held his belly, he was laughing so hard.

"All that's missing now is a health spa by the square. Or one of those new street cafés," his wife said as they pored over the postcards.

"There might be none today, but who can predict tomorrow?" said Mimi. "Look around. There's no spa town in the world lovelier than here, today." She held her arms out wide, taking in the church, the blooming chestnut trees, and the lively marketplace.

The couple nodded their agreement.

"Let's send one to Aunt Käthchen in Mannheim. And Rudolf in Possenhofen," the woman said to her husband. "He's always going on about his Lake Starnberg."

"And we'll keep another one, just in case," said the man.

Mimi smiled as she handed over the three postcards. "What about a small frame? A postcard like that looks lovely on the wall."

The couple exchanged a glance. "Why not?" the man said, taking out his wallet.

Her customers had barely finished their purchase and walked off when Josef, sitting on a stool behind the stand, said, "Child, your Laichingen sights have really hit the mark. Who would have thought?" The old man shook his head—he couldn't get over his amazement.

Mimi grinned. She was relieved they were such a success, especially since she had to present her postcards in a few baskets. As she had feared, Anton could not deliver on his promise of the wooden stand.

"I'd like one of the 'Laichingen: The Linen-Weaving Town' cards, please," said Franka Klein, whose son Vincent had been among the first confirmands that Mimi had photographed.

"Of course," Mimi said with a smile. "And so you know, from now on, I'm opening on Sundays, and—"

Mimi broke off when she heard shouting from nearby: it came from the tables in front of The Oxen. A fight?

Franka Klein also looked around. "I don't believe it," she murmured. "That's Johann! He's really come back. I must go and say hello." She paid for the postcard quickly before hurrying off.

"What's going on over there?" Josef asked. The crowd's excitement was almost palpable. Everyone had suddenly lost interest in Mimi's cards.

"I don't know." Mimi craned her neck to see better. Just then, Alexander ran past.

"Stop! Wait a moment!" Mimi called to him. "What's going on over there?"

"Edelgard's eldest son, Johann, has come home," said Alexander. He seemed resentful and tense. Before Mimi could say anything else, he ran off.

Maybe her uncle had been right when he'd told her not to do anything on Alexander's behalf. His father was strongly opposed to Alexander taking the admissions test, and Alexander was correspondingly distressed. If only she could think of some way to help him. She'd already asked Eveline whether she, Mimi, should perhaps try talking to Alexander's father. "My God, no!" Eveline had replied, genuinely horrified.

Now Mimi's uncle was also on his feet, trying to see the commotion better. "Johann Merkle, well . . . what's he doing here? I thought he'd emigrated to America."

"Who is everyone talking about?" Mimi said. She only knew Paul Merkle—that he had a brother was news to her.

"The tall fellow there. With the tousled hair."

Mimi followed his pointing finger, and her heart, for a moment, ceased to beat. She blinked to make sure it was no illusion.

It was really him. She would have recognized him among millions.

For a moment, the emotions that rose inside her were so over-whelming that she was afraid she'd faint. Joy, surprise, bewilderment. A touch of hysteria. Johann . . . Hannes?

Hannes was from here? How did he know that she was in Laichingen? Or was it just a coincidence? *They say a prophet has no honor in his own land. I'm finished with my hometown.* His voice reso-nated in her memory.

Oh my God . . . Finally, she understood—Hannes was from Laichingen. And though he had never wanted anything more to do with his hometown, he had followed her here. Mimi, deeply moved, felt her throat tighten. She could have laughed or cried, or both. *Calm down, take a deep breath,* she told herself, while she watched Paul Merkle greet his brother stiffly, his arm straight out as far as he could hold it, as if he wanted to keep his distance. Weedy Paul and broad-shouldered Hannes were brothers?

"Mimi? Everything all right?" her uncle asked.

"I think so," she said in a whisper. Everything in her wanted to run to Hannes, but how would that look? With all the self-control she could gather, she stayed where she was.

And then their eyes met, and he recognized her. She saw the flash in his brown-black eyes, saw the same joy at seeing her that she felt at seeing him.

"What do you know?" she heard him say loudly as he came toward her stand. "A photographer at the Pentecost market. All you used to get here was linen, straw shoes, and clay pots." He freed himself from his mother, who was holding on to him possessively. "Sorry, but I have to take a closer look."

Before Mimi knew it, he was heading right for her. Suddenly, she felt hot and cold at once.

"Hannes," she whispered so that only he could hear. As he looked over the postcards in the baskets, she leaned forward and whispered again, "What are you doing here?"

"Weren't you the one who said that everyone meets twice in life?" he whispered back, with a slight smile.

Their eyes traced each other's faces. His gaze felt like a light touch, as if stroking her skin. Almost imperceptibly, he tilted his head, indicating his mother and all the rest standing behind them and watching them closely. Mimi understood: this was neither the time nor the place to talk. No one needed to know that they had already met.

She held out her hand and shook his formally, and although she would have held on forever, she put on her most professional voice and said, "My name is Mimi Reventlow. I'm Josef Stöckle's niece, and I currently run his business." Her words sounded a little unsteady, and she cleared her throat. "I look forward to welcoming you in my photo studio, I hope in the not-too-distant future. A homecoming is a big event, and one that should certainly be recorded with a picture, don't you think?"

Well done! she read in Hannes's eyes, and Mimi smiled.

"An excellent idea," Hannes said. "I'll be sure to stop by as soon as possible."

Possible? Everything was possible now, Mimi thought, and she felt dizzy with happiness.

Eveline wanted to cry. *What the hell am I doing?* she asked herself as she squeezed through the crowds, holding Marianne's and Erika's hands. First the fight with Klaus, then with Alexander, who had run off. *Just like his father!* she thought. Still, she should not have slapped him like that, and she sighed deeply. Tomorrow she would write to the art school and tell them that Alexander was coming to take the exam. She still had time to talk Klaus into it, although she had no idea how she was going to succeed.

"Come, Marianne, we'll get you some new shoes first," she said as brightly as she could. She was relieved to see that not much was going on at the stall that sold the shoes.

The dealer, who'd come up from the Black Forest, explained that his straw shoes were woven and sewn according to old tradition, and were exceptionally durable. Normally, Eve would have been impressed by the well-crafted shoes, but after all the fighting, it was as if a dark cloud had cast a pall over the sunny day.

"There's a stand just ahead selling sweet treats," said Eve, once they'd found the right pair of shoes. She gave each of the girls a few pfennigs. "Go and buy yourselves something." The children licked their lips, and their eyes widened in anticipation.

How simple and how lovely life could be, Eveline thought sadly as she watched the two girls march off hand in hand to the stall selling gingerbread and candy. Beside it, the photographer also had a stall with products for sale. But instead of attending to her customers, Mimi Reventlow was standing oddly still, her eyes distant, as if her thoughts were far off. Was she unhappy? Eveline wasn't sure. She waved at Mimi, but the photographer didn't react. Had everybody gotten out of bed on the wrong side that day? A terrible thought came to her. Had Klaus gone to Mimi's stall? Had he shown up drunk and rained abuse on the photographer? Eve looked around uncertainly.

And then she saw *him.*

"Johann!" she said, her voice cracking. Eveline felt something uncontrollable and impetuous well up inside her. Tears of joy sprang to her eyes, and she wiped them away frantically. *Composure!* she told herself silently. *Don't lose your self-control in front of everyone.*

Forgotten was the fight with Klaus about Stuttgart. Forgotten were the children. Her pounding heart would burst out of her chest at any moment, she thought. Struggling as hard as she could to hold herself together, she stayed where she was and watched Johann approach, stride by stride.

"I'm here!" she cried, when only a few yards separated them. She pushed through the crowd until she was standing in front of him, and it was all she could do not to throw herself into his arms. But there were the others. His mother, old friends, neighbors. They tugged at his sleeves, everyone wanting his attention.

Eveline put her hands behind her back and clasped them together painfully, if only to resist the urge to stroke his cheek.

"You're back . . ." Her voice was hoarse with emotion.

"Eveline," he said. "How lovely to see you! Are you all right?" he asked, studying her face as if he knew how the sight of him shocked her.

She returned his gaze with an intensity that revealed almost too much. She nodded, smiling. *Yes. Yes, I'm all right now.*

"And you?" she said softly. "How are you?"

"Time will tell," he said with a lopsided grin.

Eveline's smile widened to a grin, too. How she loved his cheerfulness, the power he radiated.

"You know, I never planned to come back to Laichingen. But things have changed. I've come to realize that there are more important things than my old principles." He looked at her, his eyes filled with meaning.

She nodded. She knew exactly what he was talking about. He'd come back for her. "Things do change," she said. "*We* change."

"Johann, come along! You must be hungry after your travels. Let's go to The Oxen," his mother said.

It didn't matter if he went off with Edelgard for now. Johann was back, and they had all the time in the world.

Eveline closed her eyes. *Thank you, God.* Now everything would be all right.

CHAPTER 42

It was starting to get dark when Anton grabbed his jacket and left The Oxen. His mother and two helpers were washing the last of the dishes, and she had mercifully let him go. At the tables in front of the inn, the last beer glasses were being drained and would not be refilled—the few men still there had been drinking the whole day, and Anton's mother was adamant that it was time they went and slept off their drunkenness.

The market square was still busy, although the sales had come to an end and the customers were gone. The sellers had had a good day and were dismantling their stands, stowing tabletops on handcarts, stacking baskets, and yawning heartily.

Anton noticed the last two candy apples sitting by themselves on a tray and pointed. "Can I have those?" The man, weary from too much talk and the long day, handed them to him without a word. When Anton tried to give him a few pfennigs for the apples, he wouldn't accept them.

"Thanks!" said Anton happily. *Love apples,* he thought as he walked off with the red toffee-covered fruit. As "love apples," as they were known locally, he really ought to have given one to Christel. But she had sat a very long time in front of The Oxen with her family and hadn't given him a second glance. As far as he was concerned, she could go jump in the lake.

Normally, Anton wouldn't have so easily swallowed the situation with Christel, but he was in too good a mood to get upset because of her. Alexander would also enjoy a candy apple, he knew, and his young friend was too skinny anyway.

When Alexander had shown up at The Oxen at midday, Anton had sent him away. "No time to talk! Too much to do!" Anton had said as he rushed by his friend. They'd agreed to meet in the evening at the train station, behind the last shed, where no one ever went. Anton could smoke a cigarette in peace, and they could talk without being interrupted.

Alexander was already there when Anton arrived. He sat with his back to the wall, his elbows resting on his raised knees, his head hanging.

"You asleep?" Anton said, giving him a small shove. "Who spent the whole day working, you or me?" Grinning, he held out an apple to his friend.

Alexander looked up. There was such a look of despair in his eyes that Anton recoiled in shock. "Has something happened?"

"No, and that's the problem." Alexander sniffed. "Father is still refusing to let me go to the admissions exam. But he knows perfectly well that it's my only chance."

The art school. Again. Anton sat beside his friend, his back likewise to the wall, and took a bite of his apple.

"Mother isn't getting anywhere with him. They fight. One says this, the other says something else, then Father takes off and that's that. It's always the same song and dance. Nothing changes."

"Then why don't you just go to Stuttgart anyway?" Anton held out the second apple to his friend again.

Alexander took it, but instead of biting into it, he turned the stick the apple was on and looked at the bright candied fruit as if it were a precious artifact of gold and silver. "Do you see these perfect curves? Only nature can do that. See how this particular apple is slightly narrower at the top than at the bottom? See the dip where the stem is darker than the rest? See the shadows from the setting sun on this side—the red candy looks like it's on fire." He sounded enraptured. "I want to be able to paint all of that, you know? I want to learn how light and shadow work. For once in my life, I want the smell of oil paint in my nose. I want to feel what it's like to really work with paint. I want to have a canvas in front of me and know that it belongs to me. Just to me! And I want to have a sketchbook of my own and never draw on wrapping paper again in my life."

Anton looked at his friend in amazement. Alexander's voice grew more passionate and excited the more he said. He'd never heard him speak like that before.

"If it all means so much to you, it's even more important that you get to that exam. If it's a question of money, maybe I could lend you some?" said Anton, thinking anxiously about his own lack of exactly that. To hell with it! If he had to, he'd pinch what he needed from the register. The end would justify the means, and this was about his best friend.

But Alexander said, "What would be the point? Even if they accepted me, Father would never let me go to Stuttgart. He's a weaver, his father was a weaver, and his father's father was a weaver, so *I* have to be a weaver, too!" He spat the words out with so much vehemence that small drops of spittle flew. "I feel like a slave."

"What if you just take off? Like Johann did?" Just take off . . . his own dream. But as simple as he made it sound to his friend, he knew better.

"The same Johann who came back today?" Alexander mocked. "With nothing but a linen sack on his shoulder?"

Anton said nothing. He did not understand what Johann Merkle was doing here, either. America! The land of unbounded opportunity! If he himself ever made it that far, wild horses wouldn't be able to drag him back to Laichingen.

"Maybe he could at least give you some advice? He's a well-traveled man, after all." When Alexander said nothing, Anton went back to eating his apple. Maybe he should have given the second apple to Mimi, he thought, with a sideways glance at Alexander's, discarded on the dusty ground.

What a woman! She seemed to be having so much fun, to be so full of life in the whirl of customers that had kept her busy the entire day. In the hurly-burly of the market, she came to life, just like him. Yes, Mimi Reventlow certainly had a nose for business—in that, at least, they were very much alike. A pity they couldn't have a Pentecost market every day.

Anton thought with horror about the monotony that would return to the village the next day. The highlight of the week would be serving the businessmen on Friday. With a little luck, a traveling trader might lose his way and end up in The Oxen. And if a day went really well, maybe Christel would finally let him kiss her.

But was that enough? Just as Alexander hungered after his art, Anton thirsted for the big, wide world. The thought of having no choice but to waste his life in Laichingen was more than he could bear.

But it would not get that far.

Mimi Reventlow didn't know it yet, but she would be his ticket to freedom. Exactly how that would work, Anton did not know. Nor did he know where Christel fit into the picture, but Anton had not the slightest doubt that Mimi Reventlow coming to Laichingen had been fateful. She would not stay there forever, though, and when she left . . .

Time was on his side, he thought as he took the last bites of the apple and leaned over, tossing the core beside the apple Alexander had discarded. As he did, he saw that his friend was crying. Tears flowed down his thin face, and he didn't make any move to wipe them away.

Anton was shocked and also felt utterly helpless. What should he do? Console his friend? Get up and go? Maybe Alexander would prefer if no one saw him like that.

"Don't be sad," he finally said, and he stroked Alexander's arm awkwardly. "We'll think of some way to get you to Stuttgart. When's the exam, did you say?"

"End of June. But I have to tell them I'm coming by the middle of next week."

"Well, then we've still got plenty of time. There'll be a chance. Something will come up," said Anton.

"A chance? I'd have a chance if Gehringer was dead. Or if his damned factory burned to the ground." Alexander shuddered. "Or if everyone decided they didn't want any damned linen anymore. Then there'd be nothing holding me here. But by then my chance would be long gone."

"I like the first option best," said Anton with a grin. "A little hunting mishap, maybe an accident with his car. Brakes fail . . ."

For the first time that day, Anton saw a smile appear on Alexander's face.

"I never knew you had such murderous thoughts," Alexander said.

"Well, there's a lot you don't know about me. And while we're at it, let's send Christel's father off to hell, too," Anton said gleefully. At least he'd managed to drag his friend out of his misery, even if just a bit. He climbed to his feet, then helped Alexander up. "Let's go." He went to sling an arm around Alexander's shoulders, but Alexander stood where he was and looked intently at him.

Alexander's voice trembled as he said, "I promise you here and now: I'm going to take that exam, and no one's going to stop me."

AFTERWORD

All characters and events in my novel are fictional.

The arrangement of buildings in Laichingen, the train station, power station, etc. is not historically accurate, but the product of artistic license.

It is, however, true that for centuries, Laichingen was an important center for the weaving trade. Laichingen linenwares were quality products, like knives from Solingen or clocks from the Black Forest. Until the late twentieth century, linen from the region was an indispensable part of the trousseau of every Swabian girl.

The traditional Laichingen Pentecost market still continues today.

These days, Laichingen has a Catholic church, a Protestant church, and a Methodist church. In earlier times, Pietism was widespread in the region.

At the time my story is set, the Royal Academy of Fine Arts (Königliche Akademie der bildenden Künste) already existed in Stuttgart. Alexander's invitation, however, comes from the Stuttgart Art School, an invention of mine.

All photographs included here are from my private collection.

I've often been asked where I get the ideas for my novels. The first time I had anything to do with historical photography was in my parents' antique shop in Kirchheim unter Teck, when I was a young girl. After school, we children didn't go straight home but instead to my parents' shop. From there we all went out together for lunch, or my mother made sandwiches for us in the workshop. The shop reopened at two on the dot, and my sister and I did our homework there, too. While I wrote essays and struggled with math, I always had one ear pricked for the jingling of the bell over the shop door—I always found whatever was going on in the shop far more exciting than homework!

An antiques business isn't just about the things you sell, but also about the things you buy. I was often present when my father was offered original photographs that came from Otto Hofmann's renowned Kirchheim photo studio. Even back then, they were sought-after collector's items. If my father and the seller reached a deal, I was afterward able to look wide-eyed through the black-and-white photographs created in the local studio between 1889 and 1948. One day, my father even had the chance to buy the huge bellows camera and the canvas backdrops that Otto Hofmann himself had painted. What an amazing treasure! My father being my father, he soon passed both on to the city museum, where those valuable pieces really belonged. Today they can be seen in the open-air museum in Beuren.

At some point, I began collecting historical photographs myself, and you will see some included throughout the series. My research materials are far too beautiful to keep to myself—I simply must share some with my readers.

I hope you have enjoyed Mimi Reventlow's journey so far, and I wish you many pleasant hours reading about her—not only photographic—adventures in the books to come!

Petra Durst-Benning

IMAGE GALLERY:

STUDIO PHOTOGRAPHY FROM

APPROXIMATELY 1910

Kirchheim photographer Otto Hofmann and his wife as photographed by their daughter, Anna Hofmann.

The desire of people, for just once in their lives, to be someone else— thanks to technical innovations and a wide range of props and accessories, photographers could make this wish come true in the studio.

Even back then, one did not have to venture out into the snow and ice to create a wintry vista. The elaborate and skillfully painted snowy landscape served as a backdrop, and props like the young girl's muff and cap were all that was needed to complete the scene. With the aid of retouching techniques, the photographer could later make it snow.

I wonder what these two young men did in real life. Were they bookkeepers or beekeepers? Did they work in an office or a shop? It doesn't matter, because in the studio all kinds of different dreams could be turned into reality. Why not be a fancy pilot and fly to Paris in your single-motor machine? The props of studio photography made it possible.

This young woman looks a little unsure of herself. Did she feel overdressed in that opulent headgear? Or, for once in her life, did she enjoy the feeling of being a "real lady"?

Confirmation photographs: it was usual for youngsters on the cusp of adult-
hood to stand sternly and with no trace of a smile, so it comes as no surprise
that Mimi Reventlow tried to make this important moment in the lives of
her young subjects a little more free and cheerful.

The baby pond: it wasn't actually the stork working hard, but rather the photographer, who—employing a range of retouching techniques—conjured up all the little babies in the picture. Many customers bought and sent postcards like this one, which sold very well.

Mimi Reventlow was a little more reserved—all she added to the Hüle in Laichingen was a bevy of swans.

Gustav Rüdenberg, from whom Mimi bought her first camera in 1905, opened his company "G. Rüdenberg jun. Mail-Order Firm for Photography and Optical Equipment, Hanover and Vienna" in 1895. In 1906, Rüdenberg married the beautiful Elsbeth Salmony, and together they assembled a wide-ranging art collection. In September 1941, the couple were taken to the "Jewish House"—formerly the hall of prayer at the Jewish cemetery on Strangriede road in Hanover—and from there were deported to the concentration camp near Riga, where both died.

COMING SOON:

An Artificial Light, Book Two

in the Photographer's Saga

EDITOR'S NOTE: This is an early excerpt and may not

reflect the finished book.

CHAPTER 1

Laichingen, Swabian Jura, Pentecost Monday, June 5, 1911

Mimi all but floated into her uncle Josef's house, her feet barely touching the floor. It wasn't the success of the Pentecost market that had her on cloud nine—rather, it was Hannes, the man she hadn't been able to get out of her mind since they'd first met nearly two months before in Ulm, the man who'd found his way into her dreams.

Mimi still could not believe that he'd come for her. When he appeared at the market as if from nowhere—just minutes before!—her joy at seeing him again had nearly made her faint. Given everything stacked against them, she'd almost lost hope of ever seeing him again.

Yet here he was in Laichingen because of her, even though in Ulm he'd made it very clear to her that he was finished with his hometown, that he'd never set foot there again. She hadn't known then that Hannes was originally from Laichingen. For her sake he'd evidently put his resolution aside, she thought happily.

She cheerfully tended to her uncle—fatigued by the busy market, he only wanted to rest—and helped him to bed, then she got ready to go to sleep. Hannes had said that he would come to her "as soon as possible," but when would that be? Mimi wondered as she lay in bed.

Now that she knew he was close by, she could hardly bear her sense of longing. She sighed and snuggled deeper under her blanket.

Their first meeting in Ulm had felt predestined. The evening they had spent in each other's company had been marked by an intensity that Mimi had never known. To be with someone else, or to be free? For Mimi, freedom had always come first.

But now, with Hannes, she could imagine almost anything.

It was eight in the morning, and her uncle was still asleep when she heard a soft knock at the front door, which faced the back garden. Mimi, unable to sleep and out of bed since six, knew at once that it was him.

"Hannes . . ." Her voice was a mere whisper. "You've come." She looked at him cautiously, as if she still could not believe that he was really here. His brown-black eyes as warm as the coals of a fire. His mouth a touch too large, but just right for a man with so much to say. The dark-brown, unruly hair crowning his tall, powerful frame. The broad shoulders to lean on.

In the bright light of that June morning, Hannes returned her gaze intently, almost as if he wanted to be certain that his decision to come back to Laichingen had been the right one. "It wasn't easy for me. I couldn't shake you from my mind. I just could not accept that something that had not even started could already be over."

What a declaration of love! Mimi had never heard more beautiful words. "I couldn't stop thinking about you, either," she admitted in a whisper. She wanted to nestle against him, but Hannes took her by the hand and led her to a corner of the garden between Josef's little woodshed and the back of the studio, where no one could see them from the surrounding houses. In the shadows behind the studio, he finally took her in his arms. They held each other for a long, silent moment, enjoying each other's warmth and closeness.

"How did you even find me?" she murmured.

"I went to the guesthouse in Ulm where you'd spent the night and asked the landlord if he knew where you were going next. At first, he hesitated, but when I made it clear how important it was, he told me where you'd gone. You can imagine how I felt when I heard you'd left for Laichingen—of all the places you could have traveled, you were in my old village."

"And you still came after me. Oh, Hannes . . ."

He released himself from their embrace and looked into her eyes again. "May I ask you for one thing?"

Mimi nodded. He could ask her for anything.

"From now on, would you call me Johann? I called myself Hannes when I was traveling. Whenever someone in America said my real name, it sounded like a girl's name: Joanne. Hannes was easier for them, but it will only confuse the villagers here to hear you use that name."

"Of course," said Mimi with a smile. Names meant nothing. "As long as you don't call me Minna. That's what my mother used to shout, whenever I'd been up to something."

He laughed. "And? Have you been up to something these last few weeks? Have you already managed to catch the eye of one of the weavers?"

"Oh, wouldn't you like to know!" As if one of the pale, worn-out weavers slaving away from morning to night in the factories could be even half as attractive as Johann, she thought.

He took a lock of dark-brown hair that had come loose from her elegantly pinned hair and twirled it around the index finger of his right hand. "With all the people around your stand at the market, you seem to have made quite an impression here."

Mimi grinned. "Thank God I have, or I'd be packing my bags again already. I have to earn money for two now, you see—for myself and for my uncle, who is quite ill and needs care." She pointed to the house behind her.

He looked at her with admiration. "You're so strong, so beautiful," he whispered. "I can hardly wait to get to know you better. You and me . . ." He pulled her close to him again.

Mimi closed her eyes in sweet anticipation of his kiss. For the moment of a heartbeat, the world seemed to stand still, then his lips finally touched hers. Mimi's knees grew weak, a warm trembling filled her, and with a commitment unfamiliar to her, she opened her lips to his.

The morning after the Pentecost market, Anton was a changed man. Feeling on top of the world, he stood at the kitchen sink at his parents' inn, The Oxen, and washed the countless dirty beer glasses as if he were counting gold coins instead.

It had been good to talk with Alexander the previous evening, he thought while he polished the glasses with a clean cloth.

He was still amazed at the intensity with which his friend had sworn that he would do *anything* to take the entrance exam for Stuttgart Art School that the photographer Mimi Reventlow had organized for him. Anton hadn't suspected that such a fire burned inside the weaver's son. As Alexander spoke, one thing had become clear to Anton: It wasn't enough to complain all the time about the work at the inn—about the kitchen smells he hated so much, or about the monotony or the same old faces he constantly saw. Whining about those things was no different than making yourself comfortable in a rocking chair: yes, you moved, but you didn't go anywhere. If he, like Alexander, wanted to turn his back on Laichingen, then he had to do something about it. And that was exactly what he was planning. Even better, he already had a pretty good idea of how he could manage it. But he had to talk it through with Christel first. Christel, his secret sweetheart, still struggled with the idea of abandoning her hometown, but in her parents' house she was worse off than he was at his parents' inn. At least he got paid for his work, but Christel was no more than an unpaid maid for her parents, Paul and Sonja Merkle. Christel deserved more.

"I'm going out for a little while," he yelled to his mother, who was sitting at one of the tables in the barroom, sorting coins into small piles.

What a beautiful morning, Anton thought as he stepped out into the square in front of The Oxen. The sky looked as if it had been wiped clean, the cobblestones gleamed in the sunlight like anthracite, and birds twittered in the trees in front of the church. How good would it feel to shoulder his pack on a day like this and hit the road! *Soon,* he promised himself. *Soon.*

He wondered if the photographer was already up. She must be, he thought as he strode across the square to the house on the opposite side. Mimi Reventlow was smart and hardworking, a capable business-woman. And time was money, right? Anton laughed.

Mimi Reventlow didn't know it yet, but when she left Laichingen, he would be at her side. He would have to be patient a while longer since he knew that she wouldn't leave town while her uncle needed care. But that didn't stop him from dreaming, did it? He got along well with Mimi, as he'd discovered on their outing to Ulm. Together they could conquer the world. It certainly wouldn't be much longer, he thought as the closed shutters on the upper floor caught his eye: Josef Stöckle was likely still asleep. The old photographer was gravely ill, and God would certainly call for him soon.

Anton would use the time that Mimi stayed in Laichingen to his advantage. He would offer a helping hand here, a favor there, and make himself increasingly indispensable. When the day of her departure finally came, Mimi would have no choice but to let him go with her. *That* was his plan.

Anton went around back, swung the garden gate open, and was already at the door of the house when he saw a shadow move back by the studio. A burglar? The photographer had done good business at the market, and many had seen it. Was someone trying to get his hands on her money? Fists raised and heart pounding, Anton crept closer, ready to leap into action. But when he peeked around the corner of the woodshed, he saw only Mimi herself—in the arms of Johann Merkle!

Anton froze in astonishment.

"There's another thing," he heard Johann say as the two broke from their embrace. "For the time being, it's better if we . . . well, if we're not seen together. And no one needs to find out that we already know each other from Ulm."

They knew each other? Anton found it hard to trust his ears.

"But why all the secrecy?" Mimi asked, not understanding.

Anton risked another peek. Johann seemed a little impatient as he said, "In the weeks you've been here, haven't you noticed that things in Laichingen are a little different than in other places? Everyone hears everything about everyone else. I don't want people gossiping about you. As a businesswoman, you have a reputation to protect. It's no good if they mark you with an affair with someone like me."

"With someone like you!" Mimi ran her fingers through Johann's curly hair and smiled. "What's that supposed to mean?"

An affair? The two of them had had an affair? What was going on? Anton's head was swirling, and he couldn't think clearly.

"An emigrant. A vagabond. Someone who can't be trusted an inch," Johann said.

"A unionist?" said Mimi, teasing him.

"For now, no one needs to find out I work for the unions, either, or I won't get a foot in any doors here at all."

Johann Merkle was a unionist? Anton had recently read a report in the newspaper about a workers' uprising in Berlin. Apparently, unionists had riled the men so much that not even the police had been able to make the mob see reason. This was getting more and more interesting. Anton hardly dared to breathe—he didn't want to miss a word . . . or be discovered.

"But there's nothing dishonorable about that," said Mimi, still pressed close to Johann. "The weavers would be grateful for a little support, I'd imagine. The unwritten rule that says the son of a weaver also has to become a weaver . . . I find it incredible. And the hours they work—for a pittance! It's time someone told the mill owners that they can't exploit people the way they do forever."

"Mimi, Mimi," said Johann cheerfully. "That's exactly what I admire about you. The fire in your eyes when you talk about what you believe in. I've only ever seen that in men, never in a woman."

"And what's wrong with it?" Mimi shot back. "You also speak your mind about the things you believe, don't you?"

Johann nodded. "But to just come out and say what I really believe would be the worst thing I could do here in Laichingen. I've been gone many years. Why should the villagers trust me?"

Damn well right! thought Anton vehemently. All these years, Johann Merkle hadn't cared a bit about what went on in the village.

Mimi nodded her understanding.

"I have to settle in and show the people I'm one of them again. My first impression is that conditions for the weavers haven't improved in the years I've been away."

It's unbelievable! Johann Merkle strolls into town after years away and imagines he knows about everything and everyone, thought Anton angrily. *The self-important blowhard!*

"You've had my trust from the start. And when the people hear you speak like I heard you on the plaza in Ulm, they'll follow you like lambs," said Mimi, her voice so full of admiration that Anton had to bite his lip to quell a groan of dismay. The photographer was in love. Head over heels.

"Let's hope so." Johann grinned. "But here in Laichingen I can't simply set up in the square and talk about worker protection laws and better pay. No, I'll start as a weaver, probably with Herrmann Gehringer since I used to work for him. I'll only find out where things truly stand when I'm in the lion's den."

"You actually want to work for that monster?" Mimi sounded surprised.

"What have you had to do with Gehringer? You haven't been picking fights with him, have you?"

"Depends on how you look at it . . ." In as few words as possible, Mimi told Johann what she'd been through with the weaver baron.

As far as Anton was concerned, Mimi had acquitted herself very well indeed. Far better than any of the men, he thought; all they did was bow and scrape to Gehringer. Anton noticed that Johann also seemed impressed by Mimi's behavior. His laughter, at least, sounded encouraging.

"You and me—at least there are two of us willing to stand up to the man. But if I start at Gehringer's, there's something else to think about." He paused for a moment before he went on. "My brother will be mad as hell. He was overjoyed to see me leave back then. He thought the way I stood my ground with Gehringer was damaging his own career."

There was an intimacy to the way they laughed then, as if they had known each other a long time.

"I have to go. I have a lot to sort out today. I'm staying at my mother's place. Edelgard . . . you might know her. She's a seamstress."

"Yes, I do know her. When will I see you again?" Mimi asked, a little sadly.

"As soon as I can manage it, I promise. But I don't know how the next few days will go." He raised her chin and looked into her eyes. "From now on, we have all the time in the world, don't we?"

Confused and angry, Anton crept away. It was infuriating—and terrible timing—that Johann Merkle had decided to come back now. It seemed as if the prodigal son already had the photographer wrapped around his finger. Anton kicked a stone, which went skittering across the market square. Mimi had sounded as if she already had visions of standing at the altar with Johann. Damn it! The last thing she needed was to put down roots here in Laichingen. She was supposed to leave the village when her uncle passed away—and with Anton himself at her side.

For a moment, he thought about trying to find Alexander, whom he wanted to tell about Johann and Mimi. But he decided against it. His friend was ignorant when it came to women. And perhaps it was an advantage if he was the only one who knew about this liaison.

Anton stopped and took a deep breath. He had to keep a cool head. He had to think about the changed situation and not do anything stupid. Only time would tell how he should play his hand. One thing was certain, however: he would not give up on his plan.

Eveline stood at the well, drawing water into a large bucket as she held her face to the sun, enjoying the warmth. The sun had shone just the same the day before, when she had stood face to face with Johann at the Pentecost market. And how he'd looked at her, so intense, so sensitive.

She was impatient to see Johann again, but Edelgard would surely keep a tight grip on her son. And she wasn't the only one staking a claim, thought Eve angrily. At the market the day before, half the village had swarmed Johann—including the photographer. Mimi didn't even know him! Couldn't people give him a moment's peace? Eve had wanted nothing more than to protect him and shoo everyone else away, but they'd been granted no more than a few hastily whispered words. That had been enough, though, to give her the courage she needed to go on.

Eveline smiled. She could still only dream about Johann, but they certainly would see each other again in a little more than a month at the *Heumondfest*, and very likely before that. At the July harvest festival, Johann would ask her to dance, she knew, just as they had once before . . . And in his arms, she would forget the world around her, if only for a moment. He would whisper how beautiful she was and how much she enthralled him, just like he had back then, before he left eight years ago, when they had met secretly several times.

For a while, she really had believed that Johann would help her escape her despair. What would it mean if she ran off with a man a second time, but instead of Klaus, this time with Johann?

When Johann suddenly disappeared to try his luck in the wide world, she had been utterly surprised. It had taken almost all her strength to remind herself over and over that she was married, that she should be thankful fate had not tempted her into adultery, or worse.

Now he was back, and it seemed the good Lord had plans for the two of them after all. She knew one thing for certain: Johann would be horrified to discover how terrible things had been for her in the years that had passed, and he would do everything he could to help her.

The soft sound of crying snatched Eveline from her thoughts. She turned to Marianne and Erika, who sat on the ground, looking miserable. A fat tear rolled down Erika's cheek. "My tummy hurts so much, Mama," she sobbed.

"Oh, children," said Eveline gently. Her own stomach was growling with hunger, but Eveline tried to ignore it. "It's only a few hours till dinnertime, then we'll have a good bread soup." She still had half a loaf of decent bread. The other half had mysteriously gone moldy overnight. Her pantry was bare, nothing edible would come from the field for a long time yet, and her purse was all but empty after Klaus had spent his wages at The Oxen.

She heaved the heavy bucket onto the handcart. The young plants in the field needed water urgently to thrive and give them a rich harvest in the autumn.

"When we come home from the field, we'll collect some delicious dandelions along the way. I'll make them into a salad, all right?" she said as brightly as she could.

Marianne held her stomach and said, "Can't I eat my piece of bread now? Maybe I won't want anything for dinner tonight."

Eveline fought back the tears that suddenly threatened to overwhelm her. Johann would want her to be strong, she knew—simply because Klaus was not.

"You know what we can do? We can go to the chicken pen right now and find an egg for each of us."

Her daughters' pale faces instantly brightened a little.

The chickens were old. A short while later, with two pitiful eggs, Eve returned to the house, the children at her heels.

There were still some hot coals in the stove, enough to fry the eggs. Eveline put the heavy cast-iron pan on the stovetop, then took the moldy half loaf of bread. Wisely, or in desperation, she hadn't yet thrown it out, and she cut off the moldy sections of crust as best she could.

"Mold for beauty, as the old people here promise," she said, and gave each daughter a piece of the bread.

"Don't you want anything?" Marianne asked when Eveline put a plate with a fried egg in front of her and her sister.

"I'm still full from the porridge this morning," Eveline lied. The mere sight of the crispy fried eggs made her mouth water. To distract herself, she looked at the pictures that her son, Alexander, had drawn on old cardboard and wrapping paper from Helene's store. An owl. A swallow's nest: a mother swallow feeding her babies . . . He'd drawn every blade of grass so finely, so precisely.

Wasn't it typical of Alexander to choose a motif like that? He could have drawn the rooster out in the street or something else, but no, Alexander had chosen to draw an unselfish mother bird. The thought was enough to give Eveline new strength. She would try everything she could to change Klaus's mind about giving Alexander permission to take the admissions test for the art school. If she managed that feat, she was sure Johann would have a few good words of advice for her son about leaving Laichingen.

A ray of sunlight fought its way through the narrow opening between the neighboring house and their own, dousing the dark yard in golden light.

Eveline smiled.

Read more in
An Artificial Light, Book Two
in the Photographer's Saga

ABOUT THE AUTHOR

Petra Durst-Benning was born in Baden-Württemberg, Germany, in 1965. For more than twenty years, she has been writing bestselling historical and contemporary novels, including The Glassblower's Trilogy, The Century Trilogy, and The Seed Traders' Saga. Translated into several languages, Petra Durst-Benning's novels have sold more than a million copies in English. She now lives with her husband and two dogs in the countryside south of Stuttgart. For more information, visit www. durst-benning.de.

ABOUT THE TRANSLATOR

Photo © 2016 Dagmar Jordan

Edwin Miles has been translating in the film, television, and literary fields since 2002. Originally from Australia, he completed his MFA in fiction writing at the University of Oregon in 1995, where he worked as a fiction editor on the literary magazine *Northwest Review*. In 1996 he was short-listed for the prestigious Australian/Vogel Award for a collection of short stories. Miles's translated works include Petra Durst-Benning's The Century Trilogy and The Seed Traders' Saga, Bernhard Hennen's The Saga of the Elven, and Jonas Winner's Berlin Gothic novels. After many years of living and working in Australia, Japan, and the United States, he now resides in Cologne, Germany, with his wife, Dagmar, and their children.